PRAISE FOR

THE SAVAGE

"Think Margaret Atwood's *The Handmaid's Tale* set to the tune of Hank Williams Jr.'s 'Country Boy Can Survive.' Inventive, clever, and so topical in terms of today's American divisiveness, *The Savage* is set to become one of the year's most discussed books. As compulsive and chilling as Cormac McCarthy's *The Road*."

—Ace Atkins, author of *The Fallen*

"Frank Bill traverses the dangerous terrain of an America lost, where memory is as strong as might and where the door of humanity opens wide, exposing all the beauty and ugliness that hide inside. And in *The Savage*, Frank Bill makes this journey the only way he knows how—with truckloads of heart and soul."

—Michael Farris Smith, author of *Desperation Road* and *Rivers*

"*The Savage* strips away the comforting illusions of civilization to expose the seething heart of the beast within us all, portraying the lives of everyday men and women surging headlong on the implacable rails of capital-F Fate. I don't think I'd thrive in the world Bill conjures here, or that I'd even want to, but it's a thrilling, transporting place to visit, and you will not want to leave until you've reached the blistering end."

—Kirby Gann, author of *Ghosting* and *Our Napoleon in Rags*

"A postapocalyptic revenge tale with Southern Gothic overtones, Frank Bill's *The Savage* starts at a fevered pitch and quickly becomes downright typhoidal. With unrelenting action and a cast of characters that makes *The Walking Dead* look tame, this isn't just primal and gripping storytelling, it's twenty-first-century mythmaking. Good luck putting this one down."

—Christopher Charles, author of *The Exiled*

"Written in unflinching prose, *The Savage* is Frank Bill's brutal exploration of a kill-or-be-killed world in the perhaps not-so-distant future. Rife with the shocking violence we've come to expect from Bill, *The Savage* is a gritty portrait of stripped-down America thrashing as it teeters on the razor-thin line between survival and depravity."

—Steph Post, author of *Lightwood* and *A Tree Born Crooked*

CHRISTIAN DOELLNER

FRANK BILL

THE SAVAGE

Frank Bill is the author of the novel *Donnybrook* and the story collection *Crimes in Southern Indiana*, a *GQ* Book of the Year and a *Daily Beast* best debut novel of fall 2011. He lives in southern Indiana.

ALSO BY FRANK BILL

Crimes in Southern Indiana

Donnybrook

THE SAVAGE

THE SAVAGE

Frank Bill

Farrar, Straus and Giroux New York

Farrar, Straus and Giroux
18 West 18th Street, New York 10011

Printed in the United States of America
First edition, 2017

Library of Congress Cataloging-in-Publication Data
Names: Bill, Frank, 1974– author.
Title: The savage / Frank Bill.
Description: First edition. | New York : Farrar, Straus and Giroux, 2017.
Identifiers: LCCN 2017012725 | ISBN 9780374534417 (paperback) |
ISBN 9780374710910 (ebook)
Subjects: LCSH: Dystopias—Fiction. | BISAC: FICTION / Literary. |
FICTION / Action & Adventure. | FICTION / Mystery & Detective /
Short Stories.
Classification: LCC PS3602.I436 A6 2017 | DDC 813/.6—dc23
LC record available at https://lccn.loc.gov/2017012725

Designed by Jonathan D. Lippincott

10 9 8 7 6 5 4 3 2 1

For my two girls, Jenn and Emma, I love you each.
And for my cousin Denny Faith, with whom I roamed the woods and built a lot of fires.

PART I

THE SALVAGED

All you lyin', greedy, stealin', cheatin', hurtin' everybody
sinners
You're all gonna pay the worst on Judgement Day

—Scott H. Biram, "Judgement Day"

NOW

Clasping his eyelids tight, Van Dorn recalled the echo from the radio, speaking of the dollar losing its worth. Of a global downfall dominoing across the United States, of militias formed by the Disgruntled Americans, a group of fed-up military and police tired of the government milking the working class. They wanted change, so they'd taken out the grids, the world's power switch, eliminating lights, sounds, and anything that warranted electricity, and what followed was the images of men being kneeled in front of women and children, homes besieged by flame, a pistol or rifle indenting a face enraged by fear, hurt, and anger. Trigger pulled. Brain, skull, and hair fertilizing the soil with departure. One man's life taken by another without mercy.

Van Dorn had spied upon these foreigners over the passing months. Men who'd trespassed through the acres, raiding, robbing, slaughtering, and burning human, home, and salvation.

As he opened his eyes, sweat trickled a salty burn from his brow. Wanting to help those weak and in need, he feared risking this freedom he'd forged since the fallout, one of silence, separation, and singleness. Instead, he'd made his way back into the camouflage of the woods. Tried to dissolve what he'd viewed from his memory, though it haunted him night after night.

Hunger pained Van Dorn's stomach, as he'd not eaten in days. As he laid a hand to the heat of the broken pavement, his chest pounded with dread from the engines' bouncing horsepower through the valley; the sounds and vibration were a signal, these men were getting closer. He knew what they'd bring. Death.

Glancing back through the line of brush and briar that scripted the hillside, Van Dorn knew he couldn't drag the venison that lay before him back to shelter to field-dress it. He'd no choice but to chance his freedom. Salvage what meat he could out in the open.

Several miles back, he'd shot the doe. Tracked the beast's blood spots over the dead leaves until it gave in. Tumbled downhill and out into the open road.

Before the power devolved into a station devoid of words, the static speak on a local NPR news broadcast foretold of the unraveling domino effect that was upon the land. How the U.S. dollar had failed as one war after another bankrupted the very same government that had created the disaster with countries they dealt promises to in the first place. Countries that had been using their own currency rather than America's coin for day-to-day living. These countries and foreign territories waited for America to crumble within a digital age of gadgets, degrees, and national debt. Disorder was coming in pockets of civil unrest. Militias had formed after the Disgruntled Americans made a bold statement with armed robbery, testing the strength of the United

States' protection of its citizens. Men and women had walked off their jobs. Law enforcement disbanded. States were attempting to secede from the union. Cities and towns were being looted. Criminals were beginning to run rampant. Military had been spread thin, were trapped on foreign continents fighting other men's conflicts. Human beings who wanted to govern and police everything had lost their rules. Then came the explosions from the networking of small militias. Electricity had been cut and the everyday noise of vehicles, music, television, and people vanished.

As he took in the glassy coal eyes, trees sketched shadows over Van Dorn as he unsheathed his blade, thinking of a time before his father and he had settled with the Widow, a time when his father and he had roamed the roads like vagabonds. Stealing and scrapping. Living hand to mouth. It was preparation. Something Van Dorn didn't understand then but understood now, so many years later.

With the blade in his right hand, his left spread beneath the deer's chin. Pulled the head back. Pressed the edge into the white of the deer's throat. Watched the blood spill warm.

Lifting the hindquarter, Van Dorn stabbed the serrated edge above the genitals. Split the hide up to the rib cage, careful not to part the intestines or the stomach, taint the meat. Fluid steamed from the innards. Flies buzz-sawed the air around his one hand, severing the fat, which held the colors of plum, crimson, and pearl hanging half out. He cut the diaphragm from the cavity. Dug his arms elbow-deep up into the venison, feeling the wall of heat and marrow, gripping the esophagus with one hand, the other hand severing it with the steel.

Tugging the veined heart, lungs, and intestines free, Dorn left the bladder.

In Van Dorn's mind, he recalled the broken-speak of his father telling how the only thing of value would be a commodity: *Something of weight. Gold. Silver. Bullets. Arrows. Those things that'd break or burn flesh would render food, water, survival.*

Buzzards circled overhead. A few landed fifteen feet away, stood tall as Van Dorn leaned forward on his knees. Tawny beaks hooking the slick noodle insides. Jerking the fuming hues of organ as he tossed them their way.

Crystalline beads stung Van Dorn's eyes. Red encircled the venison's outline. Splitting the almond hide around the neck and shoulder, he dug his feelers into the fur, pulled it down the carcass, and freed it from the shoulder, ribs, spine, and hindquarter, exposing the beet-colored meat. He paused. Heard the barreling sound lessening his time for what he could cut. He'd have to make a decision.

With a fevered action, Van Dorn guided the blade down one side of the spine. Hands stained warm and slick, he carved and sectioned the loin. Placed it into the foiled insides of his satchel. Zipped it closed. Warded off the heated air and the insects with their larvae.

Eyes swiveled from side to side, keeping watch up and down the passage of the back road. Ears tuned to the vibration of distance being closed by the oncoming rumble as he worked the blade along the shoulder.

He wanted more than the loin. Something that would last longer than a day or two. Something that would ease the pangs for protein and mineral.

Across the road, triple strands of rusted barbed wire ran from post to post, bordering a barren expanse of dirt and burnt weeds where crops were once nurtured. Now it just held unturned soil that hid the scattered bones of horse, cow, or wild game that'd been set free or run down and butchered or wasted for this new sport called *survival*.

A .30-30 lever-action Marlon lay over Van Dorn's back, a gift from his father, Horace, that had once belonged to his grandfather. Rungs of brass ran across his front, a gift from the Widow a few years ago. Handcrafted by the crazed Pentecost Bill, a leather smith with three daughters spewing the teachings of the good book.

The rattle of engines replaced sound. Slick insides splatted from the buzzard's beaks to the ground. They extended their shadowy wingspan. Disappeared into the gray-blue above. Van Dorn turned. Sheathed the blade. Ran. Worked his way up the hillside.

Hands red and peeling, he grabbed small trees for leverage. Climbed his way up the embankment of splintered sycamore, gray oak, briar, and dying fern. Trundles of leaves lay upturned from the weight of his tracked kill. Hamstrings burned and forearms tightened as his heart raced.

Two ATVs humming with the knotted tread of mud and black plastic fenders throttled down. Went silent. Behind them a flatbed's transmission ground gears to second, then first, slowing its pace. Tires came to a stop and the engine found the same quiet as the ATVs that waited on the road now thirty feet below Van Dorn.

Two men stepped from their four-wheelers. Boots crunched across the road. Door hinges squeaked from the flatbed's cab. The third man dragged his leg, raking the crumbling silt of the road.

Foreign English emerged from one of the upright men. "What is this beast?"

While the other voiced, "'Tis a deer."

The hobbling man paid them no mind. Raised his head to the air like a malformed dog. Inhaling the bark, leaves, and pollen that lay within the hot air.

Van Dorn sat, ducked down behind a barrel-shaped oak. Chest heaving in his temples. Lactic acid stiffening his muscles. His hands quaking with the fear of being captured. Possibly killed by these ungodly forms of human. Criminals. Seeing them more and more over the passing weeks. Crossing the county back roads and Highway 62.

Unable to fight curiosity, he wanted to catch a better glimpse of the men. To view these savages. Swiveled his neck, peeked through the weeds that camouflaged him, took in the three shapes. Two stood, one kneeled. All sniffing the dry heat of the day.

Their arms, bulky cords of muscle connected to bone by tendon. Inked with skeletons, devil horns, daggers, and lettering, suspending from leather vests and jagged flannel. One of them had hair rifling in singed fibers from his skull. Another's face was stitched and chinked by scars.

The two who stood kept pivoting their heads. Taking in the surroundings. Studying the landscape. While the one kneeling poked the violet meat. Thumbed the hide hanging loose, submerged his index into the blood that had expanded from the field dressing. Tasted it. His eyes followed where the loin had been removed while his right digit traced it. Van Dorn heard the words that sputtered like an exhaustless vehicle. "'Tis a fresh kill."

Glancing up the hillside, the kneeling man sat patient. Eyeing the incline for a hint of passage. Watched the dead stillness of trees and leaves. His head turned oddly. Deciphered the skids of soil. Looked at the downward path Dorn and the deer had created.

Van Dorn could taste the stench of these men. They'd the air of mildew, scorched antifreeze, gunpowder, and decayed flesh. It made his throat burn from the acid that bubbled in his gut. Fighting the dread embedded within, Dorn slowly turned his eyes away from the distorted silhouettes of men. Looked behind him, upward through the tiny growth of trees and briar, forty more feet to the top. Another fifty to Red, his mule. And all at once an itch tickled his nostrils, a numb comfort overcame his mouth, and he sneezed. "Shit!" he mumbled.

Footsteps tripped across the crumbling cinder. Then stopped. The scrape of a voice with a Spanish accent: "A sneeze."

The other figure pointed to the hillside. "Upturned leaves."

Van Dorn imagined the location of the men in his mind. Twisted his neck to look one last time. The one kneeling met Van Dorn's eyes. Went from slits to wide.

The man unholstered his pistol, stood up, thumbed the hammer of a 9 mm and yelled, "Something human eyes us from that tree's flank! Can see the shape of its head."

Van Dorn did what he should've already done. Stood up and ran. Leaves mashed and limbs crunched. A voice belled, "Shoot! Shoot this shape that spies on us!"

Knees burned, hands grabbed tiny trees, and Van Dorn climbed another foot closer to the top. Then another and another. An explosion crowned through the valley. Earth exploded below him, then came the combustion of automatic carbine. Footing gave as he fell backward.

Leaf, rock, and limb accompanied Van Dorn's descent.

His twenty-one-year-old frame took the jags of land. Marring and denting his arms and shins, until he lay at the bottom of the hill.

Gathering his bearings, catching the air that'd been knocked from him; adrenaline coursed through his body, blotted out the ache that would come later, after the rush, if he lived long enough to encompass the hurt.

Moans reared from the bed of the truck in the road. Scuffed-leather-covered feet came before Van Dorn with the hum of insects and a smell that made the insides of his mouth water and his stomach buckle. He wanted to retch as his eyes made out splotched and stained clothing. Over the dented and moist chest that drew to a cryptic leathery face. Lidless orbs, unblinking. Lips misshapen, revealing teeth and tongue. This texture of man looked as though he'd eaten a plate of explosives with a chain saw and lived to tell about it.

One of the men said, "Look at the size of this man-child." The other said, "Bring him to his feet, Cotto will enjoy soldiering you." The man grasped and pulled Van Dorn by his locks to bent knees.

Feeling his hair give, Van Dorn knew in order to survive, to escape, he'd have to do just as his father had done that night long ago. He'd have to kill. And he thought of the milk jugs filled with soil or water, used as makeshift targets. Empty cans of Miller High Life and Evan Williams bottles shot from fence posts. Or walnuts sprouting from tree limbs. Offering a marksmanship that dropped deer, rabbit, squirrel, and groundhog from their life-span. Left to be carved and cleaned for subsistence. He thought of that night. Of a man's recognizable face before his father had told him to turn away. Then came the drum-crush of gunfire. And when he viewed the sheen of flesh again, it was an unimaginable sauce of flinted bone.

Like now, the tides had turned from a doe killed for eating to human sacrifice for the continuation of one's existence.

Being dragged across the road, Van Dorn struggled to find his balance amongst the memory from that time he couldn't bury. From years before, emotions of dread and the pulse of testosterone turned to fuel for his actions, for his continuance.

The one dragging him paused. Looked down at Van Dorn. His head twisted side to side. He'd an insignia branded upon his horsehide neck, a spider spread with tactile legs and a red dot upon its center.

Van Dorn had seen it before. But where was unknown.

Pawing and reaching at the hand that held him, Van Dorn reacted, palmed his Ka-Bar knife attached at his hip. Pulled and swiped upward at the arm. A line erupted with the ooze of red so dark it was black.

The man released Van Dorn, screaming, "Motherfucker!"

Another hand slapped at his shoulder from behind, tried to rein him in. Wielding the blade just as his father had taught him, Van Dorn met the digits of the man's hand. Pain erupted thick as sap spit from trees. "Heathen bastard!"

As he shuffled backward toward the primered truck, Van Dorn's back stung. The ache and scrape of his descent was weighing in. Sheathing his blade, he slung the leather strap from his back attached to the .30-30. To his front, a man bore down on him with a pistol. Van Dorn pointed at the form. Took in his beaver-skinned complexion, black hair, and acne-pinched cheeks with dead eyes. Van Dorn envisioned a deer lifting its head after eating acorns from the ground; he imagined aiming for its heart, and he pulled the trigger.

The man's expression parted out of the temporal line of his skull. Another shape came at Van Dorn; he chambered a new piece of brass. Hands bloody and pulsing, raised. Energized by fear, Van Dorn told himself to shoot. Shoot as his father had done that evening long ago.

And he did. Skull bone tarred over the road.

After many months of living out of eyeshot, watching the harm of others while dodging scavengers and this horde of Spanish-speaking men, he'd now killed two of them in seconds.

Cries and whines reached for Van Dorn from the truck. He viewed what he had overlooked: an iron cage calcified and welded to its bed, restraining ivory outlines. Visages bruised, dirty, and starved of faith. "Help us!" they cried. "Please!"

Women and children. Young boys and girls. But no men.

Towering, large, and muscled, Van Dorn was the apparition of hope. Hair smeared across his head like mud, at odd lengths. Smudged face and trembling, but not broken. Then the familiar—a female with sweaty strands and a blemished outline spoke, "Dorn, help us. Please. They . . . they've slaughtered Daddy."

The Sheldon girl from over around Frenchtown. The Widow and Van Dorn's father helped her family run fence line for separation of their cows and hogs two summers before this hell hit. Helped them build a hog pen. Butcher, process, package, and freeze their beef and pork. He and the girl had fished, hunted, rode mules. Shared the first of several kisses, groping, and adolescent lust.

The roar of more engines from the distance rattled and scoured the land. Around the bed of the truck came the third frame, dragging his leg. A pistol raised with the same spider tattoo across the back of his hand. Van Dorn trained his rifle at the outline and followed the only word that coursed through his mind: *Kill!*

—

Hidden by the tarnished chrome trunks of trees and rock, Van Dorn climbed back up the hillside, .30-30 in his grip. Heart bunched in his chest. Out of breath. Shaken by his actions of survival, he turned to take a final glimpse of his eruption from the hilltop.

Below him, the roar of more vehicles had pulled up and stopped. Men like those he'd shot stepped from their trucks and four-wheelers.

With a matte black HK33 assault rifle draped across his front, one man studied the brain and bone fragmented upon the pavement. Blood thick and drying from the midday heat. The man shook his head. Motioned to the other men who walked the road with hand signals, no words. Some with heads burred. Others with oily tresses. Inked-up arms wielding AK-47s, some pointed, others surveyed. Van Dorn knew what they were doing, looking for the one who'd slaughtered their own like an Old West showdown from the films he'd watched with his father.

Pale Rider. High Plains Drifter. The Good, the Bad and the Ugly. The Outlaw Josey Wales.

The men picked up their dead. Flung them into the bed of a rusted Chevy as though they were sacks of feed. Then they dragged the deer, hefted it up onto the pile of bodies.

The one man with the HK33 stood out. He wore an ink

of thorns around his sand-stubbled head. Several teardrops fell down his cheek. Mossy-bearded. Arms covered in smears of blanched ink and wolf spiders upon each hand. Studying the hillside, he listened for something more than silence. He and two others walked toward the mess of leaves along the road's edge. Looked back to where the deer had lain. Pointed. Motioned index and middle fingers like an upside-down peace sign into his left palm, as if legs walking up the hill, then lifted his right hand into the air and circled his index overhead.

Two men got on the discarded ATVs. Another opened the abandoned truck's door, sat in the driver's seat, the caged humans attached to its rear. The Sheldon girl screamed, "Dorn! Dorn! Come back!" Until an older female's hand smothered her speech.

The man with the HK studied her. Walked toward the cage and questioned her. Moments passed with an exchange of words. Then the man walked to his ATV. Engines roared. Others got back into their soil-specked vehicles. Drove down the road slow. Gazing and examining the hillside. Van Dorn worked his eyes open and closed. Trying to place the men's tattoos as he ran back to where he'd tied his mule.

—

Van Dorn's arm ached as he swatted the flies from the bedroom's doorway. Rot hung in the air like manure spread upon a field to treat the soil. Two bodies of bone lay in the bed. *Resting*, he told himself. The Widow's skin appeared ashen and sunken. Eyes no longer soft like her touch, warming him with comfort, but now full with the decomposition of sunken burrows.

Horace, Dorn's father, lay thick boned, hair once the

color of raven now fine as thread for sewing, his muscles deteriorated beneath his decaying cotton shirt and denim pants. Empty brown beer bottles lined the floor next to the bed. Home brew from the Widow's brother-in-law.

Backing up from the room, Van Dorn pulled the heavily grained door closed. Walked back through the old farmhouse with the insignia branded upon those men haunting his mind. A black widow with a red dot in its center. Strobing over and over in his memory. Where had he seen it?

In the kitchen, sun bleached through the panes of window. Vibrations pulsed through Van Dorn's spine, arms, and legs. He dropped into a wooden chair. His .30-30 flung upon the table. Hands pressed into his face. He'd killed those men. Their hides roasted brown like a duck's skin. Who were they? Where had they come from? Why'd they have the females and children caged like livestock being transported to their butchering?

Where were the fathers, the brothers, the uncles, the men?

They'd loaded up their dead. Tossed Van Dorn's deer into the truck with them. As he raised his head from his hands, the thought that he'd ignored for far too long came: How long before he was discovered again?

Van Dorn remembered his father telling him, "You're a survivor. A pioneer. You know the ways of the land. You'll have to search out similar folk. Educate those that have no learning to what you know. Won't be safe to hole up here forever."

Van Dorn's sockets pained and squeezed in his skull, remembering everything he'd tried to forget but couldn't: His and Horace's return to southern Indiana. The squatters. Stopping for gas. Gutt. The Widow. Gunshots. Stains to the slats of floor. Tarp. Digging a deep depression within the earth. His father's slow unraveling over the years spent with the Widow. The crazed words that fell from his tongue as time passed with a bottle in tow. Saying, "Men will cripple the weak quick as an unexpected winter frost in 1816. Know who'll survive? Ones that've been taught how to nurture and live from the land."

Standing, Van Dorn removed the meat from his pouch. Hands quivered, his mind replayed the actions that had been cast upon him without notice. Sketching those caged people's faces from memory. Worn. Crusted but familiar; the Sheldon girl. He wondered if she'd tried to fight back. Knowing her father would have. He was a hunter, trapper, labored in the blood of life. He was not weak. And Van Dorn wanted to be the same.

Placing the beet-colored loin on the cutting board. Pulling his blade from its sheath, he parted the dark meat. Cut with the muscle's grain. As was true with his father, Horace, violent actions came when his hand was forced. If there'd been a test to take a life, he'd have passed it. He thought of how easily the men dropped to the ground. Everything within them evaporated with a single gunshot. They became weightless. Their beings exhausted. Just like when his father and he met the Widow. Even before that. When they'd left Harrison County. Abandoned the working world. Lived on the road, thieving scrap tin, aluminum, steel, and copper from foreclosed homes.

—

Horace always warned Van Dorn, someday it would come to this. *Kill or be killed.*

But it haunted Van Dorn, leaving all those others behind; seeing their lost complexions saddened him. He'd viewed the dismantling of others, but never so close. He told himself he'd no time to free them. He was one against many.

Van Dorn's stomach groaned. He couldn't eat till dark. Fearing someone or something would see the smoke from a fire.

Running a forearm below his nose, he sponged mucus. Justified his choice of morals. He did what he had to do.

Grabbing a ceramic bowl from the cabinet, he placed the slices of meat inside. Turned and walked into the dining area, to the basement door on the far side of the room. Opened it, descended the old wooden steps. Outside light opened the darkness from small windows within the four corners overhead. Carved shadows down the rock walls that were lined with plywood shelves and weighted by jars and jars of canned vegetables. Green beans. Peas. Potatoes and carrots. Pickles, sliced to quarters or speared, and corn that'd been cut from the cob. A stain graphed around the rust-speckled freezer that had held dead game. Nourishment that'd been wrapped and stored till it went too long without power. He'd eaten and salvaged what he could, but most of the meat within it had expired.

For Van Dorn, vegetables served little purpose without meat. He longed for eggs and their thick cholesterol centers. He'd killed his remaining hens when too many weeks had passed without deer, rabbit, or squirrel.

The smell of mildewed earth and rotted meat rose all around him. He stepped to the wooden box that covered a hole within the floor. Where a whiskey barrel had been lowered into the ground. Gravel lined the outside of it, insulating it with cool. Creating a makeshift fridge built by his father and him.

Like his father, the Widow had learned him about the old ways. Gardening, hunting, fishing, and trapping. Loading ammo. Dynamite. Sharpening of a blade. Knowing one's direction by the rising and lowering of the sun. And now it was being used.

Opening the barrel, he laid the meat inside. Wishing he had enough room to save what had been in the freezer.

He grabbed a jar of beans, pinkie-sized chunks layered the liquid within. Laying them on top of the wooden lid, he slid a walnut chair from beneath a matching table. Sat down. Glanced at the radio that offered no sound.

Beneath the table and in the corners, coils of boneless muscle lay. Skin patterns golden brown with black slithering their way toward his booted feet. As he reached down, one of the coils came cold into his palm. Screwed up and around his forearm. Raising it to the tabletop, he let the serpent slither from him and lie facing him. And her memory wrangled within. Droplets of moisture slid from her tight cheeks where eyes the shade of sky smiled. Her hands soft, working the blade, peeling potatoes, shedding their jackets, quartering them into a liquid that steamed. Blue flames heating the pot upon the gas stove. "You're Van Dorn?" she asked.

"I am."

"Your father, he speaks highly of you and your labors."

It was Dorn's first visit to the Sheldon girl's home. His father and he had come looking to size up the property for running fence line. Dorn had stepped into the home for a swig of water.

"Does he, that's his offering of kindness, I suppose."

Dorn was hesitant. Nervous. Shy around a female near his age. But also of beauty.

She smiled, her teeth were of pearl, lips smooth, and she asked, "And you, how would you speak of your father?"

"Strong and of great knowledge. A man who fights many demons."

"Demons? Awful colorful words, dramatic even."

"Not when one's viewed all the broken pieces of the world of which we've traveled."

Running a forearm to blot the damp about her forehead, Sheldon shook her head. "You're a traveler. Not from here. Where all have you seen?"

"I's born here. Father took me to the road when my mother abandoned us. Took to Kentucky. Tennessee. Ohio. Seen those that've been relieved of their worth."

"And now you're gonna help my daddy construct a fence."

"What my father told me. Think I could trouble you for a glass of water?"

Laughing, Sheldon told him, "That's why you've stepped into our home. Not to see and flirt with the daughter. How about iced tea, is that suitable for a traveler such as yourself?"

Taking to the wonder within her bright eyes, the elegance of her pale pigment, Van Dorn smiled and replied, "Please, it's of no trouble."

Now, cat eyes watched him within the shadowed basement. Black tongue forked, jutting in and out. Van Dorn rubbed a pointer over the scaly head, whispering, "Know what I must do. Leave here. Find those faces I left behind."

Van Dorn fell silent, watching the serpent. The others gathered around his feet. He sat waiting for dark. His memory drifting to a time before the silence. A time when he questioned how much longer he could live in an existence of hand to mouth with his father. Scavenging through the rural areas of Tennessee, Kentucky, and Ohio. Where in the wee hours of night they ripped and cut bronzed wiring and piping from the walls and floors of foreclosed homes. Traded the weight for tender at salvage yards.

THEN

After more than a year of travel, their frames sketched into the truck's seat like two skeletons from a discerning past with no future. Abandoned vehicles scattered roadside from town to town. Out of gas. Broke down. Men and women out of work. Out of money. Maps lined the busted dash with Horace and Van Dorn's routes highlighted. Addresses of houses seized by banks they'd written down from the county sheriff's bulletin boards in the towns they'd visited.

Van Dorn longed for a life with kids his own age to fish with. Talk about books and girls. Something more than the wiring of a home or the best price of copper per pound. He ran a hand through the reams of hair that hid his forehead, tickled his upper lip and the rim of his neck, unable to restrain his thoughts from Horace, and he said, "Tired of this bullshit. Wanna go back home."

When the economy began to swirl into snuff, Van Dorn was fourteen. He remembered stepping from the Ritalin shouts of children who lined the green vinyl seating of the school bus. Walked the long stretch of gravel to a heat-bleached trailer and the pole barn Horace worked from, a stretch of land they'd resided upon since the boy's birth.

Van Dorn's mother had run off with another man when he was nine on what his father called the chemical path, rumor was she got clasped into a world of trading skin in truck-stop diners to afford her and her new fellow's next fix. Tap of the vein. Taking a ride down addiction.

Van Dorn had found his father sunk into the couch that day while lipping a bottle of black-label Evan Williams, two backpacks expanded and laid out on the wooden coffee table, and he questioned, "Where we going?"

Horace swallowed hard and capped the bottle, knowing that other than the one hundred dollars in his wallet, he was flat broke. Employment had dried up, no one was spending. The furniture restoration and handyman business where he'd strip and restore antique dressers and hutches, remodel a room, build a new deck or rewire a home, had sunk. He was left with nothing but splinters, tools collecting dust, and a mouth to feed. He'd procured an idea from a regular down at the tavern who'd lipped and yammered about homes being built quicker than they could be inhabited. Their worth imploded. Now they were unable to be afforded, the materials that constructed them lay in rot. A person would be better off looting the metallic conductors from the structures and setting the rest to flame. He knew what he could do and how he could do it; the wheels of survival churned ideas in Horace's mind.

Planting his palms on his knees, Horace stood up, leveled his singed red eyes on Van Dorn, and said, "Into the wilds of life, my son."

"What about school? Our home?"

Van Dorn sensed his father's tension as he grabbed one of the packs, handed it to him like an uppercut to the gut.

"The road will provide your schooling and a place to rest your eyes."

And without contemplating consequence for his words, Van Dorn asked, "What if I don't wanna go?"

It was the first time his father had laid hands to him. Bringing the calluses of his right palm to his face, telling him, "You have no say in the tutelage I'm demanding of you. You're going."

They left that day with the clothes on their backs, a tent, a gun, some tools, fishing rods, and a few books the father and the boy favored.

For Whom the Bell Tolls. The Old Man and the Sea. Tobacco Road. Wise Blood. The Sound and the Fury.

But Van Dorn's words brought the lurch of guilt for this way of life to his father. He'd questioned Van Dorn's quietness during their travels. His rolling of the eyes when talking scrap prices. Distant stares at other kids hanging out in the mom-and-pop groceries when gathering provisions. One thing Horace would not show was weakness. To him it meant failure as a provider and a father. He replaced it with anger. Feeling as if he was being tested and ridiculed by Dorn. One day he couldn't take no more. Coaled the remaining tobacco from his cigarette. Flicked the butt out the window where dark passed warm and rashy as a wool blanket. Took the steering with his left. Launched his right fist into the peak of Van Dorn's left jaw. "Dammit!" he yelled. The truck swerved off then back onto the road. Pointed out the insect-gut-sprayed windshield. Horace said, "All this here is your home. Your education. Can you not see what I'm learning you?"

Parting the hair from his eyes, Van Dorn rubbed his cheek. Felt the balm of heat. Held back the moisture that weighted his sight.

"I seen enough of this home. Of this learning. I want to go back to school, have friends. I want it to be like it once was."

Since being on the road, they'd taken shelter amongst the dilapidated houses within the valleys of shunned vehicles on cinder blocks. Where dry-rotted tires hung from limbs and unraked leaves piled to the shade of bourbon and replaced the grass. They'd back down rutted driveways that held no hint of movement, hoping for a few hours of shut-eye. Sometimes they were met by half-mongrel hounds barking, then Horace would shift from reverse to drive and speed away as the mixed breeds gave chase. Other times they'd find a stream, set up a camp where they could bathe and fish. Cat hit at night, while bluegill or bass struck at the break of morning. They'd scale, gut, and then seer the opal meat in a cast-iron pan over an open flame. Fingering and eating the oily meat.

In Horace's eyes, he'd educated and provided for Van Dorn the only way he knew. Passing on his skills of how a house was blueprinted, where the wiring and piping ran, and knowing where to begin cutting the bronze-colored metal. Then loading and hauling their wares to a place where they could burn the insulation from the Romex to trade weight for coin. To Horace, these learnings were an apprenticeship for persisting in a world that was becoming less and less kind to those like themselves who were skilled in a trade.

Slowing the truck as they rounded a lake, Horace noted how a few houses were plotted across what looked to have once been untrespassed acreage, more than likely willed to a family member after kin had died, then sold and sectioned off for new construction. At least that's what Horace believed.

"Friends?" Horace questioned. "You got me. What used to be has been banked into lies. Squandered at the price of persons like us, the working. Tell me this, how else we supposed to earn our keep?"

When money was flowing well, Horace'd splurge on a hotel, buy Van Dorn a book from a grocery, offer a good night of comfort, cable TV, and lamplight to read by. While he swam in a twenty- or thirty-dollar bottle of whiskey and their battery-powered tools charged.

"Couldn't we get us jobs somewheres, move back into our trailer?"

Horace chuckled. "Your mouth plies my ears with ignorance, boy. You know they's no such foolishness being offered. And we rent our skin for no man."

"What about joining up with a militia? Mend with like-minded people, put our skills to good use?"

They'd heard the stories when fueling up the Ford and grabbing a local paper. Jobs had become scarce. Even getting part-time work washing down the lot at a McDonald's was competitive. They'd spoken with families like them who'd become homeless and camped beneath overpasses in cities or within parks. Or joined up with rogue groups of working-class men and women, those who'd set their sights upon anarchy. Plotting to make statements all across the United States against their failed government at the right moment.

"How we know if we don't look?"

They were closer to home than they'd ever been. Had crossed the Ohio River from Kentucky to Indiana two days ago. Paid a visit to the justice center in Corydon. Scribbled down some residences and pitched their tent at the Stage

Stop Campgrounds. Mapped out their path. They'd been driving somewhere between Laconia and Elizabeth. Had entered a private area of housing, one road in and the same road out. *Maybe this return to familiarity has brought on the boy's discourse*, the father thought as he fought back with his trail-worn wisdom.

"I've taught you better'n that, Van Dorn. I've never let you starve nor freeze. And I'm not about to join ranks with a group of martyrs on a pilgrimage to dismantle and shun the powers that be."

"No, we'll just lurk among the streams of decay, take company with human crustaceans."

The father hung a right, and Van Dorn imagined Horace stomping the brake, laying a tread of knuckles upside his hard head, but his father had taught him to have a venomous tongue. To argue his point of view with strategy and facts. Hoping he'd grow sharper than he'd ever be. And for this Horace was proud.

Killing the truck lights, Van Dorn's father let the moon navigate him into a half-circle driveway. Still rolling Van Dorn's words around in his mind, Horace concluded that Dorn was correct in what he said, though there was little reason for him to treat his father with disrespect. The distance they'd traveled wasn't easy for either of them. Horace missed planing and staining wood. Hammering nails and driving screws into treated boards to frame a deck or an addition. To create something of substance. Worth. And he'd not lain with a female in over twelve months or better. But the whiskey helped to numb those emotions of want.

The brick home sat lone, devoid of vehicle or light, with neighboring other dwellings standing over a football field away. Shifting into reverse, Horace backed down the lumped soil. Tucked the truck up next to the house and killed the engine. Van Dorn grabbed his flashlight, unlatched the passenger-side door. Horace reached for Van Dorn's arm. Strained for words to better all that had been passed between them but found none as Van Dorn jerked free.

Outside of the truck, Horace stood opposite Van Dorn, fastening his tool belt. Dorn pouted, stared out into the night from which they'd come, and Horace told him. "Quit wasting the dark, get your cutter and bar, go around back, they's supporting walls, looks to be a walk-out, try the doors, start on the basement pipes."

From the Ford's bed, Dorn pulled a battery-powered saw and hexagonal crowbar and said, "Yes, master." Then disappeared around the corner of the house before Horace could acknowledge the salty-tongued reply.

Tasting the bitterness of truth, Horace knew there was no reward for the struggling. Seemed the harder one tried, the harder life came, and all one could do was keep dredging forward, hoping for a sign that acknowledged the accuracy for one's direction.

He tried the side door before committing to prying. The knob turned and the door opened. Scents of mildewed lumber and chalky walls engulfed Horace's inhale. Shining a light on the kitchen floor, he saw that tile and grout lay in pieces, had been plied or broken, coffee stains dotted the ceiling with jellyfish outlines, the countertops were scuffed to the particleboard beneath them. Cabinet doors had been sprung and removed from hinges.

Kneeling down, the father looked beneath the sink. A foul odor decorated the square space; he wanted to check the piping, see how it was connected, whether it was hard or flex. It was neither. It'd been gutted.

In its place lay the chalky bones of a small animal. Pieces of hide. Entrails. Specks of pissants and shells of dead flies. "What in the hell?" Van Dorn's father muttered. Standing up, he walked to a set of doors and opened them, expecting to find the water heater, but it was gone.

Following the warped walls from the kitchen to the dining area, Horace glanced around the open areas of shadow. Decay lingered in the air and he listened for Dorn, could hear no jarring of metal teeth against mineral pipe. Took in the drywall that held smears of handprints, had been pebbled to the floor from wire being ripped out but not finished. Just frayed ends of copper hanging as if some scrappers had been halted of their actions.

From the far left corner next to a curtainless window, a yoke hung balanced in its center from above. It held medium-sized hooks on each end where two hinds had been attached, now shriveled. The carcass they'd been connected to was no more, only sticky splotches of matted pelt and blood lay on the floor. *Looked to have been from a deer,* Horace thought. Steps printed from the mess, tracked toward a hallway where shapes flicked and strobed. Worry stirred within Horace. His grip damp around the crowbar, wanting to find Van Dorn, be rid of this place. Stepping down the hall into a windowless room that reeked of urine. A candle sat creating a static haze. Shining over the blots of shag; blankets lay twisted and piled. A doorless opening descended. Basement, Horace thought. In the corner, grimed toenails poked from boots that were attached to frayed denim. The father guided the light up the legs. Made out two silhouettes. A voice came in a sparking screech. "Dim that there light, trespasser."

The shape of a man held a length of steel pressed to Van Dorn's throat. His face looked cooked and split. One eye stared. The other was bare skin the shade of a cherry-flavored slushie.

Van Dorn gripped the reciprocating saw at his thigh.

"Don't be quaking that edge to my boy's throat, we've no yearn for trouble."

Thoughts of dying entered Van Dorn's mind. Of all that he'd seen. All that he'd not done. They'd crossed some unruly types on their journey but nothing that made him question his longevity.

"This here is our squat."

"Release your clutch from the boy, we'll be a memory."

The words *our squat* had not registered in Horace's understanding when he saw the blade making contact with Dorn's neck, but the aroma of dated cottage cheese suffused with humidity suddenly weighed heavy on him. Van Dorn's whites metered wide.

Two feet of lumber angled into Horace's nape. The flashlight danced on the floor. Horace palmed at the throb in his neck. "Shit!" Took another hit from the wood. A voice clanked over Horace with a warning: "All your kind do is cripple the foundation of its worth. Teach you not to carve and steal for density."

Tense, Van Dorn's gut knotted with the blows that descended upon his father. Knowing he should've turned back the same way he'd entered. Seeing where the plumbing had been stripped; animal carcasses and human feces littered the basement walls and floor. The blade came from nowhere, threatened him with "Yell and it'll be your last. Just watch and listen." The heathen man and Dorn waited.

Van Dorn spasmed, felt the sharpness against his throat. The laugh of words sprayed over his shoulder. "Elsner's getting his groove on your pops."

Watching Horace's outline on the floor, Van Dorn felt the heathen's chest in his back. A hand rubbed at the arch of muscle that connected to his hamstring. The other man laid a boot into Horace's ribs. The heathen relaxed the knife, began sniffing Dorn's lobe. Horace grunted. Dorn wanted to vomit. Thoughts of what to do. How to do it came all at once. Van Dorn raised his left hand up his body. Fingered the sharp line below his chin. Squeezed the trigger of the saw in his right, spun, and slanted a crosscut into the meat of the man's leg. The man bellowed, "Aw, shit! Shit!" Hot specks peppered Van Dorn's hand; he watched the man reach and pat at the dark that spread from his thigh like a busted transmission.

The one called Elsner looked to the screams. Then came the crack. The separation of foot. Then another crack and the discomfort that blistered up Elsner's shin and knee. Caused the release of the wood. Elsner squealed, bent forward at the split and give of his calcified metatarsal's tissue. Horace worked his way from the floor with a hammer. Stood heaving and leveled the straight claw into Elsner's scalp.

Fingers raked at Van Dorn's shoulder with adrenaline. "Help your ole man." Dorn leaned, supported Horace's mass as he panted, "Lead us from this goddamned layer of filth."

Van Dorn guided them down the hall, into the dining room, where several outlines emerged. Raising the tool, Dorn mashed the trigger of the saw, cut at the air, parted through something meaty; a man groaned, "Bastard." Bodies backed away barking, "No, stop, stop." Van Dorn rushed, dragging Horace into the kitchen and out the door.

At the truck, Horace swung his arm from Van Dorn, reached for the driver's-side door, and said, "I can navigate."

Firing the engine, Horace shifted into drive and stomped

the gas. Tires flung dirt till they bit hard surface. He drove out the same way he'd entered, questioned what had just taken place, trying to make sense of what they'd walked into, some unknown juncture of midwestern hell.

After surviving a near-death experience and viewing the possibility of losing his son, Horace pondered what he'd spoken to Dorn. The clenched fists he'd belted him with. Guilt of his abuse sunk in. Of their lives of salvage. Maybe he'd traveled so long that he'd lost sight of change. He felt the rhythm pounding behind his breast. Knowing what caused this beat was blood. It was the same that pulsed within Van Dorn, and as they disappeared into the raven of morning, Horace told him, "Maybe it's time we looked to settle back home, maybe rebuild what once was, create a new existence."

With the haze of dawn bringing the shapes of trees and field grass into focus, Horace and Van Dorn followed the back roads that morning down to the Stage Stop Campgrounds. Pitched their avocado-colored tent and camped. Slept like soldiers after a recon suicide mission. Woke well after lunch with the sun's glow beating down on the tent. Overwhelming them with stifling heat. Making it uncomfortable to breathe. Their bodies lacquered by damp, road grit, and a week or better without bathing.

Waking, they packed up. Horace needed fuel and Van Dorn was bit by the want for something more than the weight of carp or bluegill being snagged and reeled from the Blue River.

With the windows down, they headed west on 62, turned north on 66. Passing a Pilot gas station. Van Dorn questioned why Horace didn't stop, and Horace told him, "Wanna see the old land I've distanced us from after all this time."

Highway 66 curved and dropped, though it was less steep than Van Dorn recalled. There was a time when riding down it felt as though one were free-falling from a cliff that had been dug out. Reconstructed and widened. Trees looked as though they were dying. Their leaves turning early. The land around them weathered, not green but singed like a burnt russet.

Horace followed 66 all the way to Marengo, where it turned into Main Street. Crossing over old 64, Horace cruised by wood-sided homes. Brown shutters peeling, front doors missing and jambs rotted, and roofs collapsing. Old Dodge with doors ajar, paint discolored by sun. Trees littered what yards there were, dead of growth. Where torn garbage bags knotted and hung from limbs. White signs with red letters had been nailed on the front of each home, reading: THIS BUILDING OR STRUCTURE HAS BEEN DEEMED TO BE IN UNSAFE CONDITION AND SHALL NOT BE USED OR ENTERED BY ANYONE WITHOUT THE WRITTEN PERMISSION OF THE BUILDING INSPECTOR OF MARENGO.

Horace wheeled past the red brick of the Old General Store that was no longer in business. Metal barrels sat on the side. One mashed a decaying black, the other rusted and dented. A busted-up pay phone mounted to the building's outer wall. They turned down Water Street. Steered a U-turn in front of a powder-blue metal-sided pole barn. On the white bay doors someone had spray-painted SUPer SHInE DeTAIL ShOp. Heading back the way they'd come, Horace fired up a cigarette. Let it lie loose on his lip. Turned down 64 and drove west toward English. Van Dorn took in more of what they'd been away from for so long: the small roadside park with a rock-climbing wall that was more of a pull-off and rest area than a park. The Jay C food store and the Curby ice cream shop, an area that still had not been built up or overrun by Walmart and fast-food chains. It was still simple and small. Mom-and-pop businesses. Not polluted with too many choices. The way towns should be, or had once been.

Horace turned down 237. To the right stood a greening turquoise statue of William Hayden English, the man the town had taken its name from, an Indiana politician. Pulling to a stop next to a pair of dated gas pumps, with long metal levers on the side, Horace looked to the calico brick building with a red tin roof—it was the English minimart—and Horace said, "From 1859 to 1990—"

Van Dorn finished for his father. "—the community encountered six floods, town council bought one hundred and sixty acres, and moved everything to higher ground. Second-largest relocation for a town in U.S. history."

Evening was upon Van Dorn and Horace. Smirking at the boy, he said, "At least you've still a mind for the importance of the historical. Of learning where people come from and what they've suffered to get where they're at in life."

"It's what you learned me."

"That it is. Glad it's stuck."

The minimart's door lay steel-framed in the center with a bay window on either side. To the right sat a scratched white newspaper box. On the left, a huge ashtray sat spilling over with butts. Horace stubbed out his remaining smoke and they entered the mart.

Brass bell overhead jingled. To the left stood a female behind the counter. Ale-burnt skin. Locks thick, dark, wavy, reared, and banded atop of her head. She wore a gray T-shirt. Nodded without expression.

"Evening."

Horace adjusted his cap, brushed his hands over the stained and messed Hanes he'd been wearing for days, and said, "Evening, ma'am. Me and the boy be grabbing some provisions." He pointed to smokes lined up above her head. "I'll be needing a carton of Camels and twenty-five dollars of fuel."

"Sure. I lay the smokes here for when you's ready to check out," the female said as if she were lost in a catatonic haze.

In front of the counter stood a blanched-faced beast of a man with graying shards of beard, grease-stained trousers, a head sheared of any hair. Folds of scar lined his neck with a thick black graving of ink that Van Dorn couldn't make out. He twisted his face to Horace and Van Dorn, spoke in a rusty tone. "Is a wave of heat out there, ain't it?"

Discomfort melded through Van Dorn's body like butter to hot toast. Horace nodded to the man. Fucked him with his eyes. Said, "About the same as it's been."

Keeping his body between the man and Van Dorn, Horace and Van Dorn surveyed the aisles of shelving to their right. Upon tiers lay bags of chips, candy bars, jarred sauces, canned goods, and relishes. Sensing his father's unease—something was out of order—Van Dorn could feel Horace's protecting, keeping himself closer to Dorn than usual. Not letting him walk the small aisles alone. Horace's eyes darted to the man without shifting his view while pulling cans of chicken, SPAM, and sardines, beans, a bag of rice, and a loaf of bread from the shelves. A radio sat on the shelf behind the lady, playing Jamey Johnson's "High Cost of Living." They approached the coolers to the back; drinks, lunch meats, and eggs were enclosed, kept cold. Dorn pulled out bottles of water, a package of ham and bacon from within. Walked back toward the counter with Horace.

What Van Dorn and his father hadn't seen when they entered and passed by the beastly man was the matted black Wilson Combat .45 pistol in his right hand. The man had now turned his back to the entrance. Trained the barrel on Horace. With his left hand he pushed a nylon bag upon the lard-colored counter next to the carton of Camels.

"Pay no worry to this gun. After the half-breed cunt fills the sack and you lay your wallet on the counter, I'll be a distant memory."

The man's yellow eyes twitched wide with a fluorescent glow.

Van Dorn's father pursed his lips and said, "The lady won't be filling the sack with cash and I sure as shit won't be offering up my hard-earned efforts to nourish me and my son upon the counter."

Holding the pistol at Horace's chest, eyes bulged with anger, the man thumbed the hammer back, stared through Horace, told the lady without looking at her, "Empty that fucking machine of its worth, Widow." And to Horace he demanded, "You drop the groceries. Lay your wallet to the counter or the floor gets a fresh shine of you and your boy."

Horace looked to the lady behind the counter slowly and said, "Don't give him a damn thing."

With meanness the man said, "She shall."

"She won't."

"Testing me? That it, stranger?" He glanced over to

Horace's left, leveled his sight at Van Dorn, who was near equal to the size of his father. Ran a tongue over his bottom lip. Demanded, "Come here, boy."

"Don't move, Dorn," Horace said, then back to the man: "Place that shooter back down the hem of your denim. Walk out the same way you entered before I open you like a can of beans."

The man found Horace's words amusing. Chuckled. Van Dorn watched the man's index finger rub the trigger. Size him up. He had maybe an inch or two on Horace but each held swells of muscle built from labor and hard living. The man shook his head. Repeated his request to the lady he called the Widow. "Tired of waiting to see who has the biggest dick. Empty that fucking machine or I give the boy a new breathing hole."

The man's words carved malice throughout Horace. Van Dorn could see the red that kindled the side of Horace's face. Horace told the female behind the counter once more, "Don't give him no currency."

The man's cheeks scorched like burners on a stove turned to high. "Clip your fuckin'—"

Behind the counter the Widow moved. Reached for something low. The man with the gun caught a glimpse of her movement. Glanced toward the female.

Fury edged and pushed through Horace's insides. He came forward with the cans of food, released them, grabbed at the pistol with both hands. Pushed the gun hand up. Drove a left knee into the man's rib cage. Kept himself between the beast and Van Dorn. Shielding him. Horace and the man stumbled back and forth. Struggled for control.

Horace angled the knuckles of his right fist into the side of the man's complexion over and over. Drawing an ooze from the temple till the man slipped Horace's grip. Brought the side of the pistol against Horace's jaw. Knocked him against the counter. Standing with blood spewing down onto his shirt. Training the .45 on Horace, the man told him, "Might look Aryan by the shade of your pigment, but your actions speak otherwise."

Horace came growling from the counter, followed by the eruption of gunfire.

NOW

Violence engulfed Dorn's every reflection. Distancing himself from the memories of the food mart. The Sheldon girl's face netted around his brain with darkly pigmented men covered in tattoos that Dorn'd slain and those that came upon the aftermath. Especially that outline of a figure with the crown of thorns.

Up the basement steps he came, exhausted from the memories. Pouch of venison slung over his shoulder. Jar of potatoes in hand. *Outdoor Life* magazine in his back pocket. Through the dining room and out the kitchen door. A crippling hunger pulsed in his organs. Unlike his thoughts, the night was clear overhead. Gas for the stove in the house had run out within the first month. Paper and leaves had been piled. Twigs were tepeed over them. Lit and then kindling stacked till the singe of coal came from the small log that smoked over the open flame of orange and yellow.

Meat browned in the small skillet that lay over the thick wire shelving Van Dorn had torn from the fridge after the fuel disappeared. Placed over the wall of limestone he'd picked and piled to construct the circular fire pit.

Next to the slices of loin, canned potatoes popped within the hog fat he'd spooned from a mason. Carried from the house and laid on the ground next to him. Upon the bank, Dorn sat with the .30-30 across his knees, watching the riverbed below. Inhaling the flavor from the pop and sizzle of fat. Thinking of his grandfather, who spoke of hogs being raised on chestnuts and slop. Of how it created the toothsomest meat but made the white lard cook into a black oil, scorching the flavor. So they incorporated a diet of corn for a month or better before butchering them. Causing the fat they yielded from the hog to stay white and not cook into a black burn.

On his grandfather's farm, Dorn recalled the screams and squeals from hogs. Of them in the wooden pen, a floor concocted of shit and mud. Dorn stood waiting, watched his grandfather and father corner one after another, banding their fronts and hinds, held tight while Dorn sliced the swine's balls off. Laid them on the wooden rail where they appeared like two fleshy baseballs. Then cut the hog loose, letting it run in the pen with its bloody fold of skin hanging that looked near a rotted cloth. Mountain oysters or lamb fries, his grandfather would joke. They'd castrate the hog to help fatten it before the butchering. Once the hogs were fattened, they loaded them in the rusted bed of his grandfather's truck, metal bars welded, homemade, to jail the poor squealers for their travels to another farmer's place to be processed.

Now, forking the meat in the pan, turning it to fry evenly, Van Dorn wondered about the other faces. Thought of them being loaded on the truck, if they were being hauled off for butchering.

Sitting the fork down, closing his eyes, he made the images out, patched and filthy. Some were young boys. Eyes plumbed with sags. Lips peeled. Others behind the bars were young girls. Daughters. And older females. Mothers. Opening his eyes, he slid on the thick cotton glove, protecting his hand from the heated handle. Removed the pan from the fire. Let it lie out on the rock, away from the flame. With night he could travel the land. Maybe work his way toward English or Marengo. Search for these men who took people. Find their encampment. Where they rested. But then what would he do once he found them and those whom they took?

Knifing a hunk of loin from the skillet, savoring the taste of deer, he chewed and thought about that night they'd returned to Indiana. About the man who held up the Widow. The moments he'd tried to bury but could not. Instead they infested his mind like the enslaved faces in the back of the flatbed.

THEN

Horace never fell. A hole bored into a side wall. Somehow missing the glass of a bay-sized window.

The pistol rattled to the tile with the shuttering body that followed. Van Dorn eyed the man laid out sideways. Horace grabbed the .45. The female arched over the counter, still holding an axe handle she'd blindsided the man's skull with. Horace huffed air and slanted words with vehemence to the man on the floor. "Threaten me, my boy, now comes consequence!"

Van Dorn watched the man grit his teeth with his father's bootheel realigning his teeth. Coloring his gums. Crooking his cavity for air and words, replacing words with grunts and slurs.

Stepping back from the man, Horace glanced at Van Dorn. "Veer your face south, son." Next an explosion came like hail to a vehicle. Brass bounced onto the floor. A mess was created. The man's image spread over the floor with a mural of bone, muscle, and brain.

The female screamed.

Everyone's ears rang. Afraid to breathe, Van Dorn twisted his view back to the man. Studied his splayed features. From his perspective there was no twitch or pulse of fiber.

Horace towered over the man, held the smoking pistol in his bloody fist, and said, "Stupid son of a bitch forced my reaction."

Movement came around the counter, the female dragged the axe handle behind her. The three of them stood staring at the man's swells of crimson that had become his detonated appearance. A pool of nerve tissue and blood widened in its shape. Stained the floor with its expired tint.

Van Dorn could hardly believe the ease of violence.

"Lord God," the female said, "you showed him his end."

"Dumb-ass pointed a gun at me, threatened my son. No one lays a threat nor a hand to my blood except me."

"You've made that clear."

Quaking from neck to heel, the woman reached with the axe handle. Jabbed the man's body like a young child testing a dead animal's bloat. Nothing returned. No rise or fall from his cage.

"He's one dead son of a bitch."

"Thought he's gonna try and kill me and my son."

"You twisted the tides."

A rank smell crept among the store. An off-color pool seeped from beneath the man's center. His bladder had fallen. Horace shook his head, turned his eyes to the female, asked, "You gonna phone the law?"

"Hell no," she snapped.

"It was self-defense. I'd no other means."

"Ain't disputing the facts. He's a month out of the pen. Know'd no other skill than robbing folks."

"You know'd him?"

Walking around the body, the female studied the sinking of his shape. Stopped and said, "Know'd him, I married one of his brothers. A man who dowager'd me. But left me the family's store we's standing in."

Surprised, Horace looked to the woman. "You're telling me this retch was robbing his own?"

"Was his intentions, yes. Until you and your boy walked in on his attempt. He wasn't good for much. None of them Alcorns are unless it involves hassling a person that ain't white. Except my husband, Alex. When he married me their family tree was peppered with some culturing. I ain't white and I ain't black. I'm what they call half-and-half, or mulatto."

Horace said, "Them?"

Laying the length of wood upon the counter, the lady wiped her nervous palm against her pants leg. Offered it to Horace. "Call me the Widow Alcorn." Pointing to the man, the Widow said, "This one here that you showed his end was named Gutt."

Horace shook his head. "The boy and myself did not come for trouble. Call the law. I'll take whatever consequence they offer."

"Cain't. His brother finds out he's shot dead in my store, they'll as soon kill you and me. Hide us where no cracker-headed badge'll look."

Horace's complexion grazed confusion. "You can't leave him lying about the tile for everyone to see."

As though she'd devised it before Horace and Van Dorn had entered her store, the Widow spoke calmly. "No I can't. I'll be needing you and your boy's hands."

Passing to the rear of the mart, the Widow opened a door. Disappeared for a moment. Came back with a gun-magazine-sized cut of plastic. Unrolled a tarp next to the body that sounded like thunder as it crunched and she spread it open, created an enormous square.

"Time ain't something we got much of. But sooner you help me roll his dead ass up, I can mop his remains from the tile, toss his ass in your truck, have you and your boy follow me to my place, bury him deep."

Holding the .45 down his side, Horace looked to Van Dorn and asked, "It's your choice, Dorn. We help her get rid of this man, we're seared for life. Or we walk out. Drive to Johnny Law's, I turn myself in."

Dorn swallowed the bitter taste of decision; his ears no longer rang. But his heart pounded. Arms ached as he hugged the lunch meat that sweat a cold spot through the cotton of his shirt. Glancing to the loss of life before him, then to the Widow, Dorn wanted out of this place. He thought about his father. He'd learned him of surviving life. Never abandoned him like his mother. Dorn stepped toward the counter. Dropped the food upon it, exhaled, and said, "Gonna need some gloves."

Rushed, the Widow walked over to the shelves of food and supplies. Removed two sets of gloves from a chrome carousel. Handed them to Horace and Van Dorn.

Sliding the leather gloves on, Horace told Dorn, "Boy, sometimes life don't care much for us, beginning to believe we should've never encroached back over the Ohio River."

Horace and Van Dorn tried the best they could not to step their boots into the expanding pool of blood, and dropped groceries as they rolled the warm body onto the tarp. Taking in Gutt's ripped-apart complexion.

Pulling a set of car keys from Gutt's front pocket, the Widow placed them into her own, with a key chain dangling a Nazi swastika. Horace shook his head, told the Widow to get some tape. Grabbing a roll of gray duct tape from a shelf, she, Horace, and Van Dorn wrapped the body up like a burrito, taping and sealing the ends, snugging the canvas to the cadaver.

A sickness festered and bubbled within Dorn's stomach. The insides of his mouth watered but he held back the bile. Horace eyed Van Dorn and told him, "Let's get him to the Ranger."

Dorn got the feet, Horace the head, lugged the heft of the deceased out the door. Darkness had saturated the land. No sound could be heard other than the hum of bugs swarming outdoor lights or vehicles traveling up and down old 64 off in the distance. Horace used one hand to lower the tailgate, support the body he half laid on it. Climbed into the bed. Situated his and Dorn's gear, then maneuvered Gutt, placed him long ways, but had to bend his legs. Laid their wares atop of his body, camouflaged the lifeless passenger, and closed the bed.

Horace filled the Ranger with fuel. Backed it around to the side of the mart while the Widow sopped and bleached the blood from the floor.

Lights within the store disappeared. Out the front door came the Widow, who bolted the entrance behind her. Horace and Van Dorn sat without words in the Ranger with hunger rolling around their insides.

Through the rolled-down window, a set of keys dangled from the Widow's left hand, then a carton of smokes released from her right, landed on Horace's lap. "Camels is on the house. The food sweated too much. Can get new tomorrow. But now, someone's gotta drive Gutt's car."

From the road behind the Widow, lights came slow with the crack and give of gravel as an old Dodge wheeled in.

From inside a male voice hollered, "Widow? Guess you's closed?"

The Widow turned, Horace jerked the keys from her reach, whispered to himself, "I'll navigate." He looked to Dorn. "You ride center behind her in the Ranger, I'll follow behind you once this local gets his ass moving."

"What if he don't?" Van Dorn whispered back.

"Then we might need to help him find his route, he's thieving our time."

The Widow walked toward the man in the truck and spoke. "Yes I am, Elmer. You have to come back tomorrow around lunchtime or head to Marengo."

Elmer rested an arm on his steering wheel, poked his head out the window, trying to get a closer look at whom the Widow was speaking with. "Who's that you talking with back yonder?"

Van Dorn watched Horace slide the .45 from his waist. Keeping his eyes on the man as he mumbled through clenched teeth. "Don't force my hand, old-timer. Go on and get."

As he thumbed the safety on the .45, Dorn's heart sped back up.

The Widow said, "Just some that has lost their direction."

Elmer lowered his arm that rested on the idling truck's steering. Reached for the latch of the door.

"Ain't giving you any trouble, are they?"

Horace laid his left arm out the Ranger's window, fingered the handle. Watched the Widow's pace pick up and she told Elmer, "Lord no. They's okay. But I gotta be getting along. It's late. You need to do the same."

"Don't suppose you'd unlatch that door, maybe flip a

light and grab me a pack of them Indian smokes so I don't gotta hit a tavern?"

From the road another set of lights came. Sped on past, but slow. Horace pulled the latch of the Ford open. The interior light didn't come on as they'd removed the bulb. Keeping the camouflage of night for when robbing homes. And Horace said, "Fucker can't take an invitation, I give him a hint."

"I can't, Elmer, done told you I need to get."

The Widow turned away, her face one part anger, the other worry. Meeting Horace's eyes, she lipped *no*. Wanting Horace to stay in the truck. Gears in Elmer's Dodge shifted. The suspension squeaked and he slowly twisted the steering, pulled back onto the road, drove on until his taillights disappeared. At the Ranger's window the Widow said, "We take the back roads, shouldn't be no concern for the law."

Horace came from the truck, told the Widow, "My nerves need no more testing." He glanced back at Van Dorn. "You shouldn't have born witness to this, son. Another man having his life taken. For that I apologize."

Dorn didn't know what to say. But he guessed they did what needed done and slid into the driver's seat.

Van Dorn watched from the side mirror as Horace walked to the rear of the store, disappeared around the corner where a GTO sat. A moment of uncomfortable silence passed. Then a door squeaked, slammed shut, and the hot rod screamed to life.

Starting the Ford, Dorn waited for the Widow, who drove up in a burgundy Chevy Silverado. Yelled out the window to him. "We going to the right, be cutting over a few roads, it'll seem farther than it is but it ain't."

Van Dorn nodded. She took to the right. He and the father followed. They lined the back road like three sets of incandescents, mouth to ass.

Behind the wheel, Dorn thought of the world that was taken from Horace and him. Things he once thought genuine. The skills his father held with his hands, turning lumber into furniture, restructuring homes, hunting wild game, preparing it. Things Horace had been learned by his own father. And now they were lost in that world that drained men once good, forced their hands, wilted them to bad. Left them with a trail of wrong. Look at them, driving down this road with a murdered man in the bed of the truck. Following this female through the pitch-black night. Dorn's heart throbbed and his lungs burned and he pressed an index into the CD player, which lit up. Spun a tune, Waylon Jennings singing "Lonesome, On'ry and Mean."

Dorn wondered if they could trust this Widow. What if she was touring them into a fouler situation than already existed? And Dorn tightened his grip on the steering. His palm damp from nerves. Nosed the Ranger closer to the Widow's bumper. Taking the winds and curves, hoping she was as trusting as she appeared. Hoped for someplace to rest. Someplace devoid of worry. The harder Dorn tried to wipe the bad from his mind, the worse the thoughts of what he'd watched his father do lulled through him. Knowing if they were ever caught, they'd be charged for the murder of another, and then what would become of them?

Oncoming headlights cut shadows down the faces that navigated the three vehicles. Dorn checked the rearview for someone to brake each and every time. Worried that one of them would turn around. Follow them. Fearing somehow they knew what he carried. But none of the passers did.

Headlights drove on, disappeared into an abyss of back-road grit and timber.

The three vehicles progressed over the road as it snaked, dropped, and rose up and over the hills. In and out of the valleys. Trunks and limbs zipped past until the Widow braked hard, turned off Harrison Spring Road and onto a dead end, Jennith Lane. Where at the gravel's end a cottage-style home sat. The yard lit by floodlights that showed antique parts. Tractor. Plow. Bailer. A road of potholes took them out to a mess of shack-like structures. The Chevy stopped. Van Dorn braked and slid the Ranger into park. The Widow got out of her truck. Her frame glowing phosphorescent in the Ranger's lamps. She was attractive. Shapely, Dorn thought as she motioned for the father and him to do the same.

They were standing outside their vehicles, and the Widow pointed. "Park the GTO around back of the chicken coop. Let the Ranger ride down the rivets of tire tracks right there and kill the engine. We got us a long walk to carry Gutt, up into the woods along the river. Gonna get us some shovels from the milk house and a few traps to set after we finish the dig."

Horace wrinkled his complexion, questioned, "Traps?"

"For skunk. Need to make sure we cover what we bury, deter other animals and such away."

The Widow walked into a shingle-walled structure the same pigment as blood. Came back from it carrying two triangle shovels and a calcified pick. Propped them outside next to the door. Went back inside, came out with the burn of a lantern and several links of chain attached to rusted metal mouths. Horace shook his head and mumbled to Van Dorn, "Hell've I gotten us into, boy?"

Van Dorn dug a Maglite from beneath the Ranger's peeling-vinyl front seat. His bearings uneven but knowing he must show strength like his father. Must be strong. He pushed the light down into the denim of his ass pocket. The Widow rested the tools for digging upon one shoulder, the traps clanging from them. Her other hand led the way with the lantern. Dorn and Horace stepped to the rear of the Ranger, gloved their hands, pushed their wares from the lifeless mass. Horace motioned for Dorn to step back. "I got him, help the Widow with the tools."

Horace lifted Gutt, broke him down over his shoulder. Dorn took the shovel and the pick from the Widow, placed them over his shoulder, and she led the way.

Humidity and heat delivered the pungent and repulsive scent that wafted from those who no longer breathed as Van Dorn and Horace trekked over the land that lay foreign to them. The Widow guided the two male shapes through the wilderness, panting within the night, twigs and branches marring and scraping their hands and faces and arms until they descended into a sinkhole with the circumference of a large swimming pool but maybe forty to fifty feet deep. Where in its bottom they lay the stiffening hunk of humankind to the side, began to dig at the scorched and hardened earth.

Above them, they were surrounded by shadows of wood and limestone. It was here that Gutt Alcorn would lie in burial. Dorn and Horace rolled his shape into the hole that ran as deep as the father was tall. Man and boy stood damp and stinking. Tips, palms, and complexions smudged and printed by soil. They covered Gutt until there was no more dirt to fill the hole. No words of hymnal were spoken to send

Gutt to his Maker or absolve his connection to the world he'd once known. Only the trounce of distancing soles to earth as the Widow wandered back up the steep hill to set her traps for skunk with the father and son following behind her. Climbing back to the top of the meteor-like hole. Lungs burned while their bodies began to feel the loss of energy. The crash from being amped up on violent happenings.

Once the Widow's traps had been set in a location where she'd watched such critters trespass, Horace and Van Dorn followed her back through the woods, trampling over limbs that cracked and popped, noticing the sound of a river was nearby; each thought of running toward it, jumping in to feel a relief from the mossy film that covered their hides.

Van Dorn was spent but knew the night was not coming to an end as the Widow spoke. "Dark'll only last so long. We need to get back on the road, dump the GTO."

Van Dorn replied before his father. "We can then call it a night?"

And Horace said, "We may never know day nor night again. At least not in the normal sense."

To Van Dorn, the Widow replied, "Yes, we may call it a night after the car has been dumped far from everyone's eyes." She stopped, held the lantern to Horace's damp and salty face. "All things will come to pass with time, trust me. Was nothing so hard as losing my provider."

Van Dorn and Horace followed the Widow out to Tucker's Lake in the GTO, where they wiped the car clean of any prints, left the GTO with the keys in the ignition, returned to the Widow's home with the gray of morning cast upon them. Offering Horace and Van Dorn shelter. A place to bathe, eat, and lay their heads. They stripped themselves of garment. Saturated cotton and denim with fuel. Ignited their clothing within a burn barrel. Showered and dressed in fresh garments.

In the kitchen, the Widow prepared breakfast while the two men sat at the kitchen table that was covered by a white cloth. Glass salt and pepper shakers sat in the table's center, each the size and shape of a large goose egg with a lime-green lid. Horace was fidgeting, his nerves needing to be numbed from all that had taken place.

The Widow stood over the pearl-tinted stove, blue and orange flame heated the bottom of a black cast-iron skillet where she spooned a ceramic-colored mixture of bacon and beef fat from a used mayonnaise jar. A dozen eggs lay in a pink carton about the counter where she picked up the oval shapes, one at a time, cracked them open, and dropped the clear goo with yolk into the skillet, where it popped and sizzled.

"What brought you and your boy to English?"

"Wanted a look at what we'd not seen in some time."

"Not seen?"

"We been on the road. Far from here. Was salvaging for a living. Kinda lost my reasons, being rooted in the county when the wife skipped out on me and my boy, then the economy went to snuff." Horace looked to Van Dorn with deranged bloodshot eyes and finished with "We'd been gone long enough, decided to come back."

"Seems many a folk has lost they way in these times. Can remember when one could always find work. It ain't that way no more. Between jobs drying up, meth, heroin, and opiate addiction, people's dead 'fore they even know it." The Widow went silent, then said, "Never said what your names was?"

"I'm Horace Riesing. My boy's named Van Dorn."

"Well, Horace and Van Dorn, how you two like your eggs?"

The Widow asked this as though nothing had occurred.

"Soft in the center," Van Dorn said.

Horace balled his hand into a mallet. Unable to take the unacknowledged weight of what the past forty-eight hours had seized his conscience with, he brought the fist down on the table's center. Rattled the shakers. Van Dorn sat as though time had quit. Wanted to reach out. Clasp his father into a hug. Let him know things were as okay as they could be. That they had each other.

"A man has been murdered by my hands," Horace shouted. "Buried by me and my boy. And you ask how we want our eggs?"

The Widow swallowed hard, ignored Horace's words. "How many you two want?"

Van Dorn's eyes bugged to the size of cue balls. Starved and knowing his father would not answer until he was free of what they'd been accomplices to, Van Dorn spoke for them each.

"Let's start with the dozen."

Angered, Horace said, "Don't be a pig, boy."

"He's fine. Just me out here and I got a mess of hens. Mess of milk from my few cows and pounds of meat in the freezer. Two of you's safe here. After breakfast you can get some shut-eye. Decide what you wanna do when you wake."

"Dammit, Widow, what's your angle in this taking of another's existence?"

The Widow turned to Horace and said, "No angle. I take kindly for what you done. My brothers-in-law have belittled me since my husband's passing. And even before with their snide ways. Though it's wrong, I feel no qualms nor pity for what happened to Gutt. Don't know how many times I wished his and the others' deaths. Only thing I'm sorry for is that it was you and your son who had to do it. But what's done is done." She paused, turned back to the cast iron, flipped the eggs onto a plate covered by towel paper to absorb the discoloration of grease, cracked several more eggs into the skillet. And she finished with, "In these woods the rules can be shaped how I see fit, not how they see fit."

And then it came, the one thing Horace needed to find his calm. "Got any sauce?"

"Kind of sauce?"

"Only kind they is, that which is rendered from mash and rye or wheat, corn, and barley."

The Widow flipped the eggs as they crisped brown and whited on one side and she told Horace, "They's a half gallon of Maker's below the sink. Glasses is above. Help yourself."

Standing, Horace stepped to the sink. Bent down, slid the curtain back that doubled as cabinet doors, where he found not a single bottle of bourbon but five half-gallon bottles. He grabbed one. Reached to the upper cabinet, pulled three clear glasses from it. Went back to the table, where he twisted the red lid that matched his eyes from the squared bottle and poured himself three fingers of ginger-colored liquid, then three for Van Dorn and the Widow.

He sneered at Van Dorn, nodded to the glass. "To help you sleep." Then to the Widow he said, "I poured you a taste."

"I cannot drink this early. I have a store to run. Traps to check. Things to tend."

Horace sucked his glass empty, then reached for the Widow's glass, took a sip, and asked, "How did your fella find his end?"

Glancing to the ceiling, the Widow thought for a second and then spoke. "On his way home from cutting wood. Had our other Chevy's bed weighted full. Brakes went out when he was traveling down the gravel curves of Rothrock Mill Road, hit a tree head-on. All them ricks come through the cab. Crushed him. Died in an instant." The Widow paused, then asked, "How about you, your wife?"

"It was the dope. Lost her to the meth and the opiates."

"Some say a madness is coming to the land. If you follow scripture, it sure seems like end-times."

"Scripture or not, madness is here. Me and Dorn seen the lives of the working scattered throughout the states we haunted, hoboing, camping in tents along streams, vacant homes no longer able to be afforded. Seeing the young who've no skill. Why I've raised Dorn in the old ways. Taught him some thieving. He can use his hands and his mind. I seen this foolishness coming long ago, when he's about five we bought us a TV. Next thing I know we's going to the grocery and he wants different types of cereal with each trip, not 'cause he likes them, 'cause he sees these commercials advertising different trinkets in the boxes."

Dorn cut in with "Father takes our TV out into the field with his twelve-gauge, shoots it. Blows the tube to shards."

Fried eggs with their greased whites lay piled on a large plate while the Widow dropped slithers of bacon into the skillet. In another cast-iron skillet, diced potatoes the size of silver dollars fried with hunks of onion and specks of pepper. The smells fed Dorn's and Horace's senses. Turning to Horace as he filled his glass once more, the Widow told him, "They's no TV in this home, only a radio and an eight-track player. No need to worry. But this madness we speak of, me and Alex knew of a man who lived on down around the county forest, some say he's crazed 'cause he says that he sees things before they occur. Sometimes in visions. Other times in dreams. Claims we should all be prepping for a wave of bad. Some say he's a prophet, others a drunk with a warped tongue." The Widow paused as the food popped and she took in the shadow that rattled her back door's glass. "Shit, it's Dillard."

Van Dorn asked, "Who's Dillard?"

"Gutt and Alex's older brother."

Like Dorn's father, Dillard Alcorn was thick in size, hands similar to extra-large snow gloves, a tattooed frame similar to a shadow of a Mack truck, only it wasn't a shadow. It was a man built from labor and hard living with auger-bit eyes that screwed into your mind and forced you to look the opposite direction if you were weak in the orbs and yellow backed.

When the Widow opened the door, Dillard towered over her, seeing a man and his boy who'd not been seen before at his sister-in-law's home. He registered this information, brought his attention back to the Widow. Telling her, "Gutt never come home last night."

"And this concerns me how?"

"You know I's keeping a short leash on him since his release. His nose void of dirt. He's family. Something your half-breed ass is still part of regardless of my baby bro's passing."

"Ain't seen hide nor hair one."

"He's to have met me at Lisa's last night in Corydon. But told me he'd something he needed to take up with you first."

"Didn't take nothing with me. You check with those he takes commerce with?"

"That I did, but he's not been seen."

Dillard was no fool. Knew something was amiss. Eyed Horace and Van Dorn.

"Who might be your company?"

"Those'd be my acquaintances."

Gripping the inner jamb of the doorway, Dillard started to push past the Widow and questioned her as she blocked his passage. "Not gonna offer your brother-in-law an invite to your home? An introducing to your guests? Them flavors of breakfast is tempting my taste buds after being out all night looking for Gutt."

The Widow laughed. Clamped strong to the jamb with both hands and said, "Only time you come around is to nose into my affairs of living, seeing as Alex is no longer alive. Don't think I'm in the mood for your company nor introductions on this morning."

Dillard was still eyeing Horace and Dorn; Horace impaled him with his eyes, the bourbon offering extra fuel to his cockiness, and Dillard asked, "Wouldn't be the ones'd lost they direction, would it? Elmer says he came by the mart, seen you speaking with some folks and you wouldn't open up for him to buy some smokes."

Not veering his view from the doorway, Horace grabbed his bourbon. Sipped it and said, "Why don't you ask us who we are?"

Rage glazed Dillard's stubbled jawline. As he pressed his chest forward, the Widow's grip broke from the jamb. Teetered her back. She sensed the cockfight that was brewing. Reached at the slab of door. Began to rear it closed, mashing Dillard's fingers. "Maybe they is, maybe they is not. It's my business, not yours or Elmer's."

Dillard sized up the situation. Saved the fight for another

time. Pulled his hands away from the doorway, took a step backward. Watched the opening shrink while eye-fucking Horace and said, "Remember this, Widow, you'd not have a pot to piss in if it weren't for my baby bro or the blood that birthed him."

With that the door hinged shut.

NOW

Morning came with the threat of sounds, busted and splintered lumber. Feet trampled floorboards, heavy and weighted. Followed by the voices of men, muffled and foreign.

From the green military cot, Van Dorn rose already dressed in a knurled T-shirt and denim work pants stained by the drudge of days in search of food. Booted feet planted to the fungus floor of the basement. Hunger was a twisting pang for sustenance even after eating every cut of meat from the skillet the night before. Then digging into his memory. Memories brought on by the killing of three men with familiar engravings from his past but upon whom they'd been engraved, he could not place as it was unclear, fogged in his memory.

Gotta leave this place, Van Dorn told himself. Trying to rouse the grogginess of sleep from his frame. Pulling the .45-caliber Colt from beneath his pillow, sliding it into his holster. Still unable to shake the familiar face of the Sheldon girl being caged with those women and their young, Dorn grabbed the lever-action .30-30. Slung it over his frame.

Stiffness fired about his muscles from the fall and fight of yesterday's actions.

Snakes lay coiled in corners and about the floor like land mines ready to be detonated, but not by Dorn. For reasons unknown they'd always navigated to him like protective pets.

Making his way to the back wall of shelving where a metallic gun safe stood, door ajar, he wondered how many were upstairs, wondered if those from yesterday had tracked him. Pulling a backpack from one of the wooden shoals, raking supplies into it from the safe: Ammunition. Ohio Blue Tip Matches. Binoculars. Compass. Dorn slung it over his back. The tick of his heart was equal to an early-morning pot of coffee as he counted the steps of feet overhead, stomping from room to room, knowing that regardless of who it was he'd stayed in this home too long. Been fortunate not to have been raided or discovered long before now. Knowing that movement willed progression. Stagnation willed death.

Moving in a blistering rush across the fault-cracked floor to the slab of cedar that led outside, Dorn cursed himself, knowing he should've taken to the land long ago in search of others similar to him and his father and the Widow. Frontier types who understood their terrain. How to live from it. But then there was that fear of those who kill and rob you of all your worth.

Before the dollar had failed, and folks walked away from their jobs, formed militias across the United States to take out the power grids—after following the actions of the Disgruntled Americans—took a stand and told their government that they'd had enough, houses around him had turned to camps or rentals for getaways that never came. Beyond these homes within the valleys and back roads he sometimes hunted, he began to view men and women who went into hiding in cellars, embedded themselves into the earth, bunkered by soil and leaves. Folks who were scared. Dorn had spoken with some within those first weeks. They'd not wanted to risk lives. Traveling into town as others had and never returned. Hopes were that someone or something, be it county, state, government, or military, would come for them, offer answers. But after too many months, no one had. Only scavengers, militias, and the horde had made their way throughout the land more and more, reaping it of its commerce.

Grabbing the door handle, Dorn glanced to the corner. Made out the shape and the familiar scent of fuel. Listened to the ransacking going on from room to room. And voices that did not speak clearly.

Reaching down, Dorn grabbed the can of gas. Removed the cap, thought of the Sheldon girl. Of going catfishing late night down on the Blue River. Pouring fuel into a lantern that lay behind them on the gritty bank. Glow of a half-moon cast down upon the calm of water. Trees hung overhead. Lines baited, weighed down by sinkers with triple hooks and chicken livers. Fishing the current's bottom till the zigzag came, Sheldon jerking the rod opposite the pull and tug of the fish. Her arms lean but strong as a boy's until she fell in. Dorn dropped his pole. There was a panic at first. His struggle to help her. Hands holding her. Splash of water from limbs. "Stand up," he'd told her. "Stand up." And when she wouldn't he grabbed her hips, pulled her upright. The river level stopping at her denim knees. Laughter reddened her face in the moonlight. Locks wet. Her shirt soaked. Braless. Van Dorn turned his eyes away from the shapes beneath, trying to be respectful. "Nothing to be ashamed of,"

Sheldon told him. "I'm a girl. You're a boy. There's an attraction."

Van Dorn thought of her and the others starved of hope and he knew what he had to do. Began dousing everything. Floor. Shelves. Walls. Stairs. He'd find these men and the women and children they'd taken, and he'd free them by whatever means necessary.

Overhead, the bedroom where Horace and the Widow lay was entered. Accented muffles hollered, "Goddamn, they's dead! Rotted!"

Dorn stood by the door that led to his freedom from the house. Dug a match from the box in his pack. Waited. Listened to the footfalls approaching. The basement door was busted from its hinges, bobsledded down the stringer of stairs.

Dorn knew it was now or never. Clamped his eyes shut. Listened to his heart pump one jab after another into his breastbone as the soles of boots descended the stringers. Purging. One at a time. Dorn remembered what his grandfather Claude had told him of *soldierin'* when getting rabid on vodka. He'd served in the Korean and Vietnam Wars. Hide of one leg whittled and gnawed by shrapnel. Begged as he did to have the limb removed, the doctors would not. The man was old-school badass. Would sit sucking down one glass after another, spilling stories of traveling in small units. Before initiating combat, he and his men sat, studied their enemy. Discovered who was commanding, killed him first, and the others scattered and fell by brass, bayonet, or grenade. They were run down, hunted, and eliminated.

Opening his eyes, he flicked the match against the zipper of his jeans. Inhaled the sulfur flame ignition. Met the eyes of the man who led the others down the steps. Lifted his weapon. Dorn tossed the match to the floor. Turned. Flung the door open. Gave more air to the combustion of flames. Stepped out into the daylight, where black dirt-specked vehicles were scattered about the property. Off in the distance stood the blur of the figure with tattoos comic-booking his face, a crown of thorns haloing his temples, and the Sheldon girl within his grip.

Stone-shocked for a moment with what was happening, Dorn wondered if she had led these men to his dwelling after he'd abandoned her and the others earlier.

Automatic gunfire kicked up granules of soil. Van Dorn's veins were swamped by adrenaline, he'd no other choice but to run. Couldn't contemplate the Sheldon girl's actions, he could only react, run opposite of the mayhem, away from the screams, shrieks of shapes being ignited, and the carbine that echoed all around him. Hoofed toward the barn, where he saddled his mule, Red. Heard the shouts of men from the house. The Sheldon girl's face haunted him. Her long layers of moleskin hair. Smudged cheeks and blue eyes. Custard lips, limbs so thin they appeared ossified.

Mounting the mule, Van Dorn pulled on the reins. Guided Red out the rear of the barn.

Galloping along the river, Dorn halted the mule, turned to study the sky above the trees. Looked back to where the house was. Thought of circling back, but knowing there were too many of them, well armed and beyond pissed off by this point as he saw the hint of black rising. Smelling the burn of all that he'd known since returning to Harrison County: wood-framed windows, walls of shelves that held pictures of the Widow's people. Fathers, mothers, and grandparents. Her history reduced to ashes.

Van Dorn told himself he needed to find distance,

regroup, devise a plan, then maybe he'd scour the land. Not let the Sheldon girl lose her account of life. Not let it be taken or ended before it'd even begun. He'd start by traveling north up the worming Blue River. Cross over to the west, keep to the trees above and along Rothrock Mill Road, journey past the place of the killing, keep working his way toward Wyandotte Cave Road and beyond, hopefully find shelter amongst the rocky hills.

—

There was the uneasiness of eyes studying Van Dorn's every movement as he reined Red down the grooved soil of broken bank where a canoe launch was located at the Mill. Red took the decline along the shore of pea gravel. Dorn studied the green glass of miniature ripples still present even without much rain, and thought of the river's center and the folklore that plagued it.

The Widow had told him that a local man of the county, who was married with a boy, had drowned his lover in these waters, the lover being his cousin, though she was never found. The blame had been placed on the man's son because of an altercation between him and the father over the female's disappearance. Something the son had seen but the father denied. The Widow knew this as truth, telling that she'd been the one to have found the drowned female's stray bones downstream when laying manure nets in large holes for baiting catfish. Though it was not nearly enough to construct a body, it had given the Widow reason to drag for more. She searched the river bottoms but nothing else was found.

Crossing the river's center, Dorn's mule came from the water on the opposite shore, climbed the hillside at a slant. Clomped over a dead-end road where people had once parked to fish. Other than tracking and shooting the deer, Dorn had not hunted or traveled this side of the river since the loss of power. He'd kept to his own, hunting the fields and wilderness to the southeast, not the northwest. Refraining from as many eyes as possible, especially the hordes that'd become more and more visible over the passing weeks.

Working his way over the leaves crunching like miniature tins, Red huffed and snorted, several times jerking as though he were spooked or sensed Van Dorn's paranoia of those he'd ignited within the house.

Dorn halted Red. Listened to the woods. Read the signs: a huddle of sparrow about the ground in search of nourishment, a bush-tailed squirrel gathering nuts from below a walnut tree, and as Dorn watched he wondered, if he were to shoot a rabbit, would the fur about its bottoms be thicker than normal? It was mid-September and before he'd become a scavenger, he'd grown up with the wisdom of his father predicting the oncoming winters by the wildlife's behavior and their appearance. So far their movements hinted toward a rough winter.

Waiting, Van Dorn listened and watched to see if he was alone. Several crows perched upon a limb, another sign for a bad winter. Dorn watched the birds' quiet. Their quick blink of the eyes. Their glancing into the silence around them.

Dorn navigated Red back to where he'd begun to dress the deer, shot the men. Crows walked about the stains. Picking at the rutted remains of rot. On one of the trees below him hung what appeared to be a blackened appendage. He dug the binoculars from his pack. What he viewed was exactly that, a human limb. From another hung what appeared to be a hand.

Lowering his field glasses, Dorn thought of animals who

urinated over a section of ground to ward others off, territorial pissing, only these were humans, they'd marked their territory with the dead. *A warning*, Dorn said to himself.

Behind him leaves trundled with the clomp of what sounded like footfalls. Turning. He glanced to the ground. To the trees that climbed up into the gloom. But saw nothing and the noise ceased.

Traveling on past the killing ground for what seemed an hour, Dorn came to the edge of a property line. Stopped. Before him lay several acres of dead cornstalks, tanned and broken over. Paths made way into what had once been a yard but looked like a hayfield that coursed up to a home forged of brick. White pillars from the side. Land that had once been farmed, probably sold when the parents grew old and passed away. Had maybe been developed into the beginnings of high-dollar homes. Something Dorn's father and the Widow complained about on their late-night binges on Maker's. Something Dorn and his father had seen firsthand while jotting down addresses to rob.

Searching his memory, unable to remember seeing this residence on his way to the Pentecost's place with his father, Dorn recalled the long driveway. The home couldn't be seen from the road.

Feeling eyes dig into his back, he could not shake the uneasiness of something bad. Lifted his binoculars, searched the area for evidence of transit, something out of place. Disrupted. The heads of two Labradors lay with bodies outstretched. One fudge. One black. No rise from their ribs. Their insides appeared gored. Splayed out. Looked like fresh kills as the blood appeared red and saucy. On the front porch sat a man in a rocker. Neck bent back, mouth agape, eyes removed with a vulture on the chair's armrest, beaking at the orb holes. Split-glass flesh marred the side of his temple. A mess littered his front all the way to where parts of his legs looked to have been cut out. Sections of quad removed. The spill of the cutting painted the porch where a female lay tossed out on her back. Or at least it was what Dorn believed to be a female.

The actions were all wrong, though Dorn could not place his finger upon the wrong just yet.

Off beside the home was a matching brick outbuilding. Beside it, an indent of mossed-over land. Parked on the sunbleached blacktop was a navy-blue Mercedes two-seater with the hood raised, nose to nose with a silver Lexus SUV, its hood also raised. Jumpers wired from one battery terminal to the other, connecting the two. Driver's-side doors on each ajar. From the Lexus ran a boy. T-shirt, cargo shorts, hair matted, about eighteen or nineteen years of age. Cutting to the concrete walk that gave way to the home's front porch of cadavers.

From nowhere came a jaunting figure. A head with porcupine hair. Sunken and carved features like a totem of wood. He donned denim bibs. No shirt. He tackled the boy, who hollered something indecipherable.

The figure raised the boy to standing. The boy kicked. Threw his arms sideways. Reached, dug his fingers into the man's features.

From the porch the buzzard took to the air.

Dorn lowered the field glasses. Knew he'd need to make a choice. His heart pounded. Limbs tensed with each echo from the boy that bounced out into the woods where Van Dorn sat hidden.

But the boy wasn't shouting for help.

Dorn swiveled the rifle from his back. Butted the stock

to where shoulder met chest. Hesitated. Clasped his eyes. Opened them back up. Something was amiss. This he knew from hunting, like watching a deer being baited with a salt block.

Front door of the home swung open. Dorn lowered the rifle, raised the field glasses with his left. It was a girl. Looked to be the same age as the boy. Golden locks unfluffed. Flat and olive-oily. Stains about her face, smearing her front. She screamed, "Let go of him!" and from the weeds came another figure. Banded eye, cankered complexion, sleeveless flannel, wielding a hatchet. He hugged the female, raised her up. She rammed her head backward. The figure ran a tongue up the side of her face, laughed. The other figure dropped the boy to his knees. Laced his fingers into the boy's hair. Brought a butcher's blade to his widow's peak.

Dorn lowered the glasses. Knowing he had to shoot them now if he wanted to save them. Risk his direction. Freedom. Alert others. Raised the rifle once more. Seemed there was one, then two, meaning there could be a third, a fourth, and so on. A damn domino effect.

React, Van Dorn thought, *don't think*. That's what his father would tell him. And Dorn leveled the .30-30. Closed one eye. Let the other rest on the knife wielder. But the boy, he looked not afraid. Dorn inhaled deep through his nose. Slowing the rhythm in his chest, the nervous twitch in his arms and hands. Flashes of Gutt on the tile. Men coming at him on the road. Horace drilling into his worldview since birth: *Do what you must to others and abandon weakness*.

Exhaling, Dorn firmly pulled the trigger. Gunfire breached the land. Neck sprayed hot. Hands released the boy. The bibbed figure dropped backward, palmed his neck.

Van Dorn shelled and chambered brass. Turned to the

man hugging the female, who looked to be pawing at her pocket. She was released. Knees hammered the porch. The boy came at the man with a blade pulled from somewhere. The man turned his head upon his neck from one side to the other. Trying to hone in on where the rifle shot came from. But it was too late, Dorn sighted his silhouette between the crosshairs. Then the boy stepped into his aim. Took a stabbing swipe at the man, who stepped back. Lined himself in Dorn's hairs again. Slapped at the boy with his left hand. Brought the hatchet with his right. Another explosion pierced the man's face. Flung chunked juice, deflated his hide to the ground.

Bootheels hit Red's ribs. He clomped through the stiff and scorched stalks toward the home. Trail of dust followed.

Dorn halted the mule. Stopped short of the concrete porch. Bore down on the girl and boy who stood staring at him. Appearing ghostly pale and angered. The other figure clawed at his neck, gurgled as his life slipped away with each drop of being that'd once circulated within, moistening the chiggered weeds.

The boy looked up to Dorn with a small gash at his skull's peak. A rivulet of blood trickled down his forehead. A flaking rub decorated his plump lips. No tears dribbled from his brown eyes, which sunk into their orb holes. Cheeks appeared rashed and he smirked. "The hell are you?"

"Van Dorn. And you?"

"I'm Toby. This is my sister, Ann."

Ann studied the mule. Her skin so deficient of pigmentation she looked like a species of cave fish that never knew light as she ran a tongue over her chaffed lips.

"Who are these that attacked you?" Dorn asked.

"Trailer trash like all you, that's what our parents called

them before they discovered their endings," said Toby, as he glanced to Ann. Nodded his head. She reached to her pocket. Lifted her eyes to Van Dorn, who took in the measure of slick steel in Toby's hand, and he smirked, said, "Or supper, as we've come to call it."

Van Dorn glanced at the man in the rocker; his legs had been carved at the muscular regions. Then the two dogs in the yard. Cars that didn't run. Appearing to be jumped. Van Dorn didn't want to accept what he'd realized too late, what he'd interrupted.

Toby and Ann stepped to Dorn and his mule. Ann buried a curved surgical blade into the mule's neck, tugged downward, parted its hide.

Red squealed. Blood steamed.

Toby dug his knife into the opposite side of Red, who kicked his front legs up into the air. Bucked Van Dorn from his saddled back. Wind was knocked from Van Dorn's lungs when he hit the solid walk and a vibration moved from the rear of his skull and drove a loss of time from his mind.

THEN

Finding his way back to the Widow's home, fast as a metallic element boring from a gun barrel, was Dillard and an unknown figure. A week had passed since Gutt's GTO had been discovered at Tucker's Lake. It'd been combed for evidence. Held no print, neither hair nor hide. Nothing to suspect foul play.

The unknown figure was not the type of man Dillard was known to hold commerce with, which was typically an Aryan-skinned local or paroled felon with sawed-off teeth and a scarred jawline. Instead, with him he brought a gaunt shape who'd a bourbon hide. Oreo hair and a maze of ink about his arms that gave headache to the eyes, trying to figure out where one faded carving began and the next stroke ended.

Before word had bled through the county with the finding of Gutt's GTO, an offer had been put forward to Horace and Van Dorn. A place to lay their heads, begin their lives anew with the Widow. In return, the Widow asked for a hand around her place. Horace and Dorn accepted, as the killing and burial of Gutt had gilded a trust amongst the three.

It was after lunch when the sun stroked down upon Horace, Dorn, and the Widow. Netted beads of sweat from their tawny skin. They planted by the signs of the zodiac, meaning each day was branded by one of the twelve signs that appeared once a month, which lasted two or three days, then changed, guiding Horace and the Widow by the markings on a red-and-white calendar that hung in the Widow's kitchen. Using the constellation that was to be foremost in the sky at the time of planting, the body part associated with the planet and its closest element, would yield the best time for seeding, knowing when it would be too hot, cold, wet, or dry.

Horace managed the flaking green plow that forked from hands, reined and harnessed to Red, the mule who pulled it up and down the dirt, the rusted curve of a triangular blade cutting rows through the soil. While Van Dorn hoed lines for sowing, and the Widow came behind, dropping seedlings and pushing the dirt over with bare feet. They marked the end of their rows with a single stick. The paper packet the seeds came in placed upon it. They had lines of corn, green beans, peas, peppers, cucumbers, lettuce, and zucchini.

Dillard walked out into the loose soil, the unknown man following. The Widow stopped what she was doing and Dillard said, "Know you've heard they found Gutt's car but no trace of Gutt."

And the Widow replied, "Word is all around the county. Some say he's run off. Others say he had an unpaid debt. Regardless, it concerns me none."

Hulking over the Widow's firm and shapely outline, Dillard raised his ink-collaged arm of bullets, blades, and swastikas, steered a finger to her face. "It concerns you plenty. I know he was to pay a visit to you. Now he's vanished and you're shacked up with these two hides. Think you've indulged in more than you're letting on."

Horace halted Red in the garden. Sensed the tension that was to be unleashed from Dillard. Turned and began to walk over the fresh cake-mix soil, boots imprinting the dirt, leaving a path of his tanned muscle that glistened within the heat while the knuckles of each hand bled the color of bone.

The Widow told Dillard, "Who I keep company with is no concern of yours. Done told you he never visited the store."

"Awful coincidental that my brother vanishes when these two road rags roll into town." Dillard looked to Horace and demanded, "Who the hell are you, simpleton?"

Dorn walked up till he stood near shoulder to shoulder with his father, just behind the Widow; he was almost the exact size and shape of Horace, only younger. Hair split-ended and stenciling over his eyes. Hoe in his right hand, ready to swing if needed, back up his father. Horace kept a straight face, sweat stinging his eyes, told Dillard, "None of your fucking concern, wannabe bigot."

Dillard smirked and said, "When it concerns my brother, I make it my business." Dillard leaned to his right and told the man beside him, "Think maybe his tongue needs adjusting. What do you think, Manny?"

The tatted man alongside Dillard smiled. Jutted his head up and down. His tone was broken and foreign as he sized up Horace and Dorn and the Widow. He said, "Think they all need calibrating." Without warning, Manny stepped toward the Widow. Waved a slap to her face. Startled her as she tripped backward but didn't fall. Dorn was behind her. Caught her weight.

Before Manny raised another motion, Horace laid skin down on him with a right fist. Chiseled an ovaled opening into his sight. Pinched his eye, stumbled Manny into Dillard. Horace circled Manny, kept him between him and Dillard. An obstruction. Quick, he tugged Manny's ear, head-butted him. Then drove a fist into his throat.

Dorn had pulled the Widow away from the onslaught. Shielded her.

Arms and legs gave. Manny's knees stumped into the soil as though two pieces of firewood waiting to be split. Hands spread to catch his balance. On all fours Manny heaved. Tried to find the wind that had been cinched. Horace had started to lay the tread of his boot to Manny's complexion when Dillard raised a black Glock 19 handgun to the rear of his head.

"Enough, motherfucker."

Seeing the Widow disrespected, pistol pointed at his father, Van Dorn grabbed the hoe. Circled it over his head with a whooping battle cry of "Ahhh!" Prepared to etch a split down on Dillard's face.

Horace turned. Brought right and left hands to halt Dorn, took the hoe from him. Told him, "This is not your fight, son." With lungs fast expanding, Horace turned back to Dillard and smirched, "Seems big men need to bring guns and a Spaniard to do their bidding against road rags."

From the ground Manny wheezed, "Ain't Spanish. I am Guatemalan. And if I'd my Mutts with me you and your spawn would not be breathing."

Keeping the 19 on Horace, Dillard told him, "I need answers about what happened to Gutt."

With a jawline bit by tears, the Widow told Dillard, "You're barking up the wrong damn tree. Need to hunt somewheres else."

Dillard lowered the Glock. "They's something here but it ain't tree'd. I believe it's buried."

NOW

He woke with a belt of pain to the rear of his skull. Hands bound. Wrist over wrist behind him. Laces removed from his boots. He was in a massive opening, devoid of furniture. His eyes adjusting to his surroundings. Shelves climbed to the ceiling with medical dictionaries, anatomy bindings, and surgical doctrines combined with philosophies by Jung and Freud, an A-to-Z encyclopedia on serial killers. Appeared as though he were in a museum of books that foretold deviant theories.

In the front room, a bay window appeared with the curtains drawn. Large rectangle of an oak door, closed. Poster-sized illustrations of the human form hung beside him. Some were of the backside. Others of the front. Some skeletal. Some muscular, tendon and organ. Body parts named and dissected. On shelves sat the bones of hands, feet, and skulls from human and animal.

As he tried to work his hands back and forth, to free himself, the waft of air within reeked of something putrid, like the chickens they sometimes found in the Widow's henhouse.

Dead from the unbearable humidity. Dorn thought he'd been taken to a lair for the broken and fragmented.

Strung over the floor before his feet were the interiors of his pack. Compass and boxes of ammunition. Somewhere behind him, the sound of words being whispered drifted from a room. He needed to figure out where he was. To distance himself from this juncture. Eyes followed the blood that smeared and tracked from the front of the room, continuing on past him. Looked as though someone'd had a mud bog using a person's insides.

Everything about the home screamed grotesque. Footfalls traveled in an upward clomp. Growing in pitch till the feet were leveled beside him.

A callused nudge came to his right temple. Dorn looked up at Toby standing milky skinned and lean. Features depressed, arms casted with red, holding Dorn's .30-30.

Studying the way Toby held the rifle, gripped it like a spear, no finger on the trigger, the safety on, Dorn questioned Toby's understanding of the artillery, whether he knew how to shoulder, aim, flip the safety, and shoot.

"You near cost us our supper."

"Supper?" Van Dorn questioned.

Behind Toby, a long hallway was lit by sunlight. Pictures of deformed men and women hung from the walls. "We've watched these bands of degenerates loping about as though a lost herd of goat. Such easy prey they are, of course they thought the same of us, I'm certain," Toby said.

"Prey?"

"Prey. They're not the first we've baited with our tactics of jostling back and forth, pretending to jump the cars, acting as though we've no idea they're watching. Childish really, not much different than playing an Xbox game. Guiding them in, so to speak. It's what we've grown accustomed to in order to procure nourishment."

"You mean food?"

"Dear God, yes. Food is something we ran out of eons ago. Parents had no choice, really. Cars wouldn't run. We waited till we could wait no longer. Father and mother were morticians. We've been around dead bodies since our birthing. We were showed how they were prepared for viewing, but never for nourishment."

Van Dorn asked, "The man and woman on the porch?"

"Suicide was their alternative. Their choice."

Van Dorn questioned Toby while slowly working his hands back and forth, as the binding wasn't tight. "Choice?"

"They offered themselves. Not an easy decision for either of us. But they were old, we are young, and they weren't born blood. Better them than Ann and me."

"Born blood?"

Turning his back to Dorn, Toby walked about the fired squares of clay like a professor offering a lecture. Glancing at the walls. Running a tip up the spine of a volume that lined the shelves. Raised his voice.

"Adopted, simpleton. They were not our real parents."

On the floor, Van Dorn pushed his back into the plastered wall. Twisted his wrists within the nylon strings; his thoughts bounced between shock and dread, unable to fathom the thought of eating a human, let alone one's parents, for continuation. Thought about Jeremiah 19:9: *I will make them eat the flesh of their sons and daughters, and they will eat one another's flesh during stress of the siege imposed on them by the enemies who seek their lives.*

In his lower back he felt the cold pang of a handle, the

pistol. They'd not searched him, only his pack. The muscle that pumped blood in his chest raced. He needed out of this layer of cannibal. Adolescents turned to the ways of the vile before they took him as their supper.

"Why not hunt the land for wild game?"

"Hunt the land?" Toby's laughter recoiled from the walls of the home. "We know nothing of hunting animals other than that you need to gut them and remove the skin. Grew up learning anatomy and reading books while Father viewed the world news. Father always found humor in the bartering of beliefs for world power. How graying men shuffled papers at the expense of others' lives who actually fought wars. That's what I wanted to be, a paper shuffler. It's easier to wait, let the food come to us. To stab rather than pull a trigger."

Van Dorn kept Toby speaking. Buying his time. "And you've survived all these months on . . . human?"

"On the meat of man, woman, and child, yes. We hide when necessary. Have a panic room in the house. It's hidden within the basement. Nothing electric, just old Victorian trickery," said Ann as she came from the hallway, bare of shoes, her feet and shins covered in fluid, her arms bubble-gummed with scars from what looked to be cleaving.

"Had planned to go home. Back to the city when the power went out," she said, walking across the floor in an almost catatonic state. "Our father drained the battery on the Mercedes, trying to jump the Lexus. Ran it out of gas."

She came up behind Toby, ran a hand up his neck, licked his cheek.

Getting a cold shiver, he felt the taste of how a rotted possum smelt expand upon his tongue and Van Dorn asked, "Why would he try to jump one if the other ran?"

Ann glanced at Van Dorn with a sneer. "'Cause everyone wouldn't fit in the two-seater, what an invalid question."

Toby turned to Ann. Kissed her forehead. Stared into her eyes. Reached a left hand at her breast, ran a thumb over it, and asked Van Dorn without looking at him, "What is your story, Van Dorn, from where do you travel? You look very filthy but speak with a hint of intelligence."

Feeling the looseness within the nylon from his boots, Dorn wouldn't argue for the siblings' intelligence; they'd not tied his wrist with firmness. Wanting to live, he'd have to move, and move quick. Abandon his pack. He thought of Red, his mule. How they laid blades into his thick coat, digging at the meat, for consumption, he believed. Looked as though he'd be on foot. And he lied, "My mother and father's truck gave out long ago. Stayed on the farm till our food supply dwindled, saddled our mules, tried to make a go of it out in the wild." And he thought of the men he'd shot and the women and children they'd restrained. "Till a group of hordes ambushed us. Murdered my folks. I escaped. Been livin' off of wild berries, yellow root, and game ever since."

Across the room, Van Dorn noticed the lurk of shadow darkening outside the window. Toby and Ann were caressing each other. Pausing and studying the shelves of books, Toby said, "Ah, your mule. He had a name as though a pet. How standard. He'll be our supper this evening. Something new. Marinated in olive oil and red wine. We have a gas grill out back. The one item Father kept stocked with fuel in case of power outages. It's lasted us all this time. How many months has it been?"

Ann didn't answer but said instead, "We've still got a battery-powered radio, though it has no use anymore. Used to listen to a man on an AM station at night, ranting about madness, saying that like the United States, all of Europe went bankrupt when the American dollar fell. That jobs dwindled, militias formed, and crime escalated. People no longer trusted their government. He talked of Mayan Prophecy, of solar alignments, storms wiping out grids, and something called an EMP, electromagnetic pulse. Others think maybe a virus from a hacker could've infected everything. Just assumptions, that's what the man said. No one could prove him wrong, everyone was in the dark, living like nomads, no communication, no news. Though there was one thing he spoke of with certainty: there are no more rules."

And Toby said, "Sure miss hearing that crazy bastard and his theories."

Seeing his opportunity, Van Dorn needed to act before they sectioned him for the grill or whatever was outside the window came and enslaved or slaughtered everyone. Working the gap between his wrists, he watched as Toby and Ann warmed about each other like incestuous lovers, their eyes not watching his movements but studying each other. Toby's right hand rubbed between Ann's legs. Tongues drew wet over each other's lips. Dorn closed his eyes for a moment, wanting to curse himself for wasting ammunition on those two men. Believing he was salvaging Toby's and Ann's lives; he had sensed something was amiss. Should've trusted his instinct. Dwelling on the horror of this killing skewed Van Dorn's thoughts and psyche as he tried to keep his wits about him, and he asked, "What possessed your folks to come out here and live?"

The silhouette outside the window paused, then slowly disappeared. The door handle's latch lifted. A clicking motion that went unnoticed.

Irritated, Ann said, "Dear God, the simpleton and his questions. A summer home. Father and Mother liked to come here and recharge their batteries, relax. Get away from their jobs in the city."

Toby released a pouting breath and cut in with "Internet is slow, barely got a cell phone signal. Only thing we could do was watch satellite when it didn't rain, play Xbox, and read."

Having seconds to react, Van Dorn questioned whether he'd be forced to kill these whom he believed he'd saved. He'd be a fool if he didn't, they'd off him when the mule meat was gone and the hunger pains set in. Or they could castrate him, feed and fatten him up for a butchering like the hogs his father and grandfather took to.

Van Dorn felt the shake in his finger's ends, and stress jarred his tendons and ligaments. The front door creaked open slow and methodical. Toby and Ann looked to the intruders in surprise. Two profiles passed through the opening. Outside light gave them the appearance of faceless figurines, hiding their features at first. Once they were inside, Van Dorn saw that they were male. One wielded a cane cutter, its width discolored by something human or animal; the other gripped a roofing hammer with what appeared to be strands of hair caked between its claw. Clothing was ragged T-shirts, tainted work pants; their scents were a concoction of the earth, burnt papers, spored lumber, and sweaty socks. The whiskers upon their scratched and crusted faces could've marred the paint of a vehicle. And the sugarcane-cutter wielder looked to Toby and Ann, yelling, "You've murdered our kin!"

Freeing his hands, which were rubbery and confetti-filled from being pressed behind him, Van Dorn dug at his lower back, pulling the .45 from his waist. Toby stepped around

Ann, placing her behind him, lowered his head, tactile and wormy. Eyes evil slits, he butted the .30-30, pressed it toward the man, and said, "Killed me some supper, you invalid fuck." Ran a tongue about his lips. Tugged and tugged the trigger as though using a video game's plastic gun. His face was confused when there was no explosion of gunfire. He held no understanding of how the rifle worked.

Grinning at Toby's ignorance, the man laughed. "Fool." Sliced the air with the cutter. Knocked the .30-30 away. Came with another slice. Caught Toby's forearm. Split the muscle as if it were a squash being sectioned for a salad. Toby screamed. Blood oozed. The .30-30 clattered on the ceramics. The one with the claw gavel thumped Toby's skull like he was staking spikes, connecting and securing iron on railroad tracks. Over and over till he plopped the skull into the floor, creating a heaving mash of tissue and gore; Toby's entire frame jutted and jarred as though pummeled by electricity.

Ann stood in hysterics, screaming, "No! No! Toby, Toby!"

The man with the straight claw embedded his hand into Ann's starchy lengths of hair. Slammed her face-first into the shelves of books that collapsed to the flooring until her shrieks found quiet.

Training the pistol on the mallet wielder, Dorn thumbed the hammer, squeezed the trigger, and lit up the interior with surprise.

THEN

Upon the Widow's property, Horace took to sharpening tools or mending the leaks of the roof with heated tar from a bucket. Replaced sections of rotted stringer and joists within the attic of the Widow's home or patched pipes beneath the sinks. Hunted wild game and split wood for the oncoming winter. Each kept an eye wide for the unexpected visitor, listening for the ping and drop of gravel from the tread of vehicle while the Widow worked the mart, as Dillard's visits now came once a month after the battering of Manny. Always in search of clues to his brother Gutt's disappearance. Always he traveled with companion, men from south of the equator, the Mutts, he called them. And Horace told Van Dorn, "One can only wonder why the alien skin finds interest in an Aryan."

Day had shifted to night after the picking of beans. Seated around the kitchen table one night, Van Dorn and the Widow broke the mint-green strings that were as long as crayons. Taking them from the tin basins and placing them into large plastic dishes to later be washed, boiled until tender, and cooled with cold water, packed and layered into masons with salt water. Then sealed and stored.

Johnny Cash's tone belled from the speaker of an old eight-track player the Widow had been given by her father. Cash sang of lines walked, getting a rhythm or a boy named Sue. A crock jar of sweet tea moistened the burn lines of wood grain on the table with condensation. A ceiling fan trundled overhead. Horace sipped on three fingers of Maker's as the Widow finally told of her dead husband, Alex. Of how they'd once been. How they'd become and how he'd found burial in the bone box.

Meeting in town at Lisa's, a local watering hole, he'd bought her a drink. Conversation ensued. She lived with her parents on a farm around Crandall, Indiana. Where her father raised a small number of cows and hogs. Farmed feed corn and hay. Her mother was a black Baptist, her father a white Methodist, spiritual and hardworking, each appreciative of the land.

Alex helped his father, who worked for Olin Chemical in Brandenburg, Kentucky, farmed several hundred acres of corn and soy, but he also ran his parents' minimart in Marengo.

Numbers were exchanged.

The Widow and Alex's courtship lasted a year. They traded vows at Fountain United Methodist church. Mortgaged the place in which they now sat. Alex's parents gave the mart to them as a wedding gift. Something neither Dillard nor Gutt ever accepted. They were the seeds that spawned an alternate direction. She and Alex lived simple. Never had a phone or TV, only a radio and the eight-track her father had given her.

She ran the store, sometimes with Alex. Ordering what

was needed. Keeping the books straight with part-time help. Dealt with the brothers. Their snide slurs that funneled beneath their breath. She and Alex lived in this way for ten years until he'd gone to cut some fallen timber for Warner Stokes, one of his father's friends. A leafy-faced man with a pear-shaped build and yellowed chewing-tobacco teeth. He'd stopped by their home. Told he'd seen a hickory tree that'd been blown down after a storm. Said he'd no use for it, that it was Alex's to keep, use for firewood if he wanted to cut and haul it without help.

"Being a hard wood, it was best for winter fires, lasts a good long while," the Widow told Van Dorn and Horace. "Alex being as he was, always thinking he needed plenty for the following winter to cut, pile, and let dry till the next summer. Use what he cut from the previous year. The man was always thinking ahead. Figured it was too good to pass up. So he made the early-morning trek, worked on it all day."

The Widow went silent for a moment. Quit her breaking of fiber lengths. Then came the crack of her voice, as though it were a test of strength to speak. "Thing was, I drove the beat Ford every day to work. It was mine. Alex always drove his Chevy. But he'd not wanted to haul the ricks in his truck as it were newer, less beat-up. Was coming home that evening on Rothrock Mill Road, coming down them gravel drops and curves. Parts of the road had been washed out and ridged from some rainstorms we'd been dealt recently. Police surmised he was tired, the shoes had gotten too damp. Dozing off, he took one of the drops too quick, fishtailed, pressed the brake, slammed into a tree. All that weight in the bed came through the cab. Mashed him six ways to Sunday. Sheriff Elmo Sig later said the brakes had went out."

Coming up on the wreck that night after closing the mart,

road blocked off by the tan cruisers, the white-and-orange ambulance, their strobes of red and blue marbling the surrounding wilderness, the Widow nearly lost it when she saw the bed of her Ford truck. The cab full of lumber.

Seeing him in that morgue, swelled contusions. Purples casting to darker shades like a vegetable finding rot. Bulbous swells of pulp, the Widow told Dorn and Horace, she never seen such a sight. Couldn't help but wonder if it was Dillard who messed with the brakes. Bled them of fluid, hoping it'd be she that come across her ending that night after work, not his brother.

NOW

The gun jerked Dorn's wrist. The mallet-wielding man's left thigh spit like an eruption of sap from a tree with the ooze of fragment, caused the man to shift in surprise as though his leg had been stung by a hornet, and he screamed, "God-damn son of a bitch!"

Ann's outline wilted onto the books that'd fallen and piled. Patting at his wound, the mallet wielder focused his view at Van Dorn with rage that heightened the pigment of his face. He'd not noticed Dorn on the floor before. Dorn now looked to the door opening. Then back down at his supplies strewn about the tile. *Get out the door,* he thought, *and to the woods or risk a fight you may not win, supplies you'll sacrifice to salvage your life, live another day.*

On his feet, Dorn was stopped oak stiff by the cane-cutter wielder. Eyes leveled on each other, Dorn offered the opening of his .45 and the man kept his feelers raised, questioned, "What heathen are you, son?"

Van Dorn glanced down at Toby, who appeared put together all wrong by his Maker, his complexion a wad of gashed and battered flesh. Ann lay down beside her spewing blend of a brother. Feeble and slow, she worked her hands together like a puppet's crossed and knotted strings in an expression of grief and confusion.

Van Dorn stared through the man. *Shoot or be swiped by this idolater's blade*, he thought, holding his boot string in his left, shuffling his feet sideways toward the door opening. Keeping the pistol leveled on the man. Heart flicking in his ears. Hands felt weighted, similar to two sponges fully absorbed of liquid. The open door a foot away, Dorn lowered the pistol and ran to the daylight and the front of the home. Leapt over the female, the dead mother. From the corner of his eye he saw a massive blur. Knew it was Red. Heard the buzz saw of fly that swarmed about the sawed hide. Entrails and wasted meat. Landing, he stumbled over the one man he'd shot in the neck. Regained his balance. His boot came off. Twisting, he sat on his ass, slid his foot back into the boot. Behind him came the blade wielder. Knowing his hand was being forced in order to survive, he brought his hands together and cupped the pistol, and an explosion clipped sound. The man's paunch opened to the size of an apple. A mash of cotton, skin, and muscle sketched the air. His abdomen appeared as though several paintballs had burst in succession. Dropping the blade, he patted the fresh wound, hands pasted with the discharge of his organs.

Rolling to his feet, Van Dorn limped through the knee-high grass, kept his foot semi-stiff to not lose his boot again. Lungs flamed like glass being shaped in a kiln. Muscles ached. Worry was knowing he'd abandoned his ammunition, compass, and rifle. The .30-30 was an heirloom from his grandfather to his father and then to him. Now it was a relic to the lost and doomed.

Crossing over Rothrock Mill Road, reading the sun, he was headed northwest and was now unsure where he'd go, what he'd do.

Darting into the woods for shelter, placing distance between the house of horrors and himself, he saw the images replay and erupt in his mind, over and over with the sounds of pistol fire and bodies falling.

Wanting to break down, fall apart, blinking his eyes, Dorn felt a blistering pulse in his frontal lobe. He came to a mess of fallen hickory. Worked his way over the leaves, through the limbs, and sat as though in a makeshift deer or turkey blind, a form of camouflage. Fear and anxiety scourged him.

Fool, he told himself. His father's words. He could hear them now. *If any of those men survive, they'll hunt you down and end you.*

The pistol lay in his lap. Hands raised to his face. The shoestring was wrapped around his digits, rubbed against his skin. His body held a dampness, congealed with the odor of being unbathed. Quaking and twitching, Van Dorn wanted to omit the killing, the murdering of the savage and nomadic in order to endure and persist. The violence splashed images within his brain. Words came vehement and unflinching. With only a pistol, a blade strapped to his hip, he couldn't navigate back to the Widow's, not that there was anything worth going back for. What he had to do was continue forward. Find shelter. Rest. Decide later if he'd seek out the Sheldon girl, the others who'd been taken, and try to understand the purpose of those who hunted and enslaved the women and children.

Anger bit hard within Van Dorn. He reflected on his

leaving the Widow's as he had. Burning the shelter. Food. Accommodation. He could've stayed. Fought. But why? Organizing his actions, if he'd not done as he did, they could've murdered him or enslaved him just as they had the Sheldon girl. He wondered if maybe she was forced to lead them to the Widow's, her family possibly threatened to be murdered like the men he'd watched die. *Hold it together*, he told himself. *No time to be weak. Let everything unravel. Not after all you've endured thus far.*

Smudging the salty tears from his face. Lowering his hands. Sliding his foot from the boot, Dorn threaded the lace through the eyelets of worn leather. Slipped his foot back in. Tied it. Checked his pockets, found several wooden blue-tip matches from the night before. A handful of unspent .45 cartridges for the pistol. Two clips on his belt. Toby and Ann had not taken them. Their ignorance of guns was as moronic as his was for not retrieving his own supplies, he imagined. Seemed they knew only of blades and how to part the hides of souls and eat them. *What a grisly existence*, Van Dorn thought. *One part Old West, two parts rural apocalypse.*

The cadence within his chest had quieted. Only to speed back up when the bark of hounds traveled through the forest around him. Swiveling his head left, he listened. Then swiveled to the right. The barks, some thick baying, others low, muffled, and throaty, sounded as though there were three, maybe four dogs. Van Dorn stood. Rooted through the blind of leaves and limbs. Studied his direction. The barks were coming from behind him. Feral, he imagined. He mashed over the leafed earth. Barks came in groans that pitched and bounced similar to that of an old engine, churning and chugging, the distance being lessened.

Dorn sped up his jaunt, anticipating the tick of enamel at his heels, knowing the damage a pack of canine could tread upon a person. Or so he was once told.

THEN

She'd wanted something more than Horace could offer, that bond of tenderness, not just warmth of companion. Something she once held with Alex. Something Van Dorn's father never recognized since Dorn's mother had run out on them.

Living with the Widow for more than three years, Van Dorn was now seventeen. And with all the numbers that'd fallen from the calendar, Horace and the Widow never held words of degradation, scalding each other with put-downs. The Widow would grow silent after hinting to Horace about that next step, of becoming more than what they were. More than offering a hand to her around her place and the land after she'd given him and Dorn a new life. Human emotion toward another was there, but not the commitment of vows; it wasn't in him.

On those days or evenings when Horace turned her ideas away, of running off to Tennessee to be married, she'd retreat. Want time to herself. Held silence outside in the wooden swing held up by links of rusted chain, where she'd glide back and forth with the Maker's, telling them to Go, just. Fucking. Go! Letting Horace and Van Dorn embark on their solitude elsewhere.

Traveling with Horace to the Leavenworth Tavern for a drink, Dorn would sit and they'd talk. Horace offering his philosophies of the female. Of his understanding of their wants and desires, but knowing the complications that came with bonding by paper. Physically was another issue, a new set of rules to govern. These father-son talks were more of a release for Horace than a learning for Van Dorn. A confiding.

"They get goddamned hormonal," Horace told Dorn. "Wait one day, you'll see what I speak of. They trap you with their tools, cooking, cuddling, and that warm between their nethers."

Late evening was falling upon them at an outdoor table, looking over the Ohio River. High above its gray water they sat on the drab deck, a thick braid of rope running through the surrounding posts, connecting one to another. At a far table sat a man, hair slicked, not one strand out of place. Like the tint of a Hershey's chocolate bar with hints of silver. Arms graffitied by silky red and orange flames. T-shirt. He was hard-looking like Horace. Appeared as not one to fuck with. He made eye contact with the two. Nodded his head, raised his glass of brew, took a swig, and said, "Not seen you and your sibling round here before."

Horace nodded back. "We make our company silent."

The man slid his chair from the table. Stepped toward Dorn and Horace. "Mind if I join you and your offspring?"

Horace was on his third Maker's over ice. Looked to Van Dorn. "Up to my spawn."

Van Dorn sensed something about the man. The way he carried himself. His demeanor. Not cocky but confident.

"Makes no mind to me," Van Dorn said.

The man offered a hand. "Name's McGill, Bellmont McGill."

Horace took his hand. "Horace Riesing. This here is my son, Van Dorn."

McGill winked at Van Dorn. "That name rings a bell." He sat in the chair he'd clattered over the deck boards. Pondered on the name, then spoke. "Couldn't help but eavesdrop on your words, your knowledge of the opposite sex." He used his hands as he spoke. Continued with "Pounding the soft part of the truth. I come here sometimes. Normally bring my daughter for company and the drive home. Name's Scar. Oh, she's a wad of fury. Feel for the man that tries to settle with her. Like her mother, more tom than puss."

Bellmont slapped the table with his punch line.

"Blood's blood regardless of gender. Long as they carry the knowledge of their kin, that'll constitute their worth," Horace said.

"Your talk is in an odd tongue. Where is it you and the boy live?"

"Down off Harrison Springs Road."

Van Dorn glanced at his father, unable to believe his openness to the stranger. His becoming too lax from the booze brought on a nervous pang in his belly. His father was never an open book to others. Kept to himself. His troubles and ways were his own business and nobody else's.

"Hmm, I know near every person in the county. Hell, I own enough of it." McGill took a swig of his brew and, sounding cocky, he said, "Maybe you heard of my gathering I hold every year, Donnybrook?"

"An Irish festival?"

"Sorta, it's a festival of carnage for the working. Where men and women can eat, drink, fuck, do what drug they prefer while wagering and watching men beat the tar from one another for three days and a big ball sack of coin. Lets them forget about all this loss of wages and self that our world keeps stealing from the middle and lower."

Horace took a swallow of Maker's. "Sounds barbaric. Unruly."

"Oh, it's inhumane and pugilistic," Bellmont said. "Would you care for another swallow, the round's on me?"

"Maker's on the rocks. Appreciate it."

"Welcome. And your boy, Van Dorn, what's your poison?"

"Sweet tea. I'm not of age."

Surprised, Bellmont leaned his head back, slanted his neck, squinted his eyes. "Sweet fucking tea? You a Jehovah's Witness or some shit? Of what age are you, son, look to be twenty-one or better, almost as big as your ole man?"

"Seventeen, sir. Almost eighteen."

"Seventeen and you hold a tongue of manners." Slapping the table again, he said, "Tea and Maker's it is. Be right back, Poe seems to be lagging on his help round this fucking grease shack."

As Bellmont sat the glasses of hops, mash, and tea about the table, Van Dorn and Horace offered another thank-you. Bellmont sat down, looked at Dorn, and said, "Know where I've heard mention of your name." He threw the bone out slow. Words simple. Methodical. As if wanting to see Horace's reaction to his own. "I've an acquaintance goes by the moniker of Manny. He's connected with a runner of guns in the area named Dillard Alcorn."

Except for a heated breeze, a wave of silence passed. Horace scuffed his chair over the boards. Situated himself with caution. That pang in Van Dorn's gut caused his nerves to bleed with the same. Bellmont knew this. Eyed Horace, raised a palm. "I've no quarrel with you, nor does Manny. Any man who gives fit to Alcorn is a man to be admired. Alcorn's a wannabe racist. Proclaimed his blood to be Aryan but turned a blind eye to supply weapons to Manny and his gangs, who are Mexican, Salvadoran, and Guatemalan. One of which is run by his son, a revolutionary type down south of the border. In my mind that's yellow as yellow gets. Goes against everything he preached in his early days. He lays claim that you and the Widow somehow offed his idolatrous brother, who in the minds of most should've been buried long ago. Manny knows when his ass has been spit-shined by a man of worth. He's territorial, not ignorant, you earned his respect in many ways."

Chewing on Bellmont's words, Horace sat in quiet. Considering his cards. Dorn knew he wasn't buying it. There was something foul about the entire moment. Like trading sins the way he and his father had done on the road. Breaking into abandoned homes, stealing the weight of metal. Knowing it was wrong. Horace telling him they had to do it to get by. *If not us, then who, some other thief?*

Horace rattled the ice in the moistening glass. Brought the bourbon to his lips. Laid it back on the table. "Alcorn thought he could harass something from the Widow that doesn't exist. I recognize his misery. Wanting to find his sib. But he was warned of striking the wrong path."

Bellmont's eyes flickered. "Agreed. It's been near three years since he vanished. Never hear of the Widow going to Alcorn's place and accusing him of murdering her provider. His own baby brother."

Though Horace knew the story as told by the Widow, he questioned Bellmont, tried to shovel away more answers. "Why do you word it as you have?"

“’Cause everyone know’d of Alcorn’s distaste for his brother’s choosing to wed a stained-skin female. Then to inherit the family store. It left a taste of acidic ore upon Alcorn’s tongue, was the Widow’s truck that Alex drove the day he found his extinction.”

Dancing around information, Bellmont was offering too much knowledge. Speaking of a feud that Horace and Van Dorn had walked into unknowingly. There was a tension at the table that evening. It was as though the Widow had been waiting for Horace and Van Dorn to walk into her store at the right moment. Give an eye for an eye. From that evening on they came to acknowledge that they were the obstruction that kept the Widow alive. Kept Alcorn away from her, as though they were her guardians.

Sipping his bourbon, Horace asked, “You hold no ill ways toward the Widow?”

“No reason to. My ills are with fighters. I barter their skills and bleed them of their worth. Just as the Romans did to the gladiators. Promoters to boxers. Only I feel and know of their pain and struggles. My wife and I used to do it together. Traveling to the rural-area taverns and bars, watching the bare-knuckle fights, harvesting new blood to build my life’s dream, the Donnybrook, and we did, year after year. Watching it grow. Till her liver turned to rot from the tilt of too much booze combined with narcotics. Now I run the racket with my daughter. I’m savage to those that fail me. But kind to those that swim in the salvage and sacrifice of this land.”

“Savage how?” Horace asked as he lowered his gaze upon Bellmont, wondering if this was an indirect warning.

Bellmont thought for a moment, offered a smile that some

offer just before pulling the trigger on a monster buck. "Could I interest you and your boy in a real-life example?"

He looked to Van Dorn. Could see what he felt, an unease. Same as what he felt after the back-and-forth of words, there was something untrustworthy about McGill.

"I think not."

"Fine. Then I shall tell you. Have either of you ever seen the damage a hound can do to the skin of a man?"

"Can't say that I have."

"It's unlike anything you've ever witnessed with the eyes. More defined and brutal than a fist, knee, elbow, or head-butt. Depending on the canine's dentitions. Sometimes pelting the flesh with kidney-bean-sized holes. And the blood, black and oozing. It's how I created something called the hound round with my ole buddy Manny, to separate the men from the boys when a party decides to falsify my trust, declining my offering of a better existence through brutality."

Van Dorn watched the intensity within Bellmont's face. How it tightened and reddened with each discharge of word from his tongue. Watched Bellmont take a drink of his beer. Wipe the foam from his lips and say, "If ever you should cross a pack of wild or feral dogs, run for your fuckin' lives. They'll not stop till you're an open stream of warm, collage the earth with your skin, then stain it with your insides."

NOW

Scents of dank soil and outgrowth came in a hurried rush. Trouncing through the decay of tans, emeralds, and silvers. Trees fallen, uprooted from severe weather. Rotted and withered. Branches scraped and briars snagged Van Dorn's skin and clothing and his lungs burned. Stopping to compose and catch his breath, he listened for the barks that now came like a solid pack of uncaged beasts from the south. An orchestra of bawls that rose up into the trees and rained down upon him, punching louder and louder.

Speeding his pace, Dorn noticed the ground in the distance. Imperfections in the land, how leaves laid lower in spots and so he jumped over, or maneuvered around them, knowing they were animal traps. He was unsure of who'd set them, his mind fogged by the events that had come quick. His stomach growling for food. Blood sugar low. All he could do was react. He'd traveled too far north, unable to calculate whose property he was trespassing through.

Now, behind him, twigs snapped and the terrain crunched with hound paws, closing the distance. About the earth before him, Van Dorn took in a large section where tree limbs lay crisscrossed and lightly camouflaged by plant and leaf that covered a massive pit. He leapt up and over the obstruction with all he had in his tank. Landed on the other side. Unbalanced, he felt his left ankle give and twist. Dirt smeared beneath his nails as he reached to balance and break his fall.

The sounds of falling paws over the land ceased. Turning, he watched the snap, give, and collapse of branch. The monstrous area of terrain that he leapt over gave, swallowed the hounds whole with the yap and growl that turned to whines, yelps, squeals, and then hush.

A sensation of burning crawled up Van Dorn's leg. Trying to stand, he felt as though a dagger were scraping chips from the bone of his shin. A heave of pain came in his chest. Eyes winced. He dragged himself to the hole that'd been covered. A booby trap for trespassers like those from the jungles of Vietnam his grandfather had spoken of. Bit by bit he came closer. Seeing how the territory had snapped and given.

As he neared the earthy edge to glimpse the ruin and loss of canine, smells of shit, piss, and vital juices reeked from the large perforation. His eyes took in several short furred hips coming into view. Poking ribs with whittled spikes, puncturing through hide. Then more shapes crossed one another like a Celtic-patterned knot as he crawled past the edge to see, one, two, three, four, five dead dogs. Short-furred. Some white with spots of brown and black. Brindle. Walkers, if he had to guess. Starved, almost emaciated. Off in the corner he noticed a shoe and a boot and an action figure, a superhero or something. *Odd*, he thought.

Then came the bounce and snap just inches from his face as he reared away from the opening. One had endured the drop. Unnerved; instinct took over and he reached behind him for his pistol. Hand jerking with busted nerves. He could hear the snarl. Then a silence and the whining.

Looking down upon what had survived. A dog the color of fudge and melted peanut butter with drooping ears sat upon the expired. Its fores balanced on the walls of the pit, glancing up. Situating himself, Dorn leaned back on his knees. Leveled the pistol, taking in the sad sink of hide around its sight. He held no compassion for the mongrel, but an emotion nonetheless rose within Dorn. That of a boy and a beast. Of the bond. Of how hard it was for one to erase the other's vitality.

THEN

Knowing his time was lessening, Claude, Van Dorn's grandfather, lay in a hospital bed losing his mind. Rubbing between crown and widow's peak till it was raw of hair. Wanting to give all the lessons of his life to Van Dorn before he died. Telling of his toughest decision. Of doing what was right. On crossing that line from boyhood to manhood, even when it meant a loyal companion's path would have to be cut short.

Claude's first hunting dog was bought when he turned ten. Eight years before enlisting in the service. He named him Sam. Picked from a champion litter. Well-proportioned, his hinds and fores were muscular and white. His spine and ribs held the print of caramel that hugged him like a saddle. Ears the same shade of tan, splashing around his eyes and over his snout. He was a specimen. His grandfather had spent his farming coin on the German pointer hound. Though his own father had told him he was wasting his earnings on a dog meant to hunt bird. Regardless, he put in months of stacking hay, picking beans, shelling corn, and chopping wood to save.

To train Sam, he trapped or caught coons. Placed some in rusted roll cages, others he skinned. Always threw the tails to Sam. Giving him the scent. Watching him bark and toss the coon tail around in his pen as a pup. Other times Claude took the hides. Dragged them over the ground and up a tree to where he tacked them. Then set Sam loose to strike on the smell. Bark at the tree.

The grandfather taught commands to Sam with a steel whistle he strung around his neck with a piece of leather through its hooped end; it was about as long as a grown man's pinkie. Blowing once to get his attention. Watching the lift and perk of his ears. The upward hook of his tail, his body ready. Then with a double blow of the whistle, Claude would yell, "Here'a Sam, here'a." Let Sam know he needed to get busy, strike on the scent.

His grandfather diminishing, his flaccid skin curtained upon his frame like unfilled garbage sacks in a room that reeked of rubbing alcohol, Van Dorn listened as his grandfather told him that the hardest part was getting the pup from the dog and turning the dog to a hound. On the first hunt, Sam struck up on a scent. Took to bawling and disappeared into the wild. Leaving the grandfather to walk. Follow the barks through the wilderness, his .22 ready.

At first, it seemed a good strike. Then Sam's barks began to go kamikaze, distancing one direction, then another, for far too long. Coming across the scrape of horns to a small tree, the scratch of a buck. From the fresh pellets of tiny marshmallow-sized manure, Claude knew Sam'd struck upon a deer trail. Even with all the early training, the dog knew how to hunt, but had yet to distinguish between what he was bred to hunt and what he wasn't. Meaning, like *all* young hounds, he'd need to be broken, the old way. And it'd take only the one time, if he lived through it.

Next morning the grandfather woke early. Entered the woods with his father's, Van Dorn's great-grandfather's, .30-30. He walked with the molten plastic sky of morning overhead. Passing the sycamore and oak, over the trundle of leaves and limbs to a midpoint on their property. Where he sat. Waited next to a small swampy green pond littered with hooved tracks. Seeing his breath murk as dawn broke, a deer, almond and custard, came through the weed and berry briars to the watering hole for a final sip. The grandfather put it down, a single shot to its lung point. Parted the cords of its throat. Removed its gut but not its glands. Bound the twine around its rear legs and dragged it to the field in front of their home, where he left it to lie. Went to unleash Sam. Led him to the deer. Let him encompass its scents. Pushed and wrestled Sam to the ground, held him on his side, while banding his front legs together just above the paws, then the rear, leaving Sam immobile and whimpering. He cut the binding on the deer's rears. The dog whined and jerked but could do little more till Claude banded his snout shut. Dragged him to the dead deer's ass where he'd split it. Lifted the hind leg. Buried Sam's face in it and lowered the leg.

It was all about timing. Wait too long and Sam suffocated. Pull him free too soon, he'd not be feared by that scent, but removal at the right moment, he'd be broken.

Watching Sam's raise and lower of the rib cage. First it rushed. Then it came slower and slower. Inhaling and drowning in the backside scents of gore from the venison. Forever searing his mind with that odor. When it looked as though Sam was near death, hardly a lift or drop from his cage,

Claude pulled Sam from the deer, Sam's face caked and stained by blood. He cut the twine from his legs and patted Sam, who slowly came around. Eyes blinking, then full-bore open. He'd timed it just right. Leashed and walked him back to his pen.

It was an old way of training passed down from father to son to break a hound. And the first time he'd done it by himself. Next day he put it to the test. Walking Sam in the woods. Watching him strike a trail. Then came the yelp, running the opposite direction as though shot by electricity, that deer's redolence forever engraved within his memory; a venison's trail had apparently crossed the coon's scent he was chasing.

Sam would be the closest the grandfather could get to an animal. Placing his life's blood in the hound. Taking him on hunts and dog shows from state to state. Letting him ride in the cab, seated on the front seat next to him. Filling his family's freezer with coon meat and his coffee can with cash from the selling of pelts but also studding him to breed with bitches for pups to sell.

Within two or three years Sam developed a golf-ball-sized tumor below his throat. And the grandfather's father told him, "Eventually he won't be able to eat, breathe, nor maneuver. Know what'll need to be done. Your dog, you'll be the one to take to it when the time comes."

Most hound dogs' joints begin to give out after eight years, Sam had another five good ones. The lump had gotten near the size of a grapefruit. Claude would've liked to have had it removed, but back then it was unheard of, as money was spent on family and bills. He knew what he'd have to do. His father's words ringing ever so loud in his mind's eye every time Sam had troubles eating, and even breathing as he lay on his side in the straw-floored pen of the barn. Freckles of tan over his coat like ticks, having problems rising. He'd sit up with what sounded similar to a bronchitis fit of coughing.

In the hospital bed that day, Claude spoke of Sam as though he were royalty. Telling Van Dorn, *No dog needs to suffer, to be left without a choice*. His cataract eyes juiced with moisture. His voice cracked and he said it was the hardest decision he'd ever made. Unleashing Sam for a long walk, Claude had his whistle around his neck, .22 in the bend of his right arm. How he shook when Sam'd struck up a trail and off he went. His bark sounding clotted and broken. Every so often stopping to hack. Buckling Claude's heart. Knowing what had to be done. He was the one who had to do it. When he got to the tree where Sam'd run the coon, the grandfather looked above. Saw the marble of gray and black fur. Tiny robber mask around the eyes that peeked from a limb above. Its tail fringed and ringed. The grandfather lifted the .22 and shot the coon from the tree. Sam stood proud, looking down upon his final treeing as the whistle was blown once. Sam raised his head in the opposite direction. Perked his ears and hooked his tail. Ready for a double blow from the whistle that was replaced by a .22 shell discharged from the rifle that pierced the rear of Sam's skull. Dropped his shape to the earth next to the coon.

NOW

Bearing the .45 down on the dog with its snarls of wanting, Van Dorn now understood why Claude had told him of Sam. Of needing him to understand how hard it was to put his best friend down, so he'd not suffer.

Even with the threat of being chased, possibly mauled, something within Van Dorn would not allow him to pull the trigger. Unlike he'd done when his life was threatened by the men before, something within the madness of this hound's retina said it was not Dorn's scent that made him growl.

As Van Dorn lowered the pistol, the hound sat upon its dead brethren. Reacted by resting its melon-sized dome between its paws. The hound's eyes bored up at Van Dorn, not wanting him to splay its savagery, its way of surviving, onto the walls of the earthy pit.

Rolling to his side, maybe the hound sensed his emotional weakness. Knowing animals could smell one's fear. Holding the pistol out, Van Dorn looked at it. All he had to do was spend a cartridge on the hound and move on.

Moments passed. Van Dorn sat with his leg outstretched.

Heard the whine of the dog. Reached down at his ankle. Felt the swell of pain. Noticed a shimmer of something metallic and golden among the leaves next to his leg. Reached and pulled a chain with a locket in its center. Thought it odd to find a piece of jewelry lying out in the middle of the woods. Wondered where it came from. Slid it into his pocket. The dog whined again. Dorn wondered where the pack had come from. They couldn't have belonged to the men who came into Toby and Ann's lair of murder or they'd have been waiting on him when he ran from the property. He thought that when he'd crossed over Rothrock Mill Road, it was a coincidence. The dogs were a mob of wild creatures, on the hunt for food, and he just happened to cut into their supper time. Dorn studied the opening. Whoever dug the pit would check it, for what, Van Dorn could only guess; food, and to keep trespassers away, or possibly both. Then he thought of the toy in the pit, the locket he'd discovered. Maybe the owners of these things were like Toby and Ann, eaters of all tissue devoid of husk or shell.

Looking down on the beast, he couldn't shoot the hound nor leave it to rot and agonize or be eaten. He decided to offer the animal a choice. Salvage its life.

Glancing about the forest of foliage, Dorn searched for something vined, ropy, and something of length. And it dawned on him all at once, touching his belt, then the leather that ran over his shoulder, crossed his torso with the hem of brass casings for the .30-30 that he no longer carried. Limped to the edge. Peered down upon the feral hound once again. It lay as it had moments ago, unmoving, eyeing Van Dorn. If the dog stood, he could noose the belt around its neck. Then he'd have to tug it up by its head, hoping not to break nor damage the tendons or vocals of its throat or, even worse, strangle it. Even then, getting his belt from its nape could enrage the brute. Cause it to go into hysterics. Test his hand, leave Dorn no other choice than to end its life.

As he unbuckled the strap of leather from his waist, his skinner fell to the ground. Van Dorn ran the belt back through the buckle, creating a small snare to lasso around the spiked fur of the dog. Took the other end of the belt that he'd hold, mended and knotted it to the belt of bullets he'd pulled off. Thumbing the cartridges from their loops. Tested his tying skill's strength, seeing now that he'd more than enough length, he could only hope he'd not hang the dog before it placed its footing back on solid ground.

As he lay flat on his belly, ache ran up from his ankle, through his hip, over his ribs, and to arms outstretched over the opening. The dog raised its head as Van Dorn lowered the homemade gin toward its snout. Beneath the dog lay the piled and unmoving. Scents rose as Van Dorn inhaled their fuming discharges.

In the canine's eyes sat a pity, deep and cavernous as though bedded in a wilderness that had once been civil and overnight turned lunatic and barbaric. The dog did not snarl. It only bored into Van Dorn's vision. Letting him fling the noose over its monstrous bloodhound head. He took this as a sign. And told the feral dog, "Know that I'm offering you life, not death, can only hope you're just as generous."

Working from his elbows to his knees, Van Dorn stood and slowly tugged the belt. The dog went with the pull. Van Dorn maneuvered with its weight, going hand over hand. The knots of the leather tightened, the dog reared back on its neck, as if to keep tension from its throat, then the heft of its weight came all at once and the hound hung in the air, dangled within the pit like a monstrous drop of mucus being dragged up the side of the dirt wall, gurgling and hacking through its nose. Van Dorn above, rearing his weight backward.

Shaking and tremoring, Van Dorn's legs and arms burned acidic. His ankle a chemical reaction of pain as though vinegar and baking soda were being combined. Kneeling, he continued placing hand over hand till he could see the hound's penuche-colored skull. Leaned and lowered himself over the edge. Held tight with one hand to the leather belt. Red fired his complexion, his other hand reached and wrapped around the dog's chest. Grunting, Dorn felt the pop of his own shoulder and back muscles, giving one final heave, almost falling forward. Then taking the weight of the dog and dropping backward like a wrestling suplex.

On his back he lay, looking up into the limbs of tree overhead that roofed his vision, the sky peeked through in hints of C4 putty and cotton whites. Blood rushed to his head. A relay of inhales and gasps. His heart fluttered and his lungs scorched. The odor of retch spread over his chest. Like that of a rotted carcass or sun-baked coon found along the rutted surface of country passages where vultures fed.

The slow thump of a muscle, not his own but that of the unruly beast, vibrated against his body. Slowly he bent his neck, raised his hands to the leather that collared around the hound's nape. Removed it. Rolled the dog from atop of him. Spent and unconscious, it lay spread out on its side. Dorn sat on his knees, studied the dog. It looked to be an oversize pup, maybe nine to twelve months old. Part bloodhound, part Rottweiler. Its paws were the diameter of a large tuna can. Thick and stealthy, connected to lean-muscled fores and rears. Not starved as he'd thought.

Nails slick as rubies, rounded off. The coat smudged and crusted with soil and whatever it'd killed and ate. Reaching a hand at its riblets that rose and fell, Van Dorn rested his digits. Then slowly began to stroke them back and forth. Taking in the pulse and warmth of what he'd offered. Life.

Untying his makeshift noose, he placed brass back into the leather holdings, slid it over his torso. Looped his belt back around his waist, reattached his skinner, when from behind came the clatter of weight over leaves.

Feeling for his pistol, Van Dorn gripped the .45. Turned with the gun raised. Eyes searching about the wilderness with the oncoming snaps of twig and branch. Over his shoulder, the mongrel stirred and began to growl when Van Dorn took in an enormous shape's curled husks and dime-sized nares.

—

Rumors had spewed from hunters' mouths to the Widow's ears during deer and turkey season. Thin or sawed-off stumps of men came camouflaged into the mart, divulging the small pockets of breeding. Speaking of swine being nourished on the eggs of ground vertebrae and deer fawns. Some said they'd been taken from Louisiana, brought here some twenty years before by one mangy male on a hunting trip, released into the wilds of southern Indiana. Done over and over, letting them spore and spread.

Before now it had been just that, a rumor. But here was this appearance of blackened-rind hide and hair thorned all over with tips the shade of dead field brush, ears in rounded points, hooves digging into the dirt as the snorts scuffed sound. Van Dorn had never laid eyes upon such a creature. As he kneeled, the hound growled behind him, its exhalation of breath nearly gagging him. Smelling of something far beyond rot. Fearing this dog he'd saved would take a jag to the rear of his neck, Dorn began to turn when the hound jetted past him. Belling and kicking up leaf and soil with the pat and dig of pawed claws. Steading fast like a purebred racing greyhound.

Van Dorn trained the .45 on the wild boar; because he'd helped butcher and process many a hog with his father and the Widow, he knew that, unlike a deer, its lungs were more forward, above the shoulder area. Aiming too low, he'd shoot beneath the boar. Watching it snort and charge into a collision with the mutt that did not back down, he wanted to shoot but couldn't. Fearing he'd clip and kill the hound as it charged like a spearhead. Dug into the boar's ribs. Squeals lit up the wilderness. The boar twisted. Lowered its head, tried to root its tusks into the dog. Clawing and swaying; lock-jawed barks followed with the pierce of brutality.

The hound climbed till it looked as though it were mounting and hunching the boar as it swiveled and bucked. Took the hound for a bull ride till the dog released its clamp. Hit the ground. Yelped. Was knocked senseless. The hound tried to regain its footing. Blood oozed from the boar, dotted and smeared about its hide as it came with its second wind. The hound staggered. Dazed. The boar charged.

Van Dorn tugged the trigger. Pieces of pork spine greased the air. Van Dorn limped toward the boar, wished he had his .30-30, knowing this would've ended with a single shot as he tugged the trigger again. Ribs opened up. The boar squealed. Kept its head lowered and rammed the dog. It belled in pain.

An explosion concaved the air. Wrung the wilderness of its quiet. An oozing red jackhammered above the boar's right leg. All four gave out as it lay expelling a sound more chilling than a metal rake screeching down aluminum. As it heaved its final gasp with a silver-dollar-sized puncture within its mount, moisture drained from the beast thick as ketchup.

Van Dorn looked to where the eruption of gunshot came. Off beside the opening of earth, an outline of domed skull with wiry thistles of hair poking from ears stood holding a rifle. Remington, Model 700, .22-250. Clay gray synthetic stock with five shots and a scope. Dorn knew the weapon and the man who lowered it. The ground gave and crunched as the shape stepped forward. Skin appearing bloodless except for the ink of red and black stars about his neck, the Celtic crosses, snakes, and words of scripture engraved about his limbs. Dorn's heart was a menthol rush. Feeling the cold burn of every inhale. The man came into focus. Spoke to Van Dorn: "Be damned. Been trying to trap that son of a bitch since this rapture has crippled man, woman, and child."

The dog lay panting. Van Dorn slid his pistol back into its holster. Eyed the man known as Bill Henning, though Dorn's father called him Pickle Loaf Bill 'cause anytime he came to give him a hand he'd always be eating a sandwich of homemade pickle loaf. He was known as a leather smith. Had made the holder of brass that hung over Dorn's torso. But he was also recognized by others around the area as Pentecost Bill. A born-again with an acidic tongue of religious rhetoric. Reading and studying everything from Methodist and Baptist ways, until he settled upon being a fire-and-brimstone Pentecostal. Was believed to lead an underground movement for the Church of God.

Bill donned a pair of worn navy-blue work trousers. A knife within a leather case was looped on his side. Stretched T-shirt over his torso. His beard was a bright shade of cherry, long and pointed like an upside-down cedar tree, thick and coarse.

"Came from nowhere," Van Dorn told him.

"Hell you doing this far north without Horace or the Widow?"

Van Dorn stood quiet with the ache in his ankle climbing up from his shin to his thigh. The Sheldon girl's image flashed in his mind, dirty and helpless. Unlike when they'd picked morel fungus together, walked the woods, canvassing the ground, soft tones of laughter, her knowledge of the land and her flowery scent of flesh, lengths of hair, hand encompassing his own, her holding it, his viewing the contours of a female that awakened the hormones of his adolescence. And suddenly the remembrance was darkened, wiped away by the shadows of men pouring down the basement stringer, the flint of a match that sent the old house into a blaze.

Dorn kept mute. Didn't reply.

"Know it ain't safe to be out in these retches." Bill tromped to the boar. Brought a worn sole of boot down on the swine's throat. Bending, he kept his weight upon the passage of air passed. Worked his Case XX across the swine's throat.

The dog sat like a fawn. Unmoving, it began to growl at Bill, who leveled his eyes, told Van Dorn, "Your hound tries to break my hide, I'll end his actions quick as they started."

Van Dorn stood lost in memory, remembered the day Bill'd gotten the rifle. Had contacted Horace to help him sight it on an aluminum pie pan tacked to a maple tree. Taking three shots from a hundred yards. The first one was a few hairs to the left of center. Horace adjusted the sights. Handed it back to Henning. He shot. Hit dead center. Unbolted the gun's action. Released an empty brass. Bolted another one in. Took the third shot, making sure the second wasn't luck. It wasn't.

"He's feral," said Van Dorn. "Saved him from dying, unlike the ones in your squared pit."

"Giving the beast a second chance . . . let us hope he'd return the favor."

"He tried. Why he's tossed out as he is."

"Hog is too weighted to carry back to the house. Gonna have to dress him like a deer. Walk back, fetch the Harvester." He paused his work of the blade, twisted a glance at Dorn. "You look to have a limp. One of them hounds nip you?"

"Twisted my ankle jumping over your pit."

Bill worked the blade through the boar's thick coat. From chin to ass and said, "That would have been your end." Clearing his throat, he said, "Never answered why you's this far north alone, with all the hell that is being unleashed. You's lucky to have not been taken in by the Methodist or the Baptist."

Dorn thought on Bill's words, then spoke, "Killed a doe few days back, was field-dressing her when these men came. Forced my hand." Dorn paused. Swallowed the knot in his throat. "I killed three of them. They'd a mess of folk caged up on a flatbed. Only females and boys, no men. One pleaded to me, the Sheldon girl and her mother. Said the men killed her daddy. Before I could try and free them, more men came. I ran and hid. Waited till they left. Headed to the house. They raided me next morning. I set the place aflame with them in it, fled but not before I seen the Sheldon girl, I believe she offered my juncture to them."

Bill cut the large intestine at the ass, pulled it out warm and steaming. Severed the gullet, parted the intestines, and removed the heated weight of more entrails. Cut the liver and gallbladder free. With arms gored and slopped by hot crimson, Bill shook his head, looked up to Van Dorn. "Maybe she had to. You know, when this started I's just outside the city of Louisville. Down in Portland, getting me some bibs and trousers when news of the dollar came over the radio. It was no longer worth the paper it was printed upon. Every folk in the store started looting. Chaos. White, black, poor, and struggling. Took what I had and ran. They's people all out in the streets. Pushing on cars and choking one another. Guns being fired. Got in my truck and hauled ass. God as my copilot, as they say. Week later, power disappeared. Now they's hordes, some working the cities while others work through the towns. They's a man named Cotto Ramos taking people's kids and wives. Slaughtering the males. Seems they getting cocky now, trying to overrun the rural. But folks out here has turned wild as the animals they hunt. They's a few men, old-time preacher, the Methodist and the gunrunning racist Aryan Alcorn, they've they own clans. They enslave men to fight one another. To battle. Part empowerment, part entertainment, it's an underbelly of the new ruling class."

"I seen," Van Dorn said, "seen a brother and sister who eat humans, but ain't seen no preachers."

Bill came to his feet. "Of the flesh, or anthropophagy, cannibalism, that's ole Lucifer working his spell, so some say. The Carib people from the West Indies worked that into their religion. Course others say when man and woman feasts upon they own, it's a sign of the end. Regardless, religion is thick in these woods."

Limping toward the dog, Dorn kneeled down. The dog snarled and showed fangs. Dorn raised a palm. "It's okay, boy. It's okay."

"You's in the right state of thinking if you'd place a bullet in that hound's pan."

Van Dorn kept his tongue silent. Placed his palm down upon the hound. Caressed its prickly hide. Feeling what he'd not felt in months, the vibration of helping another. The warming bond of kinship.

"You've made no mention of your father, Horace, nor of the Widow as I've asked about them, only that you burnt the homestead and fled."

Seeing them laid out in the bedroom of flies and empty beer bottles, Dorn fought his emotion to shed a tear for their passing and told Bill, "They're no more. Found a sickness when the power went and never came back from it. And you, how is it you've knowledge of these religious clans, of this horde, their leader, and his men enslaving the rural?"

Bill chewed on quiet for a moment and said, "I've knowledge that is of no concern to you. But this sickness you speak of, was it fever flat-ironing their brains, and an ache and vomit that split they insides?"

"It was of the exact notes that fall from your tongue. But how did you befall such knowledge?"

THEN

The sickness came years after a gift of fudged glass bottles sealed in two waxy boxes had been delivered by Bellmont McGill. A *peace offering*, he'd said, from Dillard Alcorn, a man who now feared Horace. Unlike Bellmont, who paid a visit to Horace from time to time after their first meeting in the bar. Told Horace, "Longer you let the home brew sit, better taste it'll yield. Give it leasts a year or better."

And that's what Horace and the Widow did. They let the boxes of hoppy brew lie in the basement collecting dust and webs upon a plywood shelf. Waiting nearly two years after word had traveled around the counties that an unruly confrontation of mayhem at Bellmont McGill's Donnybrook had ended his legacy with robbery and his demise.

They, like most within the surrounding counties, had attended Bellmont's funeral. But years later, evenings after the dollar had become useless, and the power had twitched and clasped like an eye, never to be opened back up, Horace, Dorn, and the Widow were seated in the kitchen with Johnny Cash trolling from the battery-powered eight-track about putting a vehicle together "one piece at a time" when the music went sideways in sound and the last of their battery's supply had went dead. To ease their burden for their loss of music, Horace stood. Unable to take the creaks of the house. The sounds of inhaling and exhaling heartbeats. Went to the basement. Returned with the two wilted cardboard cases of clanging glass. Placed several in the freezer before it'd thawed to liquid. Removed two iced mugs. Laid two bottles upon the grain of wood. Pulled an opener from a cabinet drawer and pried one lid from a bottle and then another. Poured each into a mug. Watched them head with foam. Horace lifted one and the Widow lifted the other. "To Bellmont McGill, if they's a God, rest his damn soul as we're soon to follow." And then each took swigs of the metallic-colored liquid while Dorn watched, as he'd never held a fondness, never acquired a palate for liquor. Never cared for the off-center feeling it delivered to the brain and body.

Drunkenness came in a stupor of stories. Family histories from each side. A great-grandmother whose father was shot after a card game over one side's loss of funds. A bullet that missed a man's heart by centimeters, nearly causing said man to not meet a female weeks later and seed the grandmother's life. They spoke of prophecies. Of the world turning mad. Of surviving without power and Horace's worry of whether he'd learned Van Dorn enough to be a man leaving twenty, heading for twenty-one.

By morning, Horace and the Widow lay in her bed, she at a loss for speech. Empty bottles lined the slats of scuffed floor. Beads dampened the two outlines. Eyes lay recessed. Lips blued. Chests rising stiff and lowering even stiffer. Paled and retched. They complained of their insides tightening. Something heating from within, cooking them to sunken shafts of flesh. When they rose, it was a searing pain. The matter that spewed from their insides came at first in oily chunks of regurgitation and the smell of demise. The room reeked of what one would believe wounded and fallen soldiers smelled like as they lay boiling within the torridity of self.

Van Dorn watched as hours turned from day to night and back to day. He was helpless, as he could do nothing. His father lipping his final words, "Of all I learned you, never showed you how to band a man or woman who feels as though they been wrung inside out."

Dorn asked, "What is it that you are trying to tell me?"

"I'm not in the right state of mind, all I know is they ain't no brew I ever tasted was so sweet you couldn't quench your fill even whilst it twists one's insides into a knot."

And the Widow belched and said, "None that I tasted neither." And she clasped Horace's hand. And he clasped hers.

Days of silence piled up after. Days of hunting with no planes in the skies above. Few vehicles trespassing from roads to town. Of visiting neighbors who'd gone into hiding. More and more there was nothing. Though the flies came. Nesting and rooting, creating hollows of space. Sounding like hands digging in buckets of hardened beans, lifting and dropping them.

Dorn kept the Widow's bedroom door closed. Unable to remove and bury either, always telling himself, *They're resting.* While their reek filled the home.

As he walked the woods after sitting in that room, the inhale of death furrowed his nose.

Memory of squeezing his father's hand with no return of his father's clamp. Only the crunch of mortis.

Some days the silence was neither friendly nor unfriendly. It was just brainless moments without interaction.

But a month after the calm, he traveled through the wilderness to the steep overlook where below, years before, Horace and he had laid Gutt to rest. Taking the depression down to the bottom, he saw that the rock lay off to the side atop of the loose and piled soil. The earth had been disrupted. The deep hole dug but empty. Dorn couldn't believe what he was seeing. And the sounds came as those of his father but from Dorn's mouth instead. "Looks as though Gutt's body has been dug up. His bones erected."

Someone had trespassed. Dorn could only imagine as to who had done so.

NOW

Sweaty, Van Dorn limped behind the red and rusted International Harvester tractor that chugged and coughed, while muscling the hound, cradling him in his arms, the feeling of the dog's eyes following his every step returning. Only this time, he felt as though they were whittling wormholes into his spine.

Knobbed tires trundled over the land, the engine popped. Bill had winched the swine's hinds with a calcified log chain. Attached it to the hitch and dragged the weighted and hairy boar back to a shack built for the purpose of butchering.

Four cresol-covered planks of wall with a slanted tin roof sat surrounded by a graveyard of beat and wrecked automobiles. Chevy trucks. Ford Mustangs. Toyotas and Hondas. Hoods raised, engines removed. Transmissions dropped. Interiors rotted. Windshields split and webbed. Things that had not been here upon prior visits with his father. In the center of the rural salvage yard sat a stone home the color of a vanilla wafer. Its shingled roof faded and sunken in places.

In others tar paper showed like a worn-out punching bag, its leather flaking and creased with rips.

Bill killed the tractor's engine. Stepped down. Walked to the shack and slid open a door attached to a track. Romex wire rained from the rafters with pull strings and dusty bulbs. The foundation was particles of solid, with drainage holes cut that led out the rear. Muddied the earth with whatever slop or fluid was diverted from feral or farm-raised animals killed for sustenance. And the smell that wafted from the interior was demise.

Holding the hound, Dorn asked, "Where can I let him be?"

Bill studied Dorn, offering an eerie quiet, then pointed. "Over about that mess of hay."

Stringy and matted, three females came as though sprouted from the earth. Each stood facing separate directions. They were scavenger-like and rough, their clothing was denim pants, work boots, and wifebeaters. There were no curls of hair or makeup. Nails painted by grime and dirt. One carried a butcher's cleaver, the other a hatchet, and a third carried an axe. Farm-raised like the meat and vegetables they ate, they were Bill's daughters. Martha was fifteen, Myra was sixteen, and Mary was seventeen. Each had hair the shade and texture of spent bearing grease. Their lids lay blackened as though they never slept.

Dorn laid the dog in the hay. The three daughters watched his movements, studying his footfalls. Forgetting how his father always told him to never turn his spine on no one, Dorn turned his back. Fear sketched the scene of an axe lifting, a hatchet chopping, and a cleaver cleaving.

Skin drew tight and erect as Dorn walked to the boar, helping Bill remove the chain as he motioned at Martha: "Get me my gambrel stick."

Martha disappeared inside the shack, came back with a thick length of barked wood, little more than shoulder width in length, its ends pared to points and bloodstained. Handed it to her father, who worked the lumber into the rear tendons of the boar's hinds.

"Get the kettle for the leaf lard," Bill ordered Myra. He eyed Dorn. "Let's drag 'em inside the shack. Hang 'em up, ready him for scraping the hair from his hide."

Side by side, each gripped the gambrel stick. Hefted the swine over the ground. Walked backward into the shack. With the girls' help they lifted the hog to the ceiling, where a large tarnished meat hook was lodged into a rafter. Mary had leaned her axe against a wall. Came with a boiling bucket of water in her gloved hands, began dumping steaming water over the boar's hide. Loosening the hair for scraping. Bill turned to a diminutive table constructed from walnut, grabbed two knives. Handed one to Dorn and they began abrading the skin of its fibrous tresses.

"Seeing as your people found they end, I'm to believe you's up this far north 'cause of what? Boredom?"

Dorn hesitated and said, "Partly . . . to find the Sheldon girl, but also to help those taken prisoner, to find others like myself."

Bill held something in his tone, the change of sounds rolling from his mouth, through his lips, something akin to deceit. Working the cordite-colored blade back and forth over the rough hide, he questioned with "You're speaking of those who's encaged?"

"Yes. I aim to save Sheldon and the others from whatever it is these men are doing."

A fit of words spilled from Bill's tongue. "Have you lost your mind? You find her, you find death. Did you not tell that she navigated the hordes to the Widow's?" Bill shook his head and continued with "Believe you me. What needs finding is the Lord. Is the only saving any of us is getting in this hell we've dealt ourselves into."

Working the knife, knowing the Pentecost was one step away from the asylum's gates, Dorn still held suspicion; from the look of the man's stature, it seemed as though Bill'd not missed any meals as of late.

Bill's girls were only three in number but stood statue-like as if guardians or protectors, awaiting his commands or maybe something else.

Each blade gathered more and more hair and Bill spoke with tension, told Mary, "Fetch another bucket of boil."

And she did. Came back and began pouring it over the hide. Dorn chose his words carefully, held a sense of distrust, felt as if Bill were hiding something, and he asked, "You spoke of hearing a rumor about the pockets of hordes, the rural clans. From who did you hear this, you've yet to answer."

"Who?" Bill paused for thought. Spittle had congealed in the corners of his mouth as he appeared more and more irritated with Dorn's words and he said, "Was no rumor. Is real. Seen them with my own two eyes. I'd led myself astray when hunting. Came up behind a great neighborhood of brick homes. Watched from afar. Men going from house to house. The hordes looting the fathers from them. Breaking them down to their knees. Pointing a barrel to a skull and pulling the trigger in front of their loved ones. It was enough for me to mind my own."

With a look of horror, Dorn paused his scraping and asked, "Why you figure they kill the men, keep the girls?"

Pursing his lips, Bill said, "Breeding, why else." He then

lifted his gaze to Dorn and said, "Though I never eyed them killing young boys. There lays some unknown meaning in that. To kill a father but keep a son."

"And what about these religious clans, you've viewed them as well?"

"I've visited their cellars, yes."

"Cellars?"

"Meat cellars. Look, all you need to know is this: stay clear of them or you'll be enslaved to fight for another's entertainment and power to rule. You win, you eat, and if they's females about, they'll be forced into coitus."

Curled splinters of hair piled to the floor and stuck to the hands and blades of Bill and Van Dorn. Dorn believed Bill was hiding something as they scraped and scalded till there was no more growth to be removed. Then came the kettle. The removal of leaf lard that'd be used for cracklings. Bill stabbed into the boar's spine. Guided the blade down the backbone. Then Dorn helped him lift the carcass from the hook and lay it on the large walnut table planked by heavy two-by-six cuts of lumber that'd been nicked by steel and smirched by things that had once been breathing.

Myra brought a hacksaw down the swine's back. Getting to the pork chops and the fatback. Then the tenderloin that rested on both sides of the backbone before sawing and cutting at the rib cage.

"Think we'll ever get juice back to light up homes?"

"If God sees it in His plans. Otherwise be prepared for a long era of suffering. This is why wars are begun. An indifference. To rebuild what has been squandered. Too many digital dependencies. Do you think many men or women, even children of this era, can do what our ancestors did in order to hold continuance, to exist?"

"I care none, all I know is what my father and grandfather taught me, the ways of the old, and for that I am appreciative."

"But did Horace raise you by the guidance of the Lord? A better way of offering it is this: Do you believe in God? In His prowess to accept spiritual donation?"

Horace had raised Dorn with Old Testament beliefs in the Methodist Church as a boy, though he'd not stepped foot in one since his mother had abandoned them. His father had lost any hope there had been in scripture. Calling the Bible a book pasted together by a government that wanted to control the masses with fear. Letting those masses read what they wanted them to read, then interpreting it how they saw fit for control. Always pointing a finger and judging others while never judging their own ways. Horace told Dorn if there was a higher power, He was a pricey son of a bitch for all the hardships He placed on the innocent to pay for His suffering.

Dorn knew he was dealing with a man who'd been willed with religious rhetoric all his life, relied on the fear he brought to others from this rhetoric, and so he told Bill, "Never gave it much concern since my mother quit us, seems the good book is just words bound by officials."

Bill slammed a fist on the wood table. His orbs were blusterous bulges of white splintered by a rosary of vessels. Damming around him, the girls heaved air into their lungs with shock. Each held their tools like weapons. Watched Dorn as Bill spoke. "Be damned, boy, the Lord is no fool! Why you think things has turned to chaos? 'Cause God's coming back for us but first the Devil's riding in pockets. Shaping and metastasizing nonbelievers into the vicious. Then it'll be hell to pay for their wrongs. Don't be a pagan."

Dorn tasted the tension like a penny pulled from one's

pocket and put on a tongue, metallic and dirty. Thought of the pistol tucked down his back. The blade in his hand. Knowing he'd had his will tested too many times over the passing days. Dorn's stomach bubbled and he felt as though he might puke. Knowing Pentecost Bill was one crazed fuck. As were his daughters, odd as ever, unlike any girls Dorn'd seen before, and he told Bill, "I'm no pagan. Like my father, I'm a survivor, a pioneer."

A glint went from a spark to a bonfire in Bill's eyes. "How 'bout a test of this professed survival?"

All Dorn could think was, *React! React before this stone-cold-crazy son of a bitch uses you as a human sacrifice for his ill-willed God.*

But before Dorn knew what was going on, he felt a heavy whack to the rear of his thigh. A hand reached for his pistol. Though it was not his hand. Another hand placed a blade at his throat and another squared a rubber mallet to the side of his temple. Lids batted and things began to start and stop until another thwack came. Dorn's world darted and pricked like a cold wind to flesh and his face met the solid surface of the shack's syrupy floor.

—

Something sandy and wet lapped Dorn's face. Scents of coagulated seepage and sweat lay on the inhale of each breath. Of things dead and rotted. Surrounding him as his head bulged and roared. It hurt to move, but not to expand his lungs with air. His arms were not tied nor his ankles bound. The rush of fluid came quaking as Van Dorn sat up. Pushed himself to a planked wall in a room. The hound sat eye level and stared at him with its Reese's-tinted fur, panting.

"Son of a bitch," Van Dorn said. The breath of the hound

was what he smelt. He reached for the dog. Slow, guided his palm over the cold, wet nose of scars. Up his snout and rubbed his head. Focused his eyes on the room, taking in the walls of barn wood that ran up and down with no hint of light between the cracks and the high tin roof overhead.

On the dirt floor, several feet away, he made out three squared shapes no bigger than a suitcase. And beyond that was the door. As he got to his feet, the boxes looked to be honed of plywood bottoms and two-by-four sides with screens for their tops. Like dens or cages for keeping something. He could make out coils of shape. The dog sat behind him. Whined as Dorn started to approach the boxes, when a voice spoke that was of the flesh.

"Name's August."

Dorn turned his attention to a far corner, where a young boy stood up. Came from the shadows, hugging himself with a slight shiver. His features smeared of dirt, hair wild and ratted. He'd a U of L T-shirt on with a pair of jeans, Nike tennis shoes. Wormy and pale.

Dorn towered over the boy, whom he guessed to be fourteen or so. "The hell you come from?"

"Your dog let me pet 'em. Stinks, though, it's all about my hands."

"Asked you a question."

"Big crazy man and his daughters come to my home in New Salisbury. Killed my daddy. Took me, my mother, and my sisters. Locked us in here. Said we'd be traded to a man named Cotto for a higher purpose."

Van Dorn spoke his thoughts aloud, trying to understand. "Traded?"

"Yeah. Hocked my sisters first. Just came in one day and

took 'em. Then a week later, took my mother. My turn's coming. He done said, like the others."

On the dirt floor next to August's feet lay a ceramic plate. Dorn eyed it. Said, "Others?"

"Yeah, when we got here they's two girls. Was traded within a day. But they told they was a mother and her son before them."

Turning things over in his mind, Dorn's questioning of the hordes, Bill's words. *Watched. Going from house to house. Looting the fathers. Pointing a barrel to a skull.*

Was Bill who done that, not the hordes. But for what reason would he have to trade mothers and children, let alone murder fathers?

"He feeds us. Won't give no utensils." Boy went from hugging himself to palming his face, trying to hide the wet that fell from his eyes as he whimpered. "I's scared. Things is gone crazy. I don't understand."

Weak, Van Dorn thought, *this August is weak*. Exactly what his father never wanted him to become.

Dorn stepped toward August. "I'll get us from this place. But, I say run, you gotta haul ass. Don't stray from me, stay with me."

"Can't leave. I's scared what he'll do. And them woods is plum dark. Don't know where I'm at."

Taking August's hand, feeling the tremors, he led the boy over to the hound. "Pet 'em some more. Be easy. He's feral but seems in need of companion." August reached a hand slow to the dog. Began to rub its dank hide when the clicking of a padlock came and the door burst open.

The three girls came in front of Bill. The hound raised his ears, snarled. Dorn turned. "Easy, boy, easy."

"Knew I should've pierced that mongrel's plate but Mary said to let him be as he's brought no harm to us. Regardless, you got a proving to offer, Van Dorn."

Cocking his head, Van Dorn sized up Bill, his burly girth, bedrock belly blocking the opening with Dorn's pistol tucked down his front. Each of the girls held a weapon, Mary an axe, the others skinning knives. And Dorn said, "What is it that I am proving?"

Stepping between his daughters, Bill approached the wooden boxes that lay on the dirt floor. He'd changed his shirt. Rolled the sleeves of his flannel up to the elbows of each arm, where the pink of fang scars lined each inner arm between the ink of tattoos. Bill kneeled down. A hinged latch kept each box closed. Bill fingered the one latch. Levered the screen. Said, "You professed to be a survivor. I profess you must do so by proving your faith. What we Pentecostals refer to as receiving the gifts, having a triumph." Bill reached his digits below the opening.

And Dorn came with sarcasm, asked, "A triumph of what?"

From the box a slivering rattle dispelled like that of a baby's toy rattler began to tack the walls of the room. Behind Dorn, August clutched his arms around the mongrel, which held a nasal growl. Bill raised the serpent. Its head lay in his open palm like a diamond-shaped heart. Black electrical-tape tongue wishboning out while its scaling body of gold, onyx, and caramel hung down as though a lamp cord unplugged. Bill embraced a smile of foliage-marred teeth and said, "A blessing. Must receive the gifts to find salvation. My judgment and the Lord's." And Van Dorn hid a shit-eating grin, realizing that what was in the other boxes would be his and August's escape.

THEN

The first time it'd happened, Dorn had been around nine or ten, standing silent within the tall silver oaks alongside Horace, who held a single-shot Mossberg 12-gauge, shushing him of speech. Watching overhead as the bushy-tailed red and gray squirrels pounced from limbs, shook and wrangled their way from tree to tree. Bored, Dorn worked his eyes over the ground, studied the movement of a chocolate-and-margarine-decorated reptile tapering through the leaves and twigs, halted at his boot. Flicked its tongue out and in. Waited. Dorn stared in amazement. Finding oddness in the cold-blooded animal's actions. Horace turned. Eyes bugged in anger at the reptile, he raised his work boot to the muscled length. Dorn reacted, a second sense he remembered, offering a hand, and the snake coiled into his palm, weighted, cool, and scaled. Horace cursed Van Dorn. "Hell you doing, boy?" Tried to swat the snake from him.

Dorn distanced himself from his father. Ran an index over the serpent's head. Gazed into its pointed oval of eyes. Horace looked upon his son as though he were mad, came at him. Watched Van Dorn as he kneeled and let the serpent slither out from his hand and back to the ground, where it disappeared into the blankets of leaves and musk of fallen timber.

Dropping the shotgun, Horace brought a hand to Dorn's arm. Shook him with anger.

"Kinda heathen actions you pulling, could've been bit. Swell up like a tick from the venom."

Neither thought much of it. Took it only as a moment of chance, a young boy fiddling with nature.

But other times came. When gathering eggs, the Sheldon girl met the lengthy outstretched fiber of a milk snake that'd wormed its way to Dorn's feet. Sheldon watching with surprise but not fear. He treated it like a game of keep-away: step back and it'd follow. Sheldon shaking her head, saying, "You been demonized." Dorn doing just as he'd done when hunting squirrel with his father. Bending down, Sheldon's blue eyes full of amazement, Dorn offering a hand. The snake letting him lift it. Hold it as though it were a purring feline. Eyeing Sheldon, questioning, "Demonized?"

"What the old-time gospel said about those who tame the serpents. Daddy says it's much iron in the blood. My belief is reptile, carnivore, vulture, regardless of creature, it's in all's nature to wanna be a pet in one form or another, and they sense the good in those that's good and the bad in those that's bad. Regardless, you've got a gift."

Another time, as she was working the soil of the Widow's ground, she unearthed a nest of garden snakes while digging potatoes. The limbless reptiles stretched, luminous, green, and slithering, about the length from shoulder to hand. Dorn came from working a hoe. Removing weeds from around bean plants. The serpents veered their course for him. Coiled at his feet. Waited and he'd done just as he'd always done. Kneeled. Let one glide into his palm. Held one, then another. Fingering their quarter-sized heads. Watching the tongues dart out like unbraided twines of rope. Then releasing them, watching them slither back to their holes.

It quickly became clear that Van Dorn possessed that gift Sheldon spoke of, or an iron of the blood, a connection of sorts to the serpents; they continued to follow up, gathering in wait, climbing into his open palms, but for what or why no one knew, Dorn least of all.

NOW

Lengths of muscled scales hung down from each of Bill's hands like stiff shafts of rope. His daughters showed little fear.

Approaching Van Dorn, Bill was no bigger in height, only shape. Dorn was leaner and younger, and when Bill offered his right hand of two small serpents, each copperheads, Dorn did not cower, but came sure-footed. Offered his left hand. The snakes, black and gold, jutted their heads up and down, as though lying riverside, hypnotized by the wafting travel of current. Each slithered into his palm. One darted left, the other right as they parted and twined down and around his forearm.

Bill's eyes burned fiery as a butane lighter's flame, unable to fathom what he was seeing. The two snakes crossed at Dorn's elbow. Lassoed up beneath his shirt, followed his bicep, over his shoulders, and around his neck, where they rested their heads from the inner collar. Tails flanking down. Their tongues forking from their mouths.

"What trickery do you hold within, boy?"

"None."

Bill broke down another wooden box. Unhinged it. Pulled two thick hefts of elongated meat, patterned with scales of swarthy color and tarnished coins. Their ends like honeycomb, only rattling. Standing, he held them in their centers, their upper body the size and shape of flint spear-heads. Dorn had never seen such specimens of snake. Dense and long, he figured them to be timber rattlers from Kentucky. Seeing as that'd be the closest one could find such a serpent. Placing the fear of God in any taker who'd near them, except the one who stood before them at this juncture.

Offering his right hand in the same manner as the left, Dorn eyed Bill and waited. Confident and unblinking.

Bill's retinas were charred by rage as he approached. Snakes went lax in his grip as they prepared to move toward Dorn. Bill squeezed them in anger. Baring teeth in his dis-gust. Dorn smirked into a smile. Watched the tails of each snake corkscrew around Bill's scarred arm of print, twist and fang into the knotted muscle of his limb.

"Son of a bitch!" Bill screamed. His girls turned to their father's pain.

All Dorn could think was to move his hide, and he reached for the copperheads around his neck. Held them out like an offering before tossing them at the girls. Turning to August and the hound, he hollered, "Run!" Then turned back, came at the girls and Bill. Corralled them together. Giving passage to August and the hound. The girls had dropped their weapons, screamed and swatted. Two had been bit by the copperheads. The third tried to help, reaching at the serpents. Bill shook, trying to loosen the rattlers that had bitten and fanged into the meat of his forearm. Reaching at the snakes. Screaming, "Have lost the spirit. Arm has found the flare of heat. Oh, how it burns!"

Dorn stepped toward him, their eyes met. Madness surrounded them and he reached for the pistol tucked in Bill's waist. There was no fight. Only the body-writhe from the snakes.

Dorn watched the rattlers introduce Bill's knees to the ground. Release their jaws only to bite him once more and he said, "Been bitten ten times. And each time I've lost sight of the Lord!"

With the .45 leveled at Bill's face, Van Dorn fingered the trigger, thought of taking his breath. Giving him the martyrdom he longed to have. But Dorn was no killer of any man unless forced. Backing to the shack's opening, he slid the pistol down into the hem around his waist. Went out into the night. Separating himself from the voices of plead and ache. Closed the wood-slatted door and fastened the lock. Saw August and the mongrel in the distance. The haze of darkness hugging them hysterical, as August begged, "Where do we go, where do we go?"

Adrenaline rifling through his body, Van Dorn spoke as the sounds of Bill and his daughters rang out behind them. "Far from this juncture of hell."

—

Treading over land within the maddening darkness of night, Dorn's ankle no longer ached, only a slight stiffness, while hearts drummed, calves and hamstrings burned, and stomachs groaned for food. Buried within the heated dark was the paranoia of eyes surveying Dorn's and August's movements. While the sounds and images of Bill and the venomous lengths of scaled fiber haunted the boy. Glancing left and right, he'd tried to hold pace with Van Dorn and the hound. Trekking up hills and down through hollows. Carrying with them the lug of survival.

Dorn feared stopping. Imagining that Bill, his girls, or all of them would free themselves. Come bloated by poison, savage and tracking August and him. Baring their tools for splitting timber and skinning wild game. They'd come without discernment for sparing their lives as Dorn had theirs; by not rearing their brains with a single tug from his .45.

Something itched within Dorn. An uneasiness that said he'd not seen the last of Bill.

Dorn'd wondered about Bill's wife. Where was she in all of this filth and barbaric humanizing? Always attired in a floral apron. Scented of homemade cherry cobbler, flour-dusted hands, she'd offer Horace coffee and Dorn sweet tea when they came to help Bill. He'd not seen, let alone heard mention of her from the Pentecost. Only his girls, appearing untamed and without speech, as though their cords'd been severed or removed until the snakes broke their skin. Of all the fence, roof, rafter, and floor Horace and Dorn had helped Bill work and repair, of his maddening appearances and ways, Dorn'd never caught a glimpse of the wooden boxes. Of what was kept inside them. Secrets, Van Dorn thought, they were in abundance within the rural areas of life. Hidden in dank cellars, unfinished basements, closets, between mattresses and boxed springs, flooring, studded walls, in coffee cans buried within one's foundation, and in the recesses of people's minds.

Dorn and August came upon a patch of clearing. The moon made the field of clover and wildflower glow. Walking out in the open without camouflage brought on thoughts of alarm. The paranoia of wandering eyes from the edges of the dark, and Van Dorn wondered about coyotes. How they came in packs. Several'd run a deer from brush while another waited to attack. Then they took turns circling and nipping until the prey was wounded. Couldn't fend nor protect. That's when the coyotes came all at once. Feasted till nothing remained but the heated carcass.

"Think they's vampires out here?"

The words of a child, Dorn thought. *Ignorant*. "No such thing," Van Dorn said. "Is fiction, folklore from the eighteenth century of the Balkans."

"I don't know. They seem awful real at this point."

"True, they's people who want blood. Not for drinking and living for hundreds of years. What you speak of is make-believe. Out here only thing one needs to fear is the trespass of other humans."

"Never seen nothing like what happened back there. How'd you do that without getting bit? It's like you were controlling them, like a video game."

Weeds crunched and broke with the weight of their footfalls, coming on like a locomotive storming down the rails of track. Dorn thought August spoke with a much younger mind than he appeared to have, childlike and slow.

With a familiar tone, Van Dorn told August, "Wish I knew. Something I can do, I've no explanation."

"Know what I wish, wish things was like they once was."

He sounded like Dorn when he was fourteen. Dorn told August, "Things can never be like they was."

"I just don't understand what has happened."

The next words that fell from Dorn's mouth were that of his father and the Widow but also his own. They'd been fostered into his understanding over the years. Preached like a sermon by a preacher at Sunday worship. He told August, "History, or so my father always told, is doomed to repetition. Persons can only be walked upon for so long. My father and me traveled the states. Lived by thieving the weight of metal from foreclosed homes. Saw what happened to those living beyond their means and those who lived below any means. Never thought much of what my father was showing me then. Was too damn young. But now I see he was teaching me of a future. How man thinks he's building something new. When all he's doing is creating waste. Leaving a trail or history of failures or irreverence. And the working pay for it. Our fathers and mothers and when we's old enough to pay for it, they won't be nothing left. That's why what has happened, happened. Why people petitioned their states to secede the union, rioted, the dollar fell, too much unpaid debt of others. Wasn't no more money to fund the juice."

Van Dorn's face kindled.

August kept his words silent. Rolling this wisdom around in his laggard brain before asking,

"Juice?"

"Power, of the people and what kept campfire light in your home. Leasts that's how my father worded it."

"What'd your father do, other than teach you thieving?"

"He was a man of all trades. Used to do carpentry work. Could build or fix damn near anything. He learned me of most what he know'd. How about yours?"

"Mom was a secretary for an insurance place. Dad, he run the insurance place. Was a good dad to me and my sisters, though Mother complained of his attention to other females till the power disappeared and that crazy-for-Jesus man came. Took us and—"

August went quiet with those last words, as did Dorn.

When they entered the darkness of trees on the other

side, Dorn noticed the quiver in August and asked, "You can't be cold, damn near eighty degrees or better."

"My . . . my pills. Ain't had them in a long while. I get the jitters. Mind gets foggy."

"Kinda pills?"

"For my head. I'm what my father called a dull state of mind. Things rectangle rather than circle, nothing flows like it should."

Nestled into the hillside, Dorn spotted a squared structure. Walking toward it, his pistol drawn, he saw it was a small trailer. They walked past shapes of a couch out in the weeds with metal chairs. The trailer's door had been ripped from its hinges. The windows appeared split. Wooden steps strung to its opening. Inside, moonlight glowed from the outside. The metal structure reeked of things turned old, musty, and corroded. Pictures turned sideways. A bed in back with springs thorning through and cotton slobbering out like entrails. Crickets chirped, ants marched along walls, and spiders held their netting for them all. What appeared to be animal bones lay on the kitchen floor. Dorn and August spooked a nest of birds that went wild with sound. Caused their hearts to trade shock for beats.

Out back of the trailer sat a wooden shed. Opening the doors, with the peek of moonlight jousting down between the limbs and leaves of tree, Dorn made out shapes within, inhaled the smells of lubrication and fuel. An oxidized wheelbarrow and tiller sat side by side. In a corner, strands of hay lay spread about the floor. Upon the splintered walls hung a hammer, screwdrivers, hacksaw, rake, several shovels, and an axe. Dorn looked to August. "Seems abandoned. Let's settle upon the hay for bedding. Sleep. Daylight can't be far."

Rest came like plunging into a warm void with the sound of quiet. Stinking and warm, the panting hound rested between Dorn and August, until Dorn woke from dreams of having his wrists bound. Of gunfire. Knives. The pulpy and bulbous facade of Bill chanting a sermon, dancing with snakes in one hand and a Bible in the other. His daughters with their eyes rolled into gum balls. Bodies writhing and jutting while speaking in tongues.

But it wasn't the hound and his roadkill breath that woke Dorn so much as the poke of a bored-out barrel to the side of his jaw. Eyes twitched to the view of a familiar female, whose father had been a friend to Horace, a man whose funeral Dorn, the Widow, and Horace had attended; he'd seen this female, but with her *now* were two strange men training guns upon him and August. Towering over the two men, Dorn staggered up with the worn retention about his limbs from being woken. August sat, hugged the mongrel and his stink into his bony knees. Fear cast about his face. Dorn's mind streamlined with what to do to these people who trained a gun upon them. Reach with his right, fake them, get their vision upon a hand that wasn't doing the action, and when they didn't see it coming, he'd show these men his left, which wielded a pistol.

Dorn started to reach behind his back for that pistol. The one man who'd pencil-sized holes through his ears speared the barrel of an AR-15 into Dorn's chest. Shook his head and said, "No need to get tested 'fore we even get acquainted."

Dorn positioned his left hand to jab the expanded-lobed man's jaw just as his grandfather Claude had taught him to do on a military bag strung from a basement rafter. The other man, a stubbed brute with a cutoff 135 Auto T-shirt and a spongy face, went from fingering his stubble to eyeing the hound, which he then reached and patted, its tongue lapping at his hand with familiarity. He bubbled his hick words to Van Dorn: "Punch 'em and I punch ye back, boy."

Dorn relaxed his left. Studied the old man who held the AR-15 on him. Skin was loose and mangy with faded ink about his arms. Smiling; his teeth were a decaying corn-oil tint with the ring of memory.

Each man donned military pants. Wore skinning knives and holstered pistols while clutching the black metal of automatic weapons, except for the female, who was no longer blonde, she was cresol-headed and she held a Remington 870 Express Tactical pump-action 12-gauge and said, "Either you're one lucky stud or you hold some skill for the land and how to survive about it."

Confused, Dorn wiped the crust of sleep from his eyes and said, "Can't say I follow."

The two men chuckled and the female said, "Been eyeing you since you crossed our hunting dogs who was fresh on the scent of the wild boar."

Knowing his feelings of unease were correct, of watching eyes, Dorn took on a wisp of anger and said, "Been watchin' me? Why'd you let that crazed Pentecost enslave me?"

The man in the 135 Auto T-shirt quit rubbing the hound's head, clasped his hand into a fist, shook it, and said, "Remove the hostile from your tongue 'fore I beat you into surrender, it's our way, how we work."

Dorn wrinkled his eyes and said, "Work?"

The female said, "Same as the government we once paid taxes to. You know, like letting criminals buy guns, kill, and traffic them so they can track the guns while the bodies pile up, hope to net a bigger bust. It's our test of natural selection. You survived it. Anyone escape Pentecost Bill and his harem of daughters that loot families, trade they skin to Cotto Ramos, has some skill for survival." She motioned to the man with the holes through his ears. "This is Poe." And it came to Dorn where he'd seen the man. The bartender from the Leavenworth Tavern when he and his father sat with Bellmont McGill. The female gave reference to the stubbed man. "He's Wolf Cookie Mike. You can call me—"

And Van Dorn cut her off. Said, "Scar, Scar McGill. Me, my father, and the Widow met you when offering respects at your father's funeral."

"One question has gone unanswered. Who the shit might you be?"

"Van Dorn Riesing."

Scar chewed on Dorn's name. Squinted her view as though his name held a deeper meaning that he was unaware of and told him, "You'd be the one whose father shacked up with the Widow."

"Horace, my father, yes."

Looking down on August, Scar said to him, "And you're the skin that's left of those that have been traded."

Dorn questioned Scar, "What is it that you know of this trading?"

"What the Pentecost does. Working his way through the rural areas and even some on the outskirts of other counties. Studying homes. Neighborhoods. Killing the fathers. Taking the wives and children. Trading with Cotto for time."

"Time?"

"Cotto's taking territory, he's a gang leader. A captain, it's how gangs work. The son of a Guatemalan commando type. But he needs leverage from those who know the counties. The land, the people, and its ways."

"That don't make sense."

"It's what we know. Cotto holds the Pentecost's wife hostage, along with others, in order to get his bidding done. And it keeps him from the daughters. Each human he brings is payment, buys more time for Bill and the image that he'll get her back and his girls won't be taken, whored out. It's the part of how Cotto is administering vengeance upon the land. Upon the people."

"Vengeance for what?"

"For the murder of his father, Manny. He worked with my father, supplying dogs for fighting when needed at the Donnybrook and other places in what my father called the hound round."

"That don't make sense. None of these people killed his father."

Hair black as a rotted avocado, pulled tight to a leathery baseball complexion, Scar told him, "It was a working-class type that killed Manny, and now all who held faith in my father, who followed the Donnybrook, whether they're black, yellow, white, or red, if they live here, they'll pay for his father's life with their own fathers' lives."

Dorn's nerves eased, listening to the intel from Scar and the evil that trespassed.

"Only thing he don't get, man who killed his father is the same that fed mine to rabid hound dogs." Scar's arms held lean tissue, veins protruded from biceps and forearms beneath the weight of the firearm within her grip. "Cotto is taking children, the boys, uses the drugs he can no longer sell to dope them up, get them hooked, train them to be soldiers, which ain't much more than giving them a gun, showing them how to shoot it and load it, keep 'em fucked up, and the mothers who birthed them he enslaves, possibly for whoring or maybe they're already dead."

Van Dorn nodded, his hand reached at the hound, worked between its ears. Rubbing its head.

"We have word of where he lays his head. He has his horde of men from the south. Men who've lived amongst us for some time illegally. Brought here by our government. By a man they ran drugs for in the CIA. They stashed their dope. Stockpiled it. Broke it down for selling. Now Cotto's plan involves territory and blood, lots of blood."

Dorn thought of the Sheldon girl. Her mother and the others with their complexions of ruin. Eyes stamped by the death of their husbands and fathers. Maybe she led Cotto to the Widow's in order to spare her life. Dorn could forgive her for that and he told Scar, "I seen these mothers, daughters, and sons caged up on a flatbed. Starved of hope. And the men that enslaved them. I killed three of 'em."

"Where are these victims of tyrant?"

"Couldn't save them. They was more men coming. I'd no choice but to flee. They tracked me, attacked my home. I burned it with them in it. But that's part of why I'm out here. The images have marred and haunted me ever since. I'm in search of others like myself. Survivors. To regroup and find this horde of men. Want to free a girl known as Sheldon, free her and the others."

Scar laughed and asked, "What makes this girl so special that you'd venture into the wild for her?"

"I knew her and her family. She's like me. Was raised in the old ways. Understands the land. How to live from it. And I believe no person deserves to be caged and treated ill."

"A girlfriend," Scar teased.

Van Dorn felt the pulse of red kindle his dirt-smudged cheeks and said, "Never thought of it in such a way. Regardless of definition, I aim to free her and the others."

Poe and Wolf Cookie pursed their lips. Nodded their heads. Scar smirked, cleared her throat. Said, "And then what?"

"Haven't thought that far. Maybe rebuild what's been squandered?"

"Well, we got a jaunt before getting back to camp, been out hunting, scouring for intel. You fall in with us, but don't question our actions."

Believing there was a bond to be formed, Dorn offered a hand to August, helped him to standing. But he didn't know how much credence he could lay within any of them just yet. All trust had to be earned.

Following Scar, Poe, Mike, and the hound through the woods, taking more hills and flat land. Making passage above broke-down trailers, furniture gutted and thrown out into the dirt that passed as yards. Vehicles lay abandoned on back roads. Vinyl, brick, and wood-sided homes sat devoid of presence. After they had walked more than two hours, the hint of something charred lingered in the air. With each footstep, the smell grew thicker until the reek banded everyone's inhale with woodsmoke and something similar to meat, only it was not the loin of animal. Camouflaged by weeds and trees, Dorn, August, the hound, Scar, and her men kneeled, viewing a house offset from a yard where two men, pale and thin, were barbed to cedar posts. Several worn truck tires had been dropped over their hides. On the ground sat a pit of flaming lumber. A piece of rusted iron that glowed orange on one end, used to sear and bubble one of the men. Foam dribbled from the branded man's mangled lips. He looked barely alive. Favored the other man who was tactile and jerking. Coughing up words. "Motherfucker, I kill you. Hear me, I kill you, you lay that heat to him again!"

A steel pan was lifted over the branded man's head of wool strands by a third man whose frame looked combed by a steel rake. Skin carved and nicked, indented by bruise. He'd a bandana of black with dirty white skulls all about his head. Stood shirtless, sweating and laughing as he turned the pan upside down. Drained a thick ooze of motor oil over the man. Said, "Where's your nest of nourishment? Ain't your baby brother suffered enough?"

Wiggling and jerking, the man's mouth frothed with rage. His complexion appeared almost rubbery and slick. From the house, two more men joined, flaking and peeling with the wear of being rotted and unbathed, grabbing their nether regions and pig snorting.

One held a small blue propane cylinder, its brass wand flamed orange and blue as he stood in front of the vinyl-sided home, with a roof of ribbed tin and a large covered porch. Placing the torch on the ground, he ripped pieces of a shirt, wrapped them around a thick piece of tree limb about arm's length. Laid it on the ground. Wrapped another limb with more shirt strips. Then dipped the clothed ends into a bucket of used tractor oil.

The man who'd poured the oil told the tactile and jerking man, "Last time I'm asking, Lucas, your family's 'bout tuh get smoked, then wrung of dignity. The food, where you keep it."

A gob of lung butter darted from Lucas's mouth. Juiced

warm over his torturer's face as he mustered language. "I . . . look like I . . . got a stash of food, youuuu . . . fuck? I's no more than bone and skin."

Wiping the phlegm from his face, the man told Lucas, "Keep on spitting lies. Have it your way." Then he turned to the torch wielder and nodded. Kneeling, the man grabbed the propane canister in one hand. Picked up one of the pieces of lumber. Lit its oil-soaked cotton end. Walked up the porch steps, tossed it into the home. Curtains and carpet ignited.

Turning from the blaze, the man stood watching the home expand with flames and laughed.

Dorn sat with August, Scar, Poe, Wolf Cookie, and the hound, camouflaged behind the sprout of foliage. Gripping his pistol, taking in the dehumanization, Dorn pulsed with wanting to act. Scar sensed his jittering, touched his arm. Whispered, "Wait."

The man with the propane torch walked over to Lucas.

Holding the dog back, Poe said, "They ain't with Cotto. They're charlatans, scrounging for food."

"Charlatans?" Dorn questioned.

"Copycats," Scar told him. "Make their musings for torture appear like what Cotto and his narcos do. Been suspecting them for a month or better."

"How you know?"

"The tires they throw over men. Country folk use those to start brush fires, not light folks up like these wretches aim to do, like Cotto did to double-crossers on the border, he does the same here."

"So they make it look as though Cotto has trespassed through and slaughtered country folks. Still, why would anyone wanna do as Cotto does? Stoop to the level of an enemy?"

"Why? 'Cause they's some that'd like to soldier up with Cotto. Do as he does. Live as he lives. Murder they own. Just cross paths with them, they act like they's surviving, it's a trap, they's playing coy to see what you got, then they remove you, how they get by. They're slaughterers, plain and simple."

Back to the situation at hand, Dorn asked, "What're we waiting for, they're blazing the man's home, aim to cook him and his brother as well."

"That'd be a disruption to the natural order of nature."

"Natural order? They're gonna kill innocent folk."

"You ever see a wildlife video where the filmmaker saves the animal being preyed upon? Hell no, you didn't. It'd be an infringement upon their survival. How nature works. We never saved you."

"These ain't animals."

"No they ain't, they're a whole different kinda tissue eater. You need to learn their ways to survive this terrain, as it changes with every breath."

The home raged orange and yellow. Black smoke billowed from it. Children began to scream. Sound of glass shattered from the side of the home. From a window jumped a young boy, then a girl, and an older female. A man came from the wooded area around the rear of the home. Grabbed the young girl from behind. Fisted her to the ground. The boy turned to the man. Kicked at his leg. Met a hand from the man, who stepped on the boy's back. Stomped him into the earth. Kept him from crawling as he unsheathed a blade. The older female raked her nails down the man's face. Screams came. A head butt dazed the female. Followed by knuckles branding her. Blood drew from the older female's face. Digits groped her locks. A skinner pared the thick rind of her forehead.

August held his gaze in the opposite direction. Eyes dampened and mucus gobbed from nostrils.

The man with the propane flame lit the seared and branded man's greasy hide and he came to life, writhing and spastic.

Meanwhile, the torturer reached to his right leg. Pulled a small mallet hammer free. Looked to Lucas, whose face was wrought with tears as he screamed, "No! Please! No!"

The torturer smiled. Billy-clubbed Lucas's jaw. Teeth came with a thick combination of syrupy fluid that slopped from Lucas's mouth. He tried to speak but all that exited his mouth was slurs.

Dorn had witnessed enough. Words streamlined like slivers of madness and he told Scar, "Should've done saved these folks." And he stood up. Scar reached for him but he was gone.

Stomping from the brush of green, pistol raised, all Dorn could do was react, shot the canister within the flame wielder's hand. An explosion encompassed Lucas and the propane wielder. Another shot thudded into the oil dumper's skull. Followed by a shot that rang not from Dorn's pistol but from Poe's AR-15. Clipped shoulder and chest of the human torch's outline. Skin fragment expelled from the man's back. And he hit the ground like a mortal bonfire.

Screams raged from the starved man as flames replaced his appearance. Flesh boiled and oozed fatty. Dorn holstered his pistol. Ran to a clothesline where a bedsheet hung. Ripped it from the line. Draped it over the flaming man. Suffocating the ignition of heat.

Around the side of the flaming home, the female's scalp was completely removed. Hanging down the back of her neck like a laceless tennis shoe's tongue pulled away from the insole. The front of her skull, bare bone and bleeding. The knife wielder sheathed his blade. Dug his fingers into the scalp of each child and dragged them to the woods, belching tears and phlegm.

Scar, Mike, and Poe had came from the brush. The mongrel limped. Sniffing the ground, staying near Poe. Mike made his way to the side of the home. Heat rising from the flames. Melting outer walls of vinyl. Baking anything within five feet of it. He pulled the female to the home's front, his face quaked red from the heat. Tears streamed from the female's face, and a fold of flesh peeled over her skull as she crawled on the ground to Lucas, pleading, "Why? Why didn't you tell them?"

Scar reached for Van Dorn, who stood patting the sheet over the burning man. The cotton stuck to his shape like a second set of skin. Moans crept from Lucas, whose mouth had lost its elasticity. Scar told Dorn, "It's too late. We've no means to mend nor care for the wrong that's been done."

All stood absorbing the massacre. Studying the demise as though a team of forensics. And Dorn told Scar, "Wouldn't have been too late had you let us stop these charlatans 'fore they set one man aflame and the other beat by mallet."

Dorn looked to the mother, who sat on the ground before him. Blood crept down her face from the half-sliced head of hair, eyes like tracers, igniting stares up at her burnt husband. She turned to Van Dorn and screamed, "Mean to tell me you all sat in hiding? Watched what these men lay upon my husband, my brother-in-law, me, and my children that has been taken? You's as savage as those that violated us!"

As she came to her feet, swinging wildly at Dorn, a buckshot rearranged her complexion. Brain, scalp, and life dispersed. And Scar lowered the 12-gauge before the woman hit the ground. She eyed Poe and said, "Know what chore is to be done."

Dorn was without words. Everything had happened too quick. The woman lay on the ground. A pile of lifeless tegument. Muscles in her back fired with pulse and twitch. He looked to Scar, angered, and said, "Why?"

"Ordinary people do the criminal action 'cause it's become their natural means to survive, it's instinctive. You didn't heed what I told. Me, my militia, we live by a different set of standards."

Poe walked toward Lucas and his brother. Lifted his AR-15 to the body of the brother, who was now charcoaled and smoldering. Lucas stood leaning, the sheet blotted by the burn of plasma, hued brown, black, and red. Moans of ache plagued everyone's ears.

"We waited too long," Dorn told Scar.

"Nothing to do with waiting. Shoulda let the situation unfold."

"They're like us, common folk, people that's lived from the land."

"This ain't part of the plan, can't fix every spoke on the wheel."

Poe tugged the trigger, bringing a silence to his mess. Then to the other man beside him.

Dorn asked, "What plan?"

"Territory," Scar told Dorn. "Time's wasting. We gotta get 'fore someone sees the smoke, makes a bigger mess." She turned her back. Poe, the hound, and Wolf Cookie followed. Walked the perimeter of the home that was becoming a bonfire of calcium carbonate. Interior and exterior walls now dark as spades.

Dorn walked to where they'd hid. Pulled August from

the weeds, trembling. Shaking his head. "They killed them. Killed them all."

"I know."

"I'm scared."

"Keep close to me. They won't hurt you, I won't let 'em."

"We should run."

"No, we shouldn't. We're safer with them than without. They know things we don't."

Catching up with Scar. Taking in the surrounding woods, Dorn's eyes searched for a trace of the other charlatan. Listened for the pleas of the children who had dispersed into silence. And he asked Scar, "What about the kids?"

Stopping, she turned and said, "What about them?"

"That man took them."

Anger cast about her facade and she made her intentions known. "What ain't soaking into that thick understanding of yours? They're not our troubles. We's not Robin Hood and his merry fucking men, taking from the rich and giving to the poor. We're rural soldiers, here to uncast the backbone that society has broken. Not doling handouts to the weak; if you're weak you're dead. Days of food stamps and government assistance is what brought our class to its knees." Looking up through the leaves that angled from limbs overhead and into the sky, her eyes came back to Dorn's and she told him, "We ain't got time for this. We gotta get to the ATVs, endure our trek back to camp before dark."

—

Navigating his four-wheeler over the land, crossing deer and old horse trails, Wolf Cookie was the lead, with August clutching him. Overlooking gravel roads and patches of burnt grass in the centers, Dorn rode with Scar. Poe took the rear, the hound laid across his lap. Hot air dried the moisture that glazed their bodies. That'd been matted and specked with soil, leaves, blood, and death. They passed hollows littered with limbs sheared and scraped of bark from the summer storms that had worsened over the years. Ravaging any structure or organism in its path. Garbage bags stretched over surfaces of rock, wood, and soil. Magazines and newspapers, ripped and torn. Old washers, stovetops, and rusted barrels used as doghouses, hay bedding spewing from them. Ceramic dishes and figurines had been thrown and abandoned, turned into relics of oxidation from the weather or looters.

Tire tread climbed a hillside where limestone lay gigantic and moss covered. On the other side men perched high overhead in oak trees upon slatted stoops built from pallets, some with binoculars, others without; each held scoped rifles and holstered pistols.

The land flattened down into a ridge of bunkers pitted into the ground some sixteen feet long, twelve feet wide, and ten to twelve feet deep, depending on how quickly they'd met solid lime. Roofs were gabled, ply-board shingled by ten to twelve inches of mud and weed. A rock-circled fire pit had been built out in front of each shelter with a handmade spit over each for cooking; a larger area sat out in the center appearing the same, only wider and deeper for bonfire use. Men and women stood armed, eyeing Scar and her return with strange skin. Men sported beards, oily reamed locks twisted and curled from beneath caps. Some were bibbed with denim or military pants and patterned Realtree hunting T-shirts, while the females appeared with their lengths long, pony- or pigtailed. Nails unpainted. Chewed. No gloss of lips nor liner ovaling orbs. They appeared as though creations of God's earth. Simple.

Several pens strung of rectangular wire, attached to cedar posts, held hogs, while another held cows and chickens that sat guarded off to the south of the encampment. Several wood-walled shacks sat with chimneys to their far ends. Hides of coon, squirrel, and deer stretched about their exteriors. *Smokehouses*, Dorn thought. *A place to cure their meat and tan their hides.*

Scar idled her four-wheeler down, parked next to a bunker, and told Dorn, "This is where we bed and plan. We's about fifty strong. Not a weak link among us. Is of what was loyal to my father. We keep eyes from sunbreak to sunset. We got hunters. Butchers. Mechanics and farmers."

Dorn came from the four-wheeler, his bones clattered by the dip and climb of the land. His back was aching. Legs and arms hurting as well from all the damage he'd incurred over the passing days with little nourishment or sleep. Taking in the faces of the small militia, he asked, "Who are these that followed your father?"

"As I done told, some was mechanics, others was factory workers, fighters, hunters, builders of homes. Waitresses. They're male and female 'lopers that've been wrung out by their government. Once the fortitude of society. Offered one lie after the next to gnaw on and procure a vote."

Behind them Poe came from his ATV with the hound. Then came Mike with August, whose eyes were wrought with fear as they took in the smears of an unknown sanctum. Dorn met August's glare, lipped, *It's okay.*

Waving a hand, Scar motioned Dorn and the others to walk. To take in the encampment of structures built with logs that had been halved, coated by creosote to preserve the wood; she pointed to housing, told Dorn what was for storing artillery and arms. Others were for tools. Food. Told him there was a cave nearby with a spring. In its bottom lay a stream. They bucketed and heated the water to bathe. Wash clothing and whatever else. She led him to her bunker that sat next to the ammunition and weapons storage.

Several feet behind them was Wolf Cookie, Poe, and August. She waited for them to pass by areas of men and women who sat sharpening blades. Cleaning guns.

As they entered a cellar-like dwelling, candles burned, the air was cool. Two cots lay in the rear. Shelves lined the left flank of the bunker with books, CDs, batteries, jars of vegetables, clothing folded and stacked. Crates of ammunition stacked about the floor. Scar brightened the room up with several lanterns. Along the right flank sat a long wooden pew honed from hardwood. Scar motioned for everyone to sit down and Dorn asked, "Fuel for the ATVs, where do you get it?"

Scar and her men laughed. "Get it? You see all that we've built and you ask about fuel?"

Dorn raised a hand, said, "I view that you were prepared."

"Prepared? We seen what was taking shape across the country."

"You weren't the first."

"Naw, we wasn't, it started with a group of brothers. Ex-military. Lawmen. Called themselves—"

Dorn cut Scar off with "The Disgruntled Americans."

"You know of them?"

"Know of them? Their actions spawned an underground

movement. Was all over the radio. My father held a great respect for them."

"Your father sounded a lot like my father, knowledgeable." Scar paused for thought, said, "Know why my father did as he did?"

Dorn had no idea what Scar meant and asked, "Why he did what?"

Poe said, "Created the Donnybrook."

"Don't know much of it other than your father saying the Donnybrook was a dream from his childhood, that it was savage to those that failed him. But kind to those that swam in the salvage and sacrifice of the land."

Scar smiled and said, "You're correct. He was tired, had lost his job in a tobacco plant. Drained his and my mother's savings. Sold their home. Moved in with the brutality of a man I never knew, my grandfather, my mother's father."

Wolf Cookie said, "Bellmont was like every other blue-collar American at first. Had been a slave to a system that was failing its people."

Scar continued. "But he saw the ink on the wall. Of what was coming. Had a plan. Give the working something more than NASCAR and pro wrestling. Something they could invest their souls into while viewing, let them be a part of it even from the outers looking in, let 'em suck their swills, sell dope or char food, do as the working do. Live without regret. They were the Donnybrook. But before he was removed he'd become restless with hate for what was consuming the working. Was eat up with violence, money, the power it professed, a mirage. After his being murdered, people kept waiting for another to pick up where he'd left off, someone who'd offer an outlet for their rage of struggling. But more jobs was lost. More wages cut. Politicians kept promising jobs would come back. Good manufacturing jobs. But they never did." Scar paused. "Jobs was replaced with a new word, college. And kids who chose not to do as their grandparents or fathers did, they went to school. Got an education. Then the market got flooded and kids was broke with unpaid bank loans for tuition. Something that gets raised every year and they'd a degree that couldn't land a job. While the rural dealt with prescription drug abuse, meth, and heroin. Addictions that poisoned the lives of common folk."

Scar went on. "What my father gave to people every year was a gathering of like-minded souls and they wasn't judged. He offered them an outlet, some he even give work to, helping to run the Donnybrook, of course if you's a fighter, he paid you and fed you. Let the working feel alive until he was handed his ending."

Van Dorn rolled all of this around in his mind, glanced at August, who sat in the pew, head leaned back, arms crossed, fast asleep and shaking, the hound laid out sideways below his footing, and Dorn asked Scar, "What is this *plan* you speak of?"

Scar smirked and said, "Plan is simple. Once Cotto finds the one that murdered my father and his, we kill them. Then we rebuild all that has been swindled and wait."

"You know his location?"

"Yes, he's set up a large encampment along the Ohio River at the old lighthouse in Leavenworth. Smart, he holds access to water travel. We know because not all of Cotto's men are loyalists. Some are moles. Was loyal to my father and now me. They're my eyes. My ears."

Scar paused. "We know the one who murdered our fathers is Chainsaw Angus. He's somewhere within Harrison or Orange County. Some say he's taken in by a Chinaman with ties to Triads, was to be willed in the training of ancient fighting techniques. Cotto'll find him, torture him. Once he does, our eyes will be there. And then we'll remove both of them from existence."

PART II

THE SAVAGE

The global economy has brought ruin for many, and he is a pioneer of a new type of person: the human who kills and expects to be killed and has little hope or complaint. He does not fit our beliefs or ideas. But he exists, and so do the others who are following in his path.

—Charles Bowden, *El Sicario*

COTTO

Their trespass brought visions of men stained the color of rotted sweet potatoes. They'd hands that carved, sawed, and gutted others during their hunt for the wrongs brought against them. Littering Purcell's insides with retched bubbling, constricting his intestines, culling him from shut eyes that peeled wide and full of red lines. Creating a hurt that built and bonded over the course of months and months that'd piled onto years and years of nightmares. And when the rumble of engines bombed down the long rutted road of dirt, stone, and rotted limbs, Purcell sat knowing it was one man's ending, but another's inception.

But exactly whose it was he didn't know.

From the driver's and passenger's sides men stepped. Their eyes like hooked blades parting and digging deep to rip and maim those who dared cross them, armed with automatic AKs, their black-spore locks slicked, faces patched by thick moss like whiskers and jagged scars. Led by a man in his late twenties, face inked and textured to appear skeletal, head shaven like a field of bush-hogged wheat. He'd a rim of thorns running the circumference of his skull and eyes painted by evil. His moniker was Cotto Ramos.

Cotto and his savages walked past the large oak tree in the front yard where a worn and silver-taped leather heavy bag was hung from a tree limb by a rusted chain; off to the rear of the property sat a barn beneath a graying sky as the men surrounded and surveyed the farmhouse.

Inside sat a man who knew the die had already been cast. Waking early from sweat-soaked dreams of men he could not name, could only describe as earthly and savage. One was a man with a vendetta, a goal to rule territory and people. The other was young, but held skills from the old ways. And there was the man with the opal eye. The man who'd nearly cost them their lives at the Donnybrook. But what there was not to be seen in the future was Jarhead. A fighter Purcell once believed to be the leader of the struggling class in a time without guidance.

Two men held opposite flanks of a door, a third kicked in the slab, splinters came with shrieks, followed by features and ribs being knuckled and bloodied. Cotto's AK rattled the scuffed wood. He shook his head, spit blood, and lined his view to a man of proportioned muscle. Fists raised. He came with a strong left jab. Cotto ducked. Jarhead fed him a right knee, then a quick left elbow. Cotto unsheathed a blade without notice. Lined the edge with his forearm. Came swiping at Jarhead's right cross. Drawing a line of fluid into tissue, then stabbing into shoulder meat.

"Fuck!" Jarhead screamed. Staggering backward. His wife, Liz, and two children shouted, "No!" while Christi, Purcell's daughter, and David, his son-in-law, watched without fight, only horror.

Cotto retrieved his rifle. "Enough of this weak squabbling." Pointed his rifle and pulled the trigger. Jarhead Earl's thigh flowered with the pulp of muscle.

"Show me your true shades. I want to see your insides."

Donnybrook, seemed everything circled back to that, the three-day bare-knuckle brawl that Jarhead had fought in. That he and Purcell had watched go to snuff when the unbeaten pearl-eyed fighter by the name of Chainsaw Angus shot Bellmont McGill, the creator and owner of the free-for-all. Shot his ass dead. Followed by killing a man known as Manny, while the crew that followed him, the Mutts, had watched the murder of each man take place during the chaos, unable to save their lives amongst the unhinged pandemonium, the capital of hell, that had ensued when the unruly crowd of onlookers flooded the wired ring. All manner of chaos came violent and uncontrollable with bottles, fists, feet, elbows, rocks, and clubs beating any and all, similar to what John Milton had written about in *Paradise Lost*.

Rousing his men, Cotto shouted, "Each and every body I want accounted for, keep them separate." He watched Jarhead struggle about the floor. Told him, "Only fight to be left in you is on your knees." To his men he spoke, "Outside, drag him to the dirt."

Pulling the blade from his wound, Jarhead slobbered. Crimson rivered. One of the soldiers kicked the blade from Jarhead's grip. Another cleaved into his messy lengths of hair. Dragged him across the slats of floor. Swamping a mess of self from the house to the yard, bringing his wife, kids, and Purcell behind him, with Purcell reaching for his family, who were pulled like mops from buckets, by their ankles, sopped in the opposite direction across the slats of floor to the basement. The male tried kicking at the clasp of hand around his leg, bicycling his heels to fight, but was pounded about the face by a rifle's butt till his frame was dull of struggle. Facedown, the female created a scratch trail, the nails of her digits splintering across the cedar.

Tied in the basement, the man, David, and woman, Christi, were left to starve. Jarhead's boys, who numbered two, were gathered with their mineral-flaked skin and eyes of fear. Clutching their mother's arms, they were loaded by men onto a rusted flatbed, where they were caged, their eyes haunted by the beating of their father. The wife'd be used for whoring back at Cotto's camp. The children, he'd usher into soldiers. Soldiers who would abide by his goal of ruling the land, and if power were to return, he'd traffic in drugs, just as he had south of the border.

Cotto and his men would continue their slaughterous hunt for the other, who went by the moniker of Chainsaw Angus. They'd continue throughout Harrison and Orange Counties until they found him. Once they were rid of him, the land would be left for prospering.

Out in the yard, they'd sat Purcell in a walnut chair before a tree that'd been chopped to a jagged stump. Stained by black liquids. Before him, several men stood armed, with faces devoid of emotion; Purcell's graying locks and tufted beard fluttered with a brisk breeze that caused his eyes to blink. Cotto taunted about, nothing more than a murky shadow of brawn and death bearing questions. "As you were the last to hold stock on this bare-knuckle fighter whose name is Chainsaw, do you hold communication with him or claim his actions in your dreams? It is known that you rang a deal with this barbaric mercenary. Killed McGill. My father. Then robbed the Donnybrook of its worth." Purcell sat as though a serpent removed of muscles for speech; tongueless and mute. Cotto pointed to Purcell's feet with his rifle.

Nodded to his men, who bared left and right foot of boots as Purcell tried to kick at them. It did little. His feet were restrained upon the flat area of the cresoled stump. Feet bottoms were bare of boot or sock, facing Cotto, who smirked. "The hammer." One of his men came with a small mallet. Delivered the indent of fiber. The creak of bone that gave.

Purcell's eyes pumped white as fresh dairy cream. Dentitions bit and walled behind sealed lips. Tears flavored bitter down his jaws. Arms tensed and shook.

"Leave him, he—he knows nothing of which you speak!" Jarhead screamed from the ground.

And questions were queried from Cotto to Purcell once more as he smiled into Purcell's pain of wet eyes. "I've traveled miles, across desert, woods, trounced through riots, burnt bodies, crumbled lives, I've any and every intention of crumbling yours if you do not offer words, as I've grown impatient." From his pocket Cotto removed a vial. White and black granulated powder. Uncapped it with his thumb. Raised it to his right nostril. Sniffed hard. Then to his left. Sniffed even harder. Eyes batted and burned. Tonguing his lips. "Goddamn!" he raged, and continued with "I can see the feline has stolen your usage. Word about the territory proclaims you as a prophet. A sage. Well, prophet, Where. The. Fuck. Is Angus?!"

"He knows not a trait of what you question!" Jarhead Earl shouted.

Anger flushed Cotto's complexion of ink and he came swift, his boot aiming for Jarhead's facade. Jarhead dodged. Brought his wounded leg around to foot-sweep Cotto, who didn't drop but bent his leg, brought his knee down into Jarhead. Released his rifle. His thumb digging into the pulpy shoulder wound. "Ahhhh!" Jarhead screamed. Cotto wanted to see him squirm. Then he took on a second thought. Traded his grip on the wound for the grip on his rifle. Stood and stabbed the bore of the barrel into his forehead. "You've attained the softness of a crustacean. Jarhead Earl, you're no fucking more!"

A smirk decorated Cotto's face. Finger tug ended Jarhead's life.

Back to Purcell, Cotto said, "Bet you didn't draw that with your prophetic crystal ball, did you, sage?"

Limbs twisted like knotted roots of a tree by the hands of Cotto's men, Purcell nearly chewed his tongue in half, saliva and blood ruptured from the corners of his mouth. Glancing to the slab of wickedness. Knowing that whether he spoke or said nothing, speech brought death the same as silence. He was damned if he did, damned if he didn't. He rasped, "Come closer." Cotto stepped. "Your ear. Let me speak to it." Smiling. Cotto turned his ear to Purcell. The prophet nestled a thick glob of lumpy cream-cheese-like goo into the lobe of this man who'd murdered Jarhead.

Cotto did not wipe the thick spittle. He let the warm gob string to his neck. Raised up.

"What I expected of you each was badasses. What I got was mush." Pointing to Earl's wife and children, who held wailing anger and tears after seeing their husband and father removed. "Your silence brings them whoring and soldiering. It was your choice, prophet."

Purcell clasped his eyes.

Cotto told his men, "Lay him in a posture of rest, prepare him with a message before the stringing for others to know of our trespass."

"What of the other you've branded with death, Cotto?" one of his men questioned.

"Saturate him with fuel, let the prophet watch him ignite, coal and smolder."

Hands held Purcell down. Popped the buttons from his shirt. Ripped the cotton from his torso. Another punctured his flesh with a smirched blade. Inscribing the scripture of who they once were. The Mutts, the last of Manny's men. While another formed a knot that rubbed up and down for the passage that would let the eyelet tighten. The twines of fiber slid over Purcell's chicken neck while his frame writhed from the metal scraping the pectoral and center of his chest. The area became saucy as rare rib eye. Lubricating down his body until the men strung him from a tree. Face blistering. Eyes bulbous. His bare feet kicking some twenty feet above the ground. Before the wet mapped out his crotch and fecal fell around his heels, viewing the flames that cooked Jarhead, Purcell thought of what they'd endured, of his visions; it seemed Jarhead as a leader for the rural was nothing more than dreams, he thought, as the screams and cries from Tammy and her two boys grew distant and faint.

ANGUS

Pain came from the tiny spiked steel tips that numbered more than a body's points of pressure. Poking into arterial bends, the terminals of touching, walking, twisting, and breathing, leaving Chainsaw Angus's frame in a state of immobility and dark frays of unseen feelers prodding and directing his torso into unknown surroundings until a hiccup of an inhale brought a fit of coughing, and there he sat. Lids batting like moth wings to a Bic of embering light, sectioned by the confines of four concrete walls and a lean-cut Asian man with hands behind his back. One palm holding the other's wrist, starched white oxford shirt untucked, gray dress slacks down bony knees. Thick measured specs made his eyes appear like a squinting, goggle-eyed bass and his wind-parted locks were of a hue that didn't represent anything bright. All Angus could muster was "Of what breed are you, motherfucker?"

Bringing his right hand from behind him, middle finger meeting thumb, one print sliding across the next with pressure creating the clicking sound of a snapping finger. "Up!

Up!" the Asian man ordered, lifting his other hand to the ceiling above. "You must become erect, stand!"

It was the testing of Angus's abilities.

Coming to his feet from the chair, Angus was unsteady, his mouth parched and chalky with the taste of crumbling cordite and rotted eggs. His sight burned. The Asian approached him. Angus towered over the miniature frame, who did not bat his view nor flinch upon Angus's lurching shape. Angus yearned to bring pain and hurt to the ones who'd done this to him, he wanted out of here, wherever here was. And he did what he knew best, other than cooking good crank: he was a master fighter. An unbeaten bare-knuckle boxer who'd at one time been both feared and respected.

Feinting a left jab that hid Angus's right uppercut, the Asian man swiveled his hips, caught the underside of Angus's right triceps with his left knee, smiled. Created a bridge that held Angus's arm trapped for seconds until the Asian lightly grabbed Angus's wrist. Applied pressure. Extended his left leg, speared his foot into Angus's lung point.

At an awkward posture, Angus tried to twist from the Asian's hold, only to find the pause of his breath. Eyes blurred. Insides stiffened with ache. Gritting his teeth, Angus was unable to inhale or exhale without pain.

The Asian released Angus. "I am Fu. Do you not remember your beating of Jarhead Earl in McGill's barn?" Angus grinned, recalled the cloudy vision of branding a young man's face with knuckles. Until a tiny individual took to the air with a crazy-ass kick that logged down across the rear of his neck, then someone forgot to pay the light bill, 'cause they got shut the fuck off. And Angus told Fu, "You're a goddamned dead chink fuck. The loot I was in the process of robbing from McGill, where be it?"

Fu shook his head.

Angus bared his teeth and growled as he attacked once more with a strong jab. Fu angled Angus's attack away. "Anger is weakness. Disrupts your flow. Disrupts your attention to what is countering your attack. Your anger must be fuel, not your fight."

Clamping Angus's throat, Fu used his free hand to grasp Angus's testicles, gave a quick tug, Angus felt the heave in his gut. Fu smirked. Released him and asked, "Have you found sanction?"

By his third attempt, Angus was spent with irritation, dropped to the solid surface, and said, "Why've you brought me to your layer of belittlement? Is there a point to your ways of showing me your mastery?"

"In you is a fire that needs to be tamed. Your anger is your strength and your weakness." Fu palmed his heart with his right hand. "You require change internally. Your elements are disorganized. You've wasted your skills on fruitless endeavors."

"This some kinda fuckin' intervention?"

"No, it is a second chance to breathe, correctly. Internally."

"What, chinks breathe differently than redneck cracker motherfuckers?"

"Internalists call it reverse breathing. Or muscle tendon changing and marrow washing. Unblocking meridians within one's body, to create a positive flow without restriction, offering balance and building of one's internal strength."

Seated within the concrete walls, Angus'd little option. Chunks of brain matter came down the rinse cycle of his memory; last he remembered he was involved with Bellmont McGill's bare-knuckle free-for-all, the Donnybrook.

Trying to get this crank back. Which got him bartered into a deal to fight. Then all hell broke lose. He decided that McGill's loot was a much bigger gain than the crank. Chanced a decision to kill McGill and rob the joint with Johnny Earl, an unbeaten fighter accompanied by some old shape of mutton. Purcell. When the chips were tossed to the table's center and everyone showed their cards, Angus didn't wanna share the loot. Came to the conclusion that he'd kill Jarhead Earl and the old man. Somehow this razor-eyed Fu showed up and took Angus from all of that.

"Render me an explanation, Mr. Fu, how is it that you came to be my savior at the Donnybrook?"

"Only refer to me as Fu." Fu paused and said, "In due time you shall know all there is to know."

Angus's insides cinched. A clawing pain was reeling him out, he was beginning to shake. Feeling uneasy, as though he could vomit, he looked Fu in the eye. "I need a damn bump."

Fu looked beyond Angus, ignored his request. Glanced to the rear corner wall. "You've a cot. A table. Clothing in the trunk beneath the cot. Toilet and shower with amenities to the rear of this area. On the table is a bowl. That bowl is your lifeline."

Balling his fist, Angus screamed, "Motherfucker, I need to procure some crank!"

"It is what you shall eat from. With no bowl you've nothing to place your sustenance within."

"This is a goddamned concreted cell. You're the warden. That it? Let me spell it out, I don't get me a fix, I'll spoon your fucking eyes out with my nails, stomp a path over the floor with your breathing parts."

Fu chuckled. Shook his head. "You will not. I shall dismiss your pains. Refresh your tides of thought, I am no warden, I come from the Fukien province of China. And *how* I came to find you is this: I am employed by a man to collect debts. You and your sister, Liz, voided a man who owed my employer. That debt fell onto you. I hunted and studied you. We rode with each other at one point until you decided to offer reckless abandon." Fu pointed to his jaw. A dime-sized jelly bubble from a cigarette burn, the jerky colored scratches. "You treated my face as an ashtray when we were getting acquainted. Underestimation of you was my mistake as you kicked my head through the driver's-side glass. Left me tangled in barbed wire. That's when I realized your skills. Your potential. It is now water beneath the bridge. I've taken a leave from my employer to offer tutelage as I've done in the past. Once we're finished, there will be a test of oneness."

Angus was drawing a blank. Couldn't recall much more than those final moments at the Donnybrook and he said, "Tutelage?"

Irritated, Fu told Angus, "Training is another word for what I do, but also hunting and making death appear . . ." Fu cleared his throat. "*Natural*. But that's later, much, much later. For now let us keep actions simple. You must eat to nourish your strength. But to eat you must earn that privilege, and to stay strong you must train."

"Earn?"

"Yes, earn your nourishment. Shall we begin?"

With the fog slowly making its way from his mind, Angus stood with little option.

"Sure, Bruce motherfucking Lee, sure," he told Fu.

"Sure is not a positive response, it implies uncertainty.

And uncertainty implies weakness. You are not a weak man. Yes or no. That is how you shall answer from here on out."

"You're goddamned kiddin' me."

"No, I am *not* goddamned kidding you. And I am not Bruce motherfucking Lee, I am Fu. Now, shall we begin?"

Tired, hungry, irritated. Anxious for amphetamines, Angus clasped his eyes and exhaled. "Let us spur the horses for a gallop." Opening his eyes, he finished with "I've a single question." He paused. Voices, he did remember hearing other voices like Fu's when he was encased within the steel coffin of spikes. That he remembered. "Others, they's more like myself?"

"Like you? Sort of. Yes."

"No. Foreign-tongued. I recall conversations when I was in that fucking tin body sack of a tomb with sixteen penny nails pricking me at every angle."

"There are others. My students. They teach another white skin known as Pete."

That name rang a bell. Images drizzled down the snake hole of Angus's memory. Pete. Pete. Cur's Watering Hole. A shithole. A run-down shack. A house. Men bound by duct tape and covered in something sticky. Some of it was coming back to him. But most of it was tainted, seemed like one big fucking dream, the details or the meaning, his hunt for the crank, for his sister, Liz. Liz? She'd stolen what he'd cooked with that gar-mouthed pariah named . . . Ned.

Angus's eyes whelped up. "They're here?"

Fu shook his head. "Questions. Questions. Questions. No. They believe I've taken you to my senior, Si-Bok Lao, when I have not. I've kept you for my own means, that is, if you can survive. As I said, there is a test."

"Tonguing goddamned riddles at me, survive what?"

Exhaling hard, Fu stared at Angus. "My training."

That had been several years ago, before everything dissolved. When times were tough. When men and women lost jobs, but could scrap, cook crank, grow dope, do handyman work to get the layout of a person's home and their possessions in order to thieve. And then a rumor of a militia group robbing the local Walmart spread throughout the working class. A group of ex-lawmen and military special ops who'd served overseas. They'd robbed not for the money but to prove a point. The robbery spurred an underground movement across the Midwest. That's when things really unraveled. Got tougher. Debt piled up and the dollar was no longer worth the paper it was inked upon, and man, woman, and child had had enough of the bullshit laws and rules. Some believed it was these groups who took out the power grids.

Now Fu was feeble. Unwell. Seemed his early years of alcohol and cigarettes had damaged his liver, his heart, weakened his lungs. Internally he was not functioning properly. Was whittled down to the depth of a prisoner of war, more flesh than muscle and a railing rack of bones. He'd sent Angus in search of something more than those fuckin' herbs. A strong dose of penicillin, an antibiotic to kill an infection, something to cleanse and bring his mind and body back to a functional state.

Here Angus sat, in the worn leather driver's seat, hidden behind the tinted glass of the Tahoe. Dirt specked his view, taking the old road slowly, passing more and more abandoned vehicles, papers wadded about the weeds, plastic bottles of empty. He'd viewed humans beaten, shot, stabbed, or crucified, for what? Food. Fuel. Survival.

With his gut churning, Angus had a better understanding of why Fu had done as he did. Saved him from his reckless abandon. Otherwise he'd have ended up like one of these rotted specks smeared across the baked expanse of wilderness. The skills he'd discouraged himself from using for so long had been nurtured, fine-tuned him to become an ass-kicking machine.

In his search for medicine, he'd become tired and beat, wanted shut-eye. A place to rest, gather some provisions, 'cause one could never have too much; he turned down a long, winding stretch of dirt and gravel, hoping for a secure place to do all of the above.

In the front yard, from an oak tree, hung a pulped complexion leaning into a shoulder. A rope anchored around the shape's neck, stringing the frame stiff as a copper wind chime from a limb of walnut for decoration. Cherry-tomato-sized holes stitched the outline. In its chest letters patterned the words THE MUTTS. Blood had spewed and baked black, ran down to bare feet that were dirtied with bruise.

It was that old fuck from the Donnybrook, Purcell. *Goddamn, what are the odds?* Angus thought.

On the radio in his concrete living quarters where he trained with Fu, Angus remembered hearing that once the U.S. dollar lost its worth, the militia groups took the power, then the bottom fell out and a real hell had inflamed each and every state, from the West Coast to the East. Men and women would have to depend upon one another, not others taking care of them. Those who had formed militias, or gangs, they'd be the wiser. The ruling class.

Angus carried a .45 Glock, 450 Bushmaster rifle. Extra clips of hollow-point ammo and empty jugs for fuel. Fu had his hand in many black-market schemes, and guns was one of them.

Out the windows, silence and the hint of smoke passed his inhale. Off in the distance sat a barn with something scarecrow-like hanging from it. Below Purcell lay what appeared to be a charcoaled torso. *Did these men, the Mutts,* he wondered, *find Purcell? Is the body below me the infamous and unbeaten Jarhead Earl? Did the Mutts find them, believing they'd been the one to pull the trigger on ole Manny, their leader?* Purcell and Jarhead had not been the ones who'd pulled the trigger. Angus did. They'd only pulled somewhat of a heist. Taking the Donnybrook's earnings. This, Fu had explained to Angus. What robbery and murder had done placed a sizable bounty on each man's head.

Shifting into park, Angus sat. Listening. And memories came like migraines, paining his mind with visions of his recent travels through the winding and beat concrete paths of road, searching for Fu's medicine in a pharmacy in Paoli. Then Salem. Finding nothing. Witnessing gothic decorations similar to Purcell all throughout the highways and rural pavings of southern Indiana. Viewing a house or trailer busted, burned, or smoldering from flames. Men like scarecrows in a garden or pasture, mangled or ritualized. Dead vegetation, callousing heat, and the words he heard as a young boy, from his grandfather, speaking of the year without a summer in 1816. When spring came but what followed was ass-backward. No heat, just cold clothing the land with ash skies and farmers losing their crops and cattle.

Turning the engine off, sounds of heated metal popping beneath the hood as it cooled. Opening the truck door. Seemed the only vehicles that would run had to be carburetor engines due to the collapse of technology and the computer-chipped fuel-injected engines. And that was only if you had fuel and oil to make them go. Fu did. He had barrels of water. Fuel. Guns. Ammo. Blades of steel. Stockpiled plenty of rice and canned vegetables. Fu had been prepared. But he had run out of herbs and pharmaceuticals. And he was dying.

Paranoia branded Angus with the feeling of eyes watching him as he passed over the yard where, to his right, the screech of a chain braiding through the hickory slats of a swing flicked the air. A headless Captain America action figure lay with its garment snagged and torn. To his left hung a cracked and duct-taped leather heavy bag, strung by a barnacled chain that ivied up and around an oak limb.

Sliding the .45 from his side, Angus made toward Purcell's faded farmhouse with a tin roof and its clay chipped barn off in the distance.

His chest pounded in his palms. Angus hoped to find something more than squalor. Some fuel or medications left behind in a medicine cabinet.

Bloodstained planks of stringer attached to the porch gave way beneath Angus's boots. A bucket of decaying apple cores and eggshells lay next to the door, fuming with insects. He walked through the splintered front door. Hints of mold, perspiration, and struggle lined the once white-papered walls of the home. In short order it reeked of death.

Framed pictures of a man with a female and two young children hang on the walls. Jarhead Earl, he recognized, with his family, Angus surmised, out in a meadow where hogs grazed in the far.

Angus tried to remember a time before drugs spored throughout the Midwest. Wrung the working of their means. When men and women worked either in a factory for their hometown or upon the acreage for which they were born to bear something of continuance, be it a mechanism or roughage, when the worst one had to worry about was smoking too many cancer sticks and drinking too much golden hops or sour mash instead of snorting, smoking, or shooting explosive chemicals that rotted the teeth, blackened the gums, and turpentined one's body and mind. Where had it all gone?

In the living room, dust the color of burnt wood lined shelves of books, Old and New Testament, *Foxfire* books, hunting and trapping manuals, Hemingway, Bukowski, Céline, Shakespeare, Melville, Milton. There were figurines and German/Irish beer steins with lids. Pieces of memory. Dust coated. Flooring scuffed by fingernails. Stains in uneven circles, an upturned love seat with cushions hemorrhaging dull cotton.

A chill planed Angus's spine. Fixtures without bulbs, lamps overturned. Papers wadded and tossed across the floor.

In the kitchen, dishes sat in the sink smeared the shade of a greasy lemon with green hair growing. Hints of fried pork lingered. Wheat-colored crumbs speckled the peach-shaded counter. Mason jars spread with the remains of a lardy grit lined the sink. Gnats irritated his meddling. Walnut chairs numbered in three were pulled from a Formica table freckled with gold spots, an ashtray of hand-rolled smoke butts, a packet of Zig-Zag rolling papers, and a wad of cut tobacco lay next to it, redlining Angus's nerves.

Pushed into a corner was a platinum-tinted fridge next to the basement door that recessed into the stucco walls with handprints smearing unknown IDs. Faint pleas and corrugated grunts slipped from beneath its cracks.

Angus wiped the uneasiness from his thoughts. Narrowed his eyes, held his pistol high, stepped back toward the door. Positioned himself. Gripped the cold doorknob with his left. Turned it slow when the bark of a dog snorted and the front door from the living room screeched open behind him and a man's voice came with the dog. "God-damned 'passer!"

Angus turned to the tick of pins scraping across the floor in a drooling rush. A torso of ruby stood with sooty threads of hair fanning, lips a rash of poison ivy, teeth discolored pebbles with gum-ball eyes swiveling into his own, accompanied by a slick-coated dog of ash that reared and attacked.

Reaction was Angus shielding his left forearm into the dog's slobbering mouth of marrow. Dividing the teeth that gnawed skin, tendon, and muscle. Pressing the steel into the beast's belly. Pulling the trigger. Once. Twice. A quick yelp of fur, spine, and ass fragmented onto the floor. The slag-tinted beast lay strung on the curled linoleum.

The man rushed Angus, rearing a curved angle of steel. Years ago, Angus would've used fists, feet, knees, and elbows over a firearm, but times had changed. The reactive man lived, the slower man inked the final page of his existence. Angus punched the barrel into the creases of forehead. *Dumb son of a bitch wielding a blade at a gunfight*, Angus thought. Tugged the trigger. Blood spewed like a blown head gasket, greasing the kitchen's décor, and the man dissolved onto the floor.

Fluid emitted from Angus's left arm, warming his hand and dotting the curls of vinyl. Beside him, the smudged door unbarred. Feet came in stomps. A shoulder slammed his ribs. Arms circled and locked. Teeth bit through his faded black T-shirt and into the cobra-like muscle of his back. Gravity gave sideways, Angus took in the orange jumpsuit unbuttoned down to the attacker's crotch and spotted with red. Hair pubic and stiff sprouted from his chest and pathed down over his cookie-dough belly. The man shouldered Angus across the floor. Rammed him into the countertop sideways. Teeth tugged at his muscle. The pain sliced through him. Wet lubed his ribs and his mind blinked.

COTTO

The blood-baked memories of his father painted his trail of guidance from day to day. Of how he'd arrived, how he'd react, carry out direction, and sometimes kill as they'd come silt-tongued and criminal-minded from South America.

Crossing the divide, his father, Manny, walked and hitched rides over the heated land where tiny red men, Yaqui Indians, had once crossed and found their resting below footing. He led Cotto and his mother, Kabeza, to a dope-smuggling village called Naco. Cotto was all of sixteen. The three of them holed up, lived off the grid, hidden from the Guatemalan government in a breached, broken, and leaking structure with a roof patched by aluminum, where termites, ants, and roaches lined the floor and walls, became their company. Outside those walls, garbage was picked from dumps. Sold to others to eat, to earn coin. There was no school in this area, no phones, clothing, furniture, or cars; it was peasants feeding on peasants, until Manny made contact with the coyotes. Men with shiny yellow watches and grease-burger guts, contacts that'd get Manny, Cotto, and Kabeza across the border and into America.

Trained as a Kaibil commando, Manny Ramos slept no more than three to four hours a day. As a commando, he woke to the obstacles of daily tasks that earned his nourishment, such as going hand over hand up a rope, doing push-ups, pull-ups, then sprinting three to five miles. Being schooled in guerrilla warfare, map reading, counterintelligence, demolition, jungle warfare, to devour anything that moved on recon missions, be it insects, reptiles, but also foliage such as roots or herbs, even tonguing midmorning dew from various organ-shaped leaves to keep hydrated. Cotto's father was a man who'd lived by a code. Fought and struggled within the civil war of Guatemala in the late seventies and early eighties. Been involved in kidnappings and extrajudicial executions of suspected threats to the Guatemalan president and enemies of the state. When the heat escalated and numerous investigations surfaced about the commando units, Manny and several other men in his unit decided their responsibility was to protect themselves and their families. Each man abandoned all that he'd earned. Shelter, food, a job. Went AWOL to head north in search of prosperity, same as the Mayas, Aztecs, and the Spaniards before them, all had desired to build empires in America or along its border.

Manny wanted a simple existence, but that seemed fantastical. On the day of their departure to meet the coyote and cross the U.S. border, Kabeza had been anxious, had left before Cotto and Manny had woken. Unlike Manny, Kabeza was too trusting of strangers, felt all had good in them, that Manny was paranoid. She went to meet with the coyote who went by the moniker of Raúl at a dirt-walled watering hole. Kabeza was attractive. Curved where she needed to be, hair tinted to the pitch of a moonless night, skin heated the shade of a Brazil nut. And she was MIA upon the arrival of Manny and Cotto.

In a state of hysterical anger, Manny took to the dirt of the streets and alleys, asking any and all passersby if they'd seen this female graced by beauty with a binge-bellied male. Heads were shook. Mouths smirked. They'd seen and known nothing. And Raúl was missing, too.

Weeks later, Kabeza'd turned up in an alleyway beneath bean-sack curtains covering her maggot-hole eyes. Her once silk-soft flesh had been pinched by heat and welts that rang into the bones of her wrists similar to branding.

Cotto watched a choice being made, one that Manny knew all too well. One that Cotto did not want to follow, but his hand had been secured in an iron vise that tightened every time he turned his attention from it. Tugging him back, until he realized his true nature. Vengeance.

Anger stained Cotto's father's veins. The weeks that passed were learnings from Manny to Cotto Ramos. Teaching patience. Precision. How to become a man whom others dared not cross.

Cotto's father explained how he'd wanted more for his son. For his wife. To not be submerged back into a chaotic existence of an eye for an eye. The life of criminalities and organized crime. But it seemed there was no other option for him except to do what he had been trained to do. Kill, take, and eliminate any who stood in his way.

It had seemed too simple. Knowing the coyote met at the watering hole with *walkers*, those who wanted to immigrate across the U.S. border to the north. Wanted to be placed into a menial job in the States, one that Americans didn't appreciate. Saw as being too beneath them. Where immigrants could earn enough money to send back home. Pay for a new roof, remodel their shacks, build a nest egg for their families, to get ahead and return back home or maybe better themselves and one day become legal citizens.

Cotto and his father waited until Raúl returned to the watering hole. Studied this *chicken*. Watched and followed his every movement. His going into town. Coming from the watering hole where he met other men, women, and their children wanting to travel to the north. Then his going back home miles and miles from where he'd met them. Once Manny and Cotto knew where Raúl laid his head, Manny came with nothing more than a nickel-plated Colt 1877 Thunderer revolver, not knowing if it'd even discharge the .41-caliber shells from its chamber. He had used what little money remained, buying it from a villager. Entering Raúl's shack in the dry sand-blasted breach of night, Manny surprised him with "Remember me, you piece of scum?"

Cotto fence-lined beside his father. Watched Raúl, watched his eyes bore out of their coconut oil complexion. From the bone that housed them.

Manny held tight to the pistol. Took in his surroundings. A table to his left. No rugs on the dusted floor. No pictures upon the walls. Shelves to Raúl's left, Manny and Cotto's right held a revolver that lay on the center shelf within a clip-on holster. A thick square of shabby leather lay beside it with handcuffs chipped of their silver.

Raúl tensed his hands up like caution signs. "Wait, wait, señor, you never showed up, only your wife."

"We showed up. Funny thing, my wife, she showed long before us. Went missing. Was found, rotted and sour as a fresh lime in the gut of a roadkill goat."

Raúl's eyes went to his left. Then back to Cotto and Manny. "Was . . . was not me. I . . ."

Precision wasn't Raúl reaching with his left hand to the shelf, where the pistol lay. It was Cotto's father testing the stale air, parting everyone's hearing with the tug of the trigger. The explosive kick of the pistol that rifled the lead. Pinched a kiss between the thumb and index bend of Raúl's reaching hand before his palm grasped the handle of his snub-nosed .38. A thud of a scream coughed from Raúl's lips. Blood slobbered from the open wound that he pulled into his chest, pawed with his right hand, while the fresh meat of his left breathed a damp decoration about the sweaty cotton of his shirt that expanded with the pound of muscle behind sternum. His thumb hung nearly removed from his appendage.

Cotto froze with shock from his father's actions. Manny switched the Colt to his left, came with one confident foot after the other toward Raúl. Cotto followed. Watched his father's right hand rise and reach for the .38. Manny knocked the square wallet to the floor. Pressed the .38 into Raúl's right, which clutched his bleeding left hand. Pinned both hands to his chest until he screamed in dire pain.

Manny smiled. Pulled the .38 from Raúl. Cotto filmed his father's actions with his eyes. Watched the weighted revolver's butt hammer down over the bridge of Raúl's complexion. Delivering a stress crack that expelled more gore and gave Raúl's legs a new angle as he fell from his seated position within the chair, his knees thudded into the dusty wooden foundation.

Manny screamed to Cotto, "Get his wallet. Move!" Cotto came from his father's side, from his stupor, kneeled. Peeled up the billfold from the flooring and opened it. Inside was the weight of a gold shield. An Eagle over top of it with a crest of letters that pronounced SPECIAL POLICE.

Cotto offered the open wallet to his father for viewing. Manny glanced down at the two halves that lay open in Cotto's hands. Told Cotto, "In this land, no man can be trusted, every person is lawless. It is repercussion of poverty brought on by government that milks its people." He paused, then barked to Raúl. "On your fucking belly, spread your hands over the floor."

Twitching, Raúl begged, "But, señor . . ."

"You fuck!" Manny spit, delivered a boot to Raúl's gut. Watched the air leave the pain of his facade as he dropped face-first to the wood. Spreading his arms out, whimpering like an abused canine. "You . . . You don't know who it is I work for. They . . . they . . ."

"Shut your face. You can tell me what I want when I ask it of you," Cotto's father commanded Raúl. Grabbed the cuffs from the shelf, kneeled, pushed both revolvers down his waist, reached at Raúl's thumb that hung by blood, tendon, and hurt, ripped it free, tossed it across the floor. Raúl screamed until he went silent with faint. Manny snapped the cuffs around left and right wrists. Wiped the blood onto his pants leg. Stood, pulled the heavy Colt from his waist, handed it to Cotto, and said, "Tonight, you learn resurrection."

—

What Cotto learned that night so long ago, he would never forget: becoming a man, a soldier, accepting loss. But now, with the rumbling engines maneuvering through the paved neighborhoods of suburbia, that time seemed as lost and distant as the loud begging of men, women, and children within the elaborately structured brick homes, two-car garages, yards once manicured by lawn services, and hard-earned fortunes that no longer mattered. Their pleas for trade, their wads of cash that no longer held worth, their silver or gold antiques, family heirlooms, all were met with the sardonic grins of men whose only purpose was war, slaughter, torture, and rule, while keeping an eye or ear open for Chainsaw Angus. Regardless of ruling the land, which was his destiny, Cotto would not pass up killing the man who eliminated his father, Manny Ramos, while abducting young boys, turning them into soldiers to fight against their own.

Cotto and his men offered pain and death to the fathers, to the older men, just as Manny had taught Cotto: remove the strengths, and power shall fall, as the men were hindered in their ways and views. Unlike the children, the young sons whom he gathered like livestock to be broken down, built back up with training until he felt the children'd been trained enough to be soldiers for killing their own.

Some men stood begging, others defying. Only to get the same words that were offered at every hoarding and butchering: "We've come for your children. Your wives. We've no use for you males."

Some fell to their knees, pyramiding their hands in front of them. Others thought they could swing a punch as easily as they did a golf club on the golf course. Or aim a rifle or pistol for personal protection like they did on the shooting range or the yearly hunting ventures they took or viewed upon their reality TV shows. Those fell just as quick as the kneelers. Hit the ground before they'd even had a chance to touch the trigger, let alone pull it. Dropping like the previous beggars and brawlers. The weekend-warrior wannabes.

Some were hung from door openings of cherry and oak,

others were chopped and grated, left like party decorations from trees in yards or spread and spiked into the paved roads. Left for birds and buzzards to feed on, or a possum, raccoon, or coyote to snack on.

One of the Mutts told a man just before gutting him, "You got fattened by working for so long, your soft hands have lost the skills your ancestors possessed. 'Tis a shame, as you were misled like those in my country, you helped bleed the dollars while being led by a senseless blue-haired government. No bonus checks for you, gringo! Your country has turned as crooked as my own."

"Please!" the man begged. "Please."

"Ask that of your God, gringo. Ask that of your God." And then the Mutt drew a line of red with his machete from beneath his chin, down his bare chest, and stopped at his waist. U-turned the blade's angle, pressed hard, and cut upward. Letting the organs of color rainbow and splash to the ground.

Turning his back, the Mutt said, "I guess your God is busy, gringo, I guess your God is busy."

—

Within the cages Cotto's men loaded, the scared and bawling children, restrained each with zip ties, wrist over wrist behind their backs and placed upon the flatbeds. Hauled away from the suburbs within the small towns, their mothers whose soft skin and tanning-bed flesh would help them none.

Trucks were led by four-by-fours and ATVs, led first through several small towns from the north, south, east, and west. These were viewed as the easier takings. Those lined around shopping centers and fast-food dives. But there were those who were not taken, those of law enforcement or military service or sportsmen who hunted for nourishment. Those who possessed a knowledge of combat, of killing, of strategy. Those escaped. Disappeared into the rural landscape. A landscape Cotto and his men began working their way through. The back roads and farmland. Sometimes they'd gathered none in the rural areas as surprises of ambush awaited them from those who'd gathered and amassed with others who'd possessed know-how. Men and women with skills of survival. Skills of hunting and gathering like those of their pioneering ancestors. Those who'd relied less on technology and lived from the land. Farmed and gardened. Read *The Old Farmer's Almanac*. The *Foxfire* books. The mechanics. The electricians. The carpenters. The laborers. Those nomadic men, women, and children who patched their own roofs, changed their own oil and spark plugs, sharpened their blades; those who'd less and less dependency on their government or TV or Internet. These were the types the Mutts feared if they were to create a commerce and grow in numbers. These were the people they wanted cleaned from the territory. And they wanted their children.

Those who fought back were hidden, unruly but needing organization as they battled against their own. They needed someone to lead them, not rule them, like several of the religious sects that had spawned the brawling meat cellars.

But with the appointment of a person or persons always comes power and the politics of ruling, meaning what was best for all was sometimes overlooked for the betterment of one.

—

From a distance Cotto'd heard the echo of rifle fire that crowned the valley. Eyes surveyed and scouted through the single glass circle mounted on top of a metal-housed HK33 assault rifle, magnifying images, centering shapes of human or animal, just as Manny had taught Cotto after so much blood had been spilt.

Lowering the rifle, Cotto swung his leg over his ATV. Cautious, he studied the ground for answers to the weight of his three men that lay waiting for the rot that the heat delivered. Cotto let others lead, in case something of this nature occurred. His way of thinking screamed *ambush!* Something Manny had learned him when they used one of their many routes for smuggling to the Midwest. A decoy to take the eyes off another. One makes it while the other is caught.

They'd just raided several homes. Came away with fresh bodies, several young boys for training, and girls with their mothers for bargaining with their young and to satisfy a man's needs when required regardless of force.

From the road Cotto indexed and thumbed pieces of spent brass. The metal, warm. He surveyed the hillside. Saw the sets of upturned leaves. Looked over at the deer. Came toward it. Saw the tenderloin carved from the spine. *A hunter.* Excited and angered, he stepped back toward the road's edge. Prints. Several sets. But one set traveled back to the top. At an angle. *They possessed know-how, knowledge of how to maneuver terrain.*

If a hunter, he thought, *his survival had been interrupted.* Another man who would need to be murdered just as Cotto's own father had been. But what if it were not an older generation of male?

Behind him, the sounds of the begging children and their mothers came from the barred-in flatbed. He crimped his eyes with the unrest of losing three men. Too soft, he thought. Migrating to this land did that to his people, and even to Manny. Getting away from struggling to get by; getting fat from booze, food, and training less and less; not having to keep an eye over your shoulder for those wanting to take what you had away. His hordes, his father's Mutts. They lost that edge of having to earn their existence, to compete for their lives, like he and his father had done before migrating to America. Building connections with Alcorn and McGill and the others sometimes meant letting one's guard rest. And their training and hardening waned, became less and less. But not Cotto's. He never quit training.

When he opened his eyes, the crunch of tread to ground stopped beside him. One of his men pointed at the leaves with question-mark eyes. Cotto Ramos spoke, "'Twas a hunter. Maybe a *real* survivalist. What some call a *pioneer*. Is my guess. But not old. Have this feeling." He'd viewed these men who scattered themselves about the land. Preppers. Storing grain, canned goods, barrels of water. Ammunition, guns. Those were his favorites, these men wanting to be warriors. Overweight, smoking fags, they were old and living in a comic book. They'd no deep-earned desire as to what it took to have that edge. That precision. They took on some type of *Mad Max* ideology of survival from too much American television, when they'd never tasted a grain of bitter. But this was not one of those types of men, Cotto could taste that.

Scanning the hillside for movement, one of Cotto's men asked, "How do you come to this knowledge?"

His soldier was soft to the ways of continuation, to survival. His know-how was minuscule. *He's not suffered like me*, Cotto thought as he turned to the slain deer. *I shall enlighten him*, and he pointed. "Study the parting of hide. Removal of organ. It's called field dressing. They've done this action many times. Have a certainty of wielding. They got interrupted by Diego. Became rushed, moved without haste, quickly, like the young, not the old, took only the loin and—"

Behind them, a young female screamed from the cage, "Dorn! Free us from this hell! Return to—" A mother's hand suffocated her words. The young female swiveled her eyes to her mother with a look of hate. Slowly it dissolved. Cotto turned to the cage, studied the girl. A witness to the demise, the slaughter, he thought to himself.

A playful malice scribed Cotto's eyes and lips as he approached the barred flatbed. To the girl he spoke, "You hold knowledge to the one who did this."

Tremoring, the mother could not look Cotto in the face as she told him, "She speaks with fear, with ignorance. She's out of her wits. Rambling. She—"

Cotto's words shifted to the mother. "Silence your tongue, bitch, or I'll remove it quick as a winter frost. I'm the judge, the speaker to your child. Look at me, not from me, when you offer words." Back to the young female, he questioned, "Offer to me, girl, your namesake?"

"Sheldon."

Smirking, Cotto asked, "Tell me, then, what is this Dorn you bark about?"

ANGUS

Those first days were ones of vibration. Angus's stomach muscles belted tight, eyes felt scooped, his mind running soupy as gravy with too much milk and not enough flour. Hungering for amphetamines; the slit-eyed man known as Fu offered Angus a shovel.

"Hell's this for?"

"Digging."

Angered, Angus questioned. "How deep?"

"How tall are you?"

"Look, you aim to kill me, I ain't sectioning the soil for my own damn grave. Divide my brain or knife my fuckin' heart."

"No grave. How tall are you, six-one?"

"'Bout that."

"Dig to shoulder level."

"For?"

"Your head. Now quit speaking and dig so you can learn."

Once the hole was deep enough, Angus asked, "Now what?"

"Now remove yourself of garment, get into the hole, keep upright."

Undressed to nothing more than his boxers, Angus got into the hole. Looked up at Fu, who began shoveling soil back in around Angus until he'd gotten to Angus's waist. "Raise your arms out away from your sides." Angus raised his arms. Fu began filling the hole with soil once more.

Buried to his neck, Angus was immobile. "What if I gotta shit or piss?"

Fu smiled. "Nothing is obstructing you from doing so."

For several days Angus was spooned liquid with herbs from a ceramic-fired bowl. First they were spit out. Then devoured and sipped with a gagging aftertaste. The execution of ingesting such an awful concoction eventually waned Angus's ache. Rid his body and mind of the want for toxic abuse.

Soups and rice came. A ritual of curing Angus's dope sickness. It lasted days. He was immobile, couldn't move. Therefore he couldn't hurt himself. Was left to sweat the ache and pain from his pores.

When Fu finally dug him out, Angus was ropy-lean, dirt-stained muscle with little to no body fat. Tattoos of the names of men he'd beaten in bare-knuckle brawls still scrolled over his frame. Fu dragged him to a chair. Seated him where he sipped herbal tea until he regained the circulation in his limbs.

Fu shaved Angus's head smooth with a straight razor. Did the same to his bristled face. Let him shower and clean himself once the feeling of motor functions had returned to his frame. He drank in the water that beaded upon his body, washing away the sweat. The soil, the grit. The piss and the shit. He came to his cot, pulled the cedar trunk from beneath it, where he found boxers, socks, and black military fatigues; black T-shirts and black boots. All to Angus's exact measurements.

Once he was dressed, he did not sit, he stood and waited for instruction.

When Fu entered the concrete room, he told Angus, "Everything you know must be relearned. But you must know. If you were to try and go back to your old ways of cooking crank, running dope, and double crosses. If you were to defy my trust that you must earn, you would become a hemorrhage, a lump of useless matter in my world, your own self would be splayed upon the ground that you trespass within minutes of being recognized for the murder of Bellmont McGill. This you must be aware of. Am I clear?"

"Why are you offering this to me?"

"Because now you are sober of the drugs that poisoned your inner chemistry. You could leave and function with clear thoughts. Though I doubt you'd live long with a massive bounty being offered by Scar McGill. But if you stay, you will only better yourself. I want you to know you've options. That this is not a prison."

Angus stood thinking of *Shogun Assassin*. A film he'd watched at an early age with his father, about a rogue samurai who offers his son a choice between a sword and a ball. To choose the ball would mean death. To choose the sword would mean life. The son chose the sword, unknowing his fate regardless of his choosing. Angus looked to Fu. "Let's get this goddamned betterment of self under way."

From there he was shown stretches and postures. Bending and kneeling to awkward positions. Warming the stiff from his tendons, ligaments, and joints. Keeping his body aligned, holding the postures for minutes. Building toward hours of stiffness and numbness. Then came the practice of strikes. Punches executed at any and all angles, much like boxing, but much stricter, with reverse punches, vertical punches, uppercuts, hammerfists, and backfists. Followed by kicks thrown over and over. Side kicks, flip kicks, roundhouse kicks, front kicks, crescent kicks, back-leg traps, front-leg traps. All aimed from the waist to the ankles. Nothing high or flashy. The tendons and ligaments of Angus's body heated until he felt as though they were putty being fired in a furnace. Going from soft to softer, burning until he could feel nothing but confetti dotting and flowing through his limbs.

—

A numb rang through his feelers and standers from the pain given by the saber-toothed beast. Angus flipped a generator switch in his brain. Found his second wind. Became wide-eyed. Twisted and brought his elbow into the man's nape. His appendage throbbed with numb. He clubbed the missing link of man. Crimson poured from his arm till the man dropped in the slick puddles of wound.

Angus pointed the .45 down into the rear of the man's scalp. Added to the mess on the floor.

Lungs heaved and Angus listened to the faint bellow of a female travel from downstairs. Twitching with electric rage, Angus wanted to leave, but stepped over the dead man. Glanced for a rag to tourniquet the flow of red from his arm.

Gathering his bearings, he held the pistol high, knowing what he must do, what he had to know. Holding the vision with the basement opening, nothing more than a dark void as he approached. Scents of decay and chemical swam into his inhale.

As he stood in the basement's opening, wooden steps descended into an abyss with a faint glow at the bottom. Slurred speech begged, "Somebody . . . please . . . help me—"

The jar and pound in Angus's ears from the rhythm in his chest made it hard to distinguish sound when coupled with the hurt within his arm, which worsened with each breath. The voice spoke again, "Please . . . help—"

Angus took that first step down the basement steps. Creaks shifted and bounced. Eyes adjusted with glints of light scraping through the cracks. Making out objects, webbed and rusted along the joists above. Traps, rungs of fence wire, machete, axe, and hammers lay on a wooden workbench attached to the wall. Light came from the rear of the basement. Seeped and burned over legs spread, arms strapped by reeds of leather, and the body were that of a female. Marred with bruise and filth. Panty and bra removed, strewn on the floor. One eye swollen like a bee sting. Nostrils pasted with crusty fluid. She shivered, but not from cold. It was shock. Trauma. A loaded deck of all discrepancies.

Looking to the rear of the basement, where outdoor light sprayed from double doors, he saw a vehicle sat on blocks. A Ford Explorer stripped of its tires. Doors open. Angus walked toward it, glanced inside. The gas gauge was half-full. Inside, garments strung. A map spread on the passenger's side. Routes outlined. The smell of cigarettes from a tray of stubbed-out butts. Empties, wadded and thrown about the floor.

"Please—"

The female's voice behind him, Angus ignored it. Searched the area.

In the back corners of the basement, buckets were stacked. Blue plastic drums lined the walls. More than likely, rainwater collected from eaves, then boiled and cooled, Angus thought. Shelves on the walls held bags of dried beans and brown rice. Several sealed drums were labeled fruit.

Angus thought of the storms raging and tearing the Midwest a new asshole. Fu taking stock of what was about to transpire, Angus knew there would bc a price tag upon the head of the man who'd murdered McGill but also upon those who robbed the 'Brook. But once the surrounding world began to crumble and bake with the loss of work, Angus believed all would fade to a myth. Fade to little importance. Be forgotten. But seeing this female, and the so-called prophet sacrificed from the tree . . . maybe nothing would be forgotten.

"Please . . . help me."

Angus turned. Face-to-face, he tasted the cankerous air that wafted from the female. Felt the ache of his forearm. He needed fuel and medicine. Approached what had once been a workbench where sharpened blades, pistols, and shotguns had possibly been cleaned, wooden shelving constructed, Angus slid the pistol into his holster. Unsnapped his Buck knife from its holder. Cut the leather from the female's outspread wrists and ankles that'd been looped and knotted through U-shaped nails. Placed the knife back in its case. Took in her features, reminded him of damaged fruit. Matted hair. Eyeliner was smeared watercolors. Crust that rimmed her nostrils. He knew she'd become a piece of meat for sampling and resampling. Amusement for those without a moral compass. But there was something more. She was familiar and she asked, "David, Daddy? We have to find them. Help them."

Angus kneeled, grabbed her clothing. Laid the garments beside her, hands twitched as she snatched up the clothes as if an orphan who'd never owned clothing.

Angus turned his back for her to dress. Walked out into the daylight. Listened to her sob. "Bastards!" she screamed through pouting lips of gritted teeth. "Fucking bastards!" *Dignity*, Angus thought to himself, *stripped of what she once had*. He tried to ignore her tone. Felt the drama of her words glide through him.

Grass grazed Angus's knees as he stepped out into the daylight; tan and wild, the property appeared unkempt with the passing of months. He thought of those evenings after logging timber, sweat-soaked and dusted by wood chips. Sipping the custard-like foam from a cold Pabst. Watching other workers he employed, some staying on long enough to collect a week's wage, move on. Others stayed for an entire job and a few were regular labor. Studying them each and every: they were all people that time was passing by. Men whose minds were full of bad things 'cause of what they'd seen or have to entertain to get by another day or for what they wanted but could not afford. Angus'd take a swig of that beer, knowing if he wanted to survive in this canker sore of a life, he'd need to get the hell out while the gettin' was good. It was one thing to earn your keep by an hourly wage, but if you live long enough, you have to ask yourself, was it really worth all the renting of yourself, of your time for another man's riches? Angus went from logging and bare-knuckle boxing to cooking meth and then belly-up.

A strong breeze rattled the leaves off in the distance. The land sunk, then rose and flattened to where a wilted barn sat. Chipped paint with discolored wood. Decorating its front was a man, arms outstretched as if he were offering a gigantic hug to the surrounding acres. Bullet holes centered each palm. And from behind, a quaking hand grabbed Angus's shoulder.

Reaching, he turned and pinned the palm to his shoulder. Removed his pistol, twisted, pressed the .45 into the female's right eye. Her orbs glistened like jewels. Angus released her. Lowered the pistol. "My apologies. It's instinct." The girl sagged, her energy lagging as she shook and cried, "David, we gotta search out David."

Angus holstered his pistol, thought about what was behind him, off in the distance, hoped to place a wall between her vision and what he'd just seen, knowing he needed answers. Asked, "What is your identity, your namesake?"

She blinked her one good eye. The other was mashed potatoes. "My husband and me, only persons I knew I'd acquire safety with was Daddy," she said. "Savages came, Daddy told us all things'd be okay but they separated me from David, from my daddy and—"

"Us all?" Angus interrupted.

The girl paused. "They was a woman and her children. Zeek and Caleb. A man whose moniker was Jarhead."

Jarhead was a charred torso out front, Angus thought, *his prophet noosed from a tree.*

"Where are they? These savages, did they remove them?"

The lady was having problems forming speech. Angus clutched her left and right arms. Dug his thumbs into the thin aerobic meat of each bicep. "The woman and children, they took them, how long ago?"

She jerked from Angus's grip, and shotgunned a catatonic intensity of rambling.

"A beast tortured Daddy, could hear the strain of his pain from down here. They was looking for a man whose moniker was Angus, told us if we survived, to give him a message, to tell he had a hand in taking something from him and now he'd hunt him. When he discovered him he'd know pain, then death."

She crimped her lid shut. Moisture dripped down her cheeks, hardened with silence, then a switch was flipped. A paste of saliva formed in her mouth and she spit, "The savage tortured my father! Forced us to eavesdrop. Left us tied like feral hogs to be butchered. Left me and David until—"

"The savage, did he carry a name?"

"They referenced him as . . ."

"What?"

"Cotto, goddamn it, Cotto Ramos."

"Your father, he's—"

"He's what?"

Linked by his neck from a tree limb out in the yard, that's what he wanted to say. But he did not. She'd see his rotted outline when he drove them both out of this rural hell.

"Dead."

"No!" she screamed. "No!" repeating the same word, over and over.

Cotto Ramos. The name swiveled through his thoughts; he floated off for a split second, thought of the words carved into the prophet's chest. Then came back, realized he'd no time for that now, he needed to get this crazed female someplace safer. And she held a frantic madness in her eyes.

"I'm sorry," Angus told her.

"You, who the fuck are you?!"

"Angus."

She spoke like a lunatic. "My father's pain, they left us for these fuckin' lechers to feed like vultures, to give a message to others."

"Gotta venture you to my truck. I'll get you—"

She tried to fight his grip on her arms. "No." She jerked. "Let go! You ain't reapin' shit!"

Releasing his grip, Angus raised his palms up, faced them toward her, showing he'd meant no harm. "Your mind's not firin' on all its plugs. Calm the fuck down, I'll get you someplace safe. I'm only in search of fuel and medicine."

"Ain't going nowhere with you. Gotta search out Daddy and David."

David, Angus thought, *is the one I saw gutted and T-boned up on the barn*. Angus had to get the female and himself outta here, knowing there'd be more of what he'd done encountered. Criminal-eyed men with a hankering for females, provisions, and whatever else they could squander. He needed the fuel. Upstairs came the slam of the screen door. The shift of weight over the floor joists. Angus pulled his pistol from his holster. The female elbowed past him. Ran out into the daylight.

She paused, shielded her eyes against the burn of day. Screamed, "No! No!" She was running to the barn, where the man was spread over the weathered lumber like a dead deer strung up in a cryptic greeting card for what the world was turning into, a lawless proving ground for the mad.

Adrenalized air crystallized her lungs, caused her inhale to crash and burn. She sunk at the site of David, her husband. Several feet behind her, Angus came, pistol in his grip. Working his way through the tall grass and weeds. The barn door unhinged, out stepped a man in another orange jumper. Face scabbed and stubbled, one hand held a machete. Stains of human ran up and down each of his arms, Angus was beat and thought, *So much for getting some fucking rest*, fired his pistol.

The man's chest splintered like decaying wood. He fell backward into the barn door's opening.

The female tugged at her husband's body. At the wet denim of his trousers. Thick mucus rivered from the crusted openings of her nose, tears poured down her cheekbones.

Angus grabbed her, knowing if there were more, he'd just sent them a notification to their whereabouts. "Get a flame in your ass!" Not knowing how many more there were, he'd worn out his welcome.

"Remove your hands from me!" she screamed.

Angus's heart was running a relay. Taking one hurdle after the next without passing the stick. Glancing back at the house, he could make out a face looking from the kitchen window. From the basement came two more men attired in orange jumpers. Escaped convicts. The female was wasting time, she'd either sink or swim. Angered, Angus dug his hand into her buttery hair. Dragged her up the decline toward the Tahoe, feeling her strands give. Nails scraped and dug the top of his hand. Blocking out his conscience, to feel empathy, knowing what she'd been through. Seeing her husband dead. She'd probably been raped. Add that to not knowing the man she called Daddy to be the body strung up like a cannibal tribe's Christmas ornament from a tree along the driveway.

Angus's lungs ignited as he humped through the thick growth. The men came bearing tools for the land. One came with an axe, the other a rusted sickle. They were too far out of range to waste pistol ammunition on.

Making it to his truck. Pushing her against it. She screamed. "Release your grip from me!" Opening the driver's door, Angus gritted, "Get your ass in there."

The female's knee came up from the ground, trying to knee Angus in the crotch. Angus palmed it hard with one hand. Brought the pistol butt down like a sword, parted her forehead. Her single eye went golf-ball white. She went lax. He shouldered her. Took her weight. Dumped her across the front seat. Heard the squeak of the screen door behind him. Felt a presence on his heels. Turned to a man grunting. Two other men met him from the side of the house. If not for the weeds they'd be feasting on his ass like a pack of starved hyenas.

Angus segmented the first man's face with gunfire. The second man came with an axe, swung, Angus sidestepped, watched it jag into the driver's door. Pressed the pistol to the side of the man's temple. Indexed the trigger. The man's head sprayed the truck's fender with brain matter.

The third man held a sickle, only he'd turned and ran. Angus saved his ammunition.

Two men now lay in the weeds, wetting the yard with self. Turning to get into the truck, Angus felt the thud of a rifle butt across his complexion. Everything spun. He staggered. Reached for the door to balance himself. Tried to pull his world back together. His breathing sped up. He dropped the pistol. His vision somersaulted. Turned the image over and over, trying to focus. He grabbed at the rifle, felt the tension give. Then release. He fingered a forearm. Then another. Heard the rush of air fast expanding the lungs within the body attached to the arms he gripped. Eyes focused on the female. Drool lathered from her lips. *One crazed bitch*, he thought.

Bringing his crown forward, Angus met her face. Once, twice. Stunned her, released his grip. Punched her below the nose, hit a pressure point, knocked her the fuck out.

She fell from the truck, hit the ground. Angus grabbed his pistol. Took in the bloody mess of abrasions. Scooped the female up again, dumped her across the seat, face-first. Reached for the rifle, laid it across the backseat. Walked to the other side of the Tahoe to restrain and fasten her in when he heard the explosion of noise from the barn.

A lime-colored Scout truck with an assembly of motley shapes rumbled. BBs from shell shot dinged the roof of the Tahoe. A man was mounted out the passenger's side. Pointing a shotgun at Angus.

COTTO

What he remembered was how blood dripped from Raúl's hand as though it were wax being heated. Perspiration peppered his lips and eyes. His back pressed into the chair. Hands cuffed behind him. Discomfort was his posture.

Cotton cleaved tight over his chest with spots of wet. Manny had kicked the table out of the way. Stood before Raúl. Service revolver down his front. Cotto fanned off to the side, holding the wallet in his left, weight of the antique Colt in his right, watching his father.

Paling in his face and arms, the puddle from his missing thumb behind him, Raúl tells Manny, "You . . . you're making a mistake, señor."

Like Manny, Cotto would never conceive, why? Why had Kabeza left before Cotto and his father to meet this piece of filth without them? Excitement? Some unknown surprise for them? He'd never know, and his father told Raúl, "You made one the second you forced your will upon my wife."

Raúl laughed. "It was not me."

"Then who?"

"I left her with the other coyotes waiting for you and your boy to show up. To transport you across the border. To the drop, then to a safe house."

Manny palmed the revolver from his waist. Stepped toward Raúl, parted his lips with the barrel that scuffed against the upper enamel. Asked, "How do I find these men who've wronged me?"

Trying to speak into the bored-steel opening, Raúl told him, "It's not that simple, he—"

Manny thumbed the hammer back. The cylinder revolved. Raúl's eyes veered to the lead shapes. And stammered, "He . . . he . . . they . . ."

Cotto watched his father smirk. Saw a glare prism in Manny's vision. His father had crossed over to his old trade of being. Of survival. Manny stepped back. Smiled. "He? They? What? What? Speak or I shall remove that soft muscle you use for tasting."

Raúl's complexion wrinkled. "They." He hesitated again.

"They what, are on their way to here for a pickup?" Manny pointed the pistol at Raúl's left knee. "Tell me, Raúl, or I let one of our friends free."

Raúl shook his head. "No. No."

Indexing the trigger, Manny pierced everyone's ears. Laced the air with gun smoke. Cotto dropped the wallet and pistol. Pressed his hands to his ears. Watched the denim of Raúl's leg cauliflower. Knee cartilage and blood flinted and dispersed. Raúl screamed, "Son of a bitch! Okay. Okay. His name . . . his name . . . it is the Ox. He . . . he."

"He what, you piece of shit?" Manny demanded.

". . . will be here tonight with his men. He is the one."

"The one what?"

"That did to your wife the awful that you speak of."

Pressing the pistol barrel into the splayed wound, Manny demanded, "And he and his men have walkers to transport from here?"

Cotto shook. Lowered his hands. Kneeled to the floor. Grabbed the pistol. Stood up. Looked at Raúl, who was gritting with perspiration and answered, "Sí, sí. From here, from here."

"Where are you hiding them?" Cotto questioned as he glared down at the planks of floor. Then back to Raúl. His eyes locked hard on Manny's. Hesitated once more. Manny's eyes were harder. Spooned Raúl's out, scattered them beneath their footing as if they were a muddy trail of thumbs he'd removed. And Raúl glared at the foundation of the house. "Locked beneath the rug, under our boots."

Manny bit down on his rage. "You try and play me for a fool. Give my wife to this maniac, the Ox, and his men. Bring others here but not me, my son, or my wife?"

Fear baked Raúl's lips and the words that fell from them were, "No, no. Was different. Larger groups come here, I have to keep them safe. You, your wife and boy, I could do in town. You're not a fool, se—"

Manny brought the pistol across Raúl's face. Mucus, spittle, and a few teeth dotted the floor like red flung from a brush to a white canvas. "I've heard enough. Letting my wife be defiled. Treated as though she were a piece of mutton." Glancing at the shelf where the wallet and revolver lay, Manny caught the shape of José. Motioned to Cotto. "Grab that tequila. Give him a swig to lube the lies from his tongue."

Raúl twisted his head from side to side. "Señor, you will need that when the Ox comes with his men. He's a monster. He'll bury me deep and you just above the ceiling to hell."

Cotto reached for the bottle. Took the cap from its opening. Turned to Raúl. Placed the bottle on his lips and lifted it. Raúl's throat muscles elevatored up and down as he took a large swallow. Cotto stepped away from him, holding the bottle.

"Only if I let him," Manny says. "Tell me, how many does he travel with?"

"T-t-th-three, three men," Raúl stuttered.

"Counting himself?"

"Sí, sí. H-h-he is the driver. One rides shotgun. One rides center. They drive an old cattle truck, load the walkers with hay sometimes, then they get you to the border."

"And?"

"And they get you to the pickup point and make the call."

"How do they call?"

"By cell phone."

"Whose cell phone?"

"The Ox."

"Who makes the pickup?"

"All we call him is the King."

Manny turned from Raúl. Shook his head in disgust. Turned back to him with the .38, pressed it above the bridge of his nose, and said, "You took an oath to protect and serve, instead you're working for a smuggler of the flesh. Peddling human cargo."

Raúl stuttered, "J-j-j-judge how you will. It's more than humans being smuggled from this country, it's every man for himself, we're shifting between two things, drugs and those who control their routes. Law has no loyalty and little pay. If you don't shuffle dope or flesh, then you starve. You think the police department can feed a man and his family? I get one hundred American dollars for each walker I set up for transport. I only make four hundred dollars a month being an officer of the law."

"Drugs? You're packing the peasants with what, cocaine, marijuana, heroin?"

"Not I. The Ox and his men give the peasants packs to carry with marijuana, sometimes the other."

Headlights beamed from outside, created shadows for the three bodies inside the house. Manny turned and Raúl lit up with fear and told him, "Now you shall see. The Ox will dismember you and your boy while you're full of breath. Will skin and gut you. Feed your remains to his dogs. You should run while you can."

Cotto watched his father reach for a hat that Raúl had hanging from the wall. Placing it upon his head, he told Raúl, "You won't view it. But you shall hear it." Pausing, he turned to Cotto and said, "Grab a rag from the kitchen. Stuff it down his fucking throat. Then come with me, keep behind with your pistol tucked at the ready."

Out the door, Manny's boots treaded the parched earth. Cotto stayed behind him. The taste of dry heaves hung in the heated air. Two men dropped from the passenger's side of the large vehicle. One man slid from the driver's side. Lights made the outlines appear like silhouettes. And one of the men shouted to Manny, "Raúl, are my eyes deceiving me? Have you slimmed down, my friend, or is it just this light that plays tricks with my sight?"

One of the other men shouted, "And he's brought his boy."

Manny didn't waste time, raised the pistol, knowing he had four shots left. Fired once. Twice. Dead center to the foreheads of the passengers on his left. Their weight dampened the ground. To his right, the Ox reached to his body, was backing up as he screamed, "You've dug your grave, Raúl!"

Before he could shoot, Manny trailed toward him. Footfalls hit fast. Aiming where he knew there'd be a left shoulder. Pulled the trigger. He had one shot remaining as the man spun and fell. Cotto kept his distance, watched Manny cloak over top of this man called the Ox. Manny mashed the left wrist with his boot, it held a .45-caliber pistol, a steer with horns was engraved on its shell-white handle. Manny smirked.

"You're the one referenced as the Ox?"

Top teeth met bottom teeth. Slobber poured from the corners of the man's cacti-mouth. "I am. But you're a dead inhabitant to this world. Your burial is already being fashioned."

"Not tonight. Tonight, me and my boy remunerate what you've stolen from us, as it was sacred."

Manny pulled the trigger. The Ox's right palm became a messy web.

"You son of a bitch!" the Ox screamed as he drew his hand toward his chest.

Manny had no more shots left. Threw the revolver out into the dark. The Ox's face crimped with disgust, pain, and anger. Cotto came from behind Manny, lowered his pistol on the Ox's head. The Ox's eyes crimped. "Identify your shapes to me?" Manny kneeled into the Ox's throat, heard a bit of give and pop, took the man's .45 from the ground, stood up, and gestured with the pistol. "I answer to no man. Stand," Manny told him. "To Raúl's house. You have a debt to clear."

Manny kept the .45 zeroed upon the rear of the Ox's slicked-back locks. Cotto followed behind. Each entered into the house. Cotto went off to the right, watched Manny but kept his distance from the bleeding Ox. Raúl's eyes bludgeoned wide with his damp complexion. "Ox, I . . . I had—"

Keeping his hand pressed to his chest, his shoulder a blossom of skin, tendon, and crimson, the Ox cut Raúl off, "—had everything to do with this, you pathetic maggot."

Before another word was passed, Cotto's father told the Ox, "Be like a good doggy and sit." Then he smacked the butt of the pistol into the rear of the Ox's skull like a sledge fashioning a railroad spike into a cresoled six-by-six. Knees unfastened. The Ox dropped to the floor. "Roll your body. Face me with your hands under your ass!"

Cotto stood beside Manny, watched the Ox struggle to sit on his ass. Pain from his wounded palm marbled his face. Manny spoke from the corner of his mouth to Cotto. "This is the worm who took your mother from us. The woman who birthed you. Fed you and showed you hope when you felt there was none, something I can never replace."

The Ox's right arm shuddered with the pain of his parted right hand. His left shoulder the same. The Ox shouted, "The female whose eyes I removed for fishing bait, she was of kin to you? My, she tasted so lovely. I killed her 'cause I did not want another to have the same pleasure as I. Raúl, he set it up. Told her to come early. Before you two. It was to be a surprise to her husband and son."

Manny shook his head at Raúl, whose eyes were bugging. "No, señor, he . . . he lies."

"Useless outlines of flesh, the each of you," Manny said to Raúl, and then told Cotto, "Tonight you become a man. Take the pistol in your grip. End this piece of excrement's existence, quick or slow, it makes little difference, because now we hold their wrongs for our judgment."

Cotto studied this man called the Ox. The scattered ink about his knotted muscle, the bony lady upon his unbuttoned shirt, revealing his chest's center, knives and skeletons up and down his tensed, grisly forearms, and in that moment, Cotto thought of his mother. Of her loving touch, of her warmth. Of her giving soul. And he thought about losing that to this animal. A man who smirked for what he'd done to her. Smirked at him, at his father, and belittled her. And Manny said, "He's the man who has forsaken her. Taken our happiness. Every second you consider his life is another breath of air he is offered but does not deserve."

Manny went silent, then told Cotto, "Take a swig from the bottle. It will numb the butterflies in your gut."

Cotto uncapped the bottle. Tilted it. Felt the alcohol heat and ignite a trail down his throat, lighting a fire in his belly. The Ox looked Cotto in the eye and told him, "You're weak like the female who spit you from between her thighs. Like your mother, you're a little bitch." Then he broke out into laughter.

Eyes watered and Cotto lifted the bottle once more. Felt a numbness coat his thoughts. Brush his temperament into a deep anger. Raising the weighted pistol. Manny took the bottle from Cotto's grip. "Use both hands. Just as I've taught you long before now."

Hand over hand, Cotto thumbed the hammer. Pointed it at the Ox, who smiled. Ran his tongue over his lips. Cotto pulled the trigger.

After that first time, it came not easier, but there was an understanding, an acceptance that it was part of his and his father's way of existing. How things in their world would be decided. With a gun. But now, staring at this young female, eighteen or nineteen, Sheldon. Locks of hair once golden, the strands spotted by the filth that each day of struggle delivered. Her face nicked, her clothing the same. Crimson ringing around her wrists from being restrained. Skin bruised and marred from fighting off the savages, the mercenaries. Cotto snorted black and white powder from a glass vial. His eyes two damp falling stars, he wiped his nostrils and studied her. Knew she held the answers to what had happened to his men. His fallen ranks. She knew who had slain the deer. Someone monikered Van Dorn. And she'd known how to find him, or at least where he laid his head.

But she had to be comforted first. Her fear needed to be replaced with a bridge of kindness. She needed to forget her loss. Even if only for a split second, she needed to feel safe.

"Would you like some water?" Cotto asked.

The Sheldon girl did not answer at first. She stared off into an unknown mass of nothing, with shrieking and outcries of the others she'd been caged with, the sounds shotgunning through her mind. Cotto filled another nostril with powder. Tasted the chemical and carbine dust drop down his throat. Watched her lip quiver. Her fingers shake. She searched for her center to pull everything together, just as her father had taught her. She inhaled the stale air of cinder within the building where spray-painted words and symbols rose, dropped, and spread out like hieroglyphics from an ancient time. It was the top floor of an abandoned lighthouse in Leavenworth, Indiana. A place where teens and older people had hung out over the years. Drunk booze. Smoked weed. Dropped acid. Fucked and scribed murals of pot leaves, UFOs, and any and all idea upon the cemented walls.

The lighthouse sat along the Ohio River upon the north side. Once used to guide barges in the night. Now it was part of Cotto's encampment of razor wire. Dogs. Supplies, vehicles, child warriors, mercenaries, and their training. But what the child warriors needed was a leader. A man to look up to. To admire. To aspire to in their training.

Playing weak and innocent, the girl parted her lips. "Please." But she did not look at him. And Cotto snapped his fingers to a man with an AK-47 strapped across his front. His face half-covered from chin to nose with a skeleton imprint. Hiding his mouth. Hair oiled and tacked in all directions. "Sergio, get her some liquid." The man's clomping feet trailed from the room.

"My . . . my daddy," the Sheldon girl stuttered with her backwoods English, "you and your men, you . . . you ended him." The picture flashed quick. Over and over. A man's knees unhinged. Arms pruned tight behind him. Barrel opening to the rear of his skull. Loud explosion. The front of his face arced like power lines being struck by lightning and fertilizing the yard grass with burnt combustion.

Scripts of unshelled bullets, daggers, the skeleton lady of Santa Muerte, and chinked-out Jell-O scars banded tight as Cotto flexed his shirtless arms. Approached her, sniffed, ran a finger across her forehead. She turned her face sideways from his touch. "Kill. We killed him. You must understand. Your kind took my father from me. My kind took my mother from me. Killing is a way of existing. Loss makes us stronger. Black, white, yellow, or green, it makes little qualm, I will end any and all who stand in my way."

"In your way for what?"

"To rule territory."

"That's what you do here, rule territory?" Sheldon asked.

"I train children to become soldiers, savages. My band of sicarios. To help me rule. Yes. And one day set up stash houses and run drugs again. It's all I know."

Giving a side-eyed glance, the Sheldon girl looked to this man. To the skeletal ink shading his complexion. Charcoal lines rimming his eyes, teeth above his lips, and an upside-down cross splashed down his nose, a shaved skull of stub, a crown of thorns bandanaed around his forehead, and she told him, "You could've spared this man who created me like you took my mother and me."

The girl is finding comfort, talks with backbone. Not fear, Cotto thought as he stepped away from her, snorted more powder, tasted the chemical drainage in his throat. His eyes glassed and he said, "Maybe. Regardless, I did as I did, I've no use for your people's fathers."

Sergio entered the room holding a bottle of water. Raised it to Cotto. "Not me, her. Offer it to her." Cotto sniffed with irritation. And Sergio approached her.

Unbound, the Sheldon girl raised a quacking hand. Took the water. Uncapped it. Ran the open bottle below her nostrils. Sniffed. Cotto smirked. "It's clean of toxins. I've no reason to pollute something that is of dire use to my cause."

The Sheldon girl drank. Her father's words rattling her pan much the same as Van Dorn's father's and the Widow's rattled his, telling, *If things come unhinged and your mama and me is no more and bad people take you, act afraid regardless of how afraid you are or are not, gain whatever trust you can through appearing feeble and weak, and when an opening comes, seize it.*

"Three of my best men were shot dead today, killed in broad daylight for all eyes to see except mine. But you and the others, you had front-row viewing, did you not?"

Hiding her anger at Van Dorn for abandoning her. For not trying to salvage her mother and her and the others, the Sheldon girl raised the bottle to her lips. Took a long swig. The water bubbled through the ridges of plastic as did the malice and discontent within. Something her father had taught her as he'd listened and watched the world unbuckle at the seams and go belly-up, as neighbors became fools and self-centered, she knew she'd have to play sides to survive if at all feasible. She swallowed and lowered the bottle. Said, "I heard shots. Then I viewed his shape."

A breach of excitement came from Cotto. Eyes sparking, he queried, "This Dorn?"

The Sheldon girl nodded her head up. Then down. Her green eyes held Cotto's perforated shape within them. She held his trust, was turning the tides, and parted her lips. "Yes."

"This Dorn, can you guide me to his place of rest?"

ANGUS

The road came quick, the vibrancy of oak, elm, and hickory trees, blurred with the wildflowers that'd blossomed and browned on the other side of the once-metallic guardrail. Below that, the Blue River ran a soupy brown similar to a pasty stew. Cars and trucks had been abandoned alongside the road. Angus was fortunate, didn't have to siphon gas from the many fuel-injected vehicles he'd passed. Fu had placed barrels of octane back just as he'd done with water, rice, vegetables, and meat, kept cool, hidden from all intercepting eyes, along with ammunition and firearms.

From the truck's glove compartment he'd pulled a pair of handcuffs, secured Christi's wrists behind her in case she came to, irate and heaving with violent dexterity while Angus navigated down the road, caused a collision and possibly death. Glancing from her to the rearview, he caught movement. The lime-colored Scout. It was hauling ass, gaining on him.

Looking in his side mirror, he saw the man hanging out, aiming with a long weapon, a shotgun or rifle. Then he heard the explosion of slug shot shatter his sideview mirror. He swerved. Rubber barked like a dog. "Fuck!" he shouted. Pressed the accelerator to the floor. The four-barrel kicked in. Tires hugged the bend and sway of the pavement, the engine muscled loud in pitch. The world outside passed in waves of cracked and baked tans.

Angus eyed the truck, not knowing where he was going, where he was headed; he was in dire need of rest but he'd a crazed female restrained and traveling shotgun. Could use some fuel from the canister in the back. His gas was reading close to E and the harder he crunched the accelerator, the less sense the world around him made.

Another shot rang out from behind, this time shattering the back pane of window.

Squeezing his traps up to his ears, he steered the wheel with frustration, unholstered his .45, came out of the curve, and passed the road to his right for White Cloud; a dirt farm sat dry and without vegetation on his left. The charcoaled structure of a once-squared tan sandstone home lay off to his right, the bones of horses ornamented the pasture as he crossed over the Blue River bridge, and the snaking crooks tested the Tahoe's suspension and handling and Angus's navigation skills, rocking the vehicle.

Sharp and winding surface distanced the men, tires squeaked and squealed, their shapes disappeared in the rearview. Angus kept the gas mashed to the floor, knowing there was a straightaway in the distance. He'd one of two choices: keep hauling ass and hope to outrun them or lock up the brakes, pull off the side of the road, exit his Tahoe, and open fire as they approached. As he glanced in the rearview, there was nothing. To the right in the distance sat a once-white cinder structure, now mossed over with green and chipped paint. Braking to slow the vehicle, the tires slowing their rotation, Angus pulled up beside the building, parked so he couldn't be viewed. Turned and grabbed at the glass-specked Bushmaster rifle in the backseat. Came from his truck. Shouldered the rifle, leaned into the truck, listened for the roar of the Scout and the men within to enter the cross hairs of his scope.

Deep and powerful came the sound of the Scout's motor with boisterous hoops and hollering of the men within. Through the scope Angus viewed the toothless abstraction of man hanging from the passenger's side, then the navigator behind the wheel. He tugged the trigger. A webbed hole cloaked crimson, the driver's face attained to that of a smear and the Scout ran off the other side of the road and flipped.

Angus laid the rifle across the backseat of the Tahoe. Unlatched the rear, removed a can of gas, opened the tank, lifted the jug, and poured the fuel in.

Backing out across the gravel and away from the structure, Angus shifted into drive, hung a right back onto the highway, navigated slowly past the Scout that was turned upside down, the tires still spinning. Men lay half hanging from the interior, crushed and pulpy. He gripped his .45 with his right, his left on the wheel, looking for the movement of human. Saw none and stomped the gas, not knowing where he could hole up, rest, figure out where to find medicine for Fu, ascertain some meaning to all of the menace he'd incurred.

COTTO

One by one, they moved them from the earthen gut beneath the weathered house to the rusted bed of the farm truck. Men, women, and children. Ducked down, crawled in on hands and knees as though they were slaves, sat and took the ragged packs Manny had inventoried, found loaded with dope, handed to the peasants. Dirty faces took them, and waited to be transported to the land of the free.

Before freeing the men and women from the lower area of the home, Manny finished his interrogation of Raúl, patted down the Ox in between boot stomps to the face and ribs of his slain corpse, found the cell phone, his contact for TK, the King. Raúl explained how the Ox took them to Sasabe and crossed the border. Led the *walkers* out into the night of the desert. Their pickup was a mile marker to the east. Once they found it, the call was made. Then a van was contacted from nearby, waiting for the call. The van pulled up. Doors opened. Wrangled everyone inside, then they were taken to a safe house that was guarded by gangbangers who waited to place the walkers somewhere in the United States.

Raúl explained that the entire smuggling operation was run by the King and his trusted gringos. Where he lived, some said Texas. Others said Arizona. And some even insisted it was right in the area the *walkers* crossed. Raúl didn't really care so long as he got paid.

Manny knew what he needed to do to make things work. To create a new future for him and Cotto. Made a call to another like himself, Ernesto. A man who'd fled with him, was part of the unit he commanded, along with two others. Unlike Manny, they'd no wives or siblings. Ernesto kept in contact with the others. When they went their separates, he gave Manny a number, told him if ever he needed anything, or wanted to stir the pot for some action, to give him a ring, these people would get word to him, and they did.

"Manny, my friend, good to hear your voice. I see retirement has made you restless?"

"A man has murdered my wife and now I need bodies, guns, explosives, some form of adhesive, and other supplies to accompany me to America. Make a delivery to a man known as the King. The reward will be big."

"Sorry to hear about Kabeza. A tragedy. I knew that AWOLing the unit and seeking to go straight wouldn't work out. But that was something you had to discover on your own. You know whatever you need, I'm there, just say when and where. We're blood brothers, my friend. Chub and the Minister always ask me, have you heard from that crazy SOB Manny? Now I can tell them I have a big surprise!"

"Yes, you can. But what of the guns and explosives, will it be a problem?"

"You need not worry, Manny, have I ever let you down before?"

"No."

"Then it will be like old times."

"Yes, old times, only we'll no longer work for the man, we will be the man, this I promise!"

"Will you need anything besides guns and explosives?"

"Maps, compass, flashlights, binoculars, and water. Plenty of water to drink. And one last thing."

"Yes, Manny?"

"Your dress, wear clothing that is haggard, ball caps, slick-bottom boots."

"Like a peasant?"

"Yes."

Manny took the wadded bills and land deeds offered by the job-starved peasants from Raúl's scuffed metal box, stuffed them into a pack, finished interrogating Raúl. Understood the simplicity of the workings: leaving the truck at Sasabe, trekking through the Sierrita Mountains to meet the contact. Like his wife and him, the peasants came to Raúl by word of mouth. Paid what they could to be picked up by the Ox and his men to be transported to the border. Then led into the United States, through the desert by a coyote to be picked up. Transported to a safe house. Squat until they'd be driven like bleak smudges across more terrain from one state to the next. Thumbtacked somewhere in the Midwest. Given a job. A place to sleep and get on their feet as the West Coast had become too overpopulated. But new salvation came with a price. Those who could not afford the price of getting into the United States muled drugs. Others sold themselves for sex. That was part of the swap for freedom and ruin of people.

Cotto and Manny saturated Raúl's home with fuel after Manny milked him for his worth. Planted a bullet between Raúl's near-bled-out begging eyes. Tossed a match to the home's interior. Watched it engulf as they slid onto the cracked and foaming vinyl seat of the truck. Watching orange flames roast the night in the side mirror, Cotto listened to Manny's words.

"When you're going to take something, you react, hit hard. No second thoughts. You must know who is the weak link and who is the strong. Who the lures are, those used for baiting, and use them to your advantage. The strong cannot be given leverage or they will kill you when you let your guard down. The weak must be squeezed of all they're worth, then disposed of. These men we meet, they can smell fear, any that you encompass must be replaced with confidence. What we do now is for your mother, *that* you must remember. From here on out, we are our own family. And our way, our *coda* is to kill or be killed."

Cotto sat holding the pistol, the memory of Raúl's eyes lit up like wicks of dynamite sticks. As he thumbed the release on the .45, the clip dropped into his palm.

"Quit fucking around," Manny snapped. "This is no game. Slide that back in. Be sure one is shelled in the chamber, just as I've learned you over the years. Now comes the greatest lesson you shall learn. How to be a leader."

Clicking the rectangular housing back into the handle, Cotto fingered the safety. Asked his father, "We're not going at this alone, are we?"

"No, my son, we're not stupid."

"You called your friends from before?"

"Yes, from before. Men I've done many, many bad acts with."

"We can trust them?"

"Such a question from a sixteen-year-old boy. Yes. Just as

I trust you and you trust me. They are like your own father. Like my brothers."

"That'd make them my uncles."

"Yes, and your uncles are as ruthless as your father."

Those words of his father had accompanied Cotto on his missions, informed how he saw them: missions to conquer. To survive as the hit of a pin to brass sparked the lead of gunfire that came quick and unexpected. Followed by the smoke, reminding Cotto of that night Manny taught him about *true* vengeance, the separation from boy to man. And having men you could trust. Those same men who'd delivered the news of Manny's murder. Ernesto, Chub, and Minister, the same men who visioned this man, Chainsaw Angus, as he spread Manny's life across the land, same as he'd done Bellmont McGill. And the ones who stood watching all of this take place was one Jarhead Earl and a prophet named Purcell. Then they robbed the McGills of their stake. No loyalty. But Cotto had loyal men, they were now holding down the encampment. Were preparing the young he'd taken from homes. Keeping them doped up. Training them to fire weapons. To kill. To be soldiers. Savages.

Inhaling wet powder into each nostril, Cotto watched gray billow up into the sky, creating a cloud like smog that soon devoured the shape of the old farmhouse. Screams of men inside replaced sound and the Sheldon girl pointed. "There. There he goes."

Offering her food, canned fruit, and boiled grain had created a bridge of trust. In return, the Sheldon girl agreed to show Cotto where Dorn laid his head. Where she believed he was bunkered down. Knowing Dorn was skilled, all she hoped was he'd not be killed. Regardless of how angered at him she was for abandoning her and the others, she didn't want him to be taken from this world like her father. A bullet honing his skull and expelling what lay inside of it.

Repulsion coursed within Cotto, watching the home ignite, listening to the sounds of his men perish behind the walls of the structure. Seeing this shape run toward the barn. Hulking with a pack slung over his shoulder, a rifle in tow, he was young and too damn cunning. Cotto knew, regardless of how many men he sacrificed, he had to capture, not kill, this Dorn. Drug him up. Force his pioneering knowledge of survival to create a merciless soldier to help train others. Offer his know-how of the land. And then it hit Cotto. The very thought of finding another as knowledgeable as himself sent shivers and chills throughout his frame.

Before Cotto realized what had transpired, the Sheldon girl had foot-stomped one of Cotto's men, pulled his pistol free, shot him in the gut, his tone belled as he dropped to his knees. Turning, another man took a bullet to the leg from the first man's pistol, compliments of the Sheldon girl as she'd seen her window of opportunity to escape. Seized it. A third man pressed the butt of his AK-47 to his shoulder. Cotto shouted, "Do not shoot!" And he forearmed the man's rifle to the ground, watched the Sheldon girl take to the thigh-high weeds and foliage of field until her frame disappeared into the camouflage of barked ash and pollen, the opposite direction of Dorn. Turning to Sergio, he told him, "You and the others, search the area for provisions. Radio Ernesto, tell him to keep up the search-and-destroy, keep the heat in the bush till he finds the man known as Chainsaw Angus."

"And you?"

"As I do every day, I'm putting what my father taught me to use. I've my radio, will check back with details. This Dorn will be of great use and the girl will find him much easier, as she knows the land and its ways." Then Cotto took to the field to track the female known as Sheldon.

ANGUS

Muscles burned and tendons ached to reach that place so few ever arrived and even fewer held on to. Fists tanned ribs like mortar fire, fingers dug into the soft spots of tissue like carbine piercing wood, sounding off as if a hollow tanker being filled with ball bearings. Fu had conditioned Angus, over and over. Callousing his frame.

Sleep for Angus was blades threading lines across foreheads. Scalps ripped away. The sloth of men yelling, being christened for their wrongs of sin. Nightmares, they churned in his mind similar to the earth that became clumped and heated with decay ladling in brain grease.

For the most part Fu became like a father to Angus. Even with the rigors of training that delivered heated hands and feet, pulsing and swelled. The meanings of his conditioning unknown to him over those first passing months until all the bad occurred.

Fu would repeat how he was preparing Angus. Who questioned in return, *Prepare me for what?* But when the world swam in a sea of debt that could no longer be paid by the print of bills and the aid once offered no longer came to the foreign, well, by then it was too late for most. And Angus would soon understand what he was being prepared for.

Leaving Fu behind, in search of medicine, passing dwellings of the struggle, curves of smoke whisking from the surrounding wilderness, vehicles muddied by corrosion and on blocks, furniture in yards or on wilted porch stoops, Fu's words rattling his brain, *After light is banished, nourishment shall follow. Fuel will cease. Value will be something of weight. There'll be those who rape, kill, and steal, but their ways are temporary. They'll eventually extinct themselves as all men of the savage do when they do not make investments to the continuance of race or people.*

The power had absolved and the world had tilted into an unknown mode, Angus told himself as he hung a left onto north Gethsemane Road, drove beneath the overpass of the interstate, then hung another left onto Green Valley Road. He followed the long stretch of crumbling pavement, farm pasture to the right with dead stalks, rusted fence to the left where the interstate ran west and east, but no vehicles were visible except the ones that had been abandoned, all was of the quiet.

Angus wanted rest, drove to the road's end. Hugged the right curve that morphed to gravel; countryside sprouted up with several shack-like barns and an old house where a '72 Chevy truck sat in what passed for a drive with ruts of earth, vegetation, and tree limbs decorating it. Pulling up behind the truck, he looked to the female. Eyes clasped. Anger ridged his mind as though just a separate passenger, a manic pugilist without boundaries.

Opening his eyes, Angus studied the house that sat

off to the right, paint chipped from the wooden planks of siding; a rock walkway ran along the dead flowers where ceramic figures of dwarfs and Snow White ornamented the area, their colors just as shambled and faded as the house's siding.

Shifting to park, Angus sat. Tired and worn.

As he pulled the rickety driver's-side latch of the truck, the door hinge bartered for a greasing, and Angus stepped onto the property. The smell of burnt plastic heated the air. He looked at the sky above, the trees off in the distance; there were no plumes of smoke, only the scent. As he started to approach the screen door, tension replaced the blood that creaked through his body, feeling stronger than what he'd dealt with before a bare-knuckle fight. Unknown was if anyone resided, if he could find rest, recoup, and make plans for where and what to do. Then came the noise. The words of Hank Williams III blared from a distance behind the home. Punch. Fight. Fuck. Muffled almost, but recognized, the sound harnessed his attention.

Walking around the truck to the passenger's side, Angus unlatched the truck's door, reached in, and unbuckled the female, fearing to leave her unattended, fearing for her safety. Breaking her down at the waist and over his shoulder, he took her weight, walked across the yard, his pistol in one hand, his other across her ass, mashing through knee-high grass laced with twigs and leaves. Nerves panged in his belly and he'd come to a large rusted tin-sided structure, palmed open the side door. Without thinking, he entered, instead of investigating the interior for squatters, thieves, or worse. He just entered.

Inside, insects trespassed. About the floor were bones,

mangled hides, the smear of fluid and animal entrails turned green and black as drained engine oil, hardened like straws amongst crushed beer cans. Flies weed-eated the air with infinity. At the far left wall, several worn leather heavy bags lined and were suspended from an overhead rafter. Squares of foam with knuckled centers hung from walls, used for punching. The back wall was adorned with an aged Nazi flag. Below it were crates upon crates honed of wood. In the area's center, spent brass lay scattered amongst grease that spotted the dirt floor. And from behind the back wall came that tune from a radio or CD player with Hank III still jamming. Angus clasped his left hand into a fist. Over and over to lax the anxious rattle that plagued the inner workings of his frame. Held tight to the pistol in his right. Looking at the construction of the building, he studied the old six-by-six rafters, which were rough-cut, the type that was hard to sink a nail into. Counters ran along the right wall where any and all manner of tool hung, wrenches, sockets, hammers, and a jack. Tubs for cleaning with small cans of gun oil above them. And what looked to be a rusted fridge. Walking toward it, he could make out framed photos that were freezer-taped to it, they were of bruised limbs and facades of bodies that'd been beat. Teeth broken and busted within gums. Faces of men with eight-ball eyes of bruise, a scalp with locks removed, appeared like a sauced pizza dough before being cheesed and baked.

Standing there, he shook his head. *What the fuck have I stepped into?* He walked off to his left, where the large leather heavy bags hung. His eyes followed the chain connected into the dated wood, meeting a thickly gauged hook that screwed into the rafter, the bag's center was wrung by seams of duct tape. Meaning it was still being used. Several sets of bag gloves and weathered jump ropes lay upon a bench. *Racist brawlers*, Angus thought.

Wanting to release his tension from the situation that was being created, the pugilism that was coming, Angus raised his left hand to his temple, hinged his knees, tucked his chin, felt the heft of the female across his shoulder, wanted to ball his foot and come southpaw with a bone-rattling lead right hook that'd shake the ceiling, the walls, but he could not as he clutched the pistol and the unease of something amiss within the dwelling.

From behind where the Nazi flag hung came the slide of a stall door. Dust beamed in the haze of light and the music of Hank III bounced hard from within and a voice sparked with, "Who the shit—"

Angus twisted around, glared at the image of not one but two men, one holding what appeared to be an unction-stained rag in one hand, the other clamped onto a .45 handgun. Each was shirtless, bruised, scabbed, tattooed with swastikas, skulls, the SS symbols flagging their necks. Their pants tucked into their boots. Suspenders ran from their waists and up over their shoulders; each was smudged by ill living conditions. Stubbled faces, ratty locks, and their teeth were amiss, stained the colors of yellow jackets.

A feeling of dread coated and clung to Angus. He began to step backward when the track of feet patted behind him and the pound of angular steel shafted the rear of his skull. Something like electric pain sheered through his limbs. He lost sensation in his feelers. Eyes blinked and blurred. He dropped his .45. Then his thighs, knees, shins, and the balls of his feet wavered with that confetti-like inertia. He lowered himself to one knee, brought the female from his shoulder as though a sack of grain. Slammed her forward, padded the dirt floor with her back. Trying to shake the butterflies that circled his head with the tromp of boots coming before him, he listened to the high-pitched hick giggle coming from behind him with "Got his ass, I got his ass good."

COTTO

Rough as flint edge that'd been sharpened by Indians, several men eyed Manny and Cotto with bloodshot suspicion and possibility, not knowing if they were affiliated with drug lords, men on the lam, or those who had a dollar on their heads. Father and son stood beside the beat farm truck loaded down with peasants in the rear outside of the decaying-clay cantina several miles before the border.

While they were waiting for Ernesto, Chub, and Minister, the sanctum was a place where beer was warm and the women were stained by the men who batted their skin as a means of foreplay. This was a land where if a woman claimed to have been defiled forcefully by a male, she must prove her chastity before any action could be taken.

Splotches of bone-colored flesh with patches of fur marbled the skinny strays that pawed across the uneven road.

They came like shadows from the sun, Ernesto, Chub, and Minister. Ernesto announced, "It's been too long, my brother." Each offered their condolences to Manny and Cotto for the loss of a wife and a mother. Manny nodded a thank-you, asked, "You bring everything?"

Ernesto smiled and unholstered his pistol, handed it to Manny.

Manny looked over the rubbed steel of the .45.

"Nice," Manny told him, and handed the firearm back, asked, "And mine?"

Minister went back to their vehicle, came back with a worn military pack, reached inside, offered Manny a holstered pistol and several clips. "Yours."

Chub told him, "Look in the pack, everything you asked for. Even a nine-millimeter for Cotto. And more provisions in the truck."

Manny stood palming two pistols as if he were the lead in a John Woo film, one in each hand, testing the weight. Then slid it into the clip-on holster, pushed it down into the side of his waist. Took the pack, looked at the boxes of ammo, the clips and the pocketknife-sized lengths of putty, grinned at Ernesto, and asked, "How did you come by all of this so quickly?"

With a baked hide and a cast-iron jawline, Ernesto told Manny in a matter-of-fact voice, "When we left the regime, I took what I wanted, knowing I'd never be accountable for it. Thought maybe one day it would be of use."

With black bandanas over their heads, Chub and Minister squeezed Manny's shoulders and spoke at the same time, "And that day has come, big brother."

Looking to the truck bed, Ernesto asked, "And of what use are these scavengers you're hauling around like burlaps of grain?"

"That's what we will be transporting. They're our bait."

"Bait?"

"For the King, they carry his weight."

Ernesto's eyes went dental-floss thin. "Weight? You mean drugs?"

"Yes, drugs. We need to find someplace without attention. Get them rigged up with the explosives."

Ernesto smiled. "Manny, my friend, there is no length of harm I would not endure or commit for you."

"Nor I for you, brother, nor I for you." And Chub told him, "We should get before someone gets curious to our actions."

Manny nodded. "To the border."

Each piled into their vehicles, shifted into gear, and headed down the scorched road while eyes watched from the cantina.

—

The sun leveled behind the massive expanse of dirt that climbed, wilted, and dropped as far as their eyes could take them. One man after another stepped across the corroded strands of barb that separated the two territories.

Taking to the open space of heat, the peasants wore faded and hole-pierced ball caps, their locks at odd inches. Wrung by fear and stink, they mustered the packs that held in them bricks of marijuana laced with a sharpening-stone-sized piece of C4. Manny carried the cassette-sized box that would signal each of the plastic's detonation just as he and Ernesto had done when an obstruction needed moving or ordnances needed banishment.

They'd studied several maps, Manny, Ernesto, Chub, and Minister, explaining to Cotto as they inked terrain, coordinates, and miles to be taken by foot what they were doing, knowing in the recesses of their minds, as they walked with hunter-green packs walling their spines with water, ammo, and other supplies of need for their trek, where they'd go and how long and far they'd navigate by booted foot with pistols clipped down their sides, keeping eyes abound, searching the distance for the unwanted shapes while heat baked moisture from their pores. Manny's crew kept themselves blended in with the others. Wearing ball caps and ragged denim, they wrung up next to one another like germs to flesh. Each carried a jug of water brought by Ernesto and tied to their waists or their packs.

Several days by foot is what it would take them, until they were within two miles of the pickup location, then Manny'd dial the number in the phone, give the heads-up to the person who'd phone the drivers to navigate them to a safe house and then to the Midwest for work—at least that was supposed to be the plan. But Manny knew better.

Dark surrounded the travelers as they made their first stop for rest when they entered the hills, below a ridge of stone walls that'd been eroded by weather and hardened by time. Peasant walkers sat or leaned on rock with their weighted rucks, men, women, and children who chewed fear of the unknown, trying to imagine their inhabitance within the foreign surroundings. Working the jobs spoiled Americans would not, for a weekly wage that was more than they'd earn in a month south of the border.

"*Siéntense. Siéntense*," Manny told them, motioning with one hand while holding a flashlight with the other; Cotto stood by his father, without a hint of smile, his thoughts trashed with images of his mother's insect-infested torso and the man who'd robbed her from him, but not her memory.

The men sat, shielding their families, afraid to make eye contact with Manny. "Don't hold any concern of danger for me. I will get you to safety. This I promise." Pointing to the men's packs, Manny told them, "But when I tell you to drop your rucks, you drop them. Disperse. *Comprenden?*"

He was laying the salt lick. Offering thcm a hint of trust. A warm hand in a cold environment.

Each peasant looked at the other, then made eye contact with Manny and said at the same time, "*Sí, sí.*"

Trust, it was the first thing Manny had preached to Cotto. *If men trust you, see what lengths of sacrifice you'll offer or go to for them, they'll die for you. Even if it's a lie.*

Ernesto, Chub, and Minister walked the perimeter in search of unwanted movement. Ernesto came light-footed to Manny. "In the distance, I see lurkers signaling with lights."

"Head count?"

"Two by my count, one in the north, one in the east."

"Any vehicle movement?"

"None that I've spotted."

"How far?"

"Several hundred yards."

But Manny kept his eyes peeled also. "There is at least one following us."

Lifting his eyebrows with surprise, Ernesto questioned, "And you know this how?"

"Through my field glasses, I noticed a small glimmer, a shadow of human with something of reflection, glass or silver, when we stopped to drink."

"What do you make of it?"

Manny smirked. "I'll let you know."

Manny turned to the peasants, glared at each man, and

turned back to Ernesto. "I've assured these people we'd get them delivered."

Ernesto said to Manny, "And you're a man of your word."

"We need to keep distance from whoever it is, pretend we've no idea they're here until we have to do what we were trained to do."

Ernesto nodded. "I'll keep lookers on them, you rest a bit longer and I'll check back with intel."

Manny nodded back.

Cotto looked to Manny, he'd a 9 mm holstered down his waist. Twisted the lid from a plastic milk jug of water. Took a sip. Recapped it. Asked Manny, "You think these people Ernesto speaks of bring trouble?"

"Any time man, woman, or child treks across the desert alone there is concern for trouble. Stay close to me, my son, stay close."

One of the peasants, a man whose jaws held pits and eyes irritated by allergies, approached Manny. "Thank you, sir. I appreciate what you do. Your honesty."

Manny offered a hand. "Refer to me as Manny."

The man reached. "And I am Ricco."

They shook and Manny spoke, "You come to the U.S. for work?"

"Sí. Sí."

"What is your skill?"

"Agriculture. NAFTA," he said, "it came with a promise of better wages. Only thing it did was cut all good earnings throughout Mexico by two dollars on the hour." Ricco held up his index and middle fingers. Smacked them into his left palm as he rocked back and forth. "The paper that was signed destroyed any worth our crops once had."

Manny nodded. "No choice but to go north."

Ricco nodded, too. "Sí. Sí."

"More jobs. Better money." Manny paused. "Go to the country that robbed you and your land of its yield."

One of the other peasants said, "And now we have the cartels. They offer work. Good wage. But life expectancy is zero."

Manny chuckled. "And who is the biggest customer for the cartels?"

Ricco and the others all looked at one another, lost. Manny said, "The U.S. It's a conflict of interest, to kill the drug war, to eliminate the cartels, it would be to destroy Mexico's economy and even much of South America's, because that drug money is funneled back to the south."

"And how do you know of such facts?"

"I worked for the government in Guatemala's intelligence, I know the ins and outs of all economies and their downfalls."

Chub and Minister returned. Chub asked, "Where is Ernesto?"

"He's on watch. Spotted lights several hundred yards away."

"To the east?"

"To the east."

"What is the plan?"

"We wait and see what Ernesto tells. See if they're holding positions or combing the desert for *walkers*."

"Think it's border patrol?"

"Not this far out. More than likely landowners."

"Regulators of territory."

"Yes, and you know as well as I the rumors that plague this land and those who own it."

"They shoot first with no questions asked."

"Many family members take the risk to come to America, only to disappear and never be heard from again."

Ernesto returned, heavy in the lungs for air, telling Manny, "I think we should move on."

The weight of water, ammo, and concern rang with their steps over the land as they moved amongst the bite of desert cold through the night. Keeping the peasants to the center, Cotto and Manny took the rear, where Manny could keep an eye on the tracker behind them. Ernesto and Chub led with Minister in the center, each of them blending in. Every so often they looked to their maps, swung out to a rougher, longer route, keeping distance while being very much aware of the small lights off to the east flickering every so often. Trying to distance themselves from the signaling, letting each other know they'd spotted nothing, as it was the same blinking pattern every twenty to thirty minutes.

By the breach of morning, the sky came upon on them with an oceanic glow of silence. Tired and weary eyed, Manny realized what they'd entered, what the signaling of lights had been doing, corralling them to this location, an area littered by crunched plastic bottles and jugs, discarded clothing, shards of jackets, socks and pieces of rag lay strewn about as though a tornado had ravaged the land, decried any trace of human that might have once existed. It was too late.

The air tapered with the piercing of sound and the rear of a peasant's skull dispelled in chunks of hair, bone, and brain gore. Painting everyone around him to the ground with chaos, panic, and wild eyes.

Leaves overturned and mashed with the memory of that time and the sounds of what Cotto hunted now, twigs freshly broken and the hints of female tarred over the deep inhale of mossy air. Keeping his distance, Cotto tracked and spied upon the Sheldon girl, her scents clinging to his recognition, even though she was without bathing, her salty skin still held the hints of something soapy, a lotion-scented vapor masked by dread, exudation, and this crazed countryside of thc ungodly. Still, it was female.

Cotto viewed her panic through telescopic glass: her cutting strides through the brush, being grazed by briar, marred by tree limbs that swelled her pigment when she ran, trying to get a grasp on direction until she collapsed to her knees, the gasp of lungs gripping for more air, quick glances in all directions. She sat gathering her wind, covering her mouth to silence her entwined cries of rage, depletion of oxygen, and all that she'd embarked on like a sudden collision at a traffic light.

Her inhale slowed its pace as her lungs wheezed less and less. Tears were wiped on the hem of her shirt, composure was gathered, and she found her footing, began to walk quickly, using curves of rooted tree to guide her balance until she took to running once more.

Yes, Cotto thought, *yes. Lead me to this Van Dorn the same as a feral animal does to its burrowed young.*

Every so often she'd slow or stop, glance around, keep watch to her left, then right, then behind her. Listen for the sounds of tread mashing over the leaflets and twigs, everything that coated the earthen woods.

Kneeling, she'd study the indentions within the land, how it had somersaulted, been disturbed or disrupted. Sometimes it was outgrowth from the shoed hooves of Dorn's mule, Red. Other times a branch or the mold the two's weight had left. It was assurance that she was following him. Then she'd take off on a jaunt, leap over the fallen circumferences of rot.

Cotto adjusted the rounded focus of his binoculars. Drew the Sheldon girl closer. Studied her every movement, the expand and depletion of her sides, her mannerisms within the woods that enclosed her. How she sniffed the air, touched things broken or out of place, how she calmed within the vegetation the farther she traveled. This girl knew the land. *This is something that will be of great use*, he thought to himself as he pulled his vial of powder from his pack, snorted quick and hard, gilled each nostril, tasted the drop of drainage falling down his throat. As he bared his teeth, the rush shadowed over him as he watched her nearing the Blue River that ran a glassy green with hints of brown below her. Watched her walk the road. Kneel to its left flank, finger the ground. Her prints sinking into the shapes left by the trespass of mule. But still no Dorn.

Cotto imagined his young soldiers becoming cunning and knowledgeable like Dorn and Sheldon, surveying the land, how to live from it. Survive. Knowing how to battle and maneuver with ease. Help map and rule. The very thought of these two transforming the young into hardened warriors clenched within his frame an unknown excitement. An addiction to rule.

Sheldon came to a T. Jogged left. Went toward the river. Down an embankment of rock, of assorted colors of smooth stone. Whites, muds, flints, and rust. She studied the water's flow. Searched the opposite side, her head jutting up and down. With the glare of diamond-like sight, Cotto could see what the Sheldon girl was studying, taking in where Dorn's creature had traveled upward, similar to the deer that had been tracked down the hillside, up past the small cut, and made it back up the hill at an angle. They each possessed a great trait, skill to be passed onto others. To hunt and yield what is feasible. Necessary with little or no time. Quick to react during times of duress.

When next Cotto looked at the Sheldon girl, she was gone.

The crushed powder that he sniffed was heightening his reaction to detail. Blinking hard and fast. Looking again, he watched her drift into the movement of the rippling water. Crossing at a knee-deep point. Watched her straddle the river, make it to the opposite side, her pants clinging to her legs as she wrestled through the outgrowth of weeds, briar, and small trees that wormed and curved. Then she scaled the grade. Reached its summit. Disappeared once more. Cotto lowered his binoculars, came quick from the road, waited by the stream, eyeing where to enter, then crossed and made his way up the mound of expired vegetation. Felt the heat in his joints and tendons, the burn of the climb.

At the top, with his heart binding and unbinding behind sternum bone, he reached one hand after the other to limbs, lifted himself up, and scaled an oak tree, perched hawk-like on a limb. Looked for the Sheldon girl. Seeing her in the far, but also hearing the silent unknowns. Crows. Sparrow. Red or gray squirrel. Marbled tans and whites of rabbit or deer.

There was the distant echo of gunfire that rimmed the land. Then nothing. Followed by another shot. Then silence.

The Sheldon girl slowed, took in the area, searched for camouflage, found a small enclave within the ground, and burrowed into the leaves to hide. Cotto waited for her to move. His mind a concaving rush of colors wilted and worn, colliding with daylight that began to shift its hue until darkness absorbed the entire forest.

Cotto switched his binoculars to night vision. Came down from the tree. Walked. Took careful steps to where the Sheldon girl lay. Moved as though he were a ghost. Kneeled beside her. Rested a hand down on her neck. Took in the rhythm of her breath that pushed from beating heart and expanding lungs. Calm. Lax. Unlike the jittering of his. Letting his sight adjust to the ravenous surroundings of wilderness that was nothing like his homeland. Feeling the build and dissipation of frame, an increase in pulse, her lids began to flutter, her arms jerked, the stomp of blood circulating within sped up, and she opened her eyes. Rose from the indention within the earth in a pant of suffocating fear.

But Cotto was gone.

By morning, Cotto sat vein-eyed and wired awake, holding the vial of powder. Tied himself to the tree that he'd climbed up. Watched Sheldon rise. She studied the woods, then took to the land once more. Came down the hillside above where Cotto's men had been slaughtered. Where the deer had been gutted. In the rutted road the Sheldon girl kneeled to the patches of stain, glanced around. Took in a tree where a hand had been nailed, or what was left of the hand, blackened by heated rot and engrossed by insects.

Watching from a distance, Cotto smirked at this warning. His warning. He'd had one of his men nail the instrument for touch to the tree. Sheldon moved from the road, walked quickly. Cotto followed her stride for almost an hour. She stopped at a property line. Crossed an acre or more of field that once held nutriment but was now parched. From a tree, Cotto watched her bend, run her fingers over something in the field. Indentions of hooves, Cotto thought, a marking to let her know Dorn had traveled this direction. His nerves were tense. Where was this Dorn? Where and how did he keep distancing himself? He was like a fable, leaving traces of story but no shape.

Through the binoculars, Cotto took in her walking with concern from the field. Sheldon hesitated as she passed what looked to be two dogs or what was left of their bloated and scattered remains. Bone, hide, and graying bowels. She continued toward the monstrous home that sat on the opposite side. Studied two vehicles with hoods ajar. Parked in the faded driveway like monuments from a forgotten era with jumper cables intestining from one to the other.

From afar, Cotto was irritated, taking in the Sheldon girl's nervous approach. There was no Dorn as she walked toward the mule that lay upon its side. Butchered. Her hand covered her mouth. It was Dorn's mule, Red.

"An ass," Cotto said under his breath. "Where is the one who rode and led you about?"

Sheldon looked to the porch. Viewed the strewn bodies, some blackened by blood, opened up by a sharp utensil or broken by gunfire. Adrenaline built within Cotto as he took in her cautious steps amongst the flies collecting and circle-eighting around the mule. *Display yourself, Dorn, show me you're a living, breathing warrior.*

Sheldon stepped to the bodies that planked the porch like a house of real-life zombies. She seemed to have no fear, or little of it. Or maybe it was the desire to find Dorn.

But viewing the mule made Cotto wonder what troubles the boy could've crossed into. These people of the rural land were maybe more savage than he and his men when there was nothing else to lose. And that brought even deeper desire to catch him. Dorn was planning to be everything Cotto believed he was; he'd be a defining asset to his young soldiers.

Before the Sheldon girl could turn and run, the front door of the home unbarred. A female came from within. Her face an expanse of abuse, nose and lips plumbed by something durable. Crusted red with eyes raccooned, she shouldered a lever-action .30-30 on the Sheldon girl.

Viewing the actions through his binoculars, Cotto muttered, "I shall call her the ugly bitch."

The Sheldon girl seemed to be surveying the rifle that the ugly bitch wielded upon her. There was an exchange of words between the two. Then the Sheldon girl raised her hands, palms facing the ugly bitch. Cotto caught something within Sheldon's features, a smirk about the corner of her mouth, and though he couldn't hear it, she bared teeth with rage and attacked the ugly bitch. Clawing and punching and kicking her until she dropped the rifle, caved in, and fell into a fetal position. *A warrior,* Cotto told himself. A numbness for her skill lubed Cotto's insides.

Picking up the rifle, the Sheldon girl thumbed the hammer of the .30-30, stood over the ugly bitch with anger wetting her face, demanding words Cotto could not make out. As he adjusted the focus of his binoculars, fingers trembling with excitement, trying to decipher her lip movements, it looked as though she were asking *Where? Where did you get this?* By *this* Cotto thought Sheldon was asking the ugly bitch about the rifle.

The ugly bitch reached for something Cotto could not see. He caught the reflection of a blade. The Sheldon girl screamed. Then came the rack of gunfire. The ugly bitch's brain was thrown from the rear of her skull like guts dropped in a slaughterhouse's slop trays.

Cotto wanted to clap, to laugh with joy at the fast action of violence that came unexpected but was needed in order to survive the situation. *This girl is a beast!*

The Sheldon girl chambered another round, her arms

pulsed and quaked and she entered the house. Within seconds gunfire erupted once more. Cotto stood in the tree, waiting, unnerved, anticipating her exit from the house. Knowing the gunfire was from the same weapon. It had cast the same echo, but did the Sheldon girl pull the trigger?

ANGUS

Eyes blinked open to the tilt of floor level. Reek of animal carcass and the laughter of madmen. A vibration of pain welted Angus's skull. He lifted his neck, glancing at the worn black boots; his pistol lay from his reach. The boots were a barrier between the two, so he pulled himself back to standing. From the opening where the men had come wobbled a pink-haired female; she had potato-skin knees, arms vibrating, inked with daggers, eagles, and swastika tattoos, and the color of bruises lined each of her sockets. Then came the quick view of the laughing man who stood over his left shoulder. A pip-squeaking stabber not much taller than two and a half bales of hay that'd been twined and stacked, with wilted skin that held the gloss of a turnip's insides, he wore boots with three-inch soles to add height to his sunken demeanor.

Angus twisted his attention to the two men in front of him. Smiling, they offered their gums of decay. Each was wormy and fidgeting. One veered a pistol sideways at Angus; the crud between his knuckles was earthy and human. The other kneeled, reached for Angus's pistol, stood studying it.

Smirked. "This here's one of them plastic-type constructions."

The female lay off to the left, still unconscious. The man with the pistol trained on Angus spoke. "Thought you's fitting yourself up to a beauty nap."

Angus knew if he kneeled and ducked all at once, he could spin to the man over his shoulder, take whatever steel he plowed the rear of his skull with, and use it, blanket himself from gunfire with the torso, or maybe they'd not shoot one of their own; it was a gamble.

Inhaling deep to situate his nerves, Angus stood before the misfits aligning his frame, reached, and felt the bulbous knot that leaked crimson from the rear of his head. Tested their movements, reflexes. They'd not moved him. Taking in the textures of the two men. Ragged cotton and denim. Damp flesh pocked by tats, scabs, and open wounds. One holding Angus's pistol was barefoot, the nails of his feelers were glazed by grease or oil, each looked as though he'd had leeches burnt from his frame after rolling in cresol from a woodstove. The man holding the gun on Angus said, "You some kinda mute?"

The stringy female came from behind the two men, bare feet smacked the dirt floor. Slapped forward. The female's vision appeared possessed, the blacks in her eyes were expanded to dismiss all color, and she stuttered a duck whine. "G-g-got any salt?"

The man holding Angus's pistol told her, "Nip that talk from your tongue, Okra."

The female kneeled down and started touching the unconscious female, rummaging and picking through her hair as though she had burs in her locks. "Why for, I think I've discovered me some salt." She giggled.

And Angus questioned, "The fuck you plan to extort from us?"

"Whatever it is can be offered."

Shaking his head, Angus clenched each hand into bone-hardened hammers at his sides, told the man through gritted teeth, "We's just looking for a place to bed down. Let me get the female from the ground and we'll be particles in the wind."

The man wrinkled his flaky unibrow, motioned with the pistol, and told Angus, "Sure, just scoop the ole gal up and be on with your travels. Stupid shit, done trespassed into the wrong territory!"

Angus glanced at the female, her locks strung from her head to Okra's chafed lips as she jerked and chewed. The man holding Angus's pistol turned it toward his right eye. Closed his left to look down the barrel.

For a split second, the other man glanced at Okra, his orbs golf-balled, and he shouted, "Set your raggedy ass back from that piece of meat, ain't no salt, you's chewing her goddamned lengths, making a tangle of her skull."

The female was coming to. Her shoulder quivered. Cuffed hands behind her back were halted from reaching at her hair as she tried to jerk. The man training a pistol on Angus kicked Okra in the ribs. From standing, Angus reacted. Palmed the man who held his pistol. Speared the .45 into his eye. Clamped his hand around the trigger and fired. Face. Skull. Eyehole. All separated like a spoiled tomato flung against a windshield.

Angus kicked him backward. Dropped his dead weight down onto Okra. The other man screamed, "You son' bitch!"

Angus felt the other shape behind him. Felt the movement coming. Anticipated him. Dropped and spun into the other man with the gun. Knew he'd get jammed up. Didn't shoot. Centered his weight. Shinned the side of the man's bony knee. Knocked him off balance. Dart of steel came from overhead from the one who stood over Angus's shoulder. Angus mashed the gun wielder's face. "Ahh! Dumb fuck!" the man shouted as he released the pistol.

Angus reached for the pistol that fell from the man's hold. Spun and scurried backward. Looked up over his shoulder to the man who'd hit him in the rear of the head; he stood with batting lids, confused by the sudden exchange of actions. Angus shot once at the steel wielder. Splintered one knee, caused each to bend, a crowbar hit the floor. The pale-skinned smudge of blood and screams stutter-stepped and fell toward Angus. Kneeling, Angus rolled, his weight somersaulting into the two female's bodies that lay piled behind him. The metal wielder tumbled, Angus pulled his knees to chest, kicked the metal wielder backward.

Then came the squalls of Okra, "No! No!" followed by her teeth breaking the skin of Angus's neck. A rabbit punch of knuckles marred the side of his face from the gun wielder, who crawled to his opposite side, hollering, "Shot my brother." Taking the glancing fists, Angus pushed his .45 into the attachment of mouth and teeth that quickly flung and pawed at the barrel. Pulled the trigger. The pawing body of Okra went limp; right temple, eye, and cheek had combusted into smears and streaks. Flowering the cobwebbed walls like lengths of spruce spit from a wood chipper as the female's shape fell sideways and wetted onto the floor like car wash suds.

The explosion shell-shocked the drums of the breathing's ears. Decibeled the chorus of chaos. As the rabbit puncher sat staring at the parceled skull of Okra, Angus maneuvered around on his ass, drove the .45's barrel into the rotted mouth of the puncher. The puncher gagged. Slapped the pistol from his mouth, hinged a right knee to his chest, and thrusted a heel at Angus. Kicked him backward. Angus dropped the .45, got to his feet. Looked to the pistol, then back to the slog of pale-skinned heathen who glanced at the pistol and up at Angus, who extended his right hand, fingers facing the puncher; he bent toward himself. Each man held the ring of gunfire jarring within his ears. Worn and wavered, Angus needed sleep, was redlining on exhaustion, but managed to tighten his hands to fists. Told the man, "See what skills you hold for quarrel!"

From the floor, the crowbar wielder moaned, "Beat that sum bitch, Mick, marble him black and red." The man bared what passed for teeth. "You've killed my sister, one of my brothers, wounded my baby bro. Gonna make you dent and bleed. Soak yur ass in kerosene. Throw you to the meat cellar for a bonfire of flesh and bones."

On the floor the female jerked, her hands cuffed behind her. She hollered, "Where the hell have you taken me?"

"Six Flags, honey." Mick laughed.

Not looking down, Angus told her, "Hell."

"Uncuff me, you bastard. Done caused enough death."

"Sure has," Mick said.

Angus came with a left jab to the side of the man's face. Palmed the underside of his chin. The man crimped and stutter-stepped back. Eyes blinked fast. Angus followed. Flung a low roundhouse into the side of the man's shin. Something cracked. Pant, pain, and drool creviced from the corners of the man's mouth. He came with a wild right cross, which Angus evaded.

On the ground the female rolled onto her ass. Scooted toward Angus and bicycled kicks at his ankle. Angus stomped her feet. She screamed, "Bastard!"

Angus twisted a right hook into Mick's ribs. The man spit blood, clenched Angus, tried to suffocate his barrage, reared his head back, and came forward, stapled Angus's nose. Crimson oozed from his nostrils; the man delivered tight rabbit punches while his body pressed Angus backward, the hurried breath of an outhouse's shit hole in the summer wafted from the man's mouth. Angus cut an elbow just below the man's eye, then beneath his chin, chattered what mineral- and raisin-tinted teeth he held, sidestepped, and dug a knee into the man's kidney. Eliminated his wind.

The man buckled and cringed at Angus's attacks. Spit red and took another elbow across his forehead. Followed by an uppercut that crumpled him to the floor.

Angus kneeled and took up his pistol. Glanced at the array of bodies, Okra's malformed flesh. The opening in the steel wielder's knee. The half-garnished skull of the man who picked up his Glock. Angus's ears still rang, the taste of gunpowder hovering in the air and iron on his tongue. The female was going mad with insults. Mick wept for his fallen sibling, the side door swung open. Outdoor light peeked in with a man who towered thick and aged, being guided by the barrel of a shotgun that he scanned the area in front of him with. Angus raised the .45 at the man. Was rushed by the one he'd just laid a beating on. Squeezed the trigger, fired once. The thick man backpedaled and ducked out the entrance. Tin siding clunked with a quarter-sized rip. The man screamed, "Mick the Stick, you and your brothers still returning wind?"

The man blanketed his arms around Angus. Wormed his right leg behind his footing. Tripped him backward to the dirt floor. The slam of weight to his chest, air coughed from within, exhaustion was numbing his every morsel of being as the female scooted toward Angus, kicked at his features from the side with her foot bottoms. Mick punched at Angus, left and right, repeating the back-and-forth as he screamed and drooled to the wiry man, "They's not, Josiah's been knee shot, Grudge and Okra has been delivered to they Maker!"

With a heated fury, Mick blistered and bruised Angus's face. The female continued to kick and kick, cursing him. "Wasn't for you my daddy'd be alive, you murderous fuck!"

Angus's complexion was a rotisserie of jags, bumps, and welts as he took the assault, reached through Mick's punches, grunted, and laced his fingers into his ratty knots with his left and right hands, pulled Mick's face down to his own. Lips parted and he engulfed the oily nose of blackheads, bit down. Mick screamed, "Ahhh! Ahhh!"

From the door opening came booted clomps tracking across with footfalls and the pant of menace, stopping at the two men on the floor, the length of sawed-off metal formed into a point with a duct-taped handle wrapped by a beefed-up man's digits. Seeing this aged shape, the female quit kicking. Sat with a creak in her neck. Ache in her spine from being cuffed, she rolled to her side and looked up.

Blood nostriled from Mick's nose and oozed out of Angus's mouth with a built-up three-fifty small-block engine's pulse, Angus's muscles pumped, and the hacksawed barrel of the 12-gauge pressed his ear, conducted thoughts that ran rampant in his mind. Knowing somewhere along the line these people had gone from crazed lunatic to fucking turbo-charged insane.

The leader looked to the dead on the ground, strewn about as though oversize action figures, he told Angus, "Release my follower's nose 'fore I split your pan across the damn dirt." Shaking his head, he continued with "Of the years it took to create a congregation of men and women, turn them from white-trash misfits to Aryan Christians with the knuckles of my hands that I bled, beat, and killed others for, you've decimated a small percentage of them within minutes."

Tight clamp of jaw released Mick's nose. Hands fanned out. Angus's skull reared to the ground. Mick spit and blew crimson from his mouth and nose, punched Angus with a one, then a two.

The man looked to the female and back to Mick. "And who'd be this feisty menstrual of a female?"

Rolling Angus facedown, Mick told the man, "Far's I know, she's traveling with him. But she spouted something of he killed her daddy."

Mick stood up from Angus's shape. The leader clumped over Angus with shadow, the barrel's rough end digging into the rear of his head, Mick stepped from each, seized two pistols from the dirt, held each, one in his left, the other in his right, until the man ordered him, "Quit dicking about, find some twine or baling wire to figure this shitheel's hands as it appears he's a helluva brawler. Could make a powerful Aryan representative."

Glancing from his eye's corner, his peripheral taking in Mick's bristled face while the stern-eyed leader leaned over him, Angus searched for that split second in a fight, waited for that one opening that could change everything, listened to the tall shadow of a man speak at the female, telling her,

“You seem to be a feisty gal; keep that spirit ’cause they’s men here and others who hunt that can muster a firm loaf and butter you up a few shakes be it night or day, just hold your wet for us to deal this devil to the meat cellar and let him earn his keep and honor our clan.”

COTTO

Cutting higher and higher above elevation, the sun gave heat to the shadows that cowered. Manny and his men kept themselves shielded behind the peasants. Manny eyed the spread-out peasant, Ricco. Nudged Cotto, told him, "Grab the dead's ruck of dope from his body." Cotto didn't hesitate. Reached and tugged the thick and weighted pack. Manny barked at Ernesto, "You see what direction the carbine flash came from?"

Chub, Minister, and Cotto kept corralled behind the peasants. Looked over their shoulders. Were using them as protection. Ernesto pointed two fingers to his eyes, then to the northeast, where in the far distance a wall of stone lay with breaks around it. Manny pulled his field glasses from his ruck, saw the reflective glare of glass dancing around with what appeared to be two shapes. He twisted and looked behind them, a silhouette was running in their direction. The one who'd been tracking them from the rear.

Turning back around, he mouthed to Ernesto, "Dust is being kicked up, moving toward us from both directions."

Holding the glasses, Manny was tired and worn. Eyeing Ernesto, he finished with "My guess is they's two in the rocks and maybe three or four in the vehicle that is bringing a storm for us."

Ernesto held his pistol at the ready. "Do they look of gringos?"

"Cannot tell, but I'd say they're connected to the owner of these rucks of dope that the peasants tow."

Ernesto's face glimmered with the sweat that began to pour from him like a beef-greased skillet; he wrinkled one eye into his cheek. "How would they know our position of travel?"

Manny reached into his pocket and removed a cell phone. "They's a tracking device within this cell, the same cell of the men who normally transport the peasants and the dope. My belief was they never got their call for transport, checked in on their transportation, found the house Cotto and I torched."

"You've known all along?"

"I know that if I am smuggling drugs, I can't trust anyone, so I'd wanna know where my product was at all times until I get it to the customer and I get paid. I know the bodies of the men that took my wife from me would have been found in the charcoaled remains of the torched house. So, yes, I knew it was only a matter of time. They've been wrangling us, signaling with the lights, shifting us from our route to here. That's why we needed the C4, it's part of my plan."

Ernesto smirked. "Your plan?"

"To dethrone the King. We need only one of the approaching men alive."

"To show us the way?"

"Yes."

Cotto's father told him, "Stay close, my son, and when you shoot"—there was a hesitation in his words, but it was not fear, it was that of a methodical and precise leader, passing from his rimmed-out orbs to his son's—"you do it to wound first, then we kill those men who need it, 'cause they will have no pity for any of us by the time we're done with them."

To Ernesto, Manny questioned, "Can you circle back behind us, go unseen, take out the one who has been tracking us?"

Ernesto replied, "Can a tarantula not cross the desert in silence for his kill?"

"Then go, bring me his fucking head."

Ernesto kept low to the ground, distanced himself from the kneeling Manny and peasants.

To Chub, Minister, and Cotto, Manny said, "Act as if you're a peasant, keep your guns from eyeshot but at the ready, calculate your targets, when I release the peasant's locks with my hand, you do as I, react. No wasting of ammo. Clean shots. Wound them, confiscate their arsenal, and search the vehicle, then we can decide on who fucking lives."

And to the peasants, Manny said, "Any of you run, you die here." From that day of waiting on the unknown, Cotto practiced patience. Becoming composed. Dissecting. Learning. But viewing the Sheldon girl come from the house of slaughter, all he could think of was *Dorn*. Was she leading him to Dorn? Or was she playing with him, his mind? Knowing he was watching her every movement, studying her instincts to survive?

Cotto was rattled as he watched her carry the rifle, a pack strewn diagonal across her body, and a pair of binoculars. Cotto believed Sheldon was armed with more than a rifle as she trailed through the tall grass, making her way toward a thicket of cedar that swallowed her.

Scaling down from the tree, Cotto was careful. Coming across the field at a trot, passing the cars, he descended the porch, glimpsed the dead, their outdrawn shapes of disfigure and decomposition. Traced Sheldon's steps into the home only to view what appeared to be a young man. Who lay with the rear of his skull goring a wall of books. The floor was putrid with its stink of all things human and non, coating the tiles with prints and slips, smears and artifacts of what he believed to be the butchering of vertebrae. And questioned, *Dorn, could he have delivered this bloodbath?* If so, he held real grit, something deeper and darker than Cotto could have imagined, and that grooved a shiver into Cotto. Increased the course of his adrenaline.

Stepping from the home, heartbeat redlining, he maneuvered past the dead outlines. Took caution, following in the broken lines of knee-high grass that the Sheldon girl had walked through. Grazed past the cedar, scraping his grainy skin, inhaling traces of the girl's scent, nerves jittering; he attuned his ears for sounds, stepped from the cedar, from the diminished needles whose color had transpired from green to a tanning orange to the outgrowth that had fallen from other trees, searched the ground for her steps, indentions, and breaks; eyeing them, he tracked her veering of foot. Came to a road that he crossed only to search the opposite side for her travel.

Traces of her flesh traveled within the air, the sweaty soured lilac and berry, she was close. He stopped. Listening to the distant mash of her feet to the earth, sniffing, he moved forward with the caution of a feral dog in search of food scraps, not wanting to be seen.

Passing a massive, perfectly triangular-sized opening within the earth, peeking down into soiled walls of root that haired out like parasites, he found the outlines of hide, marred and filthy, sharp bone glistened from gum and flies, seeped, grooved, and laid their flutter and squirm in the digs of decomposing canines. Turning from the trapping pit, Cotto could hardly contain his emotion, seeing the onslaught left by Dorn. To be young and possess such skill astounded him. What the young man could offer to others, to pass on, was limitless. What this meant to Cotto: power to rule.

Cotto distanced himself from the grotesque shapes of carnage. Knowing how close he was to the creator of this savage obstruction, he maneuvered with caution.

ANGUS

A shiver of awkward befell the leader's stiff hold as if he were an aged bull trying to hoof a frozen pond for water; with arthritic hands he constructed a double slip knot from a thick braid of rope, lassoed one end around Angus's neck, drew it tight, the other end around his wrists behind his back, keeping him connected and restrained from any pull of limb or the area between head and shoulder that would draw a taut stringing choke, while Mick kept a clear bead on Angus with one of the two pistols.

Standing, the Aryan bore down with the sawed-off, turned to the female. Prodded the scuff of black about her one eye with his booted foot. It appeared almost synthetic or unreal with its bruising as she winced in pain. Bending down, the Aryan sniffed her, drove a finger about the hemline between shoulder and chest, began scouring her until he came to the unsupported weight of skin where mothers feed their newborn. She cringed, bared the white about her gums, and spit, "Remove your touch from me!" He slipped a tongue from his ulcered lips and battery-corroded teeth. Ran it over the lids of her eyes.

Angus jerked, the rope went tight. He gagged and coughed. Thinking that regardless of what had befallen the female, she was a spent, unappreciative cunt.

Mick pouted a laugh. "Silly son a bitch still carry some spurs in your boots for scrapping, don't you?"

The Aryan looked over at Angus, tilted the barrel toward the side of his head; fumes of whiskey spilled from the man's lurching shape. Angus eyed the man's profile, the peer of light drew his features now without any shadow as he noted the smooth scarring above his eyes, a nose that had been busted and swelled more than the count of fingers and toes on a hand or foot, never set properly, and the stench that spilt from his gristled pores, from hulky limbs that were dressed with the ink of swastikas, eagles, and skulls ranging all about as though ruined and faded stars, dotting the raw flesh of forearms, biceps, and malformed hands. He'd been a fighter or brawler or defender of whatever belief he stood for.

Coming to his feet from the female, the Aryan looked to Mick. "Get this infringer to his feet."

The man whose knee Angus blasted, Grudge, lay with blood dripping to the dirt and whined, "What of me?"

The Aryan told him, "Quit your damn yammering, we get some kerosene to your wound, get you bandaged when we get this slab of chops to the cellar. Don't need the others looking down upon me 'cause one of my followers held no taste for pain nor pugilism before the eyes of God."

Grudge looked to the Aryan, his lookers going clockwise with confusion, and Mick shouted, "Quit offering yourself to that of the weak, that's what Aryan Alcorn's speaking at you."

Kneeling down in his faded maroon Fruit of the Loom T-shirt with tiny worm-sized holes across the chest, Mick drew Angus to his feet. The Aryan reached and squeezed Angus's arms, shoulders. Ran a thumb about the curves of skin that'd been beat, swelled, and healed. Pursed his raggedy lips, pushed back the oily gray and black threads of his hair, scratched the curved bristles of insect-legged beard with the 12-gauge's barrel. Stood his ground, looking into Angus's eyes, into his soul as though a lion defending his territory, until Angus coughed words.

"Odds are a stacked and jagged concern, as you're not gonna end me."

Showing crooked and broken enamel the shade of leaf-stained water, Dillard Alcorn motioned with his shotgun toward the mess of female about the floor and said, "Correct you are, too damn squirrelly and gamey for ending, you're like I once was, what I wanted my spawn of followers to be, fighters. I see it in your hide, you'll bring damn good hawking amongst the beggars and thieves when night blankets our land and the Lord watches over us."

Angus winked one eye small, left the other big. "Beggars and thieves, the hell are you spitting, Aryan?"

Alcorn laughed. "You'll see. It took near thirty years of confronting the damnations, battling for what I believed, seeing whites, blacks, chinks, and gays mingle, adopt, and breed, infecting this land, thinking they could do as they pleased and call it freedom of choice, telling me what I believed was wrong, hateful, even demeaning, but in a world that takes till they's no more to take from the Aryan skinned, they bottomed out. Now that the world has run bankrupt and wild, well, me and a host of others can run it even madder than McGill's Donnybrook in something we call the meat cellar, where men and women tend to get crazed as leprous wolves with hunger in they blood, and it don't matter what color your skin is or who you worship, seeing as the prize is to breathe for another day, to entertain all who attend and bring respect to their clan and their followers and earn territory."

Mick's eyes glistened wild and bulbous as he nudged Angus: "You're nothing more than a pawn for nourishment, we's doing some bidding of our own, you just happen to be white and can square your punches."

Donnybrook, the bare-knuckle free-for-all that he'd fought in. McGill, the creator, a man who was something like a God amongst the working folk, that is until Angus fed Bellmont his ending. To have devised something crazier than the 'Brook, that placed a trickle of angst into Angus. "Talking crazed, this ain't about whites and blacks, this ain't about race. I was looking to rest my mind, in search of medicine."

Mick whipped Angus's face sideways with a pistol. "Don't wanna hear that sap stringing from your yapper, you're a trespassin' murderer who stopped at the wrong property, now you earn your existence. They's no more of the money masters, of the government or politicians, rules or laws, now each man regulates his own symbi, symbi—"

"Symbiosis, you stuttering retch of skin," Alcorn chimed. "You can't pronounce it, don't speak it. Quit offering yourself and our race to appear more ignorant than you are."

Mick's face kindled red. Alcorn looked to Angus. "You say you wanted to rest your head, but you travel with a lone female."

Angus swallowed hard. "Some horde removed her father, husband. Allotted themselves the Mutts. I spared her of befouling."

"Ahh. Cotto Ramos and his band of mercenaries. His father once muscled for me, he wasn't a Christian but he was a man of his word." Alcorn stepped sideways, pointed down at the female, and said, "Woman's got an awful plumbed complexion, looks as though you roughed her up a bit. Must've garnered yourself a hell of a workout ripening her features, sure she didn't seek shelter with another because of your pugilistic ways?" Alcorn chuckled and paused, looked to his wounded and deceased flock, and finished with "Or did she get untamed on you like my followers?"

As he tried to come at the Aryan, the rope cut into Angus's wrists and neck. He squeezed out the words, "Fuck! You!"

Lowering himself back to the ground, the Aryan turned from Angus, chuckled, "No, fuck you. I care little of you and your troubles. I'm about to find out what kinda warm this hen has got under that pelt."

Seated on her ass, the female shouted, "Keep your distance from me!"

Laying the 12-gauge to the dirt, the Aryan reached at her chin. Gripped her mouth, firm and tight. "You's a frisky bitch. Once we've bridled you, maybe we'll bring you out tonight, let you watch the contusions and hurt get raised about this cocky son of a bitch."

She jerked her face and screamed, "Don't lay your prints upon my skin!"

On his knees, the Aryan unbuckled his pants at the waist, and with the lot of dead kin surrounding him and his wounded watching, he told Mick, "Get him to the meat cellar. Wasted enough time with words. He's gonna need that rest he told us he come to find."

Mick steered Angus to the door, stabbed a pistol into his

shoulder blade, told him, "Move it." He could feel Mick's eyes burning holes into the rear of his skull, could hear the begging of the female bouncing about the interior. Termiting his brain with rage, offering an emotion of weakness and nausea, as he was unable to do anything. He was helpless.

Stepping out the door, to the heat of the sun, Mick walked Angus past his Tahoe, where he knew the scabbed stock of his rifle lay, his ruck of ammunition, something the inbred racists hadn't discovered yet. Something that if he could grip, he'd use to make new inhaling holes in each of them as he could still hear the faint screams and pleas of the female.

Mick led Angus to the rear of the house, where a doorless frame was an entrance. "Keep movin,'" Mick demanded.

Planks of floor creaked from the shuffle of feet, Angus took in the stacks of outdated newspapers and beer cans that ornamented the corners, walls had been beat and cracked, tools lay strewn about. More axes, sledgehammers, chain saws, and cans of discarded fuel. Scrapes of wallpaper had been peeled and torn, even blackened as though someone had tried to burn the vinyl widths from walls but never finished. They entered what looked to be a large room where partitions and dividers had been mauled out, only two-by-fours and frayed wires remained, drywall chunks and chalky dust littered the floor's curled linoleum like explosions of frozen smoke. There were counters with busted saucers, plates and mugs that reeked the air with spoil. Leaving no hint of vitality. Just a bleak surface of survival, or what had once been.

From one room to the next they passed. Then came the jagged cutout of floor, a fifteen-by-fifteen square of give. Angus stopped. Glanced past the uneven saw of wood and textile, took in the piles of corrupted bodies, limbs curved and unnatural in their origins. Pallid torsos buried by unknown hands. Earthen parapets scraped and smoothed by the scents of damage. Of those who'd not survived the meat cellar. Angus could only imagine what had taken place here and he felt the tug and pull to his throat and wrists. The back-and-forth motion of teeth, a drywall saw, and the release of the rope. But before he could react he was kicked in his lower back. Plunged forward, nearly twenty feet to the cushions of rot.

COTTO

Tension gathered and hardened within Cotto's gut. Watching the gritty particles mushroom up until the vehicle halted with the smear of dust across the truck's nicked windshield. Doors ground open from the driver's and passenger's sides. Three shapes maneuvered from the diminutive vehicle. Men stood with aviator-style sunglasses over their eyes, straw hats rolled on the sides like tongues, unshaven, with cutoff shirts frayed at the shoulders. Straps hung loose at their leathery elbows and ran down to the small rectangular weapons that they pointed toward Cotto, his father, Manny, and the others, who kept a trembling peasant before them. Manny's left feeler clawed into the rear of the peasant's skull, posturing him as though a puppet shield against any bullet fire as he held the .45 in his right.

These men were not of Latin, Spanish, or Mexican blood. They were American.

And the driver spoke. "You know what we want."

Cotto's father knew it made little difference if they

blended in with the walkers and he laughed. "Guess you found Raúl?"

"What was left of him," one of the men from the passenger's side said.

The driver told Manny, "You've fucked with the wrong person, quit now and maybe you'll get to breathe a little longer."

Cotto fought the shiver of his nerves from within. His limbs rattled and shook as he kneeled, listening to and watching the bravery of his father even though he was supposed to pick a man, hone in on a target to shoot. Fighting to keep the 9 mm in his grip steady. Listening to Manny, taking in his words, while staring death in the face and having no care in the world. It dawned on Cotto in that moment, it was confidence in one's skills and beliefs that mattered. Manny held a vision, a goal to replace the life he promised Kabeza and Cotto. What Cotto didn't realize until later was the opportunity his father had given him regardless of the odds.

"Maybe it is you who fucked with the wrong person and will get to breathe a little longer."

The driver smirked. "That how you see it, killing a Mexican law officer, burning his home and taking property that does not belong to you? That's not how the man I answer to does business on this side of the border."

Manny laughed. "Really? Does he believe in taking a peasant's money, raping his wife, and murdering her? Leaving her corpse in an alleyway like trash with bugs denning into her decomposition?"

The driver and the passengers held a distraught appearance about their complexions, and the driver said, "What the Ox does is not a reflection of how we pass business in the States."

Manny was buying time, Cotto could see this, listening to him navigate this man from what he'd come to do, by mentioning the murder of Kabeza, seeing the faces of these men, maybe they too had wives, he was getting into their heads, pulling their thoughts and concentration from being enforcers or soldiers to being husbands for a brief moment. Manny had created an opening, his opening, something that would lessen these men's reaction times. And then it came, the echo of a carbine.

In one motion, Manny released the peasant's hair, pushed his frame forward. Dropped, pointed, and pulled the trigger once, then twice; denim and knee exploded, bone and blood curled and expanded like kernels of popcorn as the left shoulder of the driver opened up. At the same time, behind Manny, Chub, Minister, and Cotto pulled from their dirty and ragged cotton the pistols they'd been gripping and opened fire. The other men dropped before getting a shot off. With them went their grasps on the automatic weapons. One of the peasants stood and ran. Manny turned. Didn't flinch nor hesitate. Pulled the trigger, drew an entry point into the rear of the peasant's skull. His face combusted with the bullet's exit. Smeared the ground with pieces of expression as he dropped.

Stepping toward the men, Chub, Minister, Cotto, and Manny kicked at the gringos' automatic weapons. Aimed their pistols down at the faces of each of the men and Chub mouthed, "Who lives?"

Manny laughed as he kneeled. Peeled the glasses from the driver, took in the expanse of his pupils that had dilated into supersize tadpoles as his body shook. Manny said, "This one, I think we've bonded."

And the driver said, "Wait!"

But it was too late. Gunfire erupted all around them. The lives of the passengers ended. Chub and Minister took to the truck, searching its interior, making sure it was clean of other men.

From behind Manny came footfalls. A peasant screamed. Manny, Chub, Minister, and Cotto turned to view Ernesto smirking. Blood rolled from his elbows to his digits, which curved into a clamp, carrying the head of a man. "I've brought you what you asked for, Manny, just like the old days."

Manny nodded and said, "A gift for the King." He turned to Chub and Minister. "Decapitate the other two also. And wrap them with their shirts." He looked at the driver, and Cotto realized at that moment what his father had been when he was soldiering, what Chub, Minister, and Ernesto were. Savages.

"What about the others in the rocks?" asked Chub.

"Let them warn the King of our coming. We've the upper hand now," Manny told him.

Reminded of those times when he and his mother were left for long periods of time without Manny. Or when Cotto was awakened in the deep falls of night. His father making a quick exit. Returning days and days later. Sometimes distant in his movements. Silent and not talkative. Other times he seemed rattled and irritated. Making only the smallest mentions of how short a person's span of life could be. How quick and easy it was to end an existence.

Cotto recognized how his father and the men were trained for killing. Manny had been the leader. Had turned that switch off to be with Cotto and Kabeza. Shunned that world only to have that same unit of measure turned back on when Kabeza was murdered. Manny told the driver, "Now you will lead me to the King or you'll end up like your gringo passengers."

And from then on, Cotto knew that he wanted to be like his father.

—

As they passed through the black iron gates that bolted and connected to the bedrock walls of privacy with the colors of gold, tan, and flint scattered about the mortar, whirls of heated dust rained about the enclosed area as truck tires trekked and mashed forward toward the structure of a baked-stucco home of dimensions. Resting like a fortress, the home sat without buildings surrounding it; horses were railed in by posts and pickets. Gringo men stood upon watchtowers or outposts, others walked the property, came from everywhere like insects to sweets toward Manny and his men. Some unholstered pistols, others pointed automatic weapons.

Manny wheeled the cattle truck that carried the peasants and the packs of dope to the circle of glossed-over concrete combined with pebbles of pea gravel. A bronzed sculpture of Pancho Villa rested within the drive's center. Behind Manny came the second vehicle with Ernesto at the wheel, the bed piled with headless men. The King's men closed in on the two vehicles. Manny came out of the truck slow, raising his hands as he slung a pack over his shoulder. Cotto came from the passenger's side with the wounded gringo, his hands bound behind him. Ernesto, Chub, and Minister fanned out from the gringo vehicle. Tossed their pistols to the dirt. Raised their hands with smirks on their faces.

One of the King's men closed in on Cotto, looked to the gringo. "Fram, the others, where are they?"

Manny glanced over the truck's hood, told him, "They've been piled like kindling for a fire in the other truck's bed."

The man looked at Manny with his burnt complexion of stubble. "I wasn't talking to you." And the man motioned with his hand to the other men and ordered, "Kay Dog, check the trucks. Anvil, get Fram off his feet. Cut his restraints. Hog Head, get these men patted down and corralled."

Three men came forward. One grabbed Fram. Helped him limp away from the trucks as he whimpered and bled. His wound seeped with every step he took. Had turned from a red to a dark liquid that was nearly black, and he cried, "They're without mind, they're without mind. These men are . . . they're barbaric." Anvil dragged Fram. Kay Dog helped the peasants from the farm truck. "*Vámonos, vámonos.*" Several other men grabbed the peasants by their arms, led them toward the stables. Distanced them from Manny and his men, who were being patted down about their legs, backs, and chests. Poked by rifle ends into the soft spots of their bodies. Stepping away from Ernesto and the others, Kay Dog viewed the bed of the truck, took in the dead. Snapshotting with his eyes the gored and veiny necks without heads. Traced their saucy stains down to desert-spotted shit-kickers. Turning away from the bed, Kay Dog dropped his AR-15 to the ground. Came with a mouthful of odds and ends he could no longer stomach, weighted the earth with chunks.

One of the men who searched Ernesto, Cotto, and the

others stepped toward the vehicle's bed, caught only a glimpse, saw the unsearched pack hanging from Manny, started to approach him from around the other side of the truck. Manny listened to the footfalls while one of the other men tried to take the pack from his shoulder. Manny held the ruck. Telling the man, "This is for the King. Not a gringo fuck." The man raised his rifle at Manny. Behind Manny, Ernesto, Chub, and Minister lunged toward the other man with the rifle, fists laced tighter than a baseball's insides as Cotto watched the men bombard the man with knuckles and knees to the ground. All rifles were raised at them. From the enormous cookie-baked home came a man with a raised hand, shouting, "No! Leave them, leave them."

Manny revealed a psychotic grin. Eyed the shape coming down the wide tiled steps of the home. One foot fell in front of the other. The clomp of his snakeskin boots punched across the rock drive with the tick of dog's paws, two hounds of black, tan, and white, who stopped when the man stopped, sat on their rears. Standing within the heat of the day, he was a medium-sized man of Spanish descent. Appeared hard as limestone, square shouldered, his black locks short, bristled, and parted down the center. A handlebar mustache plotted above his lip; cheeks looked to have been tunneled out by termites. He wore a white T-shirt beneath a black button-up that held pearl snaps, not buttons. A gold-plated .45 rested in the hem of his pants front, pushed into his gut. He eyed Manny with contempt and held no blink of fear, only power that begged mercy from other men as he arched his right arm up, reached, and pushed away the AR-15 pointed at Manny's brain. "Kentucky Colonel, lower your rifle."

The colonel's face was laced with a marathon runner's

heartbeat. "They've wounded Fram and cut the goddamned heads off the others."

Anger streaked the King's face as though he'd eaten something tart and foreign and he asked Manny, "Is what he tells me of truth?"

Manny replied, "I know not the names, but yes, the men you employ have been disassembled and strewn in the bed of their truck."

"You killed some of my best men. And my product, you steal it. Other than being a tough and malicious son of a bitch, what am I to think?"

The two hounds sat beside the King's left and right, bared taffy-pink gums and bleach-white teeth as they panted from the humidity.

"Your product I did not steal. I delivered it for your eyes to see." Manny paused, pointing at the walkers who'd been removed and separated from him and his men, standing off in the distance, being searched outside of an enormous barn. "It is with the peasants and unscathed, as you can see as your gringos are removing them from the packs. But you're a peasant short."

The King pursed his lips, nodded. Patted each of his dog's skulls. Snapped his fingers to the man who'd pressured Manny's skull with the automatic rifle, Kentucky Colonel. Told him, "Go get a count on inventory, see if what he proclaims is true." Manny watched Kentucky give him a grizzled smirk as he stepped into his train of sight. Only to step away, move toward the peasants, who stood in the heat close to the stable of horses some forty feet away, along with most of the King's men. The cellophane squares of dope removed and lying on the ground.

The King eyed Manny, stepped away from him, the

hounds followed, wagging their tails. The King caught a glimpse of his dead men, came back to Manny, plotted his stance before him. His shiny pistol removed from his waist, Cotto could do nothing but watch from the other side of the vehicle, wondering if this was everyone's end, or only the beginning.

Behind the King, Kentucky Colonel stood before the peasants. Going over the rucks, pointing and counting, kneeling down. Inspecting the huge rounded squares of cellophane. Grabbing one, he held it up for the King to view. But he had his back turned, was eyeing Manny. His face swelled with repulsion. Kentucky Colonel hollered, "The product is all here and accounted for."

Manny looked down at the hounds, spoke, "Your dogs, they're a hunting breed, walkers?"

The King spoke direct and mad. "Yes. Walker hounds. A gift from new business associates in the Midwest, man goes by McGill, Bellmont McGill. And his associate Dillard Alcorn. But we're not standing here to speak about the breed of my dogs."

Manny placed a thumb beneath the strap at his shoulder, the King lifted the .45 to Manny's face. And Manny said, "I've a gift for you."

The King stepped away, kept the pistol pointed to Manny's head, told him, "Slow."

Manny lifted the pack from his shoulder with his right, told the King, "Your people, they murdered my wife." Holding the ruck's weight before him, he kneeled and sat the pack on the ground.

Cotto could no longer keep the tension bottled up. Across the truck's hood he erupted with "My mother!"

The King pursed his lips, looked over at Cotto. "You speak of the Ox?"

Still kneeling, Manny unbuckled the ruck, said, "Yes, the Ox."

The King's voice sounded careless as he exhaled with his words, not giving two shits. "He was an ex-sicario. You know what a sicario is?"

Manny reached into the ruck and told the King, "Hitman for the cartels."

"Yes," the King said. "He had little boundaries and a taste for the attractive whether they were attracted to him or not. Your wife must've been a beauty."

Manny's eyes went to slits. His demeanor arctic as he grabbed the contents within the ruck. "I delivered him to his end."

"That you did, as I suspected this after being told of the fires that were tamed. The porous carbon of bone-shaped outlines that were uncovered. But it is enough of this bullshit. Why are you here delivering my dope, offering your hides? Is it vengeance you wish to procure? 'Cause if it is, well, you've gotten plenty for you and your pissant of a spawn, 'cause now you're as good as dead."

Manny elongated back up to standing; with the bloody mess in his right hand, he told the King, "I want a future for my son, me and my men."

"And how do you elect to have that, with one of my men's heads in your hands?"

"No, I'm not asking. I'm telling."

The King chuckled at Manny's words. "You think you, your men, and boy can drive to my land, think that I will just let you take all that I've created? You've killed my men,

men with families, what am I to tell their wives and children?"

"The same that my son and I were told when my wife was taken from us. That the man who took her from us had little boundaries." Manny let his words soak in. Then he finished with, "But we're not of the cartel, we're ex-Kaibil commandos from Guatemala."

The King was an aged sculpture in a museum. Posturing a solid but silent opposition. Looked down at the mess of a head that Manny held at his side. Then across the hood at Cotto, where something had fermented and taken shape within him. Something meticulous and calculated. Something methodical. The days of violence and loss had congealed. A tear spilt down his cheek. Separated the young boy who was pushing toward a young man. Something had snapped.

Manny caught the movement from the corner of his right eye, knowing what was being executed. Cotto started to step from the truck's passenger's side, walking past the headlights and grill, toward the King. Manny reacted. Swung the decapitated head at the King's pistol. Knocked it from his grip. Then pulled the transmitter from the mouth of the decapitated head, hollered, "To your knees, to your knees!"

Confusion ran over the face of the King until Manny thumbed the button on the bloody black box. Screamed to Cotto, "Down!"

One explosion after another decimated the packs. Arms, legs, heads, and insides of the peasants combusted with the King's men. Particled about the air. Creating an anatomy of bloodshed and dust. The dogs ran from the entropy, back up the steps of the home. Cotto crawled over the ground, felt and reached for the King's pistol. Ernesto, Chub, and Minister felt their way to the vehicle they'd wheeled in with, reached beneath the headless bodies, and pulled out the automatic weapons. Manny had the King by his locks. Grasped and groped him to standing. Cotto pressed the pistol into the King's mouth. From a distance, horses reared and screamed. Those men who'd survived the blasting moaned. Ernesto, Chub, and Minister ran toward the barn, began sweeping the area, filling anything that moved or breathed with bullet holes, shooting men from their outposts. Manny looked to Cotto. "It is time for a new King." Took the pistol from Cotto's grip, thumbed the hammer, watched the King's eyes burn like comets in the night, and told him, "This is for Kabeza." Tugged the trigger. A mess of organ, bone, and fluid smeared over the grit or earth. The King's weight dropped. Manny stood with Cotto. Listened to the growl of the hounds who sat in the home's entrance, watching. Cotto questioned Manny, "Father, should we silence their snarls, show them their endings too?" And Manny told him, "No, we should fillet the King, let the new master feed them their old master."

That was the day Cotto's apprenticeship was sealed. A day of bloodshed. Killing most of those who'd worked for the King except for Cutthroat, a human interrogator and butcher. The King's wife and children were fed the same fate as his, a bullet. It was part of Manny's madness. Someone lives on until someone stronger comes along and takes all that another has built. That someone was Manny Ramos.

He ran drugs and humans from south of the border, implanted them in the Midwest. Enlisted the help of other commandos he'd served with. Taught Cotto the trade. Trained him in soldering. In tracking and recon. In killing and fighting. Once he'd had the reins to uphold the rules of the savage and the salvaged, Manny migrated to Indiana with Bellmont

McGill. A man who at first wanted quality drugs. Something more than a rural outhouse cook could offer from separating cold medicine and battery acid. Something he could purchase. Resell for bigger profits in surrounding counties. He also wanted to add flavor to his bare-knuckle boxing tournament with dogs fighting men. And Manny did all of this with the help of Ernesto, Chub, and Minister. Muscled others. Delivered drugs to the small backwoods bars where bare-knuckle free-for-alls were held amongst the surviving class throughout Kentucky and Indiana.

Cotto recruited gang members from Guatemala, El Salvador, and Honduras, young men who knew the routes of smuggling and survival. Kids long abandoned by their families. Young men who wanted more than the streets they ran upon but held no mercy to others. Those who understood territory. And he thought of that day when word came from Ernesto, as he sat in a leather chair, the buzz of ink vibrating from a needle that lined and shadowed textures about his forearm in the Southside Tattoo parlor as Bart Willis created the shapes of faces without meat or eyes or hair. Bony and skeletal. Symbols of death. And Ernesto told Cotto, "Your father has been murdered."

Through the door he stepped, those memories of their time before all of this ruin. Plotting and planning, he came back to the Midwest not just to reap vengeance upon those who had a role in his father's slaying: Purcell the prophet and Jarhead Earl, thieves who'd robbed the Donnybrook, viewers to the man who shot his father dead in the face, Chainsaw Angus. The man who'd take Bellmont McGill's life as well. But also to scourge the Midwest with *his* drugs, to overshadow a deal with Plato Reign, a CIA mercenary, and rule the territory with his own brand of soldiers and whatever he deemed necessary. No outside gangs or dealers could do business unless they went through him. Used his drugs. His prices.

But it'd taken so much time to track these men down. Angus being the most difficult. Unseen. Unheard. Rumor was he lay hidden in Harrison County with a Chinaman. Purcell and Jarhead had been a different story; every so often rumor of their trespass came about, letting Cotto know they were bunkered down somewhere in the surrounding counties until Cotto spotted, followed, and erased their existence, thanks to the Pentecost.

Now, entering the confines of Bill's chicken coop, a place where he was known to detain women and children for Cotto. Forced to become a pair of eyes and ears after Cotto'd taken his wife while Bill begged for mercy.

The waft within the barn-sided walls was suffering. Smells of piss and shit and the eruption of bloat and bloodshot from the heft of man who lay about the hard earth with a thin coating of dust. Complexion seared with sweat, his arms blown up like lengths of zucchini or squash that had overripened, sat too long before picking. Only it was not from the labor that creates muscle but from venom. Around him one daughter kneeled, the others lay looking worse than their sire. The one daughter held a cold, ragged square of cotton and a bucket of liquid to dip it within. Horror glazed the girl's eyes as she took in the shape and appearance of Cotto, who raised his eyebrows, with his skeletal complexion and the ink of thorns around his head as though he were a deity.

"The Pentecost has fallen."

Bill's chest rose and dropped as he looked to Cotto. Wheezing escaped from his mouth as though he were finding his breath in a kazoo; amongst the sweating and slobbering, his lips parted with words salivating from his tongue. "It is another devil who has arrived. I've fought the other and survived his magic, but if I must battle another, God will not be so kind as to spare me, but He will surely take me to the heavens, and for that I am prepared."

Cotto shook his head and laughed. "Who might this devil that you speak of be? Is he the one who has brought disfigurement and bloat to you and your offsprings' appearances?"

Bill struggled to speak. "A boy who has grown into a man, a man whose father and himself helped me more over the years than the count of hog I've gutted and butchered in my life. Boy goes by the moniker of Dorn, Van Dorn."

Cotto's eyes lit up like two bonfires infused by propellant. His pulse ignited to heart-attack beats and he asked, "When?"

"When what?" Bill rasped.

"When did this Dorn encroach you?"

"Long . . . long past the disappearance of this day."

Cotto shook his head. "I need not your hick scripture of dialect, one day or two hours or more? How much time has elapsed?"

"You . . . you raise questions like that of . . . the Sheldon girl who crossed within my misery only moments before you. Why must you hunt and bring harm to all these characters I've known? Enslaving my wife, making me do deviances for you. All you're doing is placing these people's backs to a wall and they will not surrender, they will duel till they've nothing left."

"Maybe if you'd have made known sooner the whereabouts of Jarhead Earl and the prophet, you'd still be in the company of your wife. Now what words did you offer the Sheldon girl?"

Bill wheezed. "How was I to know that it was he you searched out? You spoke only of Chainsaw Angus at first, a man who has been wiped from this earth. Unseen for years."

Enamel nearly chipped with the grit of Cotto's anger-streaked tone. "Your words to the Sheldon girl—" Pausing, he clenched one hand into a fist, the other gripped and rested on his sidearm, and he finished with "What did they convey of Dorn, his direction, did he travel alone, armed, what did you offer her?"

Bill's nerves rattled with fear. Fear of living. Fear of dying. With the venom browning his veins, poisoning his stream of air, he no longer recognized which was worse. "Th-that this young man known as Dorn, he's of some form of devilry. He's of one with the serpents."

Standing up, Cotto shook his head. He would have this young man as his own, a master warrior-soldier, much like Cotto and his father. Eyeing each of the Pentecost's daughters, the fallen and the lone breather, taking her curves of skin, pallid as goat's milk, he aimed his rifle end between Bill's eyes, his finger tickled the trigger, and the girl's eyes ignited like fresh embers with an abundance of air. "You have gone blitzkrieg in mind, Pentecost. I will not repeat myself, the Sheldon girl, what exchange did you have with her?"

"They's nothing to be told as you'll only refer to me as a fool. The boy held snakes as though he'd magic bound within his marrow, we'd a standoff, a test of the spirit, he was the victor. I was bitten in abundance, he fled with a ragged 'loper of a boy I'd kept for you and your soldiering."

"Where, where would they seek shelter?"

"Remove the rifle from between my sight, let me re-collect in peace."

"Cipher me an answer or I shall splay you into pieces and let you rest in that manner."

"You are an evil just as Van Dorn, only a different shade."

Exactly! Cotto thought to himself. Dorn reminded him of himself. Only younger. More skilled.

"I am a perversity unlike anything you've ever known, now speak to me of shelter and not sins or blasphemy!"

"To the west of here, amongst stones, they's military types of bunker. It was a donation from the army back in the mid-seventies for the youth of a church, a place that pastors and their minions could take their young to camp in the summers and be left to God and nature, learn their Bible scriptures from the Methodist teachings. It's no longer used. Word is it's now fortified by Scar McGill and her militia that grows by the day."

"Bellmont's daughter? How long have you known of this?"

"Learned of it not long after your last encroachment. They's also word that the militia clans are seeding in numbers. Been enslaving men of strength and skill. Building fighters. Men starved like animals until they victor in bare-knuckled battles. They've grown heathen and restless without McGill or the taverns and their back-lot brawls. You're gonna have a sack full of pissed-off serpents when you least expect it."

Cotto said, "Tell me more of these clans."

"They's the Aryan clan. The Chicken Foot Tharp clan. The Methodists, and many more. They're a mixed mass of men and beliefs who once fueled the counties with weed, whores, guns, and old-time religion until the dark came and crippled the rules and laws. Now they've regrouped and are creating their own clans that are about their own devices, tossing men into pits, forcing them to do harm to each other or be shot face-first, the man who wins is the man who can eat and bring his owner territory. It's savage."

Bill halted his words, sweat taffied his frame, he'd a deep hurt, an ache that pulled him in and out of reality, and he told Cotto, "Some say this chaos, it is the result of the Donnybrook fallout. New game. New rules. Similar to those in the cities who start fires in abandoned houses. Hide and watch them burn from a distance, cheap entertainment. Others preach this new system is an offshoot of the Disgruntled Americans, as these people are looking for a new outlet, a new decree, a man to follow." Bill waited, let his sayings curve his tongue, swim about Cotto's intellect, and he told, "But it shall not be you."

Gunshot filled the area. Hearing was deaf and the particles of bone, skin, and the muscle for human thought was splayed about the girders, planks of wall, webs and the faces of the Pentecost's daughters, as the only one who could muster a scream cried for her father. "No!" she shouted. "Why?" She turned at Cotto. Wanted to do something, a defense mechanism, he sensed it. Then she cowered within his demeanor. And began to bawl.

Pink had broken the surface of complexion, expanding over Cotto's cheeks, forehead, and nose. It was anger, and to the girl he spoke, "Hide or flee, it makes no difference, me and the Mutts will return and take you. But not until I've found this Van Dorn and pressed his skills and his worth onto my own soldiering horde."

ANGUS

Without light from day the shower of heat coated Angus. The stink of men bearing torches and guns, smelling sulfurous and rancid, their reams of tobacco drool running from furred lips and down chins. They pushed their fighter into the squared pit, egg-shaped head with hair removed glaring like a full moon of nicks and jags beneath flames from above as he came from hands and knees. Appeared as though shaved with a dull razor, cankerous scabs oozed, one side of his lower lip bulged out as the other'd been bitten or chewed off.

Dumas, the scavangerous announcer, stood in bloodstained carpenter pants and a moth-holed flannel devoid of sleeves and about ten years of unshaved whiskers; he watched from the wall as each man sized the other up.

Angus ignored Dumas, studied the handmade jewelry around the neck of the fighter that hung about his torso like unspent shell shot with barbed wire threaded through shriveled hides of dander. The bulk of man removed the human necklace, tossed it up to his keepers. He trembled with hurt from both hands, which were nothing more than swells of damaged bone and cracked cartilage. Angus took note of his hurt, his inner ruin, his weakness.

Knife wounds, bruises, and laceration was all he had of a chest. Angus knew why the denim sheathing his legs was no longer blue or faded. He knew it was muddy with the blood of battle.

Tensing his fists, he glanced above the pit, taking in the Aryan Alcorn, who stood with his followers, greasy and grimy; each kept a weapon either in hand or tucked in his waist. Christi kneeled like a mistreated stray, so out of tune with the reality she was surrounded by, her arms crossed at the wrists and bound behind her, half-clothed but looking even more ragged and despondent, her one eye soldered shut, the other wandered like a light in search of a barge on a river in dark, and on the opposite side of the pit stood the keepers of the man who stood before Angus. They numbered five in count, thin as malnourished dogs, veiny and warty, their heads shaved except for the centers, which boasted spikes of lock laying or standing. A pistol or sawed-off in hand; their eyes hemmed as each wore a chicken foot calcified from twine around their necks to signify their clans' label.

Lowering his vision to the man's feet, Angus focused on the stance that weighted the dead floor of limbs and torso; he was grounded, not arched on his heel or the ball of his foot. From the wall Dumas announced, "Here before us the Alcorn clan shall cross with the Chicken Foot Tharp clan in the meat cellar. Dueling till one man can no longer release air from his lungs, victor takes the weaker man's cap, gets to eat and live for another day while bringing his owner territory."

From the opposite side, one of the Mohawked men came forward and asked, "Who is it that represents your skin, Aryan?"

"Pardon my ignorance, Corbin, but I've not acquired a name from our trespasser." Pausing, Alcorn glared down to the rear of Angus's skull. "What label did your mother give you at birth, brawler?"

Feeling the Aryan's words shimmer down his spine, the eyes from the other side burning into him, Angus smirked and said, "Angus."

There was a mute stupidity that fell over every keeper standing above. Alcorn spoke once more. "*The* unbeaten Chainsaw Angus? One to have robbed the Donnybrook, to have lynched the life of Bellmont McGill?"

"'Less they's more than one of me, you'd be correct."

A madness came from his mouth. "For the church of my Aryan followers, don't know if I should shake your calloused hand or cut it off. McGill gave us much, could've been even more had he not mixed races, if he'd grouped with his own skin, of course the real question is would we be doing as we are if he was still breathing, or was it because of him that we're doing as we are?"

Heated by anger, Mick spoke through gritted teeth, "Have you forgotten this Angus killed my kin?"

"So he did. But at this juncture every organism is expendable, and in the meat cellar all wrongs are wiped from memory." Alcorn eyed Corbin and Corbin nodded. And they bellowed together, "FIGHT!"

COTTO

He'd tracked her through the night with the words of the Pentecost severing the binds of theory within his psyche. *People are looking for a new outlet, a new decree, a man to follow. But it shall not be you.*

They can look all they want, battle amongst themselves, but when I finish what I've begun, they will not know what has taken them, Cotto thought to himself. *More blood will soil the earth and it will be that of the rural. They shall lower themselves to my ways, and Van Dorn will be the first.*

Kneeling with a small light, he fingered ATV tracks, inhaled the scents in the air. Meat. Vegetable. Woodsmoke. Somewhere near was nourishment. An excitement pursed within Cotto. His imagination danced with visions of killing, taking out more men, taking in more women for whoring and more children for soldiering. And his neurotransmitters rang hard to a glow within his barbaric brain, imagining Van Dorn teamed with the Sheldon girl, their combined skills, once enslaved and doped, would be of great use in the field of slaughter. Of drilling the others into killing machines. Only younger. Faster and deadlier.

In the sky above, the moon was glowing coral and shifting across the sky. Cotto bear-hugged up the girth of a tree, his frame numbed by endorphin overload, making his way through the maze of rough limbs until he could see the land in a wider, fuller view with his night vision. Studying the landscape, he found a shimmer of smoke several football-field-lengths away. Could make out the shape of the Sheldon girl crouching beside a tree for rest not more than fifty to seventy-five yards to the west. Lowering his night vision, he pulled his vial from his pocket. Removed the cap. Finished off the powder. Waited a bit. Watched the darkness fade. Looked to Sheldon once more, she was moving with caution.

Climbing down, Cotto followed, took to the land once more, treading the direction of the indentions, which soon became a path that he veered from, but still held the scents of food and the girl in his nose, Van Dorn in his mind feeding his hunger to rule, along with the chemical taste that drained down his throat.

With morning came a dampness about the bark of timber and the mold of the ground with leaf and twigs as Cotto watched squirrels jump from branches overhead, bridging them from one tree to the next. Letting the colors of wilderness come into view. Cotto sat, his frame beginning to ache; muscles sore, growing tight, he studied the expansive hillside where the wafts of smoke were dying down. Taking cover behind a mass of cedar, he watched through his binoculars, men upon stoops of pallet, drawn to knees, and like him, they were watching for movement within the surrounding terrain. When one looked away, Cotto moved to take in the sanctum. Watched the Sheldon girl climb the hillside, young, frail, dirt-covered, and possessing the .30-30 rifle in her hands; men whistled from one tree to the next like the squirrels who jumped overhead until a group surrounded her.

Pause was shared between the two along with words. The pointing of fingers. Cotto lay upon the foliage of ground, glanced at what they pointed to—trip wires, traps for the trespassers, the unwanted like him.

One of the persons left after several minutes of speak. Walked through the open cedar gates to the ridge of bunkers nestled into the rocks. Cotto could make out only the rooftops. The rest was hidden by molded cinder. A female with uneven locks of hair returned with Van Dorn. Cotto could hardly contain himself. The female wore a Ray Wylie Hubbard T-shirt. She was thin. Veiny with the complexion of Ivory soap. Cotto's heart raced. His pressure rose and he kept watch while they stood eyeing each other. No words were exchanged. Only a stare-down. A hand raised at Dorn's face from Sheldon. A slap echoed from Dorn's flesh, waved the land. Followed by an embrace that lasted for what seemed like minutes until all walked back into the encampment. The boy had a weakness. Sheldon.

Cotto sat, waited. Manny would've been proud, proud to see what his son had accomplished. At his skills of tracking. And what he would do next to build his strength for ruling.

Careful and quiet, from his pack, Cotto pulled a leather-bound tablet of unruled pages. Began making drawings of the area. From the direction he'd traveled. Roads he'd crossed. Where the Pentecost lived. How far he'd trekked to this location. Then began sketching a profile of Dorn. Lean. Muscular for his age. The darkness to his locks and the bone structure of his face. Sharp as a Bellota cane knife. There was a rugged purity to his form. Stopping. Taking a deep inhale, Cotto placed the bound booklet back into his pack. Waited. His stomach ached for nourishment, felt hollow as he watched evening sway in. Movement came from afar, it was the powdery pigmented female. She was accompanied by two men, each armed with pistols and shotguns. They walked through the woods in a southeasterly direction. Cotto followed. Stayed hidden amongst the brush of briar and rotted tree. Halted every so often. Kept his trounce and distance unnoticed. Waited for the falls of foot to quiet, then pick back up. Feeling as though he were being watched, the paranoia of being ripped open by unknown carbine, blade, or booby trap.

Limbs pained and Cotto's mind ran with madness; he was jonesing for a fix. Had run out of cocaine. Stopping, he watched the female and her men squat at a run-down cabin the shade of weathered barn wood. Looked to have been standing since the 1800s, with a roof of thick bark. She sat upon the small porch, a door in the frame's center, windows on each side. The two men bent to her left and right flanks, each homing in on the landscape; one chewed and spit tobacco as the other sprinkled the same into a crease of tissue. Then rolled and licked the length. Lit a cancer stick with a wooden match. Through his field glasses, Cotto tuned in a close-up of the female. Recognized her to be Scar, McGill's daughter. He'd met her only once when visiting Manny. The Pentecost was correct in his intel. There was a bunker of people. And they were being led by Bellmont's daughter.

Sweat grained down Cotto's brow with the swarm of gnats, heat weighing just as heavy as the wait to overthrow her and capture Dorn and Sheldon. Cotto grew manic as he lay on his gut, torso buttering over the ground, watching. Then came the tromp of footing through the woods. From the right of the cabin it sounded like a freight train pushing over tracks, growing louder and louder. Scar's men raised their rifles. One stood, the other kept kneeled. From the green and tan brush sprung a man who stopped just ten feet from the aiming men. Cotto's heart tightened with anger. He blinked repeatedly through his bloodshot sight. Adjusted the focus on his binoculars.

Remembering those he'd brought across the border. Those whom he employed, those whom he dealt into the United States. This man he viewed was one of his own. Handpicked. Sergio. A mole. A fucking mole.

Cotto's belly burned a rage so deep and repulsed, his blood bubbled acidic and oxidized. Questions engulfed his thoughts. As he balled his fist, a slobber foamed from his jaws, and he reassured himself these questions would be answered not with queries but with spasms and distress.

ANGUS

There was the grunt, pant, and heave from the nameless gouge of disfigured man who charged Angus with a lineman's power. Standing upon the dead bodies until the last second, Angus circled to his right, pruned a hooking left uppercut to the man's ribs. The man's face met the dirt wall. He chewed and spit soil. Angus shuffled around to the man's back. Dug a cross behind his ear. Then a hook to his kidney. Legs gave. The man dropped. Lungs hugged for air. Snorted and slobbered like a heifer.

Coming forward, Angus hammered the man's shoulder with his knee. Felt the stoutness of skin, muscle, and bone give.

The man growled and barked on all fours. Twisted into Angus, reared on his knees, clamped hold of Angus's legs beneath his pits. Dug his footing into the mounds of flesh, muscle, and dirt, charged Angus into the ground flat. Eyes blinked and the wind was removed from Angus's lungs.

The man pressed to standing, taking with him Angus's legs, which wrapped around the man's waist, with both arms bent at the elbows and shelling his head. Angus's neck careened into the rot of the soil and body parts, the man dropped his weight down into Angus, punched wild and crazed at Angus's face.

Deflecting the attacks, Angus felt the swelling ache of bruise, reached through the ground-and-pound assault, caught the man's wrist, pulled it to his chin, tucked and tugged, swiveled his hips, hooked his legs around the side of the man's neck and shoulder, arm-barred the man's left between knees, applied pressure until cartilage creaked, muscle tore, and the bone snapped like a stick being stomped for kindling.

The man went soft as a cotton pillow, bared his teeth and rage with sounds that held no structure for words, only syllables of hurt, "Aghhh! Arrrr!" and the spittle that grossed through his teeth and down his lips.

Angus rolled from the man, stood up. Watched the man work to standing, holding on to his limp appendage. Let it hang, swivel back and forth like a cat's broken tail; he lifted his right hand into a fist. "Come now, you heathen fuck!"

Do or die, adrenaline was all Angus held within his cavities. He shook his head, offering the sentiment of no, don't do it. The beast of man came forward once again. Angus counted the short steps. Waited till the stench of flesh filled his inhale. Weighted his senses with presence. Grabbed his arm, went across the man's throat, curved to his neck's rear, clamped down, bent the man to him as if he were headless, cranked hard. Kept the man's throat beneath his pit, until the gagging for wind quit and the man was dead weight.

Angus released him. Let his shape litter the floor of dirt and dead gladiators.

Angus looked to the torches that were held by silhouettes from above. "Now what? I've beat what you're offering."

Alcorn laughed. "Ain't done yet."

He looked to Mick. "Toss him the blade."

From his side, Mick unsheathed a ten-inch length of steel. Dropped it into the pit.

"Ain't killing him. He's weak, spent."

"Nobody's asking ye to kill him, the winner scalps the weaker."

"And if I don't?"

From behind Angus, shell shot rang out. Pieces of black soil wall crumbled before him. And Corbin spoke: "If you don't I'll part your pan with a twelve-gauge slug. And all this'd been a waste of time and I can keep my territory."

Angus thought of Fu, his sickness. The medicine he needed to find. To coax him. The man had saved his life from ruin. He was indebted to him for that. Had to offer the same action. Couldn't do that if he were dead. He retrieved the blade. Took in the bloodstains of rust, scalp hairs, and hardened plasma from the fallen. If ever he was to see Fu again, save his existence, he had to do what must be done in order to see another day.

Rolling the man-beast to his chest, Angus bent over his wide back, reached down and expanded the man's nostrils with his fingers, reared his head back, met the man's peak of forehead with the sharp edge. Parted skin from skull. Didn't stop till he'd cut a fold of flesh that was nearly twelve inches long and six inches wide. And all the surrounding men from above cheered with a mad and heated debauchery.

COTTO

Stringing out from its socket like a rubber ball banded to a wooden paddle, the eyeball hung in the air and Sergio begged and pleaded. "Please . . ." His nose had been rearranged with a small mallet. Cotto straddled him, his Mutts watched, he laughed. "The pain you've brought is of your own devising. You fuck me, I fuck you a hundred times harder."

"Please, Cotto. Please! What you are doing, it is lunatic. Clamoring revenge for your father, enslaving others to rule. You . . . you need me."

"Need you? When you're spouting of my father, it is of one man's opinion, your opinion. Of which I find no agreement. He would've ruled this territory with or without McGill or Alcorn. My father held a fondness for these gringos, a fondness that I do not even consider, except for Dorn. To place pain upon them brings me pleasure. Our people, where we come from, all we've known is struggle and belittlement from a class of people that didn't govern; they ruled and stole and killed to appease their indulgences. I'm only spreading the gospel of what some in this country have seen as never affecting them."

Blood bubbled pink from the uneven lips of Sergio as he told Cotto, "You . . . you've gone mad. This vengeance to conquer, to capture Dorn will lead you to your death."

Coming from straddling Sergio, Cotto approached a metal table of flaking colors and corrosion where instruments were laid out: knives, handsaws, machete, hatchet, hammers, clamps, and forceps. From it he grasped a hooked blade. Stepped to Sergio, pressured it into the corner of his mouth. "Tell me, what is the plan that Scar has devised with your intel?"

"She . . . she awaits your capture of Angus. Then—"

"What, what?!"

"I . . . I inform her of his capture. She and her militia attack your encampment. Kill you. Your men, the remaining Mutts and Angus. Free those that you've enslaved."

Laughing, Cotto says, "That is all? She waits for me to do the hunting, using her mole? You're as pathetic as she."

Sergio mumbled his plea once more, "You need me."

Cotto cackled. "Need you, for what?" Looking to Ernesto, Cotto said, "I know what you need, get me Cutthroat. We need to end this clemency as it is unacceptable." Then he turned back to Sergio. "Tell me all you know of Van Dorn."

—

His skin lapsed, folded, and webbed like chunks of chewed and spit taffy, pink and slobbery. His legend was that of a bad birthing from a matron and sire addicted to the dope that was sometimes needled into the veins, other times fired in a smudged glass bottle, fired from the bottom and freebased.

It was an explosion of the caine being butaned from the bottle's bottom while the mother held him that disfigured him as an infant. Skin grafts weren't much use where he came from; regardless, his eyes rang blue as the Pacific, but his flesh was corncob rough and spiraled as if he'd been branded by the devil's flame. His hair grew in patches of outgrowth, splotched here and there; he lived in an orphanage until a villager named Juan, who'd worked for a major cartel, growing the green stink of gummy bud, adopted him as his own, raising the boy to wield a blade, for which the boy developed a fondness, helping with those early harvests. Juan taught the boy the age-old art of slaughtering and butchering, of becoming immune to the squeal of swine or the bovine losing its moo.

By the time the adopted father had passed, the boy was old enough to earn his keep, taken in by a cartel leader known as the King; the boy was schooled by a man in the lessons of what happens when men and women deceive their employers. That man was the Ox, and the Ox named the boy Cutthroat. When Manny took out the King, he offered life to Cutthroat, letting him nurture his skills as he lived within a basement beneath the King's barn. A room of tools, some blunt, others sharp. With the years he'd honed his trade. Now at his disposal were drums of acid. Steel tubs and areas for boiling, pruning, carving, and draining. He'd become a professor of death.

Sergio sat bound, the one eye hanging, tears pitted down his cheek, mixed with the blood from his busted features and serrated lips. He'd listened to the clomps climbing the steps behind Cotto. While candlelight bounced over the concrete walls of spray-painted graffiti, until an eerie shadow lurched through the entrance. And Cotto's eyes shifted to the right, then back at Sergio. "What do you know of Van Dorn?"

From behind Cotto stepped the shape of a bony and slumped figure. Cutthroat. He carried a square case that was laid upon the steel table of tools. Flame jumped and rimmed about the room, shadowing the singed skin of the man. Over left and right hands he wore black rubber gloves, a matching leather butcher's apron over a shirtless body of mangled and knotted creases. Thumbs flipped the locks of the case. The lid opened.

With his back to Sergio, Cutthroat's lips parted with a raspy tone. "When a line is drawn across the gut, everything on the other side drops and splashes to the floor. In order for this to happen, a sharp instrument is required. A person's life is then measured by seconds as blood exits from the wound, the head becomes light while existence is a blurring rush of events, shadows painted with a brush." Pausing, Cutthroat turned to Sergio, holding a blade to his throat. Ran it across his neck without touching the skin. "Quickest is this swipe. The parting of one's box for sound. When the jugular is parted, everything a person has done to that point in life becomes one heated pool of red." Cutthroat held the blade over the candlelight. Heated it. Then turned back to the table behind him, laid it down. "I've removed nails. One after the other. Submerged digits with fuel. Shit burns, stings, blackens. I've ignited fingers. A body can only withstand so much pain before the numb overtakes the nerve endings and the person passes out."

Cotto watched from the entrance, hands holding open his leather-bound pad of notes and paper, working a coal pencil, the face of Van Dorn coming through in profile; he waited with a glint of amusement and frustration.

Turning back to Sergio, Cutthroat's face was lit by candlelight as if a jack-in-the-box had jumped from the dark splotches devoid of incandescence. Skin connected to the corners of his lips, which were jagged and greasy. Cutthroat had no brows, no whiskers, his face was like a papier-mâché mask created in art class. He approached Sergio again. Leaned toward him. Grasped his chin, the one eye still hanging loose as he lifted the face to meet his glare.

"Cotto has questions. It is best to answer."

"They's nothing to tell. He . . . he . . . Van Dorn was raised by his father, who was poisoned by Dillard Alcorn. He's a survivalist. A young man who was raised from the rural land by the older-time pioneering ways. Th-th-that's all Scar has offered."

Cutthroat asks, "And?"

"And what?"

"There's more. You're holding back. Your kind always holds back truth."

Pause.

"There are rumors of others. They're . . . they're gathering. Building hierarchies in the woods."

"Who?"

"Men, mostly, survivalists. Some have lost their spawn, their wives. Others have never been touched. Have been bunkered. They're in clans being led by warlord types of religious congregations. They're territorial. Tribal. Residing in different counties. Battling amongst themselves, pitting one man to represent them, their people, in some blood feud they call 'meat cellars.' Their numbers are multiplying. They're armed. Unruly."

Cotto came forward. "I heard this rhetoric pronounced by the Pentecost. I possess something they do not: their futures, their children. They will not kill a child in battle, and because of that I will remove every one of them from existence. And I'll do with the help of this Van Dorn and Sheldon."

Cutthroat looked to Cotto, who backed away, waved a hand in disgust and anger. "Do with him as you've done with many, he's lost all worth to me."

Sergio tried to kick his legs, which were bound to the chair legs, his torso jerked. "You need me!"

And Cutthroat questioned Cotto, "Your judgment is final?"

Cotto came back toward Sergio. "Tell me what it is I need of you?"

Sergio drooled a Pepto-Bismol froth from his mouth and told Cotto, "I can get you into the encampment without battle. Without sacrificing numbers."

"You're an idiot. I know where it is, how do you think I tracked you?"

"You . . . you don't know where the traps and trip wires lay in camouflage. You can bait me . . . bait me with explosives. They'll let me in. Then you can detonate me . . . they . . . they won't know what hit them . . . it'd be—"

Cutthroat said, "Unexpected."

Cotto cleared his throat, thinking of Manny. Of how he'd baited the King with the immigrants to enter his ranch, and a smile laced with vehemence shaped his lips. And he asked Sergio, "Why would you defy me only to turn around and help me?"

"To save face before being removed."

"Martyrdom. Aren't you the clever one." Cotto paused and contemplated Sergio's offer. Closed his sketch of Dorn and said, "We must move now. Hit hard. Hit fast. I'll get

Chub and Minister to rig you with C4. I'll call upon my soldiers for their task of demolition."

—

Over the months he'd multiplied them in numbers. Some had long hair, some medium length, others colored pink, fire-engine red or moss green on their ends, while their natural colors grew back. They'd piercings, concert shirts, or bright-colored cotton worn to holed and ragged. Some were skinny. Lean or athletic, those who had been obese had been whittled down in stature. Starved of sugars. Nourished with rice, beans, and mystery meats. Their frames wafted vinegary and tart from bathing in the river. They mirrored the others who had followed direction, those who formed ten lines of five. Their hands at their sides, watching and waiting to learn the discipline of soldiering. To be prepared for raids and the slaughter of their own.

They were children, boys, younger and older, ripped from families. Their fathers murdered before them. Their mothers, enslaved and unseen.

Day after day. Week after week, the young boys were awoken at the crack of dawn. Fed. Shuffled into groups of five. Shown how to shoot their rifles, how to load the banana clips of the AKs. Given cocaine cut with gunpowder. Sometimes heroin or marijuana. Shown how to ingest the drugs through snorting or smoking. Cotto had to put his drugs to good use, considering they'd no longer earn him tender. They'd yield him blood and territory.

At first some would not give in. Take the drugs. They were forced. Some died immediately, as their bloodstream couldn't handle the rush rocketing to their hearts. They were hidden deep beneath the soil of a mass grave dug by the hands of the orphaned males who could handle the excitement. Their bodies able to withstand the surge of potency. Those were the ones left with the pang of addiction shotgunning through their young arteries, and they soon found a way to numb the hurt and shock of what they were living within, exiled as junkie soldiers in a rural hell.

But now, after weeks and months of training, it all came down to the survival of the strongest, and Cotto had lined the young men who could not meet his demands to become soldiers, lined them up in front of those who could and had survived his training; the weak ones stood snot-nosed and scared. Bloodshot eyes, smeared by dirt that rimmed their cheeks and nostrils, meshed with bruise and confusion.

Cotto pointed. "These that stand before you are those that would not heed my words, week after week. Would not listen to command nor follow direction, month after month. Now they will kneel, pay the tokens for their stubbornness."

Each stood, their hands zip-tied tightly in front of them. Shirtless and pale. Some with lips busted like spores of bacteria. Others with red encasing and running from their nostrils. Cotto's men stood behind each boy. Kicked them from behind in the bends below their hamstrings, helped them kneel quicker. Then the men backed away as another man came behind the first boy, whose hair broomed down over his eyes, cheeks gored by pus that expanded like terrain on a U.S. map. The man stood with a length of leather. Reared his arm back, snapped the leather over the boy's back. The boy rolled his lips to bare his teeth and gums, while his eyes juiced moist and he screamed, "No, please! No! I'll do as you tell, I'll—" He tried to stand, was popped by the leather once more, and dropped down face-first to the ground, whimpering and slobbering in pain. Cotto told the boy, "You'll do as commanded and this is your reminder."

All of the boys' faces filled with tears, those watching and those being corrected. Their cheeks watered in front of one another. Torsos twitched as if being surged by electricity. A learning tool that bad things happen in a world turned to ruin. When rules have been omitted.

The man who wielded the leather pulled the first boy up by his locks, lashed him five times, bringing swells and blood. Then he moved to the next, who tremored about the bony indentions of back, tactile arms, and green hair. A puddle of warm spread down the inner thighs of the boy's legs. The first lash dropped the boy to his chest. Cotto stood, shaking his head. "Weak," he muttered. "When I was of your age, fifteen or sixteen, I was on the front lines with my father. Earning as a man. Each of you are worms who've had a spoon held before your mouths for too damn long."

Afraid to move, to turn away from what their minds were registering, all of the boys mashed their eyes shut for long jags of time. Hoping the sounds of cruelty would end. Lessen. That this nightmare that they'd found themselves within would cease so they could get a fix and uncover silence. Recess into the caves of their consciences. Find that time before everything went so wrong. Only it was about to get worse.

And now all of the training came down to this as Cotto told the young soldiers, "Those who've followed my words shall have their first mission tomorrow morning led by me and my men. Each shall administer at least one kill or be killed themselves."

—

Morning dew coated leaves, limbs, and ridges of farmland and forest greens and tans like fresh fluid from a ruptured artery, while the band of men and boys dug into the perimeter of hillside surrounding the encampment of Scar McGill and her militia.

Fingers rested on triggers, eyes followed those who stood within tree stands in ragged clothing bearing high-powered rifles, keeping a lookout for the threat of unknown and unwanted trespass.

Cotto had handpicked five teams of ten boys led by his own Mutts, each heavily armed with AKs, ammo, and explosives. Their complexions painted like humans devoid of tissue or fiber, just coal blacks and chalky whites, similar to the ink that decorated Cotto's appearance. Sergio had ridden within the dark of late morning, sat center, guiding direction, the way he'd traveled behind the backs of Cotto and the Mutts. Warm country air twigged his face, offered the last remnants of feeling or sight, elements of a life that'd been taken for granted, a nature he'd never know again once the ATVs they rode were finally parked more than a mile away from McGill's encampment. Five men led ten boys spread out into a web of dope-induced bodies anticipating their first kills below the stone embankments.

Settled where Sergio had told them they'd be out of eyeshot, away from trip wires and traps that would alert the militia to their presence.

Sergio had been stopped by Cotto's hand gripping hard at his shoulder, his one eye duct-taped over from the torture; he staggered at the sudden halt, the plastic that lined his body like thick sponging leeches in a stagnant pool of pond was rechecked, the restraint cut from his wrists, Cotto armed him with an empty rifle and pistol, shook his head.

"This is how you repay the loyalty you've lost with me. You could call it martyrdom, but it is only the beginning of your demise."

Sergio stood tart tongued, duct tape and ripped cloth rounding his head to patch his sight, wanting to say, "Or the end of your reign."

But he did not. He only bowed his head in acceptance with daylight peeking behind him, the sounds of bird, squirrel, and unseen wildlife within the surrounding woods. Sergio walked the path, placing one foot before the other, imagining himself upon a high wire, crossed the grooves of dirt where ATVs, horses, and booted feet had trodden, concentrating upon the air he pulled into his nose, pushed from his lungs, and out of his mouth as though a vacuum being started and stopped; he thought of why he'd come upon the decision as he did, growing tired of the struggle, the fighting, murdering, killing, and what it settled or created, nothing but more of the same. Blood. Bodies, death of others and no future for quiet, for rest, only unrest. The loyalty he'd discovered within Manny and Bellmont McGill was much greater than what he now held for Cotto, who was unrestrained, lost in the old-world ways; the man would rather gut you, toss your entrails to starved coyotes, than have words.

Before he even trod close to the large gate constructed of rough-cut cedar, Sergio was stopped by four men armed with Bushmaster rifles who looked upon him. One man questioned, "Why the hell do you trespass without warning?"

Sergio spoke. "Scar holds the answer."

Two of the four men nodded, their eyes glancing to the surrounding woods, feeling the burn of unseen but camouflaged sight upon them. "Bring yourself."

Within the recesses of morning, blemishes of bruise and

disfigurement were viewable upon Sergio's face as he was led into the encampment. And one man uttered, "The Mutts had their way with you."

"Was lucky to extend my breathing to now."

Outside the encampment, surrounding the perimeter, the others waited for Cotto's command. He sat with the Mutts, remembering how Manny had taken down the King. And now he'd do the same with Scar and her rural militia types. One step closer to capturing Dorn. Using Sergio to open the encampment, create a distraction of disorder and the unexpected attack.

From his side pocket Cotto removed a detonating device. Smiled. Waited for Sergio's outline to disappear into the encampment. Walked with him in his mind's eye. Waited. Waited. Imagining Dorn learning the young to hone the land and its ways. Cotto'd not been this anxious since being left by Manny to run his own clique of bangers, to transport drugs from the south, across the border and into the United States.

Cotto pressed the button.

An explosion did not ring out. He pressed the button once more. The signal the Mutts had been waiting on did not come. Before Cotto and his men and the doped-up boy soldiers could move, the ground opened up all around them. Men came camouflaged, pointing Bushmaster rifles; the air around them lit up, was peppered like sections of firecrackers at a Chinese New Year celebration. Complexions parted and split. Blood sprayed around Cotto from the veins of limb and face, warmed the land. Some of the young boys fired their rifles. Others ran. Mad, scared, and screaming. Some were shot point-blank without discernment. It was hell and it had broken loose with the slaughter of Cotto's men as they returned rifle fire. They were surrounded.

It was a trap, Cotto cursed to himself. With the HK33 assault rifle strapped across his torso, he grabbed at one of the boy soldiers, motioned for several others to follow him. Looked to Ernesto, motioned with fingers to a thicket of trees. Ernesto motioned with his head until a bullet pierced his jaw and his face became a puddle of blood. Cotto ran toward the thicket of trees, kids followed. The ground exploded all around him. Heaving hard, pressing his back into the bark, he rummaged into his pocket, removed a vial of dope. Inhaled hard to clear his thoughts. To level the hazed anger that adrenalized in his head. Ears rang with rifle fire. Thoughts of Van Dorn saturated Cotto's mind. He'd become obsessed with this young man and his skills, overlooking what was beneath his nose this entire time, this fucking mole. And here he sat. Ambushed. This was not how he'd envisioned his situation. Several of the boys turned, opened fire at their surroundings. That's when Cotto caught a glimpse of Van Dorn, the Sheldon girl, a loping young man, and a feral hound fleeing toward the woods, away from the firefight. This was his moment to pin them each, take them back to his encampment.

PART III

SIRENS OF LIGHT

Oh, my God above, save this faithless, wretched sinner
Oh, my God above, I don't see myself in this here mirror
I see rage and fire and brimstone

—Lincoln Durham, "Rage and Fire and Brimstone"

RAGE AND FIRE AND BRIMSTONE

No words were spoken at first. Only actions from a raised hand. A slap. The reverberation of sting. Stabs of pain. The embrace of arms that hugged with the wet of eyes.

Van Dorn felt the urge to ball his fist or raise his palm to the opposite sex. Kindle his emotions just as she had, across her skin. Feelings were that of roots that'd dug in. Overlapped. Braided a bond. Connecting with another. This he understood.

With that bonding came the parting of root by a blade or a weighted edge. Severed. That's how he'd felt of the Sheldon girl. A deep connection to her that'd been split when he'd viewed her with the tatted man. When he'd laid sight to her outside of the encampment, he knew she'd felt the same weight bearing down upon her as she swelled his cheek with her sentiment.

Inside the encampment, they were left alone except for the dirty hound and the young boy he'd saved. Each lay with a belly filled by nourishment and lost to exhaustion and worry for what the world had become. Van Dorn sat rubbing the swell that warmed his features from the slap he'd taken. His mind undressing and dressing visions of the Sheldon girl being enslaved. Crying out his name. Footfalls descending the basement stairs of the Widow's home. The rush he met. Grabbing the fuel to bring flames about the structure. His forced departure and the glimpse of the Sheldon girl standing with that pallid man of ink. "Why?" was all he could ask. "Why did you lead the same man who'd enslaved you to my juncture of safety and quiet?"

"'Cause you abandoned us. Me. And my only way of finding you was leading the man named Cotto with his savages to your home, hoping you were still taking shelter within. When you ran, I found opportunity, ran and tracked you to here."

Seeing the .30-30 in the Sheldon girl's grip, something he never believed he'd hold in his possession again, Van Dorn grimaced and then smiled as she gave it to him and he asked, "Where? How did—"

"I get it? Told you I tracked you. Know of all the terrible you found. The boy and girl who lay with the slaughter of your mule, Red, the crazed Pentecost with his daughters and their strife with snake venom. Seen it all." The Sheldon girl paused and asked, "What about this Scar, is she of trust?"

Van Dorn placed his index finger to his lips. Leaned to the Sheldon girl. Cupped a hand over her ear. Inhaled her scents of electrolytes and earth, there was still that hint of powdery skin and feminine softness beneath the surface and he whispered, "This female, the daughter of Bellmont McGill, she's as crazed as Cotto. The one from whom you escaped. The death of her father has willed worms of madness in her brain. We need to make a plan of departure. Escape."

Sheldon sat back. Eyed him. Studied the walls that surrounded them. Leaned to his ear and cupped her hand in the same manner, "Then let us leave. Together."

She and Van Dorn took turns speaking in this way as he shook his head. "Not that easy. Can't just up and walk out. These are vengeful folk. Kind who'd just as soon place a bullet in your skull if you can't carry your own weight. I watched them let others be tortured for no damn good reason and then killed them."

"So what'll we do?"

"Scar's got moles within Cotto's people. She'd been waiting on him to smoke out the man who'd murdered her father and Cotto's. But Cotto followed you."

"Dammit."

"They spotted him as quick as they spotted you. One of her moles beat the two of you here. Alerted her. They let the mole be viewed exchanging intel with her and her men. Planted a seed of deception. If it takes, the mole will return with Cotto and his men using him as bait, that is, if Cotto lets him live. If Cotto snags this pod, the seed sprouts, the mole returns, then Cotto will be the bait. When all hell breaks loose, we part ways with this tribe of crazies."

"Where to?"

"Things have changed. I was coming back for you and those that'd been taken. But now you're here. The others, I don't know. But ole man Polk's place seems close enough. Regardless of if he's alive or not, he has supplies buried in a storm shelter that's hidden. A well that's fed by a spring. We can rest. Plan. Seek out others like us."

"What if it's been sacked and looted?"

"I have my doubts. But if so, that's the chance we take."

"What of the others that Cotto has enslaved? My mother? Neighbors? The boy soldiers?"

"Like I've said, I don't know. But we need others like us."

"Those that wanna help rather than hurt."

"Yeah." Van Dorn paused. "Look, I'll get you a pistol or a rifle. We're to be armed at all times in case shit hits the fan. I'll get some extra ammo. Other things we may need. We'll be ready when the time comes, only question is, can you take the life of another if need be?"

Lean and whittled by survival, she sat on the dirt with caked denim, T-shirt, and work boots; her face was stern with confidence, and she smirked. "Can I kill?" She laughed. Shook her head. "If that's your question, after watching the murdering of my father and the enslavement of my family, then, yes, yes, I can kill whatever blocks my trespass."

All Dorn could do was sit up straight and strong with a vengeful smile about his lips.

That morning, when the air was lit up by carbine, dirt was rifled into specks, leaves and limbs splintered. Blood watered the wilderness and Van Dorn and the Sheldon girl took to the woods. Leaping and dodging booby traps and trip wires with August and the hound following. Taking to a direction far from Scar's encampment with eyes following their departure.

—

Angus sat staring at the nightfall out a busted window of glass to his right; before him a fire burned. The structure in which he sat was worn and whittled. The walls beset by rot, mold, and the gathering of bugs, some digging, others shelled.

The fireplace was constructed of barnacled stones. A greasy iron spit sat before the bouncing of orange flames with the turning of several shapes, meat once the color of beets that had been roasted to tan, dripping and sizzling.

Angus's arms were bound behind him by wire, a leather dog collar had been placed around his neck. A chain attached to it. The other end of the chain connected to a crooked stud of the bare wall.

Glancing over to his left at Mick, who sat beside Hershal and Withers; each was mongrel in appearance with a shaggy beard, skinny, and a loam-smeared face. Each slurped and sucked on the game, cleaning it from its bone. Before Hershal lay an axe, before Withers lay a machete.

Off from them was an open door frame, two hounds sat gnawing on the bones of what appeared to be dead cattle. Their heads black and tan, their bodies ticked of white and blue-gray with legs of caramel and powdered sugar. Bluetick coonhounds.

Hershal dug his hand into Mick's mess of hair, jerked at him. "Quit pigging the damn shank of tender wounded fuck."

"Fuck you, Hershal. I eat how I wanna eat."

"Bastard, in a moral world you'd have manners."

Angus shook his head. Felt idiotic for falling into such a situation. He needed to get into these mongrels' heads. Light their fused tempers, get free of them, and find medicine for Fu. He'd been hidden within Fu's cabin, upon his acres for years. Training and learning of Asian ways. He even carried out his purpose, his test, and yet here he sat facing another.

"Manners would entail pedigree, something none of you has ever known."

Withers looked to Angus. "No one is speaking to you, 'loper. Lucky Alcorn told us to keep you restrained or I'd give you a beatin' you wouldn't soon forget like the others we've wrangled."

It don't take much to fester up an inbred, Angus thought;

he'd hired and worked side by side with many when running his father's logging company, then sold crank to them after he sunk the business.

"Release me, see how long it takes to have your brain tanned like the hare you're slopping up. I'll show you my pecking order."

From the dark door opening came Alcorn, the collage of tattoos about his hands. "Withers. Leave the 'loper be. He'd kill you before you could unbuckle your denim and drop a deuce."

"We can see about that."

"No we cain't. He's bloodied one, he'll be our ticket to more food, territory, and power for our race, our color of people, to rule within the madness that is plaguing this land."

Withers slowed the chew of meat in his mouth. "You've offered these declarations to all us white skins before, said that about all of those that we've enslaved, ain't one brought us anything other than a hot meal and embarrassment amongst the other rural clans and colors of people."

Alcorn looked to Angus. Dug his dirty fingertips into his chin whiskers. "This one differs. Possesses real skill." Pausing, he questioned Angus, "Are ye a Christian?"

Angus smirked to himself, thinking this was the brains behind the band of heathens.

"Of what does it matter?"

"In these times it matters plenty."

Angus laughed. "I find doubt in your words."

"Why do you laugh about such a question of the beliefs from the good book and the Almighty Himself?"

Fu had taught Angus more than how to use his body as a weapon. He'd trained him to use his mind. Fighting was ten percent physical and ninety percent mental.

"That *book* has brought rules to govern men and women, rules that none seem to heed except when they wanna curb those rules to meet their selfish gains. You're either weak or strong. Run in the light or slither in the dark. Falter in the rain or prosper in the shine. Like life or death, they're cycles of nature. Positive and negative forces, it's not about a *God* or deity, every man fears death, all *God* does is coax man's yearn for something he can't explain, place an ease to his fear of dying and forgiveness to his weakness and sinning."

"Remove your tongue, nonbeliever."

"I was learned by a man who taught the elements. The positive and negative ways of being and living. How one can outweigh the other, disrupt the natural order of life. The book you speak of has been taken out of context, twisted to make others follow another so that one can absolve himself of wrongs and live a life of hypocrisy while man, woman, and child follow his doctrine of lies."

Withers and Hershal came from the floor. One wielding the axe, the other the machete. Hershal barked first, pistols tucked down their fronts. "Tired of your tongue, 'loper, how about I remove your head that throaty gutter you keep spilling ill words of respect from?"

Angus grimaced. "That'd be an interesting thing to see you fail at after I take that axe from your grip and break it off in your anal cavity."

Withers pointed the machete at Angus and accused him. "You're a goddamned Antichrist, ain't you? Come here to fill our heads full of jargon. Mislead and defy us of our beliefs so we'd fail."

Angus thought to himself, *The almighty disciples for Christ have figured me out*. He chuckled. "First off, I tried to turn away, abandon your layer. You wouldn't allow it. Second,

I'm a man of flesh and bone, removed of ignorance. I was once toxic and heathen, unruly with little guidance; now I'm just determined." Angus held pause, needed to keep the meter running, keep the pulse of blood jagging their hearts, guide them to create mistakes. He looked to Alcorn, "For a man who calls himself a Christian, you've got some unruly ink about the tops of your paws."

The man raised each hand to Angus. "Like you, I was once a sinner. A man with wicked ways about him. All the time drinking. Robbing gas stations. Casing persons' homes. Stealing their wares to pawn for cash for my cause. Then came the collapse, the tides of Rapture, and I realized the error of my poor choices in life."

Angus smirked. "Let me guess, all this madness is the work of the devil, and God is coming back for His minions, His sacred soldiers in this time of dark, and He shall offer the light?"

"Don't mock me, 'loper; when the sirens ring over the land and fire falls from the sky, he will come, and when He does, we'll be the ones laughing at men such as yourself."

"You're as misled and ignorant as these other two butt-fucking inbreeds you're bedding with. You realize the man you follow was sacrificed on another continent, not on this land here where Indians and criminals roamed and settled?"

Hershal was slobbering with anger. "Ain't none of us bedding with one another, you son of a bitch."

"Coulda fooled me, way you keep battin' eyes at your boyfriend Withers there. Shouldn't have hocked the female for food, would've saved some face, looks to me you're battling fantasy of same-sex coitus."

Hershal began to raise the axe. Alcorn reached at him. "He's tightening your restraint, Hershal, needling into your scalp." He pointed to his temple with a gnarled digit. "He's of the clever, let him use his smarts again tonight in the cellar. We can all dine on fresh swine afterward if he survives."

—

Gunshots rimmed the trees midway and lower. Bark and root combusted and flaked with the explosion of carbine. Van Dorn and the Sheldon girl hugged tight to the land, leading August and the mongrel hound. Bootheels and paws dug into soil and leaf, snapping twig and limb. The pant of adrenaline, each armed and alarmed to the sounds that men and children create when playing war. Baying and rearing in the air, only they weren't playing. They were killing one another.

Tread indented the ground and Van Dorn pointed and spoke with a winded voice to the Sheldon girl, "Keep movin', they's a hive of footfalls coming up the rear."

Looking back, the Sheldon girl caught a glimpse of a string of what looked to be young boys. Some with faces painted skeletal, others with what appeared to be masks stringed and stitched by skin, armed with guns and cutting up the distance.

Huffing, she said to Van Dorn, "Think they's of harm?"

"My thinkin' is they could do harm. I'd rather we pull distance from them, so we don't gotta make the choice of who lives and who dies. Just keep a jaunt to the east here. There's a steep drop that we can go down at an angle, walk its bottom for a mile or two, and it'll open up to flat land next to where they's an old log trail. Can follow it to Polk's place."

Dorn knew the terrain. Horace and he had hunted the land with the Widow in April for morel mushroom. The honeycomb fungus of fudge and vanilla shades, picked and placed into empty bread bags. Taken home. Sliced and soaked overnight in salt water to remove bugs and earth. Rinsed the next morning. Sopped in buttermilk. Then a flour, cornmeal, and pepper concoction before being placed into a skillet of sizzling bacon grease and butter until crisp.

Sweat beaked from the face of each along with the burn of their lungs elbowing for the intake of air that combined with the rush of energy. Of the not knowing if they'd live or die.

The air lit up with the distant crack of gunfire. A hail of bullets biting trees. The rear of August's skull parted. The front of his face meteored forward into patches of skin, muscle, and bone tossed through the air. And his shape warmed the soil with dead weight.

Van Dorn took cover behind a tree, bent his knees, shouldered his rifle, turned to scope the area. Saw to the unmoving outline that was August splayed over the ground. Felt moisture cloud his vision. "Dry it up," he muttered to himself. "Ain't no time for getting wet eyed. They's someone upon you, upon us."

The hound sat before August, whimpering. Tried to lap its grip-tape tongue at August's unmoving body. Sensing his loss of shape and temperature. Van Dorn went, took the dog's hide into his fist, tugged him to cover. The Sheldon girl kept hidden behind several lumps of rock painted by moss some feet away to Van Dorn's right. Each looked to the trees and wild wintergreens of plant. Studied each for movement. Eyes batted wide like the wingspan of a buzzard. With her long streaks of hair combed tight into a ponytail, she no longer looked stripped of self but streaked with a means of continuance.

"I don't see no movement," she told Dorn as she lay with her rifle pointed.

Dorn watched the blood drool from the ream of flank around August's cutout shape. Wet crimson patterned outside of his neck and shoulders, tipped the ground. "The decline to the holler ain't far. About two hundred yards or better."

Crunch of feet came through the woods. Van Dorn caught two young boys scattering toward them. He sighted one. Hesitated. Nothing more than a young kid. Ten, maybe twelve. Disheveled. Madness streaked their faces. A blast crowned the air. The slapping pelt of lead expanded one of the boy's chests. He dropped his AK. Patted and screamed at the heat distressing his body as he followed the AK's descent to the earth. Dorn glanced from his crosshairs to the Sheldon girl. She'd shot the boy. "That answer your question on my taking another's life?"

A tight-lipped grin stamped over Van Dorn's demeanor.

Each lay waiting with their chests heaving. Bodies glazed by perspiration. Van Dorn shook his head. "They're only kids. What we need is tuh get us some distance 'fore this gets uglier."

The Sheldon girl told Dorn, "It's done got ugly. Now it's kill or be kilt."

As they moved from their shelter of tree and rock toward the downward shuffle of the hollow, gunshots sounded. Held the crack of being close. The linger of smoke on the air and above the trees fragranced the woods. The crunch of more feet came, scattered with the climate. Dorn, Sheldon, and the mongrel ran until they stood before the downfall that led to the hollow's bottom, where cinder formations lodged into the hillside, as though they were once meteors that'd fired down from the heavens and uprooted lengths of tree growth, creating bridges of walk and cover.

Dorn pointed. "There, we get to the bottom, they's plenty of rock and broken tree for camouflage and shelter. We can maneuver at a slower pace if need be."

Descending, the Sheldon girl, Van Dorn, and mongrel hound leapt and trounced in a hurry until Dorn lost his footing. Slipped with his weight proning face-first into the dirt covered by dead growth. Hands spread and reached for ground. Dorn tumbled like a weed carried in a flat desert wind, taking in the curves and jags of flint, tree, and briar. A large formation leveled out from the decline and it was here that Dorn stopped, bloodied and bruised. The mangy hound trekked toward Dorn's outline, the Sheldon girl sliding in beside him.

Over him she stood, short of breath, muscles full-on ache and burn. Van Dorn lay on his back. One leg crooked and tucked up behind his ass, he rolled it out, straightened it. His face a mess of scrapes and jags. He'd a shoulder wound, a formation wetting down his right appendage. The hound licked at it. A stick had pierced and broken into muscle. Dorn shook his head and spoke. "Ain't them some soured persimmons."

"I ain't gonna leave you as you did my mother and me."

"You ain't gotta. I can still navigate. I got two arms and the stiffness ain't set in yet."

"What of the stick that's broken off in your skin?"

"When we get settled I'll pull it free and smother its wet."

Behind them came the halt of feet. The fall of rock pieces. Dorn looked, the same as Sheldon. Above them stood a mess of young boys, their faces covered by hide masks, and in their center was a figure devoid of welcoming. He'd a face of ink, and as he raised his rifle the boys who held ground with him did the same, giving in to the hyena-like whoop of battle cries.

—

There was an acre of stained farming posts with a six-inch circumference cut and lodged into the earth like some crazed alien spectacle; beginning at a height of twelve to sixteen inches, the farming posts were arranged to create a rolling-dice pattern for the number five or that of a plum flower. These patterns ran twenty-five posts to an area, then the posts' height grew taller, some at two feet, but keeping the same pattern and numbering twenty-five. Other posts were cut to three feet, stair-stepping higher, building on up toward six feet. All were spread out, two feet from one post to the next.

Those that measured six feet had wooden spikes driven snug through bored-out holes from their sides. On the earthen floor, below the spikes were red ants, broken shards of glass, and sharp jags of flint. To fall was to implement injury. To test one's mentality for failure.

Angus was taught first to walk them. Began on the lower rungs. Then came the kneeling, bending, twisting, and holding of postures. Throwing kicks and punches from them. Working on balance and foot placement. Trying not to fall. Sometimes standing on one leg. Jumping to a post. Squatting straight down, keeping his torso erect. His spine aligned, no forward slanting or arching. Other times he'd kneel low on one leg, the other was extended, held out to build tendon and ligament strength. He worked from these various movements, increasing his balance. Then came the bending forward, sideways, and backward. Sometimes reaching for an empty clay wine jug. Picking it up. Holding it. Curling the bottle toward him, the back of his hand facing away.

Angus trained in this manner, worked up to the taller posts. Then came the picking up and holding of saucers and plates on his palms, flat, as if serving food in a restaurant. He held these out from his body, balancing them, curving his torso, mimicking the posture of a drunken individual, a mime, staggering from post to post, mannerisms, Fu called them, but never dropping the plates or the cups.

"One must be well rounded. Know his surroundings. Be cautious of his footing, of where and when to step. Learning to open the *six harmonies*."

Angus looked to Fu with confused amusement. "Six harmonies, kinda shit you spittin' now?"

"Your body has three internal and three external harmonies. You shall learn them for combat. And when you've mastered them, you will be unbeatable, but now that you've mastered the poles with your eyes open, we move on."

"To what, my fuckin' burial?"

"Angus, you may be clean of toxins, but your mouth is as filthy as your fighting."

Leaves crunched like withered bones beneath a maul with the memory of training. Of knowing when and where to step. Of sweat stinging into cuts and scrapes of flesh, burning tissue, sun beating down on a man's hide for another day of learning.

With Angus's pistol butt rimming the hem of the Aryan's pants, he was led by the men with lantern light. Shadow suffused with dark, making each man's jaunt appear hunched. The air about them was earthen, rotted wood and sooty smoke pollinating everyone's intake of breath.

Choosing his steps carefully, Angus stayed near weightless. Walked in the center with his hands bound behind him. Hershal had a single bolt-action rifle with a clip strapped over his back; he tugged on the chain attached to the collar around Angus's neck. Angus clasped his eyes with each tug, breathed deep through his nostrils, into his belly, taking in the woods and its musky scents that mingled with the odor in front of him, spreading its human nature within his body, creating a watermark to his memory; he'd know each of these men by their odor if he were ever to lose his sight. Withers walked beside Hershal, carrying an axe in one hand and a machete in the other.

Having pressed the buttons of each ash-assed shitheel, Angus hadn't broken their strides. Hadn't caused them to lose their focus, offer him an open invitation to rid the world of their trespass and free himself. Ignorant and foolish is what he'd been. Should've left well enough alone. That he knew now. He needed to be free of these men for the sake of Fu, who would be or could only be measured by the withered pattern of skin and bone he'd leave behind if not treated with medicine. Some form of antibiotics, Angus thought as they walked about the hoofed-out path of dirt, an old horse trail. After all that Fu had done for Angus. This was how Angus repaid the man. What a sorry son of a bitch he'd attained to.

Through the dark, along the trail's flanks, trees lay uprooted. Left to rot. The call of a bird rang out every so often with feet throwing the echo of smashing steps over the tough soil. Alcorn broke the rhythm of feet marching over the land and spoke to Angus. "Do you have people, 'loper?"

Angus found humor in the man's words. "That's a helluva

question to announce at a man you've enslaved and marked as the devil." Angus paused, let the man chew on his words before finishing with "My people are beneath the ground."

Behind Angus, Withers said to him, "You're lucky we've not skinned you and placed you upon a spit."

Angus laughed. "For a Christian man, you talk awfully vehement."

"Fuck you, 'loper."

"You'd find pleasure in that, wouldn't you, heathen?"

Hershal jerked the chain, reared Angus's head back. "Watch that serpent tongue."

And Alcorn told Withers, "Careful with him, we need food and territory. From that we yield respect. Know it's how these woods are now run. The weak perish. The strong are given privilege, why we need his skills, case you've forgotten."

Angus shook his head. "Sounds like a helluva congregation you're gathering with."

"You'll see, 'loper, you'll see."

They dredged from the horse path. Made their way over the land of fallen limbs, where the leaf floor crunched beneath their footing. Crossed over a shallow point of the Blue River. Took to a road that ran into farmland with the fluorescent burn of the full moon overhead until they came upon a small blur of light that grew in depiction, until everything was sketched and carved and shapes became separate from the dark. Angus made out the sanction of campers, some beat, rusted, and dented, lining each side of a back road but surrounding an old white chipped and flaking church that climbed high into the navy-blue sky. In front of the church burned a monstrous bonfire of rotted logs and limbs.

Men, women, and children stood within the area, those

who'd not been discovered by Cotto, armed with tools for gardening and hunting. Hoes, shovels, shotguns, axes, rifles, and revolvers. Scruff faced, bruised, pale, and ragged were these run-down people who eyed Angus and the fallacy of males he traveled with as a slave. He felt as though he'd entered another dimension. Stepped back into a time of traveling carnivals with Gypsies, barbarians, and Vikings. The only value was skin, and these people's entertainment depended upon the blood and fists of two men.

Alcorn stopped before the concrete steps that led up the double hardwood entrance doors of the church, where two armed men of long hair braided with faces nettled by whisker stood, clothed by dirty white cottas over their postures, golden crosses stitched into the center of their chests, eyeing him.

"Tell the Methodist Aryan Alcorn awaits with a 'loper for the meat cellar."

"Refresh my recollection with what ye are?"

"Me and my men are uplanders, migrated from down around White Cloud some years back before the government milked our souls and tossed us to the coyotes to be picked raw."

Winking one eye bold, the other thin, the one man told Alcorn, "You'd a familiar way about you, couldn't recall it. Been here many nights but never have you walked away with territory. But your fighter, what is his namesake?"

Alcorn's face stiffened. "Chainsaw Angus."

Angus's insides tightened, his nerve endings fired madly, and a chill bumped down the vertebrae of his spine. There were numbers that surrounded him, not just a few fingers of men, but many. He feared if any recognized his name, knew of what he'd done, murdered McGill, a man looked up to by many within southern Indiana, they might end his breath at this moment on these steps. Or it could bring friction, stir up a shit storm that'd free him. *Fuck it,* he thought, *the meek ain't gonna inherit the earth anytime soon.*

—

One by one rifles were raised. Crosshairs filled with those shapes of dented aluminum. Triggers were tugged and shapes gave, holes expanded through the cans of Old Milwaukee and Budweiser that lined the rotted posts of corroded fence wire and fallen sycamore.

How many evenings had Van Dorn and the Sheldon girl spent taking in the homemade targets? Forging bets from a distance with each shot that grew and grew. Starting with dreams of what one would do with the other. Where they'd take the other to see things they'd never eyed. Going to a movie. Buying a book that'd yet to be read. And the flirting that adolescent boys find with young girls, saying you missed, you owe me a kiss.

And now they stood below this savage man and his doped-up miscreants. Young boys whose faces were hidden behind masks, their eyes lost and catatonic, each gripped and lugged an automatic rifle. Some donned Slipknot T-shirts, others wore button-down flannel or seared cotton. They were a mix of small-town suburbanites and rural kids whose fathers worked in a factory, a mill, as a mechanic, farming, or selling insurance or real estate.

Dorn lipped a low-level voice to Sheldon: "When I say run, follow me through the holler."

"We cain't outrun them and make it to ole man Polk's place with you hurt."

"They's a cavern on down a ways hidden by some fallen

sassafras, it'll take us out the other side of the hill, in behind an old Methodist church."

"That's a ways down. He'll follow."

"That's my hopes, that he follows. Follows us to the end."

"We don't got no means to see in a cavern."

"They's lanterns on each end."

From above, Cotto spoke, "Van Dorn, you've attained to my cause, become my goal. You possess knowledge. Skill. Have killed my best men. You've become my addiction. My craving. Reminding me of myself at an adolescent age. Time has come for me to take you and this Sheldon girl. Enlist you to help lead my slaughtering of the rural."

"Run!" Van Dorn shouted. And young boys flinched, raised their rifles, and tore through the surrounding vegetation and woody perennial with gunfire.

—

It was how Angus woke every morning.

From a seated posture with lids pinched shut, Fu instructing Angus to relax. Inhale slow through his nose. To let his mind focus on one area, the lower gate. Expanding the space below his navel and above his dick. Build the internal glow as he exhaled, gradual. Releasing the air. Repeating this reverse breathing, over and over. Deliberate and controlled. No squeezing. No forcing. Relax. Imagine a small ball of light budding and swelling with each breath.

From day to day, Angus sat. Focusing and building his breath. Training his mind to guide his breath through his body. Up his spine and to his brain. Through his chest. Out to his arms. His hands. Down his legs, to his feet. Unblocking any stagnation within his meridians or gateways. Creating a positive flow. Feeling the tingle that built within during the seated meditations that sometimes lasted hours. Gradually he was constructing his internal energy or, as Fu called it, his Chi.

He sweated. Tendon and ligaments burned and shook through yoga postures. Held until Fu decided Angus's foundation had been erected and the real training was to begin.

It was what Angus recalled and focused on as the paint-flaked doors of the church unbarred. Footsteps ricocheted into the foyer, where a long braid of knuckled rope hung down. Up above, it attached to a monstrous iron bell. Once used to signal the beginnings of church services. Now for something barbarous and untamed.

Beyond the foyer, candles burned from walls and lanterns within the open space of the church, offering a grainy glow where the floor'd been sawed and chinked out. A twenty-by-twenty squared pit, shoveled and constructed some ten feet deep.

Around the squared sinkhole, wooden pews sat like bleachers for the unruly to watch the brutality unfold. At the pit's far end lay an upraised platform upon which a man sat robed in ragged black silk. Golden crosses decorated his chest. Tall, pallid-skinned; his eyes recessed into the rotted folds beneath each orb. He'd patches of purple and red about his cheeks and hands with a rice-crispy crust similar to hardened soap scum. Tangles of hair looked to have been clipped using a large cereal bowl, drawn on one side as if parted by an axe's edge.

Ten young boys surrounded him, none looked under fourteen or beyond the age of eighteen. Like his, their locks were flaxseed-oily and separated. Pigment was chalky. Thin. Starved of sound unless it was hymns or fighting with eyes wrenched into their skulls. They were dressed in flannel buttoned to their necks with dirtied white cottas over top. Each bore a hatchet in his grip.

Behind the Methodist, upon the wall was a large brass crucifix accompanied by a tarnished framed portrait of Jesus Christ.

Alcorn made his way around the wooden pews. Walked toward this outline of man, the heathen boys beside him. Angus followed with Hershal and Withers in the rear. Stopping before the Methodist, who questioned, "And who is this 'loper you've amassed for battle?"

"Calls himself Angus," Aryan Alcorn exhaled.

Eyes gazed. Unblinking. The mind chewing on thought. "Just Angus?"

"Chainsaw . . . Angus."

There was a moment of pause. Of eyes widening, then narrowing. "The man who showered Bellmont McGill with his last rites?"

Angus looked at the sickness before him. His gut churned. His mind wondered about the adolescent boys. Their ages and their use of sexual favors for a higher purpose to such an old wannabe sage drew a molestation of disgust to Angus. Was he a divine man of the cloth, one of those types who had a congregation of mad believers who'd hand their children over to this professed divination of the holy, a man who preached divination, milked his minions, and lived in sin and sloth behind closed doors? Angus felt the answer in his gut. Felt the storm manifesting. Fu had taught him to control his misanthropic desires and behavior. His anger. His savageness. But at this venture, he was rage barred only behind skin.

"One and the same," Angus told the Methodist.

"And to think some folk spoke of you to be dead."

"Some used to say Santa Claus was a pagan. Can't believe all the words you hear."

"You'd a hearty bounty about your head."

"I've had many, no one has yet to collect . . . or lived to tell about them."

To the Aryan, "Does he follow our rules?"

"He does."

Soon after, Angus faced the pit from one side. Another man faced the opposite with his wrists bound behind him. Each man waited as the old church filled with the shuffle of feet, smells of earthy-retched body and breath bouncing from the once-chalky walls that were now stained and marred by fumes, smoke, and blood.

The ceiling was the same, an off-tinted hue with webs and mud dauber and wasp nests. Folks once congregated here to worship and pray for the goodness and well-being of man, woman, and child. Now it was a sanctum of slaughter.

Hershal removed the rusted chain from the collar around Angus's neck. Left his hands bound, same as the man opposite Angus on the other side of the pit. Two long slabs of board were dropped into the pit, one on each side, creating an entrance, Angus on one side, his opponent on the other. Two men came. One held a pistol to Angus's skull. "Move," he threatened, "and your memories will shower this soil." The other man cut the tines of rope from Angus's wrists. "Walk," said the man. And Angus did, wondering how long Fu would or could last without medicine. If he knew of some way to meditate and take himself away from the pain and lengthen his life-span and ward off infection. The man had culled Angus from addiction and killing. Showed him another way to use his energies in life. But it seemed Angus's biggest test would now rear its head, and if he were to fail, Fu wouldn't keep his existence.

Standing, Angus inhaled the stench of sours. Of coagulated blood. The reek of skin that lay rotted and smeared in the dirt floor. There were laces from shoe and boot that had once bound feet, there were prints from those feet digging down, bracing their stances for pugilism. There were remains of teeth, fingers, toes, and nails. Even something that maybe resembled tongues or ears, either bitten or pried, shags of tresses or mane scattered like large blotches of ink, as though a person had carved the rind from skull. But Angus knew their means of removal. It was by confrontation.

Angus stared unblinking over the remains, sized the other man up, a seven-foot beast. Tattoos lined each veiny limb with lines that looked like stitches, curving and wiring over forearms, biceps, and shoulders as though the ink gun had gone dry in places. Began working again with spots of fade, plot marks and names all about, jagging and slanting. Creating a hand-drawn map of the county over his limbs. He'd a Mohawk the shade of neon yellow and the width of a knife's sheath. Thick patches of sideburns brushed down from his ears and over his jaws to where his face had been coaled to black with white around his mouth like teeth. Eye sockets the same. His torso shirtless, appearing as if he'd swum in a hole of outhouse waste; his pecs and ribs were a parch of wet cotton that'd been stretched and burnt. Scars created from battles won with a string of dried and hardened scalps running horizontal over his body.

Angus did not blink. Knowing he'd take the hominid out quick. Figure on a way to release himself from this maddening fit he'd found himself enslaved within. A world and all its folk swimming in the downfall of existence.

Because of his size, Angus knew he'd need to go for the Neanderthal's legs. Cut his height. Take his air. Then his strength and maybe his existence. The way the man twitched, his feet antsy, like his hands, which gripped and opened, Angus knew the man would come at him full force. Just a brutal surge of retard strength devoid of means or reaction.

Angus looked to the man's knees, the lumps and knots that poked out as if chunks of gravel, busted cartilage, with veins worming down the sides of his shins, varicose working into work boots.

When the Methodist stood, all eyes were on him. "Tonight, we've two unbeaten conscripts, Sadist Samhain and Chainsaw Angus."

Heads of men, women, and children turned, looked to others. A tide of disquiet and whispers stood on the air as eyes went back to the Methodist.

"You hear me correct. Chainsaw Angus. Never beaten. A man many believed dead. I'm as bewildered as you, but here he is. Representing the Alcorn clan. And if he keeps his skull skin intact, well, he has my respect and earns a partition of territory for the Alcorns."

All sight bore down on Angus and Sadist Samhain, who stood nearly fifteen feet away from each other. Sadist was growling and running his tongue over his chinked lips, waiting for a word. A signal. Something to alert the two men that it was time to battle.

And it came from the man who stood over the pit. The same man who'd held a pistol to Angus's head. Raising the gun to the ceiling, he fired. Pieces of discolored plaster crumbled and dropped from the roof and he yelled, "FIGHT!"

Angus stood with an ease of relaxation, followed the rhythm of his breath. Felt the earth thud beneath him with the Sadist's footsteps. Angus raised his hands, palms facing himself, left foot and hand forward, upper body slumped back. His hands appeared as if he were holding small cups of tea, his arms hugging a barrel as he waited.

—

The first time Van Dorn had entered the cavern, smells of parched brain, cold, thick as animal fat and moldy, spewed from the opening of a cranium and laced deep within the the space's air. The shape tilted upright with hieroglyphic tagging from a gun barrel that doubled as a brush, supported by the makeshift canvas that was a limestone wall, but nothing could be seen, as the outline of this suicide artist was hidden by dark.

The shape's name was Clyde. He'd been missing since the loss of wages. Since the layoff from the car frame plant down over the hill below the old Burger King. A place that once carried a good bit of the county's people with the promise of decent wages, providing a mortgage, a car, and groceries. A good middle-class job. But also the transference of drugs from one employee to another as the meth and oxy craze blistered the minds from one county to the next.

Those mouths that yearned for nourishment could not be filled as they once were. Even Clyde's side gig with his guitar on the weekends, playing old bluegrass tunes and folk songs he'd written at coffee shops and bars, turned south. People'd no jobs. No money to be entertained. Disappointment turned to failure. A letdown of a father who no longer felt as if he was a man nor husband. He was a man defined by struggle.

Disappearing as he had, words traveled, eyes looked, phones were picked up, and fingers dialed numbers. Mouths asking if he'd been seen. Had stopped by. He'd went from running late to missing. County browns, the cops, were called. Lines were traced. Searches began. Where he'd last been seen. Whom he'd last visited or spoken with. What they'd discussed.

His vehicle was spotted some miles away, parked in an old pull-off of black dirt and beneath an acorn tree on the back side of ole man Bently's property. Across the seat lay a box of opened .40-caliber shells. His uncased acoustic guitar. The trudge of path he'd taken, followed up the hollow, deep into the woods where he entered the opening hidden by trees. Found some weeks later within the cavern's center by Van Dorn and Horace. Looking as others had for this man. By lantern light, they'd followed the sunken prints into the dark and found the man's shape. Temperatures of cold had kept his freckled body intact. Pistol in hardened hand. Crust of explosion about forehead. Skin colored ruby, white, and waxy like a crayon. A flashlight lay beside him.

His body was tarped, Dorn and Horace carried the dead same as they'd done Alcorn's brother. Carried him through the cavern and out the other side, as the terrain was easier to navigate behind the church. There were no ridges or hollows. It came out of a hillside onto flat forest.

And now Dorn and Sheldon ran and maneuvered toward the cavern, toward its opening not much farther. The spray of bullets stopped with the command of Cotto, screaming at the boy soldiers. Calling them dumb sons of bitches. Dorn not glancing over his shoulder. Only creating distance from this madman. Dorn's heart raced. Taking the uprooted trees, climbing over the gray moss-coated rocks. The pang of hurt from his fall. Adrenaline spurring through his veins. The ache from the stick that parted and jabbed muscle.

With the mangy dog following, it was an obstacle course for the rural. Leaping upon and over tree and grabbing of limb and stone, the give of vegetation beneath foot until Dorn's lungs were speared with burn, exhaling; his shoulder throbbed and he said, pointing, "There. Behind those windbreaks and vines."

Sliding past the blinds of outgrowth, Dorn pointed to the beaded moist cavern wall where a mercury and rusted lantern hung. Below it a small can of fuel and a bread sack. "Hard to believe, ain't it?" Dorn huffed, sweat immersing his apple-red face as he tried catching his breath, staying within the opening.

The Sheldon girl reached for the lantern. Shook it. The fuel splashed inside. She asked Dorn, "What's hard to believe?"

Turning to her, he said, "That some uncivil son of a bitch ain't found this hole and stole the matches and fuel."

"Maybe they's still a few like us left."

"Maybe."

Dorn leaned outside the cavern wall opposite the Sheldon girl, the hound sat looking. Watching. And Dorn told Sheldon, "Get a pack of them matches. Be sure that lantern is full. It'll take a good thirty minutes to command light to the other side, 'less someone has holed up or sealed the opening and corked us in."

"Why you standing out in sight of gunshot, wasting time?"

"So Cotto and his soldiers will view our direction."

Dorn had made clear where the cavern was. Where Sheldon and he had disappeared to, by breaking limbs and stomping his feet into the soil. Moving loose stones about.

"Why for?" asked the Sheldon girl.

"To end him and save a kid or two. Keep telling myself

they's once like us in some form or another. If we's to keep believing they's no good no more, then what hopes do we possess?"

The Sheldon girl nodded in acknowledgment, kneeled, took a worn pack of matches out. Checking them for dampness. She wrapped the bag back up. Placed it to the ground where a flat rock sat. Visible. Shook the lantern once more. Then pulled the glass back, removed a match from the small box. Fingered out a small wooden match and struck it. Placed it at the wick and the flame took. Standing, she looked at Dorn. "That's the chance we been offered."

Dorn nodded. The Sheldon girl held the lantern up, and into the darkness they walked.

—

Within seconds of Sadist Samhain swinging a wide-rounding George Foreman right hook, Angus focused on his breath. Took his anger. Hardened it into energy. Felt the wind of movement coming at him, and his own building on his insides. Knees bent. Body arched backward as if doing a reverse somersault. The bones of Angus's back popped. He whipped and spun his body. Swiveled his hips and rolled like a disjointed wooden art figurine. Attacked the side of the Sadist's right knee with the index knuckle of each fist supported by the thumb, a phoenix-eye fist. Shotgunning a stair step of punches. Piercing his way up the thigh, kidney, and ribs. Sadist bared his yellow teeth. Dropped to his knee. Hurt peeled his complexion.

Above the pit people reeled shouts. Cheers and roars. Spitting and tossing hooch from used bottles and cups. Below, Angus came with the backs of his hands at Sadist's temple. Patting and slapping his face away. Masking his movements, like a boxer readying his jab he was setting up his range of attacks. Reversed one hand's motion, turned it to a claw, dug into Sadist's throat. Felt the softness of skin. Ripped away from Sadist, who tried to stand. Came mad at Angus, swinging wild and coughing froth.

Angus rolled his arms out. Spun backward. Dropped and fed a hard-angled kick into the side of Sadist's knee. His endorphins raked his entire body with sensations of rage. Angus was working on Sadist's weakness, his give and bend. Keeping him to the ground, while deflecting the onslaught of haymaker attacks.

Catching Sadist's arm as he fell in pain, Angus clenched Sadist's wrist. His dopamine was chugging on high gear. He felt pumped with an uncontrolled strength and power. *Stripping this man-child's respect from his peers.* He rolled his arm. Locked Sadist's elbow. Made eye contact with the ridged bloodshot orbs and told him, "You're fucking weak." And snapped Sadist Samhain's arm. Bone pierced flesh, followed the man's descent forward to the ground, pinned Sadist's arm behind him. Beneath Angus's ass and calf. He sat with Sadist beneath him, branding the crowd with his screams. Angus's body flamed with shivers of rushing endorphins as he studied the lost faces of rural men, not many women. Their scrubbed-out features and lost souls. He wanted out of here but needed to find the soft spot. The breach of weakness.

Then from the lookers above came the shouts and screams, and the man who bore a blade. Who'd released Angus's wrists. He tossed the same blade down to Angus. He looked up, wanted to return the blade to the man by separation of skin, through the cavity of his chest, and stop the pulse of his heart. Instead the man told Angus, "Remove his scalp."

—

The belt of sound funneled from the holler and to the cave's mouth, hemming ears with whoops of battle, caused Dorn's heart to peel and juice like fresh citrus. Lantern light cut through the dark where walls of rough-textured rock tunneled. Rushing feet and paws sunk into mud. Cold air dampened their hides, while the scents of mollusk encased Dorn and Sheldon's inhale, the hound pawed alongside, whining every so often.

"What if the lantern fades?"

Rubbing the red-kraut wound about his shoulder, Dorn told Sheldon, "My worry surrounds Cotto with his juvenile militia bringing us our end. Here I thought I could save those who was enslaved, I's crazed in my beliefs." Dorn paused, patted his pack, and finished with "I've positioned us a backup light."

"Lantern?"

"A Maglite. Ain't fired it but it's got batteries. Snagged from the supplies of Scar. Regardless, this cavern is a straight shot. No bumps, just a cut that opens out the other side of the hill."

Ache and throb fell upon Dorn's arm. Baring teeth, he tried to flex his shoulder. A tear traced down his cheek. He'd need a means to solder the wound. Heated metal or iron, he thought, remembering his father, Horace, mending to a hog's wound once from a puncture. He'd heated a flat square of alloy till it rang orange with the hog fastened down about the fores and the rears and melded the flesh. The hog's squeals still tattooed his memory. And Sheldon said, "That kid spared your life."

Snapping back, Dorn said, "August." The wilt of the hog's

image lying in that barn morphed into the boy's outline, weighing his thoughts, August's weight about the ground. Eyes open. The loss of blink. Blood fertilizing leaf. Innocent, Dorn thought, never hurt a fly. "What of him?"

"Where did you cross him?"

As he kept tread with the Sheldon girl, there was the brief rupture of sound. A change in air. Dorn couldn't put a figure of recognition upon what it was. Maybe his ears needing to pop. But there wasn't a drastic change in altitude, Dorn thought. He stayed attentive. "Pentecost Bill. Captured by him for the crazed Cotto. Been trapping and holding folks for him."

"Why would a local do such a trade?"

"Why would neighbors bound and burn another with motor oil and smoke out a family for slaughtering? Why not ban together and re-create all that has been squandered?"

Sheldon's tone changed. "What are you speaking about?"

Everything that Dorn had witnessed over the days and months had gotten heavy on his soul. He wiped the images from his thoughts. "It's no mind now. What August told me, Cotto'd wrung out Bill by enslaving his wife. Having Bill do his trapping in hopes to see his wife again. Reason for this, Bill knew the terrain and many in the area. Was trusted. And he's crazy as two starved copperheads in a ten-gallon bucket fighting over a rat."

"And August was alone, with no mother or sibs?"

Lantern light hovered in front of Dorn from Sheldon's grip, showing hints of the cavern like a yawning mouth. The slouch of pain was cramping while an unrecognized sound grew. "No, they'd yet to take him but had removed his mother and siblings along with another female and her children."

"Sad to view others doing to another as they are. Like

the well water has been tainted by rabies. Making everyone rabid."

Light shadowed onto the lumpy ceiling, where bats hung amongst the cordite of caramel grit. Water formed moist nipples, damp ran pasty down walls, and Dorn told Sheldon, "Like my father always told, some folk is like sketch lines, just black and white, never know a person's true shade till shit hits the fan, only then is they true colors scratched between them lines for all to see."

"Like a coloring book?"

Dorn shrugged. "They's things he used to offer to me that never rang no sense until now, and all these barrels of shit has came rolling down the decline and ain't stopped yet."

"He'd a wealth of experiences. Knew what people was about. He was a good man. Though he always scared me, 'cause he rarely smiled."

"Wasn't much for him to smile about once Mother panned out on us, he seen the writing on the wall after that. Knew of the world and all of what it wasn't. Taught me best he could till he's poisoned by Dillard Alcorn and his gift of home brew."

"How you know he's poisoned?"

"'Cause he said he was after receiving them bottles delivered by Bellmont McGill from Alcorn years and years later, he'd let it sit and sit, holding out for who knows what, a special occasion."

"How you know it wasn't McGill? Some says he was a crook of man not to be crossed."

Sheldon's phrasing lit a matchbook beneath Dorn's demeanor. "My father never done no wrong to McGill and McGill never done no ill to my father. Was no reasoning. They'd a mountain of respect for one another. He visited often. Shared conversations and brew to the wee hours of morning. The stories those two told. Naw, it was that fuckin' Alcorn."

The light before Dorn jerked violent. Squeak of swiveling lantern. The trek of footing halted. Sheldon raised her tone with "Don't move." She paused, extended her arm above her height. "They's a mess of something shifting about our feet."

Dorn looked down. His eyes searched for the adjustment of pitch-black. From behind came a rush of sound and flapping air. Sheldon said, "Serpents is all about the cavern's floor."

The mangy hound growled. Dorn watched the slither of reptile muscle scale over his boots. Some lay outstretched. Others coiled. Their tongues forked in and out. Their colors of black and gold. "Rat snakes is all they are."

"Why the hell they gathering at your feet?"

"Wish I knew. Won't none fang you. 'Sides, they ain't venomous. Keep moving."

Sounds from the rear grew and grew. Similar to an oncoming locomotive and Sheldon said, "You hear that?"

Screeches and the clap of veiny wing turned the decibel knob of sound and Dorn shouted, "Run!"

The slither of serpent stayed grounded. At a halt. Didn't follow the trek of feet and paw that pushed forward with the hail of bats coming overhead. Snakes sensed and waited on nourishment that could not be seen within the dark but only heard or radared by the split tongues. The pat of rats' feet trundled and squealed at the squirm and entrance into each of the serpent's mouths. Dorn slapped at the air above his head with his good hand. His rifle jarred against his back, he tried to keep the winged creatures from his hair. The

Sheldon girl did the same while holding the lantern light that bounced and bounced as they ran and ran. Moments and moments passed. Lungs burned. Mouths huffed and the air of light began to open more and more. From the mouth they came that opened into the forest of trees. Dorn grabbed Sheldon by the arm, jerked her to the outside wall of vegetation and small stones. Smothered her face into his chest. A hint of pain willed in his shoulder and the bats passed out into the day, the dog crouched down beside him.

From inside the cave came the sound of carbine. Shouts of a child's youth. Dorn released Sheldon. Looked into her eyes. No hint of fear, only the rush of his heart. He told her, "They's close. Must've interrupted those that mill in the stagnation."

"You mean they come across the serpents?"

Dorn nodded. Still in Dorn's clasp, unblinking, the Sheldon girl waited for something more. Never got it and she pulled from him.

Dorn pointed. "Straight downward is the church."

And the Sheldon girl engulfed huge rungs of air through her nostrils, told him, "That it is, but they's much noise and scents of nourishment that I'm digesting."

"Let's take a gander at what we may or may not wanna cross."

She didn't hesitate. "Lead the way."

—

When he was training in his past, Angus's arms were marbled with purple bruises, knuckles swelled and flat. Until Fu brought him lemons. Cut them in halves, had Angus press and rub the pulp and juice over his hurt, letting it dry and tighten and heal the flesh each night during sleep.

All of it was repetition. Building one's strength through external training in order to discover the internal. But these who surrounded him now had no idea what he was capable of. All he could think of was Fu. If he'd live long enough, if he'd be able to maintain until Angus's return.

The boys sat pressing their hatchet edges and knife blades to oiled stones. Scraping and working one side, then the next. Honing their weapons of weight to fine tools for cutting, chopping, and splitting. Some sat behind Alcorn, Hershal, and Withers. Others stood beside the Methodist. Several boys cut healthy portions from the monstrous tarnished silver plate of pork meat that lay upon a scathed wooden table in the room's center with jacketed potatoes and carrots. Masons were being passed with a ruby-colored wine and the Methodist spoke: "Angus beat my best. Nearly twenty hides of men he battered and carved."

Molded around the heat of wood flaming within an open-faced woodstove, Angus was leashed, sweating, with hands bound before him, chain anchored from hardwood floor to his neck. He ate and listened to the foolish words of a man acting as a prophet but nothing more than a rural grift.

Chewing the fatty meat, the Aryan replied to the Methodist, "That he did."

Hershal and Withers sat slurping food. Grease smacking from their lips about the mushy carrots and meat while the pale-faced boys watched. Unsmiling; their fingers were stained by oil and stone sharpenings. Their vision was unclasped walls of madness and twitch.

The Methodist took a sip of wine and told Alcorn, "I can't let you keep Angus. I will barter you provisions for his skills. Can keep shelter with me and the congregation, have your ten acres of territory to do as you wish. Maybe capture another fighter. Win more territory."

Alcorn and Hershal looked up, each with food pieces about his lips. Chewed piece of potato fell from Alcorn's lips and he said, "Horseshit!"

The Methodist shook his head. "This is not a query nor a plea, it's a direct telling of what you will do."

Withers came from sitting, was about halfway erect when the Methodist nodded. His boys restrained Alcorn. Slapped and pounded Hershal and Withers while Alcorn was forced to watch the swift onslaught of what took place quicker than a lost breath, as six young men dropped their sharpening stones. Cut the air. Testing their edges. Driving them into limbs, backs of legs, sections of back, beating and creating fault-line cracks that spit blood from skulls. The boys did not waver nor stop until Alcorn's men were thuds on the floor in a mess that appeared like spilt paint, but it was human fluid and scalp, teeth, and death.

The only sound heard was Angus's jaw moving with the swoosh of tater. The Methodist broke the silence with "Never say I didn't offer. Remove the slugs from my sight. You now align me, Alcorn."

The boys were outlined by their red-specked cheeks and cottas. Arms and hands moist. They dragged Hershal and Wither's battered and bleeding bodies from the room. Angus kept eating the meat, carrots, and potatoes with the Methodist eyeing him.

"Do right by me, you'll have food and women at your leisure. Used to be the Pentecost was more willing to share the offerings of his daughters until he found his last breath from a man believed to be one Cotto Ramos."

Alcorn was stricken with silence. Angus set his plate down before him. Swallowed his food. Forearmed his mouth to remove particles of nourishment from his lips. "I've little use for females as they've no loyalty. And food, I've had plenty. What I desire is medicine for a friend who fell to illness." Angus paused, chose his words carefully. "There's nothing to be gained from this. Eventually someone smarter and stronger will arrive. All you're doing is waiting to have that torch taken and turned into a gavel."

"I do God's bidding. Like others, I'm building something to take the torch from another and then another and another. I fear no man."

"I get it, whoever has the most toys wins."

"No, it's the survivalists. Those who've lost everything have nothing more to lose. As of now, whoever has the most followers can amass an army to protect his territory, create new laws, a new regime to fight this rumor of a man called Cotto, a foreigner who's killing men, enslaving our women and children."

"And why would a person of foreign means have an interest in slaughtering men in the Midwest?" Angus asked. "What would he have to gain?"

"What does any man have to gain by invading another's territory? When there are no more rules to be enforced, fear delivers power, things turn tribal, much like those in prison. It's not the government who runs the prison, it's the prisoners, the government is only sheltering the weak from the barbaric. But to answer your question, rumor in the whisper mill of derelicts and other congregations says Cotto's reaping vengeance to rule the land, for what, power, because you murdered his father, Manny, or because he can."

Alcorn sat listening as Angus steel-eyed the Methodist. "You saying the world went to shit and now it's gonna be rekindled by a mean-ass Mexican, a man not much different than you and me?"

"No, you and I are plenty different, I am a Christian man, your beliefs are uncertain to me, but what I know is the world became unshelved with the help of the devil and his adversaries banking too many lies, and too many hardworking folk put up with this leprosy until it was too late."

"Bandages can be changed, wounds can heal. Unless the wound isn't cared for, then it'll find infection and rot is soon to follow."

The Methodist nodded. "Shit rolls downhill. But what I am saying is, this man is a hunter. He's murdering everyone that's not part of his network. Cotto was on his way here when the fall of the dollar and the loss of power came; those were coincidental to his plan. My belief is he'd pay a hefty sum to have your head placed on a halberd."

A rain of disgust cloaked Angus as he told the Methodist, "That it, you're gonna trade my being for unknown salvation? Very Christian of you."

"Don't flatter yourself. I've no intentions of bartering you to any man. I've seen this devil's work. Where I've amassed many of my children from Cotto, my adolescent soldiers, I've rehabilitated them to do God's work."

Angus felt anger bubble inside him. "I was minding my own when those three fucks who followed the creed of we're-killing-in-the-name-of-Jesus attacked me for wanting to rest my eyes. I want no part of what you're creating. You can either let me go or pay the price when I find my opening."

"Watch your tongue. I could place a bullet between your eyes as we speak."

"But you will not or you'll lose whatever it is you've pyramided here thanks to men like me."

Smirking, the Methodist said to Angus, "Truth falls from your tongue, and that's why you'll fight for me, that is how men now earn real salvation for other men."

"Through enslavement, battle, bloodshed, and biblical words twisted into end-time prophecies? Sounds like terrorism to me. You got a wall of virgins hidden beneath that robe. Funny how you take the laws of the land away from men and they forget where they came from, forget everything it took for their ancestors to build something that they always seem to destroy."

"You seem awfully wise for a man who once cooked crank to earn his way."

"I have my moments."

Angus wanted to wrap the chains that bound him to the flooring around the Methodist's neck. Watch his lookers bat. His mouth froth and his throat snap. Angus needed his hands free. The chains removed from his neck. But what would he gain by murdering this man, what did the removal of another person's life really accomplish in the end? Other than quiet, nothing. He inhaled deep and pondered on a saying, *Assist people, but do not attempt to control them.* Teachings of Lao Tzu, principles taught to Angus by Fu. Question is, was old Lao Tzu ever taken prisoner and forced to fight to earn another day's breath? The Methodist paused, then continued with "You speak like you fight, not a wasted movement nor word. I shall help you find *God.*"

It'd be interesting to watch you gasp your final breath, Angus thought, and he asked the Methodist, "Who says I ain't already found Him?"

"You speak as though—"

"I speak as I speak. Never said I'd a loss of faith in a higher power. Only testing your beliefs of your placing words in another's mouth."

Slapping his knee, the Methodist said, "It shall be entertaining to see you battle again. What do you think, Alcorn, has your tongue been swallowed?"

Alcorn's posture was silent.

Angus postured a question. "And when would that be?"

The Methodist grinned. "Within the hour, we meet another clan who travels to here, my reconnaissance tells me their fighter is strong-willed and eager."

—

Hunkered down behind outgrowth. The denting pulse of shoulder pain, the buzz and hum of fly and gnat that swarmed about Dorn's blackening wound. A hint of rot was not far from the thorn and honeysuckle from which he and Sheldon sat hidden. The squawk of blue jay fell with the sweat from humidity that moistened their bodies as the hound panted.

They'd watched the encampment around the church. Men and women, armed with rifles or shotguns. Some sat sharpening knives. Cleaning their weapons. Others read from hymns. Looking up every so often, keeping eyes peeled for movement. Sometimes the blast of gunfire rimmed through the surrounding forest from an odd direction. Moments would pass. Then came the tread of foot. Crunch of vegetation, an outline of human gripping the weight of muscle covered by pelt, the killing of wild game for feeding.

Dorn dozed and tremored in his sleep off and on until evening. The Sheldon girl whispered, "We must get that wound cleansed. Bandaged 'fore infection sets in."

Dorn waved a hand. "Soon."

In his mind things were sporadic. Mad. The ache of fiber. Feverish visions of Cotto hunting him with his tribe of doped-up killer kids. His chest tightened. Nose ran with mucus. Thoughts of roller-coastering down an unending decline and he awoke. Sheldon stared at him. He rolled to his stomach. Leaves mashed. He glanced to the church. Lights were flamed around the encampment of campers, outbuildings, and the road lit up when the rumble of sound came from engines. Tires knobbed and the jaunt of men armed to the teeth with automatic weapons came slow. One was leading by poke and butt of rifle to a man bound by rope. From stomach to knees Dorn came. Reaching. From his pack he pulled binoculars. The Sheldon girl queried, "What is it you view?"

Taking in each shape, Van Dorn looked at complexions. Searched for the familiar. The bound man was of color. Skin dark as a walnut. Lean. Muscular. *A fighter,* Dorn thought. Then came rage. The pulse of anger infernoed his veins. Crystallized the arteries with a melding of hatred; twisting the knob on the magnification of glasses, he saw the dome of shaven scalp. Rounded shoulders, veiny arms of ink that cloned one racist symbol after another into a collage of shapes and braids. And Dorn whispered with disgust, "A murdering racist."

"Who would that be?" the Sheldon girl asked.

"Alcorn."

They treaded on by foot to the church's door. People came one by one from campers. Fires. Outbuildings. Turning into a maddening crowd. That began to chant as Alcorn and his followers led their slave to the church's entrance, where they stopped. Passed words with several men guarding the entrance. Then they entered. Moments passed. The ringing of the large bell housed within the church's foyer rang loud and piles of people filed in. Dorn lowered his glasses and Sheldon asked, "And he is—"

Dorn pressed to standing. The hound sat looking up at Dorn. Waited. "The man I believe to have ended my father."

—

Pain was nothing more than a word that would come and go like teeth being pliered from gums, filled back in with partials by a dentist, it was something that one could replace. Meaning each was temporary. Those final months of training, that's all Angus could think, when will this end? When would he be replaced? When will one test after another be the final?

But it never ended. He was never replaced. Training became tougher. Demanded more mentally and physically. And the tests pushed him to dig deeper within his skill set. But he endured. Became a hardened human being.

Fu used liniment to soak Angus's hands nightly, pulled from Fu's refrigerator along with his needles that were submerged in alcohol. His fine-tuning of each, twisting the pin-needle lengths of steel into meridians about Angus's hands. Offering the release of tension. Meditations and breathing were guided by Fu. The clearing of the mind. Keeping the positive flow of energy throughout the body. The mental aspects of strengthening Angus's insides. Creating and building his iron palm training.

Angus sat with Fu in his kitchen one evening after training, sharing sips of black tea, and Fu explained, "As strength and confidence in one's ability are built, they are tested, time and time again, to demonstrate the use of what they've built, created."

Wanting a beer or some rice wine, Angus said, "Like your internal and external strengths?"

"Yes."

"Have I not demonstrated that, over and over? Busting concrete blocks? Snapping dow rods and two-by-sixes?" Angus questioned.

"You have, but one must yearn to seek the highest levels of fighting. In feudal times great masters showed their mastery and power of internal strength upon animals that were ready for butchering in villages. Some directed their attack at the skull. Others at the heart. The lungs. The animal would collapse. When cut open, the organ that was attacked would be an explosion of shapes. Unrecognizable."

"You wanting me to go out cow tipping?"

Fu shook his head. "The watching of a man who saved a life. A life that I want to be rid of, to erase my debt, as this man holds no good to anyone anymore, only pain. I am finding age now, I needn't settle his payments for his saving of my life. He's been repaid a thousand times over. I'm no longer indebted to him."

"Why don't you fucking do it?"

"One, he'd expect it from me. Two, it's the next level you must attain, your mastery of your internal energy. And with a local, he'd never acknowledge it."

At the time he'd not grasped what Fu was doing, but afterward he realized it was a test to his training. To pass on what he was being taught, he must master himself and all that he'd been taught. It was the next test of his progression of Fu's teachings.

To hurt, maim, or wound another human being was simple. Hardest part was to strike someone, injure him internally without his knowing it, break down his organs, like passing a germ or infection to someone, he appears all right on the outside, the external, but as days pass, the infection slowly breaks down the immune system, his internal, and then all at once he just falters. Only this wasn't a virus, this was a strike with one's palm to a certain area of the body, the lungs, the heart, kidney, or liver. To damage it with internal energy.

Now smells of fresh kills sunk from the air. That of swine, venison, and hare branded by the inhale of flame from birch and cedar. The odors of unbathed flesh lingered. If Fu were still among the breathing, Angus believed it'd be a miracle. To have gone this long without the use of actual medicine to diminish the infection would be Godly, if such an entity existed.

Passing the shapes of men and women, all foreign to his sight, a slab of rough-cut timber declined into a gangplank to the pit. The rubbing of bindings about his wrists and neck were released. He stepped down into the lowered earth. Waited. Not even glancing above him. Inhaled deep and slow. Exhaled the same. Clearing his thoughts. Searching for an out.

From above he could hear the trample of feet. The rustling of men and women. The sounds of rural chaos in land once governed by rules that all had forgotten. Behind him the lumber was removed. Across from him, lumber was lowered. Booted feet came soft until they met the rugged soil of stink and human fluids. Working his sight up the outline's mocha torso, Angus made eye contact. Sized the beastly man up. Found familiarity.

—

Wars always began because one man's idea differed from another, so he'd sought to overthrow another. To submerge his will with the support of like-minded souls, force his beliefs upon another's ideology. Another's way of being. Simply put: someone wanted power. To be in control maybe because one felt threatened. Didn't agree with the moral or unmoral. The closed-minded ways of others. Mostly it was all bullshit; men are power mongers and sadists. Want to rule others and what they think, feel, and do. To be in control as long as they are doing the harming. That'd be the simplest way of understanding Alcorn's intellect, Horace had once explained to Dorn.

As Dorn made his way through the woods, down the slant of earth coated by leaves and timber, Horace's words rang through his mind. Of why Dillard was the way he was. Territorial pissing. Like a carnivore marking its territory. Though Dillard wanted little to do with the Widow, he wanted no one to be in commerce with her. He tried instilling fear within her. Keeping others who knew of him at bay with her. It was all about control. Narcissism. And when Horace and Dorn showed up, she took a liking to them and they took interest in the Widow. Alcorn lost that edge. That constraint. Especially when Horace showed Alcorn he wouldn't be restrained by Guatemalan muscle.

Coming from behind an aluminum-sided outbuilding and campers bleached of their color, Dorn, Sheldon, and the mongrel worked their way through the lines of looters, made their way to the church's entrance. To where Dorn had watched Alcorn enter, leading a man of color bound by rope. It was an outline of the familiar that Dorn hadn't seen in some time. An outline he knew was responsible for the removal of his father and the Widow, and all at once, it consumed him. Alcorn was among the living. Surviving however he wanted. Needed.

A burly outline of man guarded the church's entrance. Approaching him, the man eyed Dorn, Sheldon, and the mongrel hound.

"Ain't seen you around here, what be your intentions?"

He had seen a man bound by wrist and neck, so Dorn knew that whatever they were doing was barbaric, possibly pugilistic in nature. Regardless, his objective would be sidelined until he dealt with Alcorn, and he told the man, "To see the primates and their games."

"And what do you have to hock?"

Dorn didn't hesitate to react, reached to his pouch. Pulled out the binoculars. The man grasped them, looked them over. "Nice. You, the girl, and the hound enjoy the wagering of skin."

Defiled, angry. Lost. Starved of reason. The men and women within were unsightly. Their pungent scents clung to the air like two-week-old skillet grease. Dorn made his way to the right, hugged close to the wall where a pew ran. He was on the hunt. Followed it to the center of the church. Told Sheldon below the chattering mouths of broken teeth and split lips, "You and the mongrel keep yourselves here."

Sheldon grasped his arm. "Where's you going?"

"In search of a clean shot. Then we run like a feline with turpentine on its ass."

Confused, Sheldon questioned, "What is this place? Who are these people?"

Dorn took on a serious tone, told her, "I've no idea, but at this moment, all I know is the man who murdered my father and the Widow is here, and I aim to avenge each of they's deaths."

"What about Cotto? The kids he's enslaved? My mother, the others?"

"After I remove Alcorn, we focus on Cotto, find your mother and the others." And he went off.

As he stood upon a pew, Dorn's mind would not quit. Seeing Alcorn had rattled his nerves. Brought back a hurt he'd not realized was buried. Had thought was gone. It wasn't. He worked his way behind the clamp of jaws slurring speech and the shadows of the wrecked, the absence of hygiene and kinship unless it involved the harm of others. All he could see was red. Wanted Alcorn centered between his crosshairs. He stopped and stood, waiting. Looked around. Over top of the mass of bodies, took in the hole. Floor that had been cut. Removed. The pit that had been dug out. The two lean hulks of men who stood within it, glaring at each other. Almost whispering back and forth. Far off to Dorn's right, to the front of the church was an altar. A man came before it, children guarded him. Within their grips were tools for dividing and mincing. They appeared bloodless. Pale as intestines. The man was robed. Frail. And when he spoke, mouths ceased speech. Sound clamped. "Tonight we see two old adversaries. One of which murdered Bellmont McGill. The other was unbeaten till he met this murderer. They's two men who've been under the wire. Hidden from sight and sound for many, many years. But they've a flame to rekindle tonight. One represents me and my followers, Chainsaw Angus."

Men and women clapped and hollered. The Methodist stepped away. From behind him came a man with arms of spilt ink, skulls and insignias that represented death. Racial divide and hatred. He'd a female with a mashed eye, barely clothed. Several men sporting red suspenders and rifles. Van Dorn could close his eyes and still recognize the tongue. The image from where it came. Shape of age. Still stealthy.

Thick. Sculpted. This lurch of man placed himself before the crowd that beckoned for pugilism. Anger fed Dorn's confidence, he shook his head, *you son of a bitch*, took in the hint of age beneath his eyes, the purpling sags. Head like a kiwi's rind. Rough and whiskered. Alcorn spoke, "Though I'm less agreeing upon the mixing of skin pigment, I'm all about the parchment of flesh. The brutality of two hides wrecking one another in the name of dominance. But in these times without filament, it's all we got."

Alcorn paused his words. Took in the mass of men and women. Eyes glanced back and forth amongst one another. *Killed my father. I'm no killer, but wrongs has got to be righted.* Dorn pulled the hem of his rifle's strap. The butt nestled into his swollen ache of shoulder. The .30-30 was pointed down. No eyes were upon him. Dillard the Aryan Alcorn began to speak once more in some crazed oration, "And tonight the Alcorn clan is represented by Ali Squires. One of the most brutal and savage—"

Dorn lifted the rifle slow. *This is for you, Father.* Blacked-out sound. Viewing only Dillard's shape. Pinning his complexion within his crosshairs. *You can do it, Dorn, you can do it.* Syllables fell from lips like a television with no volume. Memories of Horace floated. The smile he rarely showed to others, but always to Dorn. The roads they traveled, his map of life and all the lessons it held. The warmth of a father's protection. Dorn's index weighted the trigger.

—

Angus was riddled by the pulse of taking one's life with the swipe of a single movement. Traffic wheeled outside the panes of glass with scents of grilled meat reeking from inside, where the kitchen's rusted and banging exhaust fan distributed the scents.

He'd watched this man eat here on Thursdays. Short. Locks the shade of a tire tube. Skin stained the shade of canola oil. Tailored in a black suit, he entered at the same time each week. Ordered a rare cut of marbled rib-eye soaked in pineapple. Seasoned by pepper, garlic, and soy sauce. With a side of sweet potato, butter, and cinnamon. Bud Light Lime bled from a tap, frothed over the rim of an iced mug. Something Angus'd not tasted in years, beer.

Entering Fredrick's, a mom-and-pop restaurant, Angus wore a John Deere ball cap over his shaved head, white Hanes with lean tatted arms hanging from the sleeves. Sight covered by aviator glasses to mask his opal sockets. Seated, he ordered black coffee. Waited with clock hands calculating in his mind.

After weeks of watching. Sitting outside the restaurant where inside, walls were decorated by paintings and photos of surrounding nature, old cars, and men shooting pool, huffing on lung cloggers, Angus was ready for the test. Zhong sat several tables away, glancing at the newspaper, wiped his lips. Folded his paper upon the table. Scoot of chair marred across tile. He went to the restroom. Angus waited for the bathroom door to close. Followed. Stood outside the hall's entrance. Clatter of dishes from the kitchen behind him. Thump of heart and rattle of nerves. When the sound of the bathroom door's lock clicked, Angus timed the exit of Zhong. Made it appear accidental, the hallway was small, room for a single passage. Zhong ran into Angus. His head meeting his pecs. Angus's left palm met Zhong's chest. A quick pat against the skeletal bone that protected his heart. Exhale of air. Release of vibrating energy. His right guarded just below the navel. Zhong blinked uncontrolled. Stood unbalanced for a split second. Fought to gather his bearings. Knowing he felt something. Tried to shake it off as he eyed Angus. His own eyes reflected by aviator lens. Coughed. Excused himself. Angus apologized. Went into the restroom. Washed his hands. Looked in the mirror. Inhaled deep. Exhaled, slow. Waited for a count of thirty Mississippis. Exited. Sat at his table. Never made eye contact with Zhong. Could hear the man eating. Coughing. Clearing his throat. Angus finished his coffee. Laid a Lincoln on the table. Walked out the door.

In his vehicle he waited. Timing. It was all about timing. When Zhong came out, he reached to his jacket's pocket. Shook a smoke from a pack of Winston Reds. Then his eyes wadded to the scope of baseballs. Crimson split the whites. The pack fell from his grip. Hands lost grip strength. Something the shade of ketchup spewed from his lips. Both hands met his chest. Orbs sought confirmation on the sidewalk from trees. The sky. Then the parked vehicles. Found Angus's outline in his truck. Dress-slacked knees cracked against pavement. Zhong screamed, "No! No!" Tried to point. His frame went face-first into the sidewalk. He lay flaccid. Loss of movement. People came from inside the restaurant. But found no flux or action within his frame as Angus drove away, understanding the surge of energy he'd transferred from one body to the next. Had timed the kill. What Fu had trained him to do. Mastery of his internal. But also to kill Mr. Zhong. To free Fu from this man's restraint. Just as he freed Angus from his restraints. But also a test of his skill thus far in his training. It would be dishonorable for Fu to murder the man who'd freed him.

Now, with the oration of Alcorn overhead, Angus approached Ali. A once unbeaten bare-knuckle god until he fought Angus. Who now pondered if he'd do the same to him, or if they could work together. Rid themselves of this enslavement. Angus had no other choice. He spoke to Ali. "You and me, we can bond. Toss this barbaric blood feud for rural pleasure. Be rid of this ritual. Go our separates."

"I know what transpired last time I made contact with you. My ass got pulped."

"Time brings change. I ain't the same man I used to be."

"So says the man who beat and left me for dead, handed me my only loss in a bare-knuckle fight way down in the hills of Kentucky."

"You appear to have healed pretty fair."

"Fuck you!" Ali coughed as he snapped a thick herculean left jab. Torqued his hips. Angus turned his cheek, dodged the attack. "Looks like you still train," he said to Ali. "Quicker than last time."

"Ten times better than when we first crossed skin," Ali spit back.

Oration of the Methodist's words rang overhead with the badgering of feet and mouths.

"All the more reason to work together."

"No doing. Trust your cracker ass about as far as I can throw you, that ain't too goddamn far."

Angus came with the backs of his hands, knuckled Ali's chest, knocked him backward. Ali coughed, swung a wild right hook. Angus rolled his elbow, came forward, drove a claw into Ali's throat. Eyed Ali. Whispered, "If it'd redeem you, I'll let you beat my ass. Just get the goddamn blade from above for scalping. That's our tool for exiting the pit, you knucklehead motherfucker."

Ali bared teeth. Raised his head back, flexed his throat.

Brought his hand atop of Angus's wrist. Applied pressure in a single motion. Angus rolled his elbow. Circled his hips and came with a backhand as if holding a teacup. Made Ali's lips juice with blood. An explosion pierced the air. Stopped Ali and Angus dead in their tracks. Tense, each looked up. Caught a glimpse of what used to be Alcorn's face. A smear of skull and organ painting the Methodist. Alcorn fell forward. Hit the podium, bounced to the floor. Everyone looked to where the shot rang from. Angus ran to the pit's wall. Kneeled, laced the fingers of right and left hand, shouted at Ali, "Step your ass in, I'll anchor you up. You can pull me out."

Ali hesitated for a split second. Metered the situation. Ran. Placed his left foot into Angus's hands. Angus lifted. Ali sprung. Grabbed a leg from above. Pulled himself out of the pit. Turned. Laid upon his stomach. Didn't think twice. Returned the favor. Couldn't reach Angus. Looked. Viewed the lumber used for a bridge. Grabbed it. Muscled its rough-cut heft down into the pit. Angus came up it. People were disheveled. Total chaos. Looking for where the carbine fire came from. The Methodist pointed to the fighters. Words never escaped his lips.

From the entrance came automatic gunfire. Limbs. Faces. Screams. Chests parted in a maddening explosion of reds. In the frame stood an outline of stubbled skull leading what appeared to be rural children, only their faces were covered by masks made of skin, hand stitched. The leader'd an archaic amount of ink about his face and arms. In his left grip he held the decapitated head of the man who'd guarded the entrance to the church. In his right a machete dripped the said man's insides from the blade. He'd an automatic rifle strapped over his back.

Angus made eye contact with the man, a hint of familiarity. The name *Manny* scissored in his mind, expanded into paper cutouts, and imploded his identity. The man tossed the head out into the church, where it ricocheted off kneeling and falling bodies, landed in the pit. His eyes scanned the room. Glazed over Angus. Came back and metered into him. The leader was Cotto and he smirked. Pointed his machete at Angus, offering the recognition of knowing he was the man he'd been hunting all these months. And from the pulpit the Methodist screamed, "It is he, the man bearing the crown of thorns. He's the one who's slaughtered fathers, whored our women, and took our children, enslaved them. Trained them to be killers!"

—

Sometime after Horace handed Manny's ass to him in front of Alcorn, Horace told Van Dorn, "Taking a man's life offers nothing for the soul. Pressures the psyche of the moral. Lifts the status of the immoral. Pushes the good-natured to cross that line of the criminal, the bad-natured, helps them to realize what they already believed, that the removing of another's life holds the next tier on the status ladder, that's how men become cold-blooded killers."

And Van Dorn asked, "Think he'll come back to kill you?"

And Horace told him, "Being belittled in front of another drives some men to think irrational, to commit vengeance. In the end, it's less about retribution, more about ego than power. No, it's not Manny that concerns me, it's Alcorn."

"But why?" Van Dorn asked.

"'Cause Alcorn saw himself through Manny, a reflection, not the other way around. Alcorn lost face."

Now, all these years later, spent brass glanced off the

pew to the carved and scratched floor, surrounding sound was crazed static and lost breaths hanging in lungs. A live round was chambered into the .30-30 with the pulse of hand on the lever and index on the trigger. Viewing the combustive spray of Alcorn's profile. The slow slant of frame, the actions were reminiscent of Gutt long ago in the mom-and-pop mart with Horace and the Widow.

Dorn lowered the .30-30. Expanse of heart vined blood through his frame with the noise of his environment slowly arcing louder and louder with chaos. His ending the air that came from Alcorn's lungs had to do with all that his father had taught and told him. Taking away the life of the good while the bad kept breathing was immoral, and how Dorn felt was neither good nor bad, only a rush of knowing he'd seared his father's killer.

With the return of sound, the explosion of carbine rang in Van Dorn's drums. Turning away, eyes of the shocked men and women looked to him, coming across the pew. Sheldon and the hound were waiting on Dorn while all around them bodies were bumping, elbowing, men and women shouting and reaching, and then more gunfire lit up the church.

Frames parted and poured to the slats. Others took cover. Looked upon the entrance where medium- and short-statured silhouettes stood. Some with faces painted black. Others red as the blood being drained from a rabbit hung by its rears. Then there were the taller ones, who bared masks that looked like folds of flesh stitched together with eyeholes and mouths. Crooked and parched. They were children. The young boys who'd given hunt to Van Dorn and the Sheldon girl, they stood savage, worn and doped up like their leader. Scratched and bruised with dirt about their lengths of arms and legs as though they'd lived within a mine shaft, laboring coal from dusk to dawn. Never bathed. Just heathen maniacs living on soot.

Some of the clansmen and -women drew weapons. Pointed. Then the Methodist barked his words of who the man leading them was. Who they were. The men and women feared shooting a child, believing it could be their own. Or one whom they'd once known from a neighbor or familiar face in town.

In the chaos of Cotto's entrance, Dorn maneuvered to Sheldon and the hound, kneeled with her beside a pew. "You killed that man?"

"He kilt my father. Hard as it was to take his life, I had to do what needed done."

Anger and confusion at the situation followed Sheldon's features and she questioned, "What'll we do now?"

"What we've been doing, kill or be slaughtered."

"But one of these boys could be my baby brother. These is kids."

He thought of when he'd wanted to help them. To save or rescue them. If they wanted to survive they might have to kill their own. But he took that as a last resort of hope as they watched the chaos ensue.

"You're correct. We wait. See how the situation sorts itself out."

—

Cotto came with the scream of bullets and clatter of brass pinging the floor. Was making his way to Angus, his hands pulsing red as he cursed. "Wretched fuck. You. You're the one who took the life from my father!"

Ali looked at Angus. "The fuck is that inked psycho?"

Angus told Ali, "Damn gangbanger wanting to settle an old score."

With gunshots from the child soldiers, men and women lay about the floor, drowning in their own pools of blood, fighting amongst one another, becoming more and more unruly.

Walking amongst the dead and wounded, Cotto kicked and smashed those who reached and squirmed, twitched or searched for speech. A streak of anger painted his complexion as he turned to see his young-maniac militia falling as some of the men and women had decided to kill the young soldiers.

Ali told Angus just before gunshots opened his shoulder and chest, "Beat his ass bloody!" Ali hit the floor gasping, patting at the holes of red that leaked from him. And Angus made his way through the mad energy that surrounded him, inhaling deep, exhaling slow. Over and over. His flow of energy hulking his insides, radiant and atomic-like. Heating his hands. His feet bottoms. Ready to release.

Seeing a good cluster of the rural clans either wounded, bullet riddled, or taking cover, Cotto screamed. Pointed amongst the gunfire and bloodshed across the room to where Angus approached. "The man I've hunted and hunted. Here he stands, hidden amongst the dying!"

Behind Angus, with a face of clotted blood, the Methodist shouted over the fray, "This man that trespasses within my congregation, my gathering of rural clans bearing a crown of thorns, I command that Chainsaw Angus brings him the same death that he has brought to us!"

Angus smirked. Shook his head. Muttered, "Silly son of a bitch thinks he's a deity." Saw what was coming before it happened. *Gonna get that thought tested real quick-like.* Offered no warning.

"My birth name is Cotto Ramos, you pedophilic sage." And before another sound etched from the Methodist's lips, Cotto lifted the machete. Bent elbow at ear. Shouldered it forward. His hand released the weighted blade. Eyes watched it cartwheel in the air. Watched it meet skin. Cranium and forehead bone halved like a cantaloupe. The Methodist's heartbeat ceased as vertebrae, neurons, and fluid spewed. His protectors came from the pulpit. Hatchets and blades drawn for battle like young Ronin behind Angus, who shuffled and pushed through the shock and retch of disgruntled bodies, some on the floor, others standing. Waiting and watching. Fearing to pull their gun triggers on the young doped-up adolescent killers backing Cotto.

Cotto and Angus kicked, palmed, elbowed, and punched obstruction from their paths. Pews and bodies dropped into the pit until they'd room to end the hunt, to clash like gladiators. And Cotto told Angus, "Your ending is here for what you done to my father. For what you took from me. I've wanted you to beg and burn all in one fucking breath."

From the far side of the church the .30-30 of Dorn had been raised. Cotto's upper profile filling it. An index finger graced the trigger. Cotto's hands balled into fists. Angus anticipated every flinch of Cotto's body from footing to face.

Right fist came up from Cotto's hips. Half uppercut, half hook. A beeline to the side of Angus's jaw. Angus adjusted his hips. A simple swivel. His right forearm deflected the attack while left palm came heated. Lifelined Cotto's arm. A vibration of energy made Cotto withdraw his arm. Slingshot it back to his body. A shock or charge of something similar to electricity plagued it with bruised weight. He lifted his left arm. Elbow bent. Shelled at his face. What he felt he couldn't explain. His mind went from straight lines on a graph to horizontal and scratchy. He searched for air. Felt as if he'd been electrocuted. Angus stepped forward. His left hand guarding center, his right gathering air, slapping from the side as he stepped to Cotto's left, his right palm making contact with Cotto's kidney. A surge of heat lit up Cotto's insides. Baked tendons and ligaments. He lost feeling in his legs. Angus circle-stepped backward. Waited as he counted down in Mississippis.

Across the room within the chaos, Van Dorn kept his rifle shouldered. Following Cotto in the crosshairs, not wanting to shoot Angus. Losing his profile amongst the bodies that gathered around the struggle between the two men. His aggravation grew.

Cotto's hands dropped. His mind was fogged. Thoughts and emotion were that of days without sleep, like being hungover in a field hoeing potatoes, humidity pressing down with no shade or water. The body drained of electrolytes. Fighting the death that eased within his torso, organ by organ. Limb by limb. He looked to Angus. "What have you done to me?"

"Not near what I done to your father or—"

From the church's entrance came the trample of feet sounding off like horse hooves along with the words of Scar, whose temperament ran Freon-cold, her militia backing her, their weapons bearing on the rears of each child soldier's skull. Some were beat down by rifle butts. Those who tried to fight were removed from creation by gunshot. Seeing the masked children fall, Cotto screamed, "No!" And Scar raised her .45 Colt at Angus from across the room of carnage, as she finished his words for him, fingering the trigger from across the church's bloodied hall, "—my father when you removed his face from his shoulders."

—

Break of twig upon the forest's floor. Coat of almond and pearl with the breach of sun upon the hillside, Dorn sat his rifle pinning the chest within his hairs, Horace watching beside him, waiting. Whispering, "Up to you. Kill it now or wait."

Rush of blood expanding the arteries. Heart increasing with pulse. Pressure rising. Ears slightly ringing. Crack of leaves. Antlered head raised. Four points branched on left and right side. Eight-pointer. Neck swiveling. Eyes a cold sapphire matching the shade of the nose. Dorn could fight the rush no more and squeezed the trigger.

And like that first kill for betterment, for survival and continuation with his father, that rush would bear no difference with a human when it meant extinction of another. Dorn held the shape of Cotto in his crosshairs, realizing that even after shooting Alcorn, it was no easier a decision to take another's life a second or third or even fourth time. Though he'd done it, more than once, he was still human, held emotion, but those killings gave the confidence to do what must be done, take Cotto's life, end his slaughtering of men, enslaving women and children. And he pulled the trigger at the same time the Sheldon girl raised her gun to save the life of another.

—

High-caliber explosion raked the drums of all eyes watching and battling. Muscle meat parted from Scar's right forearm. Took her weapon from being aimed at Angus. Vein and tissue ripped and seared. "Ahh!" Scar shrieked.

Jawline burned and ripped in Van Dorn's crosshairs with the ooze of Cotto's face.

Scar's pistol dropped with the spray of blood. Fluid the shade of fresh cranberries dabbed from Cotto's face, painted his lips. First in tiny specs. Then in droplets that grew into an overfilled bucket of liquid. Then all at once, Angus's attack took Cotto's organ. His kidney mangled internally. Then his insides erupted, split and broke by the warmth of Angus's touch.

Wolf Cookie Mike reached for Scar, who dropped to her knees, screaming. The rest of her militia stood with guns shouldered, pointed to where the Sheldon girl had administered the bullet across the room.

Dorn could take no more of the lunacy, of the killing, of what the simple rural folk were doing to one another, and he shouted, "Stop!"

Angus watched Van Dorn with everyone else. "Enough. The past is the past. Nothing can change what we've all done. What we've incurred." Van Dorn pointed to Angus, the Sheldon girl reached, held on to Van Dorn's arm. "What this man done is the past. What everyone is doing now is savage. Has nothing to do with bettering any person's life. It's all about killing and ruling. It's a struggle for power. And ain't nothing good come from murdering your own, from war, 'cause there's always another one building somewheres else."

All around, the blink of lights within the church popped and buzzed.

Dorn and Sheldon watched as everyone forgot about Dorn and his words as the spark of wires frayed with no caps glittered orange from the walls, fountained in sparks. The hum of bug lights outside attached to poles flicked and fluttered. Then came the sirens. Nerve-damaging loud. Eyes from those still among the living lit up like clouds of atomic explosions; some stayed on knees, others dropped. Began to recite prayers. "Our Father who art—" Others screamed, "God have mercy on me. Please spare me. Please."

"It's the seven seals. God has come to save us!"

Dorn and Sheldon looked at each other, astonished at what they were viewing, even after all the pandemonium bloodshed, these folks thought they could be forgiven for their wrongs.

As the sirens blared, Angus had kneeled down, helped Ali to his feet, a mess of blood about his body, unknown if he'd survive his wounds; he was still breathing and looked around with fogged eyes at what was taking place. Angered and pumped, Angus was no longer able to withhold his pestilence. Shook his head. Made eye contact with Van Dorn, Sheldon, and the hound dog across the room. Then to Scar and her militia, who still stood bearing their weapons at the ready, waiting for command, one man holding the wounded Scar upright, her arm bleeding, but none aimed their guns, as they were confused by the return of electricity. Angus eyed the children soldiers, their tremoring. *What has become of us, of this land, of this people?* Angus questioned. Some of the children's faces were covered by paint. Others by masks. Their leader, Cotto, shot dead. And glancing to the madness of the kneeling clan of followers, Angus shook his head, was sickened by their stupidity, wanting to slaughter anyone in a single instance and now seeking forgiveness, and he shouted, "What you all is hearing is tornado sirens, fuckin' invalids. No wonder you all are in the shape you're in."

EPILOGUE

Scabrous and vile, the land was burnt in places, staked with male bodies, limbless and without head. Devoid of child or women. Where homes once stood, now wrecked, littered, and rummaged. Dryers, washers, and busted screen doors, dressers upturned and set aflame. Clothing scattered and children's dolls without eyes thrown and left lying. Remnants and refuges of times condemned by the massacres and onslaught of vehemence when time had lost light and humans forgot about neighbors. Instead they massacred their own. It decorated Angus's, Van Dorn's, and Sheldon's travel with the group of clans from the Methodist's realm to Cotto's compound.

Some took by foot. Others by vehicle or four-wheeler.

Wounded, Scar and her militia sat at their compound. Dragging their dead to burials. Wolf Cookie asked, "Now what?"

All Scar could say was "We do as we always have, just as my father did, we build. Create something new."

"What about Angus?"

"I'm sure we'll cross again someday."

"Then what?"

"What happens, happens. I'm done fighting for a while."

Rides were bumpy and coarse. Small groups had come through the valleys. Volunteers reaching out sent by a fallen and stalled government. Helping to place things disassembled back to some type of order.

Some hoped to find their loved ones. Others sought nieces, nephews, aunts, sisters, brothers. Some connection they'd thought gone forever.

In Cotto's compound, children were holed up in bunkers with madness in their eyes and drugs in their veins. Piles and piles of drugs strung across metal tables. There was no firefight. For all the followers of Cotto and the children he'd taken, enslaved to soldiering, had become too strung out or had OD'd, couldn't raise claim to a rifle. The children had been robbed of youth. Of kindness. Of family. Of values. Same as the land.

There were rooms of antibiotics. Of bottled water. Of family heirlooms. Dead bodies spread and piled with insects laboring. Things burned. Crates of automatic weapons and ammunition. MREs. Things Cotto and his men had robbed in their raids.

At one end of the compound was a long, rectangular concrete building where the lock was cut from the chained door. Women had been found, ragged and rotted ivory. Locked in. Starved. Dead spread upon dead and were covered in a white powder like lime. On the rear wall, spray-painted in large block fluorescent graffiti, was FUCK YOU GRINGOS!

All stood lost. Gagged by the smells passing. Walking amongst the others who looked for their own, walked with Sheldon and Dorn, gazing about the spoiled and raisin-skinned. Wet coursed Sheldon's eyes. Her mother was no more. Starved and withered with the other females. Dorn held tight to her frame as they walked.

In the lighthouse's top floor, young boys lay limp about the floor like a deck after 52 Pickup. In the room's center was a table. Six boys sat around it. Eight-ball-eyed. Each had a box of brass shells beside him. A revolver in the table's center. One was Sheldon's baby brother. Each resembled the next, their minds blasted of wits, playing spin the bottle. Only it wasn't a bottle. It was the "lucky one of six." One child spun the revolver. The child the revolver stopped on picked up the pistol. Loaded the chamber with a single bullet. Then wheeled the cylinder. Pointed it at his temple. Pulled the hammer and fired. If it was an empty chamber, the soldier wasn't shot. That child then spun the revolver. If he was shot, another child stepped in. Spun the pistol for the next. The game went on until they reached the sixth soldier, then they started over, played until they had another sixth survivor, and so on and so forth.

It was part of Cotto's crazed psychotic protocol. To create soldiers who faced death. Survived and no longer feared it. Created a stir-crazy in their minds. Each child's eyes were rimmed with shock. Drug induced. Pupils the size of marbles. Sheldon ran to the table, stepping over the dead. Took the weapon from the table's center. Scooped up their loved ones. Offered comfort. Let them know it was over. But it wasn't. It had only begun. The world they'd once known was no more. Things would be different. Much different. The United States was now no different from the war-torn third-world countries they'd aided over the years, the ones that'd been on the world news. Or written about or photographed by American journalists.

Sheldon clasped her brother tight. "It's over. It's over." Flesh around his eyes bulbous and rashed, the boy was in a state of numb to anything said. And Dorn walked them away from the lighthouse. To a vehicle that drove them to Sheldon's parents' farm.

—

Angus would find an antibiotic, penicillin. Was offered a ride. He took it. The man driving told him, "We been trying."

"We?" Angus questioned.

"Yeah, National Guard. Red Cross. Everyone's been trying to get to as many as we could. They's just too much unknown, things is no longer safe, too damn many people. Many has gave up. No one knows how long it'll take to sort things out. Restore all the power. They's much uncertainty."

"Too many crazy sons of bitches. I wouldn't call them people no more," Angus said, and the man kept silent, then said, "Guess you seen some shit?"

"That's one way of coining it."

When Angus came from the truck, he thanked the man for the ride. Walked the long drive to Fu's home. Entered. All sat silent. Fu was no longer lying in rest. He was gone. A letter written upon a chalkboard in the kitchen read:

> Angus,
>
> If you've found this writing, you've survived. Returned. Brought back medicine for me. Though I was not sick. It was only a final lesson. Meaning I've taught you what was needed. You're now free of me and my ways. It is up to you to pass what you've learned on to another.
>
> Fu

Angus held a grin of shit-eating and lipped, "Mother. Fucker."

—

The land sat uneven and scorched in places where field grass once spread. Bones of hog and cow lay in the daylight spread out over the grounds and the wind stirred with a future for the young. With hair clean but messed from going uncombed, Dorn smelt of lilac and his T-shirt was scented by soap. The months had been hard, the loss of his father and the Widow even harder, but now Dorn looked out from the wood-slatted porch that connected to the barn-red farmhouse with a tin roof. The brindle hound, which Sheldon and Dorn had agreed to name Fury, lay on his side, at ease, resting. A soft rise and fall from his rib cage. Dorn's arm hung and clutched around Sheldon's shoulders as she sipped hot tea. Her locks beyond shoulders, the cheeks of her face sharp and smooth.

Sheldon swallowed and questioned, "Think it'll come again?"

Within the house in a back bedroom Sheldon's brother lay. His mind rattled. Worse off than a soldier with PTSD. He slept most of the hours that filled a day. Given medication from a doctor who worked for the government. Going around helping those in need. When he was not sleeping, Dorn and Sheldon worked with him, read to him, and took him on walks through the woods when his confidence wasn't questioned.

"The darkness? The neighbors killing neighbors?"

Sheldon's brother would never be right in the head. Not from the scarring of what he'd incurred. He'd need care till the day he passed.

"All of it."

Dorn and Sheldon had begun cleaning up her family's farm. Received a great deal of aid from the county, state, and federal government for all that had gone wrong. And there were others all over the United States that received the same. Regardless, they had each other. And they had skills. For food, Dorn had been hunting wild game and fishing the Blue River. Filling the freezer with meat. He'd gotten an old tiller's engine running and they'd worked the soil, used seeds Sheldon's father gathered and stored for the following year's planting, and made a garden.

"I can only hope not. But if it were to occur, we're more prepared than before."

"Think you could kill again if you had to?"

Each suffered the aftereffects of what they'd been dealt. Having nightmares of the slaughter. The enslavement. Waking in cold sweats and shaking. Each embracing the other. Soothing and reassuring that it was only a dream.

"I hope I never have to take another human's life again, 'cause I care none for that dark place it took me, but if it comes down to fending for you or your brother, I'll do what's gotta be done."

Sheldon turned to Dorn, pressed her face into his chest, and they embraced, an uncertain world lying out in the distance, knowing they'd always have each other.

ACKNOWLEDGMENTS

Writing a book is a solitary endeavor, but it cannot be done without support from family, friends, fans, agents, editors, and publishers. I'd like to thank my father, Frank Bill Sr., and my stepmother, Julie Bill; my mother, Alice Weaver, and stepfather, Tom; Carrie Bill; Brandy and Casey Robertson; Jack Bill and John Bill; Terry Crayden; Sharon Crayden; Gayle and Israel Byrd; Amy, Jamie, Abigail, and Eli Pellman; Bob and Donna Pellman; Becky and Dennis Faith; Denny Faith; Matt and Allison Faith; Stephanie Bill and Stephen Glaspie; Rhonda Abbott; Thad and Dana Holton; Kevin and Rebecca Reed; Larry Byrd; my big brother, Donnie Ross, and his wife, Amber; my friend for life, Lou Perry, and his wife, Molly; my other brother, Rod Wiethop, and his wife, Judy; Steph Stickels; Barbra White; Brandon Crayden; Jim and Ella Baker; author Kirby Gann and his wife, Steph Tittle; strength coach James Steel; Life Is Good buddy Jake Patrick; photographer Christian Doellner; Joe and Mary Lou Trindeitmar; Sara Trindeitmar; Tammy and Tony Kruer; Laura and Alan Muncy. To my coworkers—George Savage, Greg

Ledford, Kirk Vormbrock, Casey Heishman, Ted Kessinger, Randy Brightman, Glenn and Tammy Beanblossom, John Clark, Gary Miller, Roger Tharp, Darrin Harris, Larry Brooner, and everyone else I work with—I really appreciate your support. Thanks to the authors Christa Faust and Benjamin Whitmer for their early readings. Also, thanks to Ray Wylie Hubbard, Scott H. Biram, Lincoln Durham, and Tyler Childers for reading my books and for making kick-ass tunes! Huge thanks to my kick-ass book agent, Stacia Decker, and bad-ass film agent, Shari Smiley—your efforts are greatly appreciated. Thanks to my hard-as-nails editors, Sean McDonald, Emily Bell, and Jackson Howard—your input really helped reshape my words and make this one gut-punch of a book; and, of course, a huge thanks to FSG—you're the best publisher!